Praise for the Miss Julia series

"Written with Ross's signature Southern charm and wit, the newest Miss Julia will delight long-time fans of the series and will entice new readers to get to know her."   —*Booklist*

"As fast, feisty, and full of personality as its heroine."
                                                      —*Kirkus Reviews*

"Ross has a gift for elevating such everyday matters as marital strife and the hazards of middle age to high comedy, while painting her beautifully drawn characters with wit and sympathy."
                                                      —*Publishers Weekly*

"Ann B. Ross develops characters so expertly, through quirks, names, and mannerisms, that they easily feel familiar as the reader is gently immersed into the world Miss Ross has created. . . . A delightful read."   —*Winston-Salem Journal*

"Miss Julia is one of the most delightful characters to come along in years. Ann B. Ross has created what is sure to become a classic Southern comic novel. Hooray for Miss Julia, I could not have liked it more."   —Fannie Flagg, author of
                                    The All-Girl Filling Station's Last Reunion

"Yes, Miss Julia is back, and I, for one, am one happy camper."
                                        —J. A. Jance, author of *Cold Betrayal*

PENGUIN BOOKS

MISS JULIA KNOWS A THING OR TWO

Ann B. Ross is the author of twenty-three novels featuring the popular Southern heroine Miss Julia, as well as *Etta Mae's Worst Bad-Luck Day*, a novel about one of Abbotsville's other most outspoken residents: Etta Mae Wiggins. Ross holds a doctorate in English from the University of North Carolina at Chapel Hill, and has taught literature at the University of North Carolina at Asheville. She lives in Hendersonville, North Carolina.

Also by Ann B. Ross

Miss Julia Takes the Wheel

Miss Julia Raises the Roof

Miss Julia Weathers the Storm

Miss Julia Inherits a Mess

Miss Julia Lays Down the Law

Etta Mae's Worst Bad-Luck Day

Miss Julia's Marvelous Makeover

Miss Julia Stirs Up Trouble

Miss Julia to the Rescue

Miss Julia Rocks the Cradle

Miss Julia Renews Her Vows

Miss Julia Delivers the Goods

Miss Julia Paints the Town

Miss Julia Strikes Back

Miss Julia Stands Her Ground

Miss Julia's School of Beauty

Miss Julia Meets Her Match

Miss Julia Hits the Road

Miss Julia Throws a Wedding

Miss Julia Takes Over

Miss Julia Speaks Her Mind

Miss Julia
Knows a Thing or Two

ANN B. ROSS

PENGUIN BOOKS

PENGUIN BOOKS

An imprint of Penguin Random House LLC
penguinrandomhouse.com

First published in the United States of America by Viking,
an imprint of Penguin Random House LLC, 2020
Published in Penguin Books 2021

ISBN 9780525560531 (paperback)

THE LIBRARY OF CONGRESS HAS CATALOGED THE HARDCOVER EDITION AS FOLLOWS:
Names: Ross, Ann B., author.
Title: Miss Julia knows a thing or two / Ann B. Ross.
Description: New York : Viking, [2020]
Identifiers: LCCN 2019046072 (print) | LCCN 2019046073 (ebook) |
ISBN 9780525560517 (hardcover) | ISBN 9780525560524 (ebook)
Subjects: LCSH: Springer, Julia (Fictitious character)—Fiction. |
GSAFD: Humorous fiction. | Mystery fiction.
Classification: LCC PS3568.O84198 M5654 2020 (print) |
LCC PS3568.O84198 (ebook) | DDC 813/.54—dc23
LC record available at https://lccn.loc.gov/2019046072
LC ebook record available at https://lccn.loc.gov/2019046073

Printed in the United States of America
ScoutAutomatedPrintCode

Designed by Cassandra Garruzzo

*This book is for my granddaughter, Ramsey Ross,
who said that I should write a story about
a little girl named Penelope. So I did.*

For you, Ramsey, with love.

Miss Julia Knows a Thing or Two

Chapter 1

❧

After taking a good, long look at myself, I've realized that I may be a little too outspoken in putting forward my opinions, just a bit too quick to judge others to their detriment, much too inclined to think I know what's best for someone else, and entirely too skeptical of every claim to better my life made by salesmen of all stripes, including politicians. So I've decided to turn over a new leaf, and I intend to do it before I get so set in my ways that I can't turn over anything.

And here's the cold, hard truth: I am in danger of becoming a crabby, sharp-tongued old woman who has allowed her worst attributes to become her defining characteristics.

I have, however, recognized the danger in time to do something about it. I well recall being a student in what was then called a Health class in high school—this was long before those classes were enlivened by the use of vegetables as visual aids. During a period on personal hygiene, the teacher informed us that when we begin to smell ourselves, we have been noticeably reeking to others for four days.

That makes me wonder if the same holds true in different situations. I mean, even though I've only just recognized some unbecoming traits in myself, is it possible that they've been obvious to others for much longer?

One never knows how one is judged, so it behooves each of us to be prepared for the worst assessments and get ourselves ready to deal with them. So for me, that means strengthening my better impulses and diminishing those that are unseemly in a lady, and if that term puts me back into an archaic age, then so be it. Actually, no one seems to think that being a lady is worth anything these days. What is now wanted is to be WOMAN—a status that affords all the perquisites of ladyhood plus the benefits of manhood as well.

But I'm off the subject.

After taking that hard look at myself, I didn't like what I saw. So I have determined to smile more, compliment others more, allow others to have disagreeable opinions without consigning them to idiocy, be more sensitive to the needs of others without wondering why they don't help themselves, and refrain from questioning any and all motives that issue from the mouths of people trying to sell me something I don't want or raise funds for something I've never heard of, or run for office, be it local, state, or federal.

And what brought on this change of heart? You may well ask, and my answer is two-pronged. One occurred when I picked up a book that Sam was reading and a short sentence jumped out at me. It was a sentence attributed to Saint Augustine, who lived a long time ago but who could've been speaking directly to me. "Pride," he said, "lurks even in good deeds." Now, I'm sure that he didn't speak in English, certainly not with a southern accent, so I am relying on an unknown translator as most people of faith have to do anyway. But that sentence went straight to my heart, and I think it was that word, *lurks*, that had the sharp point. It means to lie in wait, to be concealed—*unseen and unsuspected*.

Reading that forced me to recognize the pride I took in my opinions—so much better informed than most—and in my actions—so much more appropriate than most. Pride, in fact, had ruled my life and it had done so by lurking, unseen and unsuspected, in every thought and deed.

I'll tell you, that was enough to shake the very foundation of my life, and I have resolved to do something about it.

But the second thing that contributed to my change of heart was witnessing what happened to Mildred Allen, my next-door neighbor and longtime friend.

Chapter 2

❧

Mildred is a law unto herself, and she doesn't mind who knows it. In fact, she glories in it. Having been brought up an only child in a privileged household, she had been her father's darling. He had raised her in great wealth and to assume both the freedom and the burden of great wealth when he was gone. He had, in fact, reared her as he would have reared a son—teaching her to read financial reports, to understand stock options, to play the futures market, and to manage the Ed and Eleanor Beasley Foundation that seemed to exist solely to sponsor British television shows on PBS. I could be wrong about that, for I certainly did not know the extent of Mildred's financial interests. All I knew was that her father had taught her well, which put him years ahead of his time in my estimation.

But in the doing, he had also put her in the unrealistic position of expecting an entire life of ease with every desire fulfilled and every problem resolved before reaching her. You may wonder, as I occasionally had, what in the world a woman like that was doing in a small, almost rural, town like Abbotsville. She could've been living among the beautiful people of California or New York—even, for goodness' sakes, of Paris or London. Well, apparently at times in her youth she had, if the occasional offhand reference to her early life was any indication.

Now, though, a yearly shopping trip to New York which included a few Broadway shows was the extent of her travels. By the time of which I'm speaking, she seemed perfectly content to stay home and queen it over our local society, such as it was, and do exactly what she wanted to do—which was next to nothing because she had Ida Lee to take up the slack. Ida Lee was a New York–trained professional housekeeper, personal manager, and hand holder who ran Mildred's household with unfailing competence, while Mildred fiddled with stock portfolios, various charities, and rewriting her will.

I liked Mildred and enjoyed her company, but not every day. Even though we were next-door neighbors, we weren't the constantly visiting kind. We could go for days, even weeks, with no contact at all, yet know that the other was available when needed. We got along well because we were on the same wavelength about most things in spite of her being an Episcopalian, although not a very faithful one. "I can't do all that kneeling anymore, Julia," she'd told me, "and I hate to just sit there while everybody else is bobbing up and down."

Not a very good reason to skip Sunday services, if you ask me, but then, we Presbyterians are known for our upright stance on any number of things. I could understand Mildred's problem, though, for she had over the years put on a good bit of weight. To be frank, she was a large woman who blamed her size on a nonexistent glandular condition. But then, we all find excuses of one kind or another for our lapses, so I accepted hers for being as good as any.

Mildred's other half, who often seemed only a fraction of that, was Horace, a man of few words but of attentive service. I never knew what to think of that marriage since Mildred so obviously ruled the roost, but of course it wasn't up to me to judge. I couldn't help but wonder, though, why Horace put up with having to dance to her tune. Frankly, I thought the less of him for it, but gradually came to realize that he was not only amply compensated, but perfectly suited to the role.

He often wore an ascot and occasionally spent a week or so at a gentlemen's spa somewhere in Arizona, getting high colonics and a suntan. In spite of Mildred's easy-come, easy-go attitude about most things, she kept him on a fairly tight leash.

And even more so since he'd recently suffered a heart attack which, according to Mildred, had left his memory slightly impaired. He had no recall of the days spent in intensive care or the weeks in a physical rehabilitation facility. By now, though, he seemed his old self with no concern about the gap in his memory. The only symptom that something was slightly off was his obsession with his little red Boxster car which he was no longer allowed to drive, but which he visited every day out in the garage. Other than that, he was his same pleasant self, impeccably dressed and ready to be of service when Mildred snapped her fingers.

As far as I knew, the marriage worked and, insulated by Horace and Ida Lee, nothing had ever disturbed Mildred's self-absorbed life. Nothing, that is, until her son, Tony, left Abbotsville for New York and came back the result of surgeries and hormone injections a changed man.

That happened a few years ago and, after several days of gasping and chest patting, the town gossips absorbed the news as part of the cultural shifts we were living through and thought little more of it.

It affected Mildred and Horace, of course, much more than any of us. Mildred took to her bed for a week or so and Horace flew to Palm Beach. I think he had viewed having a son as proof of something, maybe of his own manhood. He had certainly been of no help to Mildred in her hour of need because he took one look at his child in a pink Chanel suit and called Delta for a reservation.

When I heard the news, I didn't know whether to send a condolence card or show up with an almond pound cake. Amy Vanderbilt had not covered this particular contingency, but I certainly didn't run over and offer a shoulder to cry on. Mildred wasn't the kind of friend who shared her feelings, and I wasn't all that eager to know the details.

So, after the first numbing shock of seeing the results of Tony's life-changing surgeries, as well as accepting the fact that he was now Tonya, Mildred showed her true mettle. She got out of bed and began smoothly—to all outward appearances—to accommodate the idea of having produced a daughter instead of a son.

Chapter 3

❦

A few years have now passed since Tonya made her first stunning
appearance in Abbotsville, although she continued to make the
occasional brief visit now and then. But Mildred, who loved any
excuse to host a tea, a soiree, a dinner party, or even a backyard
barbeque, was always strangely silent during those visits. Although
most everybody was dying to meet Tonya face-to-face, no phone
calls were received and no invitations were forthcoming.

Having been in a similar situation at one time, I understood
Mildred's reluctance to put the new member of her family on
display. When I learned of my first husband's perfidy—after his
demise when nothing could be done—I had often wanted to
crawl into a hole and hide. Being the focus of every gossip in town
is nobody's idea of fun, but I had chosen the opposite tactic from
the one Mildred was taking. I had welcomed Wesley Lloyd
Springer's kept woman into my home, along with their illegitimate
son, then flaunted them both in church and at every social occasion, and ended up blackmailing those aloof, holier-than-thou
souls who happened to owe money to the Springer estate. After
that, Hazel Marie and Lloyd were quickly accepted at face value,
and no one has dared say a word against them or me ever since.
What they might've had to say about Wesley Lloyd is another
matter and of no concern to me.

Several days after the most recent of Tonya's short visits, Mildred asked me over for tea one afternoon in the early fall. Seated on chintz-covered cushions in white wicker chairs in her sunroom, we could see through the windows the glorious golden mass of color of Mildred's prized ginkgo tree.

Since we rarely met just to visit, I knew she had something specific on her mind and that her outward equanimity was perhaps not so deep after all. I vaguely wondered if I should ask after Tonya's well-being in a neighborly sort of way, as I would normally have done when she was Tony, or just leave well enough alone. Mildred made the decision for me.

"Julia," she began, setting her cup in its saucer with a clink, "I have got to talk to somebody, and I've decided that you are the most likely to understand and the least likely to spread it around town. I am driving myself crazy by keeping it all inside and pretending that I don't care one way or the other. But I *do* care. I've tried to talk with Horace to no avail. But of course he hasn't fully recovered from his heart attack and I don't want to burden him with more problems. The fact of the matter is that Tonya seems to have cut us, well, *me*, out of her life, and it is tearing me up. So I am going to impose on our friendship and discuss it with you even though I'm not in the habit of revealing personal problems."

"I know you're not," I said as warmly as I could, "and I appreciate your trust in me. You can rest assured that it will go no further, but it often helps simply to talk about whatever is troubling you."

Mildred picked up her napkin, gave it a shake, then laid it across her lap again. Then she said, "Horace refuses to talk about it or even to listen to me. He gets green around the gills whenever I bring up the subject. And Ida Lee, well, you know how she is—professional to the core. She just agrees with me and never says what she really thinks. But you, I know you'll be honest with me and tell me exactly what you think."

My first thought was that she was giving me too much credit. Like any socially oriented woman, I could lie with the best of them—it's called good manners. How often have I complimented someone on a dress that looked like a flour sack? Or told someone wracked by a recent illness how well she looked? Or exclaimed with admiration over a newly but tackily decorated room? Or accepted with pleasure an invitation that I didn't want, or with great and piteously expressed regret refused one that conflicted with nothing more than that I'd rather watch reruns on television than accept?

My second thought was that here was a chance to practice my newly determined intention to hold my tongue since no one—regardless of what they claimed—really wanted to hear the truth as I saw it.

"I appreciate that, Mildred," I said, knowing I had to say something, "and I'll do the best I can, but you might do better to discuss your feelings with your priest."

"Ha!" she said with a wave of dismissal. "All he'll do is tell me to pray about it."

"That's not bad advice, you know."

"Oh, I know, and I am. But I just feel that I'm going to explode if I don't let off steam in some way. I am so full of resentment that I don't know what to do. I've tried talking to Tonya about it, but she just waves me off and tells me not to be silly. And her careless attitude cuts me to the bone."

And, indeed, Mildred seemed deeply affected, even pulling a handkerchief from her sleeve and dabbing at her eyes. I felt honored that she wanted to share her burden with me.

"Then tell me," I said, assuming a warmly comforting tone, "what exactly does she do?"

"Well," Mildred said, heaving a great sigh, "it's more of what she *doesn't* do. I don't know if you've noticed or not, but Tonya's visits have gotten shorter and shorter, and fewer and fewer. In fact, I have to beg her to come home, but she is so busy with first one thing then another that her father and I are way down on her list of things to do. I call her, but she has company or she has an appointment or someone is at the door, so she can't talk. Then she forgets to return my call. I invite her home for something special, and she has a conflict. Why, Julia," she said, leaning toward me, "she didn't even come home when Horace was in intensive care. Oh, she called once to see how he was doing, but I could hear others talking in the background and ice tinkling in glasses, so she was entertaining. It's as if her life is so full that there's no room for us. And I don't know whether to be hurt or angry about it." She sighed again. "I think I'm both."

"I'm so sorry, Mildred, especially since you were once so close."

"And that's another thing," she went on, "Tony and I used to talk all the time. We'd pile up in my bed and watch reruns of *Sex and the City*, and talk and laugh and discuss everything and everybody under the sun, and just enjoy each other's company. But not any longer. When Tonya comes now, you could cut the silence with a knife all because I don't know what to talk about and, you know, Julia, I am never at a loss for words, particularly in a social situation."

I nodded, for it was true. Mildred could draw out the shiest of guests, ensure that everyone enjoyed themselves in her home, and send them off feeling honored for having been invited.

"It's as if," Mildred went on, "her mind is still in New York even when she's here and she can't wait to get back. Her life there is so full that she can't bear being away."

"Oh, Mildred," I said, "I am so sorry you're having to go through this. I always admired the close relationship the two of you had. You seemed to enjoy each other so much, discussing plays you'd seen, books you'd read, and so on. Maybe Tonya has so many interests that it's hard to decide which one to tell you about. You might try to draw her out by asking about a particular one." I mentally patted myself on the back for coming up with such an encouraging suggestion.

"Maybe," Mildred said, dabbing at her eyes. "Maybe so, who knows? But you're right, Julia, Tonya is multitalented. But she can't seem to settle on one thing. She's bounced from one enthusiasm to another. You may recall that at one time she was so sure that her future was the stage, and off to New York she went to study acting. That lasted barely a year. The next thing was to express herself in art, although she couldn't seem to find the right medium. So she tried one class after another, and none of them lasted. Except I give her credit for one thing—she threw pots for almost two years until she got tired of having clay splattered all over herself. And then I thought she'd finally found her métier in interior design, because she's stuck with it for the past several years. At least, I thought she had, but who knows now?"

It was certainly true that anything goes these days, and when it does, those of us who look on are supposed to smile and pretend that it's not only natural, but physically and emotionally healthy, even if it's jumping from one job or marital mate to another. If it feels good, then do it. *Wellness* seems to be the operative word and, I declare, I don't know what that means, especially when I hear of running a marathon for wellness which would just about kill me, or doing wellness exercises, or, for goodness' sakes, insuring financial wellness, or going to wellness clinics. If you're well, why do you need a clinic?

But holding myself in, I said none of that to Mildred, determining instead to let her vent without adding my own views on the subject.

"And," Mildred said with a roll of her eyes, "you know what else she's done, or *not* done? Birthdays have always been important to us. You know, there's just the three of us so we've always made those days special among ourselves. We try to surprise each other and celebrate in unique ways. In fact, that little red Boxster car was my birthday gift to Horace this year. But do you know what Tonya did for him? Of course you don't, so I'll tell you even though it shames me to say it. Nothing, she did absolutely nothing—no gift, no phone call, not even a Hallmark card!"

"Oh, my," I said, imagining how hurtful that would've been. "That's really thoughtless of her, especially with Horace having been so ill."

"Yes, except he didn't notice. I declare, Julia, he is getting so forgetful and it's just one more thing to worry me to death."

And, indeed, tears were welling up in her eyes, and my heart went out to her. *Sharper than a serpent's tooth* came to mind, although I didn't know where it had come from.

"Well, Mildred," I began, although hesitantly since I was treading ground on which friends rarely ventured, "it takes a lot of money to flit from one enthusiasm to another. I, of course, don't know Tonya's financial situation, but if you control the purse strings you can also control her."

"Oh, I wish it was that simple. Believe me, I would've already done it. But Tonya has a trust fund set up by my father, and she's long come of age to use it as she pleases. Although," Mildred said as a light seemed to dawn, "the way she's been spending could mean that she'll be scraping the bottom of the barrel real soon. Thank you for reminding me, Julia, because all I have to do is wait her out. I'll suddenly become important to her then."

"Oh, Mildred," I said, "that's not what you want! Surely Tonya wouldn't do that."

"Oh," Mildred said as her eyes began to fill, "I don't doubt it at all. All I can say is that I must've been a terrible mother to have raised such a thoughtless child."

"But, listen," I said, "she's always had your approval of whatever she wanted to do. Maybe she assumes she'll always have it. And," I quickly added, "that's a good thing. Think of all the children who grow up feeling they can never please their parents. They go through life thinking that they don't measure up. You, on the other hand, have always expressed delight in—"

"Maybe too much so," Mildred cut in mournfully. "Maybe I should've put my foot down on occasion. Tonya doesn't have time, or she refuses to *make* time, for her mother, and I just resent it from the depths of my soul."

"You mustn't give up on her, Mildred," I said. "One of these days Tonya will need you, and at that point she'll realize how important you are to her."

"Ha!" Mildred said in a stronger voice. "Probably when she needs money! Well, she may also realize that I'm not always at her beck and call, either. What goes around usually comes around. Right, Julia?"

Recalling that somebody once said that home is where, when you go there, they have to take you in, I could do nothing but nod half-heartedly.

"But I will tell you this," Mildred said with a determined note in her voice, "Tonya has to have made a dent in her trust fund. Thank you for reminding me of that, Julia. The way she's been living is not inexpensive, so," she went on, "if she thinks she can come to me, she'll have to think again." She grasped the arms of her chair and began to rise. "I am going to change my will."

Chapter 4

❧

Suggesting that she sleep on it before making any drastic changes, I soon took my leave of Mildred and went home. Who knew, though, what she would do. In her current state of mind, she could easily make a change that she'd live to regret.

Well, that wasn't quite right because if she changed her will to indicate her anger, she might not live long enough to rectify it if she changed her mind again, and if that happened, she also wouldn't have time to regret anything. Or something like that.

Nonetheless, I went home in an agitated state of mind. I felt for Mildred and sympathized with her. Having no children my-self, I could only imagine the pain of being cut out of a child's life. But then, thinking of Lloyd, maybe I could. If he went out into the world on his own, then behaved as if Sam and I didn't exist, I would be devastated. Just because someone grows up shouldn't mean that the people who helped him get that way no longer counted.

"Lillian," I said as soon as I entered the kitchen, "the Lord knew what He was doing when He didn't give me any children. I don't think I could put up with them."

"What you talkin' about?" she asked, whacking a spoon against a pot on the stove.

"Tonya Allen," I said and plopped down in a chair by the table, realizing how sapped I was from listening to Mildred's tale of woe. "That's who I'm talking about. I declare, Lillian, it seems we've raised a generation of ungrateful children, although I thank goodness that I had nothing to do with it."

"You're not countin' Lloyd?" Lillian asked with one eyebrow cocked. "Look like to me you had a lot to do with raisin' him."

"Well, yes," I said, smiling at the thought of my deceased husband's illegitimate son who had been thrust along with his mother upon me. "We've done pretty well with him, haven't we? But see, Lillian, what if he goes off to college and gets indoctrinated with all kinds of stuff and decides that he's too busy or too important to bother with us?"

"Well then, that jus' mean something was wrong before he went."

"Hm-m, you may be right. Mildred put up no boundaries, that's for sure. But it's still hard to fathom how Tonya can treat her parents as if they're of no concern to her. What does it take to pick up a phone now and then?"

"Well, here's the thing, Miss Julia. You an' me don't have to say yea or nay to anything anybody else do, 'less it be against the law. So if it don't mess with me an' mine, I always say, live and let live."

"Yes," I said, nodding in agreement, "I do, too. But it really distresses me to see what it's doing to Mildred and Horace. They're having a hard time coming to terms with the way Tonya treats them. At least, Mildred is. Who knows about Horace? He's in a world of his own these days, anyway."

"Yes'm, I hear he's havin' a hard time knowin' what day it is. Somebody said he went to the grocery store the other day and stood in line at the checkout, then handed over a prescription to be filled. An' got real upset when they wouldn't fill it."

"My word," I said, straightening up upon hearing something else to worry Mildred. "I hadn't heard that. He must be in a worse way than anybody realizes. Mildred didn't say a word about it."

"She may not notice," Lillian said with the assurance of knowing of what she spoke, "'cause they usu'lly all right at home where they know where everything's at."

"Who's this *they* you're talking about?"

"People losin' their mem'ry. You know, ole people gettin' so they can't take care of theirselves."

I sat up straight, my eyes widening. "You're not talking about Alzheimer's, are you? Horace could just be a little absentminded. I hope that's all it is. Mildred has enough to deal with without adding anything else."

"I hope so, too, Miss Julia," Lillian said, but not very hopefully. "But Ida Lee tole me how he keep askin' if she his sister, and that don't sound too good to me."

"Oh, my, I thought his memory problems were just an aberration from having been so sick." I drummed my fingers on the table, thinking. "Do you think I should mention the grocery store thing to Mildred? I hate giving her something else to worry about, but if he's doing strange things like that, she should know about it. What do you think?"

"I think she gonna know sooner or later 'cause folks like that don't get any better."

"You know," I said in a musing sort of way, "Mildred is suddenly having to face all kinds of changes. If you're right about Horace, that is. If he's getting so that he's not himself, and Tonya, well, who knows about her, I just don't know how she'll handle it all. Mildred is used to waving her checkbook and having problems disappear. What she may be facing now aren't the kind that can be paid off."

"No'm, but a checkbook helps."

I nodded and began to rise. "You're right about that. It helps but it won't solve everything, and I'm afraid that Mildred is about to learn how limited it can be. Well," I said, pushing my chair under the table, "let me go see what Sam's doing. He still upstairs?"

Lillian stopped stirring, looked up at the ceiling, and said, "He's comin' down now."

I laughed. "You know everything that goes on in this house. I haven't heard a thing, yet you know when anybody moves. How do you do that?"

"Well," she said, smiling at the compliment, "this ole house creaks when anybody stirs around, an' he's been workin' in the sunroom all afternoon, an' he's the onliest one up there, so . . . ," she shrugged her shoulders, "it's easy."

After supper, Sam and I retired as we usually did to the library, which is what we called the former downstairs bedroom now that it had built-in bookcases around the walls. Lillian had left to pick up Latisha, her eleven-year-old feisty great-granddaughter, from an after-school program. Latisha occasionally ate supper with us, but on this day she'd announced that she had a project she was working on and didn't want to be interrupted.

The television was on, but neither Sam nor I were paying much attention to it. We'd heard all the news we wanted to hear, and none of it had been very edifying. Sam was reading the newspaper as he waited for time to go to bed, and I was going over in my mind some of the things that I could've said to Mildred. I had told Sam about my afternoon as Mildred's confidant, and we'd agreed that there were no easy answers in the situation in which she and Horace found themselves.

"Just be available," Sam advised me, "as I know you will be. Having someone to listen will be helpful, and, I'll tell you this, she doesn't have Horace to lean on. I saw him for a few minutes the other afternoon and he asked me three times if I had any children. I don't think he's doing so well."

I agreed and told him of Horace's attempt to fill a prescription in a grocery store. "Which," I continued, "makes me wonder how he came to have a prescription in the first place. Ida Lee usually does those kinds of errands for them. I guess I should mention it to Mildred, although she surely has the Lord's plenty on her plate already."

"Hm-m, yes, maybe you should," Sam said, turning over a page of the newspaper. "I'm really not sure that Horace knew who I was, but he was friendly and talkative at the time. It was only later that I wondered about it.

"By the way," Sam said, lowering the newspaper, "have you heard anything about the business that Etta Mae Wiggins works for?"

"The Handy Home Helpers? What about it?"

"I hear it's going under, closing shop, selling out, or something. None of it may be true, but it was mentioned at the Bluebird the other day." Sam often ate breakfast, or sometimes lunch, at the Bluebird café with a few friends with nothing else to do now that they were retired. It was the way they kept each other abreast of what was going on in Abbotsville.

"I hope that's not true," I said, immediately concerned for the young woman who had been so helpful to me at various times in the past. "What in the world would Etta Mae do? She's worked for Lurline Somebody for years."

"I expect she'll be fine," Sam said, his attention turning back to the paper. "The caregiving business is thriving these days with so many of us living longer."

"That may be just you and me, Sam."

"Could be," he said, with a wry smile. "But look around at all the retirees who've moved here. There'll be an increasing need for hospices, assisted living facilities, and the like to take care of them."

I nodded and let the conversation lapse while I continued to think of Etta Mae and what effect the loss of her job would mean for her. I started to tell Sam that I would call her the next day, but he seemed absorbed in some article in the newspaper, so my attention wandered to the television.

"*Sam!*" I said, sitting up straight as a sentence flashed across the screen. "Did you see that?"

"No," he said, looking up over his reading glasses. "What was it?"

"It said there're sixty-three million Americans suffering from constipation." I patted my chest in consternation. "That makes me afraid to leave the house."

"Julia," he said with a bark of laughter. "Honey, that's the funniest thing I've ever heard." He dropped the newspaper and gave himself up to full-blown laughter.

"Well, it's not so funny if you stop and think about it. We could all be in danger."

He just laughed harder. And finally I joined him, although I did think that the general public should be warned of such an impending disaster.

Chapter 5

❧

I had just gotten up from the breakfast table the next morning when the phone rang. I picked it up, ready to click off if no one immediately responded—it takes a second or so, I guess, to switch on a recording. I just have no patience with people who ignore the Do Not Call list, so I also have no qualms about hanging up on them.

"Julia?" Mildred Allen asked, although she knew my voice as well as I did. "I've decided what I'm going to do about my will, and my lawyers are coming up from Atlanta later this week to implement the changes."

As Sam began to put on his jacket, I mouthed, "Mildred," to him. He smiled, shook his head in sympathy, and left for a meeting of the zoning board downtown.

"Well, good," I said into the phone, while waving at Sam, and thinking that the longer Mildred had to wait, the more likely she was to change her mind again. "That will give you plenty of time to really think it through."

"Oh, I've thought it through, all right, and the thing about it is, Julia, I've realized that if I make Tonya my primary beneficiary, I will just be encouraging her to keep on doing what she's already doing, which is thinking of no one but herself. And I just do not want to reward her for the way she's treating me. I mean us. I intend to put a stop to it.

"The problem, though," she went on, "is that Daddy wanted his estate to extend to future generations, but there won't be any future ones. The Beasley-Allen family will end with Tonya."

"Oh, my," I murmured, "I hadn't thought of that."

"Well, me, either. But I'll tell you, Julia, I haven't really thought much about grandchildren in general, assuming that eventually there would be some. But now that I know there won't be, I am just devastated." She sniffed loudly then went on. "What am I going to do with all this money and no family to leave it to?"

"I'm sure you'll think of something," I said. "There're so many worthwhile causes . . ."

"Well, I'll tell you this," Mildred said in a tone that meant business, "Tonya's selfish lifestyle is certainly not one of them."

"I am so sorry, Mildred," I said, "but you know that I don't have any grandchildren, either, and—"

"But you have Lloyd!" she exclaimed with a catch in her voice.

"Well, yes," I said, conceding what I'd long felt toward the boy, "but think of how I got him. He's not kin to me in any way, shape, or form. But if you're attached to someone emotionally and spiritually, then you have a kinship. So, see? You may well end up with family in an unusual way, as I have."

"Well, I hope to goodness," Mildred said with some asperity, "that a child of Horace's doesn't show up on my doorstep. I'm not like you, Julia, I'd slam the door and call the police."

I smiled to myself, recalling my reaction to the sudden appearance at my door of my deceased husband's paramour and the child who looked just like him.

"Don't give me too much credit," I replied. "What I did was not done out of the goodness of my heart—far from it, in fact. I acted out of anger and a burning desire for revenge even though Wesley Lloyd was out of my reach by that time." I paused as a memory of that anger flashed across my mind. Taking a deep breath to dispel it, I went on. "It was that child himself who touched my heart.

And, of course, in the final analysis, it was the working of the Lord that changed everything between us."

Mildred sighed. "I just wish the Lord would take pity and start doing some of that work in my situation. Anyway, what I've decided to do is to provide a barely living income for Tonya that will fluctuate with the economy. She'll never starve, but she'll have to work. And she'll never, ever, have access to the capital. That will be a source of scholarships for deserving students for years to come."

I was silent for a few seconds. Then, with great care, I responded. "That's a thoughtful thing to do, but, Mildred, as far as Tonya is concerned, consider that you might be acting out of that resentment you told me about. You may be punishing Tonya more than you mean to."

"Oh, I mean to," she said. "As far as *I'm* concerned, Tonya can learn to get along on her own. After all, that's what she's doing now. She gives absolutely no thought to her mother and father, and we are *aging*, Julia. Who knows how much longer we'll even be around? So I'm going to fix it so she'll know how it feels to be ignored and overlooked. That's what I've decided, Julia, so don't try to talk me out of it."

"I wouldn't dream of it," I said, backing off. "It's yours to do with as you see fit."

Mildred certainly and self-righteously agreed with that, and we soon ended the conversation.

Turning to Lillian as I hung up the phone, I said, "I declare, Lillian, Mildred is so upset with Tonya that I'm not sure she's thinking straight. I can't really blame her, though, because of the shabby way Tonya is treating them, especially Horace. You'd think she'd be concerned about him, but all Mildred can think about is changing her will to punish her after she's dead. After Mildred is dead, I mean. Does that make sense?"

"No'm, not much."

"Well, I can't explain it any better than that, except I'm afraid she's acting out of anger. Let me tell you something, Lillian, don't ever make changes in your will when you're mad or hurt or feeling resentful in any way. If you ever do, make sure you live long enough to regret what you've done and have time to change it back."

"That don't bother me, Miss Julia. I don't have a will to change or to change back, either one."

"Why, Lillian," I said, turning to stare at her, "do you mean you don't have any kind of will—nothing written down at all?"

"No'm, I don't have enough to worry 'bout who gets what. I got burial insurance I pay on ev'ry week so I don't burden nobody with my final expenses. Nothin' much left after that."

"Oh, my word," I said, sitting at the table again, stunned by my lack of care for her. "Why, Lillian, you have a sizable estate—you own your house, your furniture, and your car, all free and clear, and, knowing you, I expect you have a savings account as well." I pretty much knew what she owned for I'd made sure of most of it.

"Yes'm," Lillian said, "but it's not like I'm rich or anything."

"All the more reason to have a will so that what you do have goes to the one you want it to go to. Listen," I said, hitching forward in the chair, "do you know who'll get it all if you don't have a will? The next of kin, that's who."

Lillian turned away from the sink and stared at me with a dawning realization on her face of what was in store. "Latisha's mama?"

"That's right. Your daughter passed years ago, so your granddaughter is next of kin—the one who abandoned Latisha and never comes to see her or you. Is that who you want to get everything you have?"

"No'm," she said, shaking her head slowly, a somber look on her face. "No, ma'am, I surely don't. That girl done ruint her life, an' she's still doin' it. I want Latisha to have whatever I have, 'cause she's gonna make something of herself."

"She certainly is. She's as smart as a whip, Lillian, and she needs to know that her great-granny loved her enough to keep on looking after her. I don't mean that she needs to know now," I hurriedly explained. "But she needs to know after you're gone, because you know your granddaughter would fritter it all away, and Latisha would be abandoned again."

"Oh, my Jesus," Lillian said, leaning against a kitchen counter. "What can I do, Miss Julia?"

"You can make an appointment with Binkie to make out your will so that it can't be challenged. Then you can rest easy, knowing you've taken care of Latisha. But listen, Lillian," I went on, "you ought to cancel that burial insurance you're paying on every week. It's doing nothing but making somebody else rich."

I didn't mention the fact that most pay-by-the-week burial insurance policies issued a check to the next of kin, who could spend it any way they wanted to spend it. Knowing Latisha's mama, I doubted that Lillian would get much more than a pine box.

"In fact," I went on, "you don't need to worry about final expenses. I'll see to that."

Actually, neither she nor Latisha needed to worry about any number of things, but that's something one shouldn't disclose to one's supplemental beneficiaries. It would change a number of current relationships that were just fine the way they were.

Chapter 6

❧

Have you ever had so much on your mind, so many things coming
at you from all directions, that all you wanted to do was sit down,
lean your head back, and take a quick nap even though it's only
the middle of the morning? That's what I did, sinking down in my
favorite place at one end of the sofa that offered a clear view of
both the television set and the fireplace, as well as providing a
protruding wing for my head to rest against.

Unhappily, I didn't get much rest. Three worrisome matters
took turns jumping to the forefront of my mind: Mildred and her
daughter, Horace and his failing faculties, and Etta Mae Wiggins
and the possible loss of her job.

I set Mildred aside, assuring myself that I was already doing
all I could for her, which was to listen and to gingerly suggest that
she do nothing that would sever family ties that were already at
the breaking point. As for Horace, my only concern was whether
or not to further burden Mildred by telling her of his unusual
behavior.

Finally, though, it was Etta Mae on whom I settled my thoughts.
It had been a while since I'd even spoken with her and all that
while I'd assumed she was getting along well—no news is good
news, or so they say. But there were some people, and Etta Mae
was one of them, who kept their problems to themselves, so
silence was no assurance that all was well. And, of course, so

much had happened to those who were closer to me that I had let her slide to a back burner. Yet that young woman had been available to me on several occasions when I'd badly needed help, and, here, I'd all but blocked her out of my thoughts for the past year or so.

Actually, though, I had given her a few warm passing thoughts when the monthly checks arrived.

One of the best business decisions I'd ever made had been to hire Etta Mae to supervise the Hillandale Trailer Park out on Springer Road, a mile or so from the township of Delmont. You may wonder how I had come to own a trailer park, of all things, and the answer is that it was a minor part of the estate that Wesley Lloyd Springer, my late first husband, left when he expired in his new Buick Park Avenue out in our driveway. How he'd come to own a trailer park, I didn't know—probably, I speculated, taken in lieu of an unpaid loan.

When I took over the ownership, Etta Mae was already renting a space in the park for her single-wide, which she referred to as the only relic from a bad marriage, although, as I later learned, she had had a number of those. We first met after she nearly drove me crazy with phone calls about the other residents, the poor upkeep of the grounds, the blown-out security lights, the erosion of the drive, and a dozen other things. To put a stop to the constant complaints, I had hired her to supervise the park, collect rents, and keep out the trash—her word, not mine—human and otherwise, and she'd proved an able administrator. I'd given her full authority to hire help if she needed it and to decide who could rent a space in the park and who couldn't. It took a few months to clear out the troublemakers and the slow payers, but the arrangement not only put an end to her complaints, it also freed up the county sheriff's deputies.

So, I reminded myself, even if she loses her main job, she would still have some income—a small percentage of the rents she collected—although it certainly would not be enough. Her home would be safe as well, for her single-wide occupied a rent-free space, another perk of her supervisory job.

With concern for her well-being, I called her, using her cell phone number since I knew that she was most likely following a strict schedule of visits to the housebound elderly, sick, and ailing. As a certified nurse's assistant working for The Handy Home Helpers, she was inordinately proud of the education she'd received at the county technical school, telling anybody who would listen that she was the only member of her family to go to college.

After five or six rings, a recording urged me to leave a message, so I did, then hung up and began to worry about her again.

Etta Mae had had a checkered marital career, having discarded at least two husbands and buried one, although that one might not count since his heart had proved unable to take the anticipation much less the consummation. There might have been more for all I knew, but I didn't hold multiple marriages against her. I'll admit that at one time I might have—in fact, did—but the older I get the more I live and let live without criticizing everything that happens. It makes for a more serene life.

It suddenly occurred to me that she might have finally married the man she really loved—Bobby Lee Something-or-Other, a sheriff's deputy who was a mixture of Mr. J. D. Pickens, P.I., Hazel Marie's husband, and Sergeant Coleman Bates, Binkie's husband. That was a very attractive but volatile mixture, if you ask me, and you might as well because I, even at my age, had felt his magnetism at our first and only meeting.

My spirits began to lift at the thought of Etta Mae safely and happily married, ensconced perhaps in a lovely bungalow with a white picket fence, and living the dream of every young girl before the urge to climb the corporate ladder displaced that dream.

I may have dropped off, but if so, it had been for only a few minutes. The ringing of the phone jerked me awake and I hurriedly answered it, hoping it was Etta Mae returning my call.

It wasn't.

"Julia?" Mildred asked. "Are you busy?"

"Uh, no," I replied, trying to sound as if I'd been busy doing something besides taking a nap. "Not really. How are you, Mildred?"

"Not so good. Julia, if it's not one thing, it's two more. Here I am, trying to figure out my will, and Horace is worrying me to death. Do you know what he's done now?"

"Uh, no," I said again, although several things flashed through my mind that I was reluctant to mention.

"Well, Ida Lee brought up my breakfast this morning and told me that Horace had not been down to eat and that he wasn't in his bedroom. Well, of course that meant I had to get up, put on some clothes, and help her look for him. His calendar was clear, so I knew he wasn't at some meeting or another. We're both meticulous about keeping our calendars, don't you know, so that we always know where the other one is. You and Sam do that, too, don't you?"

"Well, no. We just tell each other what we'll be doing each day."

"Oh, well, I guess you both get up early. By the time I get up, Horace is about ready for his afternoon nap, so we find that keeping accurate calendars is a tremendous help. But," Mildred went on, "Horace has gotten slack with his. Today was absolutely blank, yet he was nowhere to be found. I know that he's been a little absentminded here lately, so my first thought was that he had gone downtown and let the time get away from him."

"Uh, Mildred," I said, preparing myself to tell her a few other worrisome activities that Horace might have been engaged in. "It might be worse than that."

"Oh, tell me about it!" she exclaimed. "It *was* worse than that. Do you know where he was? He was out in the garage, sitting in that Boxster car of his, and, Julia, there's no telling how long he'd been out there. It had been so long that he'd practically *frozen* in place. Not that it was that cold, because, of course, the garage is heated, but when Ida Lee and I got him out from under the wheel, he couldn't even straighten up. He was still in a sitting position when he was standing up! I really think he'd been out there all night, and both of his legs had gone to sleep so they kept caving in on him. You know what it's like when one leg does it. Imagine what it'd be like to have both of them as limber as a wet rag. It was all we could do to get him in the house, and we didn't dare let him sit down. Ida Lee and I had to walk him round and around the foyer until he could manage on his own again."

"Oh, my goodness," I said, picturing the three of them shambling around Mildred's elegant foyer. "That doesn't sound too good, Mildred. Did he say why he went to the garage?"

"That's the thing, Julia!" she said. "He doesn't remember why or even *when* he went out there. But it had to've been after Ida Lee and I went to bed because neither of us knew he'd gone out. All I can say is thank goodness I have his car keys. I guess I'll have to start hiding the house keys now."

We discussed that for a few minutes, both of us wondering where Horace would've been found if he'd been able to start his car. I decided against adding to her concerns by telling her of his grocery store episode and his unfocused talk with Sam.

"You know, Julia," Mildred continued, "that my plan was to employ some young man as a companion-caretaker of sorts until Horace fully recovers. But I've not found anybody who's willing to do that kind of work. And you know that I pay well, yet still, such hands-on personal work does not draw the kind of individual anybody would want. I don't know what I'm going to do. One of the first things I thought about was if Tonya would come home, she would be the perfect companion for her father. But you can throw that idea out the window. She's too busy." Mildred stopped with a catch in her voice and said again, "I don't know what I'm going to do."

"Don't let it get you down, Mildred, you have to stay strong," I said, offering platitudes because there was little else I could offer. "I'll ask Sam if he knows somebody who could help. In fact," I went on, as a sudden thought came to me, "I might know somebody, myself."

Chapter 7

❖

As soon as I clicked off the phone, it rang again and this time it was Etta Mae returning my call.

"Hey, Miss Julia!" she said, sounding as carefree and breezy as she always did. "I was so glad to get your message. How're you doing? How's Mr. Sam and Lillian? I've been meaning to call and check up on you, but you know how it is. I stay so busy that all the things I want to do just drop by the wayside and, first thing you know, weeks and months have come and gone."

"We're all fine, Etta Mae," I said, finally getting a word in edgewise. "And I apologize for letting the time get away from me, too. It's been too long since I've heard from you, and I've had you on my mind lately, so I just thought I'd call and see how you are. I hope I didn't interrupt your schedule, though."

"Oh, no. No, you didn't interrupt anything. In fact, I'm on my lunch break now, heading for McDonald's for a McRib sandwich. They don't always have them on the menu, but they're really good. Oh!" she said, breaking into her own flow of words. "Why don't I swing by and pick you up? We can have lunch together—my treat—and get caught up with each other."

"Well," I said, not exactly thrilled at the thought of a drive-through lunch, much less of letting someone who might soon be jobless pay for it. But I had long ago learned to occasionally allow someone else to host a meal instead of always insisting that I be the one who treats—it makes for a more equitable relationship. "I'd love to, Etta Mae. Come right along. I'll be waiting."

After telling Lillian that I wouldn't be sharing the tuna salad she'd made, I slipped on a light jacket and waited by the front door. The little red Mustang that Etta Mae drove soon slid to the curb, and I hurried out.

Getting into the low-slung car was a feat in itself, but I managed, wondering as I closed the door what the appeal of small red cars were for people as different as Etta Mae Wiggins and Horace Allen.

"How *are* you, Miss Julia?" Etta Mae exclaimed, as she headed the car toward the south end of Main Street. "I'm so glad you were free. This is just making my day."

Delighted that I could so obviously and easily please her, I settled back to enjoy our time together. Glancing now and then at her as she drove, I could see little change since I'd last seen her. Her blond hair might've been slightly longer—she had it gathered in a ponytail so it was hard to tell. She wore a scrub suit and sneakers, her usual uniform, although she avoided white in favor of various colors. The one she was wearing was navy blue with a green cardigan over it against the chilly late November day. As she turned the car into the McDonald's lot and pulled into the drive-through lane, she gave me a quick glance.

"I hope you don't mind eating in the car," she said. "It's quicker and a whole lot quieter than going inside."

"This is fine," I said, although eating in a car wasn't my usual idea of a ladies' lunch. "I'll enjoy it."

Etta Mae gave our orders to a disembodied voice—two McRibs, two medium Cokes, and two small cheesy bacon fries. After receiving our order from the second window, she whipped the car around to park in the side lot.

"If it gets too cold, let me know," she said, cracking our windows. "I'd rather eat inside, but you can't hear yourself think in there this time of day."

"Lots of customers?"

"Yeah, all under five. Moms pick up at preschool and bring 'em here for lunch. They go crazy, yelling and crying and spilling and throwing things. It can get dangerous." Etta Mae laughed. "Some McDonald's have an outdoor play area like the one over near the airport, but not this one."

"That sounds like a good corporate idea," I said. "At least the mothers can eat in peace."

"Or a good way to work up a picky eater's appetite and sell more hamburgers," Etta Mae said, as she leaned around to the back seat. From the conglomeration of medical supplies, newspapers, extra pairs of shoes, raincoat, a couple of sweaters, and stacks of folders and papers, she pulled out two towels.

"Spread this over your lap, Miss Julia," she said, giving me a towel and keeping the other one. "McRibs can get messy."

Then she emptied the two console cup holders of tissues, change, and receipts, placed our drinks in them, and handed me a straw, a McRib sandwich, and a container of dressed-up fries. It was my first meeting with everything but the Coca-Cola, but I will have to say that the Tete-a-Tete Tearoom's famous chicken salad couldn't hold a candle to the zesty taste of what she had ordered. Everything was delicious, and the towel was a welcome replacement of a paper napkin.

"So tell me how you've been," I said between bites. "How's your love life going?"

"Oh," she said airily, "don't ask. I've decided that I'm snakebit when it comes to men, so the thing for me to do is steer clear and look after myself."

I smiled. "That's not a bad way to go. I'm Presbyterian enough to believe that what's meant to be will be, regardless of what we do. And when it comes down to it, we all have to look after ourselves."

"I guess," she said in a pensive tone. "I keep thinking I ought to get out of Delmont, go to a big city like Charlotte, maybe, and try my luck there."

"Oh, I'd hate for you to move away, but there're probably more opportunities in a bigger city." But, I thought, more opportunities for what? Trouble, most likely, but far be it from me to give advice. I'd given that up.

"Well," she said, wadding up the sandwich wrapping, "looks like I'll have to do something sooner or later. Lurline Corn is trying to sell the business, so that means my job is on the line."

"Oh, really? That surprises me," I said, although of course it didn't. "I'd think that anybody who bought the business would keep the employees—they'd be considered an asset, especially you with your training and experience. Actually," I went on, "what does she have to sell if not the employees and the contracts with patients?"

"Good grief," Etta Mae said, "I hadn't thought of it that way. But you're right. That's really what the business is, isn't it? Of course she does have that little house on Main Street in Delmont which she uses as her office. That's where she keeps patient records, makes out our schedules, interviews potential patients, and does payroll and all the tax stuff, so I guess that would be part of the business, too." She glanced at me and smiled. "I think I'm feeling better."

She reached for the key in the ignition, but pulled back before turning it. "I just thought of something. There's a rumor that the Dollar Store is looking for a place to build in Delmont, and Lurline had an appointment with a real estate agent a couple of weeks ago. I thought it was to maybe list her home, but now I'm not so sure. If she can't sell the business, she could sell where the business *is*. Maybe I don't feel so good."

"Why is Lurline selling in the first place? What's she planning to do?"

"Move to *Florida*!" Etta Mae said with vehemence. "She's been poor-mouthing so long that I believed her when she said she was just barely making ends meet. Instead, she's looking at half-a-million-dollar condos *with amenities* in Orlando—so that, she says, she can go to Disney World any time she wants to." Then with just a touch of bitterness, she added, "And she knows that's my favorite place in the whole world."

"When is this supposed to happen?"

"Any day, Lurline says, but she's been saying that for weeks. I think she's trying to scare us all into quitting so she won't be expected to give us severance pay. So maybe she's planning to sell the property and just close the business." Etta Mae sucked down the last of her Coke, rammed the empty cup into the sack, and said, "I'd quit right now if I had something else lined up. Then I wouldn't have to hear her talk about *Florida*."

"Have you tried the hospital? A doctor's office? Or some of the health service nonprofits? Sam says there're a lot of assisted living facilities around. You could check those out."

"Miss Julia," she said, leaning her head back, "I've tried every one of them, and they all pay next to nothing. Not that I'm doing that well with Lurline, but at least I can pay my bills. But that's only because of seniority or longevity or something, and because I've threatened to sue her if she didn't pay a living wage." She gave me a twisted smile. "I know I wouldn't get very far with that, but Lurline always worries about her reputation and she knows I'd put it in the paper and talk about her all over the county.

"Ah, well," she said, then heaved a long sigh, "I haven't starved so far, so I guess things will work out some way or another."

I busied myself with cramming my cup and wrappings into the bag and folding the towel in my lap. Then I waited a second or two before making a proposition that I had no business making since I hadn't discussed it with anybody else who would be affected.

"As it happens," I began, "Mildred Allen—you remember her,

don't you?—has a great need for some immediate help. You might not want to be limited to one patient, but I can assure you that Mildred would pay well. It could be a nice stopgap for a few weeks until you find something permanent. But," I quickly added, "I've not spoken to Mildred about you—not knowing, of course, that you would be available or even interested." I went on to tell her of the difficulties that Horace was having and of Mildred's concerns.

"Hm-m," Etta Mae said, "sounds like dementia, which could just be age-related. But if it's Alzheimer's, Mrs. Allen will eventually have to think about long-term care, maybe in a locked facility. Those folks don't get better."

"Yes, I've looked around on Google, but as I said, this would be just a stopgap for you anyway. That is, if you really want to leave The Handy Home Helpers before you have to, and if you have a plan for a much better situation in a few weeks. Or maybe a few months."

She laughed. "That's the problem, Miss Julia. I don't have any plans at all—all my options are for something that's worse, not better."

"Don't be so sure about that," I said, my mind whirling with a number of possibilities. There was, however, a niggling little memory of promising myself that I would stop trying to run the lives of other people. I quickly shut down that line of thought. This was different.

Chapter 8

❧

My intention was to go straight across our yards as soon as I got home and acquaint Mildred with my perfect solution to one of her problems. Instead, I waved goodbye to Etta Mae and hurried up the front walk and into the house. An icy wind had picked up considerably while we'd had lunch, and I needed a heavier coat, maybe a head scarf, and a pair of gloves before venturing out again.

As soon as I stepped into the hall and closed the door behind me, I heard voices in the kitchen. Striding toward the back of the house, I smiled to myself. One distinctive voice made itself heard loud and clear—Latisha was on the premises.

"Hey, Miss Lady!" she cried as soon as I walked into the room. "Guess what! My teacher had to call Great-Granny to come get me 'cause I threw up right in the middle of Social Studies. So now I don't have to go to after-school class. I get to come see how you been doing."

Latisha was sitting at a small table that Lillian kept in the kitchen for her. It was covered with crayons, Magic Markers, scissors, and construction paper, all of which were designed to keep Latisha entertained while Lillian worked around her. Lillian called it her Keep Latisha Quiet table, but it rarely did.

"Well, it's lovely having you, Latisha," I said, removing my jacket. "I'm sorry to hear that you've been sick. How're you feeling now?"

Lillian, drying her hands on a dish towel, answered for her. "She's fine, Miss Julia. No fever or sneezin' or anything. I think something jus' upset her stomach."

"Your stomach would be upset, too, Great-Granny," Latisha said, "if you had to eat in that school lunchroom. I don't know what they cook in that place, but one boy said it was roadkill, and I believe it."

"Latisha!" Lillian cried. "I hope you don't say such a thing to them nice lunchroom ladies. They real good to you, an' you better not be hurtin' their feelings."

"I'm not going to hurt their feelings," Latisha said, unperturbed by the possibility. "I like 'em all. I just don't like what they give us to eat, 'specially when we're starving and have to eat whatever they dish out."

"You know you like hot dog day. You tole me you do."

"Well," Latisha said, subsiding, "that's the only one."

Looking at Lillian, I asked, "Are you sure she's all right? Take her on to the doctor if you're concerned."

"No'm, she's all right. She jus' had a big bowl of soup and thirteen crackers, an' she still talkin'. She's fine."

"I think so, too," Latisha said, and began to cut out a picture from a coloring book.

"Well," I said, "I'm going to run across and see Mrs. Allen for a few minutes. I just came in to put on a heavier coat."

Lillian said, "How's Miss Etta Mae doin'? I was hopin' she'd come in an' visit with us for a while."

"She's having some problems with her job," I said, wrapping a scarf around my neck. "I'll tell you all about it a little later. Right now, I need to talk to Mildred and get back. I don't know what the weather's going to do, but the temperature's dropping and that wind is just whipping around."

"I hope it snows ten feet deep," Latisha said, barely looking up from her work. "And we have to stay here forever."

Lillian's eyes rolled back, as I laughed and headed for the door.

"I don't know if it would work for you or not," I said, summing up my presentation to Mildred. We were in her sitting room, each in a wing chair beside the fireplace, both of us alternately gazing at the gas fire licking around nonflammable logs and glancing at the occasional pinging sound of sleet against the Palladian window.

"But," I went on, gathering myself to rise and get back home, "I had to at least give you the option. I know you wanted to find a gentleman to be Horace's companion, but when you mentioned that you'd not found anyone suitable . . ."

"*Suitable!*" Mildred exclaimed. "Julia, you wouldn't believe the kind of men that agency sent to be interviewed. The absolute dregs of the earth! One skinny little man who reeked of the bottle, and another one who was so shifty looking that I had Ida Lee count the silver when I sent him packing. And the third one—my Lord, you should've seen him! *Covered* in tattoos, and I do mean covered. He even had one between his eyebrows." Mildred shivered as she described the applicants for the job of moving into her home and keeping a watchful eye on her wandering husband.

"I wouldn't sleep a wink with one of them in the house," she went on, "nor would I trust any of them with Horace. You know how fastidious he is, and I can't *imagine* him appreciating their company. But Miss Wiggins," she said in a musing sort of way, "is another matter altogether."

"Well, I know," I said, "that you'd probably not considered a woman for the job. But she is well trained and accustomed to patients with memory problems. But, I hasten to remind you, she may not be available. She has a full-time job now, but it's looking somewhat shaky. The owner intends to sell, so Etta Mae isn't sure if she should go ahead and leave or wait and see what happens. And possibly, at least in her mind, end up on the street."

"I'll tell you the truth, Julia," Mildred said, "it's a very attractive idea, but one I've not really considered. I thought a man would be ideal, being able to help Horace dress and bathe and so forth. But Miss Wiggins is accustomed to dealing with men patients already. And the more I think of it, the better it sounds. Horace would be much more amenable to the company of a woman than that of who-knows-who off the street. He does like the ladies, you know."

She smiled with indulgence and so did I, for it was true. Not that Horace was a flirt or a skirt chaser, he wasn't. He simply enjoyed the company of women and their discussions of parties, fashion, and who was mad at whom among the Real Housewives. Sports or politics left him bored and unsettled.

"I'll leave it up to you, then," I said, handing her a slip of paper. "Here's Etta Mae's phone number. She knows that you might be interested, so a call won't surprise her. But let me issue a caution again, Mildred, she may be too dependent on her job to risk leaving it before she has to."

"Oh, I understand," Mildred said, nodding, but of course never having had to depend on a job in her life, she didn't. "I'm thinking of just asking if she'd be interested in sitting with Horace on her days off. Just to get a taste of it, you know, and see how Horace likes her, and so forth. That way, she wouldn't have to make a decisive move until she was absolutely sure it would work for both of them."

"That's a perfect idea, Mildred," I said, surprised that I hadn't thought of it. "Now I have to get on home. It's doing something out there, and it looks as if we're in for a night of bad weather."

"Be careful, Julia. You don't want to fall and break something. Let me call Ida Lee to walk you home."

"Oh, no," I said, shrugging on my coat and going to the window to look out. "I wouldn't dream of doing that. Look, the grass isn't even covered, so nothing is sticking. I'll be fine, but just in case, call the house in ten minutes or so to see if I got there in one piece."

Urging her to stay where she was, since I knew she had difficulty rising, I hurried through the foyer and to the front door where Ida Lee waited to see me out. How she always knew when and where to be, I could never figure out, but I appreciated her lovely manners.

"It's nice to see you, Miss Julia," Ida Lee said. "Be careful going home."

"Thank you, Ida Lee. I will."

As she turned to open the door for me, I said, "How do you think Mr. Allen is doing? You're around him as much as anybody, and I know Mildred is worried."

She hesitated for a second, then said, "He's not doing well at all. We don't dare leave him alone or he's out the door before we know it."

"Don't hesitate to call us if you need to. Any time at all for either one of them because I'm concerned about Mildred, too."

"Yes, ma'am," Ida Lee said, a frown appearing on her lovely forehead, "I am, too."

I left then, and picked my way slowly across the crackling grass until I safely reached my own door.

Chapter 9

❧

Sam had come in by the time I got home, so we had a few minutes together in the library before supper. Before I could launch into the plans that were bubbling around in my mind, he smiled and said, "Guess who I saw downtown today."

"Who?"

"Ernest Sitton, looking the same today as he's looked for twenty years. A little grayer, maybe, a little paunchier, but wearing the same three-piece suit he always wears. He must have a closetful of them. Good lawyer, though."

"I don't really know him," I said, not one bit interested in Ernest Sitton, but Sam enjoyed people, the more individualistic they were, the better. Fortunately for him, Abbotsville had a gracious plenty of eccentric characters who kept him entertained, but I had too much on my mind to appreciate another oddity like Lawyer Sitton. "I've heard he has the first dollar he ever made and plenty more to go with it."

Sam nodded. "He's not a spendthrift, that's for sure. I once heard him tell a client that time was money and he didn't plan to waste it on a scoundrel charged for the third time with the same crime when he hadn't been paid for the first time." Sam laughed at the memory. "Then he left the courthouse. Drove all the way from Delmont just to tell him that."

"My goodness," I said. Then, unable to wait any longer to tell him of my day, I quickly brought him up to date on my luncheon with Etta Mae Wiggins and my visit with Mildred.

"So," I said with justified satisfaction, "it could work out that Mildred gets excellent help and Etta Mae has a job regardless of what that Lurline woman does."

"Uh-huh," Sam said, frowning. "The only problem will be the timing—Mildred needs someone now, while Etta Mae has a job which may be permanent no matter who owns the business. And you have to consider that Horace might not take to a woman companion or Etta Mae may not be able to handle him if he gets worse." Sam stood before the fireplace, rocking on his heels, as he thought through the problem. "If he has to go into an assisted-living facility, Etta Mae would be jobless again."

The air in my sails began leaking just a little, but I rallied by saying, "I don't think Horace is anywhere near having to do that, and I doubt Mildred would put him away even if he were. She has the means to keep him home regardless of his condition, mental or otherwise. If, that is, she can find the right kind of help and the kind of which she approves. And you know," I went on, perking up at a happier thought, "I'm just not convinced that Horace is that bad off. What he needs is some entertainment, a little distraction from thinking about driving his car. It's likely that he hasn't regained his strength after that heart attack and that his mental condition will improve as everything else does."

"That's true," Sam said, nodding. "But if he does get better, Etta Mae will still lose her job."

"Oh, my goodness, Sam," I said, rubbing my forehead, "here I was, thinking that I'd found the perfect solution to two problems, but I see now that it could add to Etta Mae's."

I was thoroughly deflated by this time, so it was with great effort that I reminded myself of my intention to stop trying to solve the problems of other people. Having recognized my unattractive tendency to manage the lives of others, I'd promised myself to let them flounder around on their own. Yet I had jumped in with both feet with a solution that could end by making things worse for Etta Mae.

That should've taught me a lesson, but I could no more stop worrying and thinking about that young woman's dilemma than I could fly.

Maybe, I thought, I could ask around and find out who was interested in buying The Handy Home Helpers outfit, then find out what the new owner would do—keep the present employees on or start with a clean sweep.

And, of course, there was the Dollar Store to look into. It would be nice to know just what their plans were. If those executives only wanted Lurline's property—a large, convenient lot on Delmont's Main Street as I recalled—she could simply sell it and shut down the business.

Of course if she was a businesswoman as I was, she'd be loath to close an active business and walk away without getting anything for it. And who could blame her? Not I, that's for sure.

The following morning, after a restless night, I dressed warmly but down, not up. Here's a tip: if you're looking for good terms on something you're interested in buying, don't go dressed to the nines. No use flaunting your financial status.

I had looked out the window when I first got out of bed, half expecting to see tree limbs weighed down with ice. That would've changed my plans considerably, but sometime during the night the weather had changed its mind. According to the Asheville weather report, we had gotten the tail end of a cold front the afternoon before, and by now it was dropping snow on Virginia and Pennsylvania. Better them than us.

Sam had a meeting at the church that morning, so he'd gotten up early. He was still at the table by the time I came downstairs, so I joined him and waited as Lillian broke an egg into a skillet.

"What's on your agenda for the day?" Sam asked.

"Oh, nothing much. I may do a little shopping. Christmas will be here before we know it, so I need to start on that. I declare," I said, leaning my head on my hand, "we barely get over Thanksgiving before Christmas is upon us. Although I must say that Thanksgiving this year was unusual, but very nice." I put my hand on his arm and smiled, for we had spent the day together without having guests or being guests. The Pickens family, with whom we normally spent holidays, had gone to Williamsburg that week, and I had given Lillian several free days. We had had Thanksgiving dinner at the club, and the day had been spent in the best of company—our own.

"Anyway," I went on, "our gift list gets longer every year. It's not that I dislike getting gifts for so many, it's more a fear of forgetting somebody."

"I'm happy to leave that concern with you."

"That's interesting," I said, smiling my thanks as Lillian placed a warm plate in front of me, "because I had already decided to leave all the gifts for men with you."

Sam's eyebrows went up. "How many would that be?"

"Well, there's Mr. Pickens and Coleman, maybe Bob Hargrove and the preacher, if you're so inclined."

"An hour or so at The Home Depot should suffice for them all."

"Oh, Sam, do put a little thought into it," I said, although I knew he was half teasing me. "And I've just thought that Horace might like something under the tree, although we've not done anything for him specifically in the past."

"Don't you want to give family gifts? That would cut the number in half, making it easier all around."

"Not really, because everybody would do the same for us, and we already have three popcorn poppers."

Sam laughed. "I see the problem."

"Anyway, we need to think of something special for Lloyd and go in together on that. It's just that the older he gets, the harder he is to buy for."

"Maybe something for his car?"

"I can't imagine what that would be. When you shop for the men, look around for something for him. I'll probably get him one or two things, too."

Sam smiled again. "I'd be surprised if you didn't."

"Well," I said, "you know I don't believe in spoiling children, but he hardly qualifies as a child anymore. Lillian," I said, turning to her, "what about Latisha? What would she like for Christmas?"

"I think they all want the new things that ding and have pictures on 'em and games to play, but . . ."

"Oh, yes, electronic things. That's what you can look for, Sam. See what's new for the twins' age and Latisha's and Lloyd's, as well. Oh, and for Gracie, too." Little Gracie Bates was Binkie and Coleman's daughter, and the twins belonged to Hazel Marie and Mr. Pickens, a man who always had to outdo everybody else.

"What about you, Lillian?" Sam asked. "Wouldn't you like one of those vacuum cleaners that cleans on its own?"

"Lord, no, Mr. Sam. That thing would scare me to death, it come sneakin' up on my heels, nudgin' at my feet, an' followin' me all over the place."

"I feel the same way, Lillian," I said, rising from the table. "We're about to become overly automated, if you ask me. Did you know that you can even answer the doorbell when you're under a hair dryer at Velma's? I just don't need to be in touch that badly, especially since it's usually a Jehovah's Witness at the door."

Sam laughed and got to his feet. Walking over to me, he put an arm around my shoulders. "You've about given me some badly needed Christmas spirit, and I'm going to get my shopping done early. Have a good day, honey."

"And you, too," I said, fully intending to make it so.

Chapter 10

❧

As I drove into Delmont, some ten miles or so from downtown Abbotsville, I was amazed to see how it had grown. I'd not had reason to visit the little town in several years, so I slowed to take in all the changes. Small houses dotted the hillsides, new streets opened onto the main road, and a huge apartment complex covered several acres. Where had all these people come from and where did they work?

I figured out the answer as I slowed even more for the three blocks of downtown Delmont. There were fewer **CLOSED** signs in shop windows than when I'd last been there. The street was lined with parked cars, indicating that business had picked up considerably. I noticed a new gas station right across the street from the old one, and glimpsed a huge new Food Lion grocery store on a side street.

Delmont, I realized, had become a bedroom community. As house prices had increased in Asheville, and Abbotsville had filled up, Delmont was receiving the overflow. They'd even added a traffic light on the main street—one that had red and green lights instead of only a flashing yellow one.

Seeing an empty parking space, I pulled in, then out, then back again, hating parallel parking but finally getting the car reasonably situated. Holding my head up high, I walked away, ignoring the two feet or so between the car and the curb. I strolled along, glancing in shop windows as I held my coat closed against the cold. I was aiming for the drugstore that I knew had a small fountain area. As it was the middle of the morning, I was counting on finding few customers and a bored waitstaff.

Entering the drugstore and sitting at a tiny metal table, I slipped off my coat and glanced at the menu while surveying the store itself. It was not doing a lot of business, so when the not-so-young waitress ambled over for my order, I knew I had timed it correctly.

"Coffee?" she asked, holding out a cup and saucer in one hand and a glass coffeepot in the other. She smiled, showing a gap between her two front teeth.

"Yes, thank you. It's nippy out there."

"Yeah, it is," she said, pouring my coffee, then setting the pot on the table. "But I'd rather have cold than ice any day. 'Course the kids was disappointed. They'd hoped the school buses wouldn't run. But to my mind, we really dodged the bullet last night."

"We surely did," I agreed, pleased that I'd found what I wanted—a talkative waitress. "Do you live here in Delmont?"

"All my life and don't intend to leave. You want some pie? We got cherry and it's fresh."

"That sounds good," I said, although it didn't.

She was back in a few seconds, setting the pie, a fork, and a paper napkin in front of me. "You visitin' in Delmont? Don't think I seen you before."

"Yes, just visiting. Well, no, in fact I'm here to look into The Handy Home Helpers. You see," I went on, putting a worried frown on my face, "a friend is getting where he needs help, and his family doesn't know whether to keep him at home or find a place for him."

"Oh, honey," she said, leaning against the table, "everybody's havin' that problem. But I'll tell you the truth, I wouldn't count on The Handy Helpers if I was you."

"Oh? Why not? I've heard good things about them."

"Well," she said, lowering her voice and bending closer, "from what I hear, they're about to go out of business or something. Lurline Corn, that's who owns it, is dyin' to take the money and run. Only thing is, nobody's got the kind of money she wants."

"You mean it's for sale?" I pretended to be both surprised and disappointed. "That's too bad. I was hoping it would be a possibility for my friend to stay home and get the care he needs, as well. But, I guess, if it's actively on the market, his family should wait to see who the new owner will be." This was where I expected to hear the details of the sale—who was buying it, when the sale would be finalized, and some of the new management's plans for the business.

"Yeah," she agreed, then went off on a tangent, "but here's the thing, she—Lurline, I mean—she's got that prime lot right here on Main Street, and word's out that a Dollar Store's looking at it. Listen, she could make a killin' if they was to buy it, and I hope they do. Can you believe it? A Dollar Store right here in Delmont. Why, this town would set up and take notice with something like that. It could draw other stores right along with it. We might even get a Walmart one of these days."

"That would be nice," I said with a slight shiver down my back. "So convenient, you know."

"It sure would," she agreed. "The way it is now, we have to drive all the way to Fletcher to do any decent shopping. I'll tell you one thing, though, Lurline better do something soon or get off the pot. I heard them Dollar Store people're thinking her lot's not big enough. They're lookin' out on Springer Road, too. I know, 'cause a couple of 'em came in here and I heard 'em talkin'."

"*Sherrill*," a voice from behind the pharmacy counter rang out. "You got a customer at the front counter."

"Oh, good grief," she said, "I gotta get busy. Nice talkin' to you. Enjoy that pie, you hear?" And off she went, after confirming what I'd already heard, as well as dropping some new information, both of which was exactly why I was sitting there trying to eat cherry pie that was as dry as a bone.

Springer Road, I thought as I sat in the car, letting the engine run to warm up the interior. Named for my late, unlamented husband, Wesley Lloyd Springer, not because of any particular honor bestowed on him, but because he had owned the only business on it—the Hillandale Trailer Park. Springer Road was paved, but just barely. There were no sidewalks. The pavement, chipped and broken on the sides, simply fell off on either side into fairly deep ditches. It was what was once called a farm-to-market road, running perpendicular to Delmont Road, then winding around curves, up and down hills, and eventually connecting some miles away to the road to Brevard.

Pulling out of the parking space, I drove slowly on, catching the green light, and easing along until I came to the end of the three-block business district. And there on the left, just as I remembered it, was the small brick bungalow with a metal railing around a cement front porch. A sign, almost as large as the house's facade, read:

THE HANDY HOME HELPERS
CARE YOU CAN TRUST

And under that was a smaller sign that read **OFFICE** with a large red arrow pointing toward the porch. It was a corner lot, so I turned left and, as there was no traffic behind me, slowed to get a good look at the grounds. There wasn't much to see—two large trees in the front yard, and a small gravel lot in the back. Two cars were parked there, and another sign pointed to a rear entrance.

It was a nice-sized lot, probably listed as two town spaces on the tax rolls, but if my mental picture of your average Dollar Store was accurate, it wasn't the ideal size for another one. Still, it would draw foot traffic, although I'd not seen very much of that on the sidewalks.

Circling the block, I came out again on Delmont Road and followed it on to Springer Road. Since I was in the area, I decided to look in on the trailer park, having left it totally in Etta Mae's hands for longer than perhaps I should have. Turning in onto the lane that led into the park, I was pleased to see several evergreen azaleas planted by the small, tasteful sign. The twenty or so trailers, a mixture of both single- and double-wides, looked neat and well-kept. There was no litter and only a few of those large, plastic tricycles that were a blight on your average family lawn. Etta Mae's trailer looked as if it had been winterized—the striped awning had been put away, as had her two lawn chairs. The only potted plants were two small cedar-looking bushes on either side of the doorsteps.

On the whole, I was quite pleased with the way the park looked, having seen no full clotheslines strung from trailer to trailer, heard no loud music blaring from any of them, and seen no overturned garbage cans. One of the most consistent problems at the park—besides domestic disturbances—had been scavenging animals from the heavily wooded areas near the park. Raccoons, possums, and the stray dog or cat had depended on garbage cans for their livelihood. Early on in her employment, Etta Mae had charged me for the purchase of a BB gun and an inordinate amount of ammunition, but she'd put a stop to the nightly raids, as well as, according to rumors from the Delmont deputies, cut down on the number of domestic calls they'd had. An armed woman, even with only a BB gun, had been an effective deterrent.

In fact, the entire park, I noted with satisfaction, situated on five-plus mostly cleared, level acres and bounded by a cornfield on one side and a forest on the other, all of it less than a mile from downtown Delmont, should be quite attractive to the Dollar Store's real estate committee.

I had not gone to Delmont with a real estate transaction in mind, but when one jumps up demanding attention, I generally pay attention. I drove home, smiling to myself.

Chapter 11

❧

My smile had dwindled by the time I pulled into the driveway at home. What in the world was I thinking? I had gone to Delmont to see the lay of the land with only the intent of helping Etta Mae in mind. Now here I was considering the sale of what could be the only means of income for her, to say nothing of selling the ground out from under her.

Of course, I told myself quite firmly, the undeveloped acreage that surrounded the Hillandale Trailer Park would be more attractive to the Dollar Store committee than the trailer park itself. To situate a store within walking distance of so many families would be better for them than the eviction of those same families.

Still, it was hard to let go of the possibility of turning a pretty penny with the sale of something that had little intrinsic value to me. A trailer park had not been the jewel of Wesley Lloyd's estate, and I would not miss the meager monthly returns from it. Its real value lay, obviously, in an eventual sale to someone who wanted the land.

I had, however, been led down the primrose path by similar rosy thoughts a few times before and had learned to ignore the promise of a windfall. The sale price of a piece of property might make you sit up and take notice, but once you subtract the realtor's fee, the lawyers' fees, the prorated property taxes, and the capital gains taxes, you'd usually have been better off to have kept the property.

So, I told myself, get selling the trailer park off your mind entirely. It wasn't as if I needed to sell it, and besides, it wasn't as if the Dollar Store even wanted it. I had been putting the cart before the horse, and I immediately began to mentally unhitch it. Therefore, the Hillandale Trailer Park was not for sale, no matter who might want to buy it.

With that firmly decided, I reaffirmed my intent to help Etta Mae and to do it in a way that would not embarrass or humiliate her. What I'd have to do to accomplish that would be to engage her to help me, not the other way around.

And, as I left the car and headed into the house, I thought that I knew how to go about doing exactly that.

"Lillian," I said, shedding my coat and gloves as I went through the kitchen, "I have some figuring to do, so if Mildred or anybody else calls, take a message. Tell whoever it is that I'm in the bathroom or whatever, and I'll call them back in a little while. I'll be in the library."

She turned to look at me as I sailed past. "What if it's Mr. Sam? You want me to tell him you in the bathroom?"

I stopped. "No, if it's Sam, let me know. I'll take it, but for now I need some time to see if what I'm thinking of doing is feasible to do."

"That sound like something you might not oughta do."

"On the contrary. The more I think of it, the better I like it. And when I tell you what it is, I know you'll agree. I just need to think it through, because you know I don't go off half-cocked on anything."

"Uh-huh," she said with a slight tinge of skepticism which I ignored.

Entering the library, I went straight to the fireplace and turned on the gas flame, then I retrieved a pen and a yellow legal pad from the desk. Sitting on the sofa, I began a list of things that should be done, and the first one was to contact a real estate agent. No, I'd not changed my mind about selling the trailer park. I was now interested in purchasing, not selling, so I needed someone who would act for me and in my best interest. Nell Hudson, the agent I'd used a while back, was out—she talked too much. Like most people, I did not want my business discussed around town before it was done.

I jotted down the name Joe Blair, the agent who told his clients what they needed to hear, rather than what they wanted to hear. I could work with someone like that, especially since in real estate matters, I was occasionally inclined to go off half-cocked in spite of what I'd just assured Lillian that I did not do.

I wrote Mr. Blair's name at the top of the page, added his phone number, then came to a full stop as I realized that a major decision had to be made. Should I proceed with my plan before discussing it with Etta Mae, i.e., present her with a fait accompli, and take a chance that she wouldn't like it? Or should I first get her approval, then risk the possibility of failing to make a deal and end up badly disappointing her?

It was a dilemma, no doubt about it, even though my sole purpose was to do something good for someone else. Considering that new leaf that I'd so recently turned over, one would think that everything would fall into place when one's intention is good. But I found myself stymied before even starting. It was clearly a problem to be discussed with Sam.

Sam wasn't home, but Lillian was. I put aside the pen and pad, and went to the kitchen.

"Lillian," I said, as I pulled out a chair from the table, "if you wanted to help somebody and had a very good idea of how to do it, would you tell the person what you were *going* to do or would you just go ahead and do it and then tell her?"

"What?"

"I mean, I don't want to risk getting her hopes up if things don't work out, because when dealing with a third party you never know what they'll do, so if you promise something and then can't follow through, that could be worse than not doing it at all."

"Miss Julia," Lillian said, standing by the counter with a ladle in her hand, "I don't know what in the world you're talkin' about."

"Etta Mae Wiggins, that's what I'm talking about. See, Lillian, the word's out that the business where Etta Mae works is about to be sold. Nobody knows what the purchaser will do with it—keep the business going with the same employees, fire the employees and hire new ones, close the business entirely because they only want the property, or all of the above. So, see," I said, hitching forward on my chair, "I'm thinking of buying the business myself and hiring Etta Mae to run it, thereby ensuring that she has a job, and if she does as well with it as she's done with the trailer park, everybody'll be happy. Now the problem I have is this: Do I take Etta Mae into my confidence *before* I proceed or do I tell her *after* I've done it? Either way, I run the risk of disappointing her or me if things don't work out."

"How would it disappoint you?"

"Why, Lillian, if I go ahead and buy something that she doesn't want to run, it would leave me with a business that I have absolutely no interest in owning. What in the world would I do with it if *she's* not interested? I mean, what if she decides to move to Charlotte?"

"Why'd she wanta move to Charlotte?"

"It beats me—looking for new opportunities, I guess. I certainly wouldn't want to, but she's mentioned the possibility."

Lillian leaned on the counter, thought about it for a minute, then said, "She's not gonna move to Charlotte. Not now, anyway. Not as long as Miss Granny's still livin', an' don' look like she's gonna slow down any time soon."

"Of course!" I sat up straight, wondering how I could've overlooked Etta Mae's sprightly grandmother who helped Hazel Marie with the little twin girls that she and Mr. Pickens had produced. "You are absolutely right, Lillian. Granny Wiggins is her only living relative—as far as she knows, anyway—so she's not about to move away. Well," I went on with a laugh, "that puts a different light on things, but I must've caught something from Horace Allen to have forgotten Miss Granny."

"Oh, that poor Mr. Horace," Lillian said, shaking her head. "He's gettin' real pitiful, Miss Julia. I saw Ida Lee run out and bring him back in the house yesterday. He was on the sidewalk, headin' for town, it looked like."

"My goodness," I said, "I didn't know that. Poor Mildred, she has to do something, and do it soon. I keep hearing that people with memory loss are prone to walk off and not know where they're going or where they've been."

"Yes'm, an' the fam'lies have to put out a Silver Alert so everybody can look out for 'em an' bring 'em home. It's real sad, Miss Julia."

"Yes, it is, but Mildred says that other than worrying about his car, Horace doesn't have a care in the world. So I guess it could be worse, bless his heart."

After thinking along those lines for a few seconds, I said, "Lillian, if you ever notice me getting in that condition, let me know. I like to think that since I've gotten this far without any signs of dementia, I won't get it at all. But I guess the one affected is the last one to know it, don't you think?"

"I 'spect so, but you're sharp as a tack, Miss Julia. I don't see nothin' to worry about in you or Mr. Sam. Or me, either."

"I agree," I said, reassured and just a little prideful in the smooth working of my brain. Then, rising from the chair, I went on. "Well, this is not getting anything done. I'd better get up from here and get back to work. But what was I doing?" I stopped, frowned, and tried to recall why I had come into the kitchen.

"Oh! Of course! I came to ask you what to do about Etta Mae, and you reminded me of Granny Wiggins, and that answered my question. Or at least it clarified a few things. I declare, half the time I don't know whether I'm coming or going.

"*But,*" I quickly added, "that doesn't mean a thing, Lillian. I've always been like that."

Chapter 12

❦

When Sam got in later that afternoon, I laid it all out for him—what I wanted to do and how I thought I should go about getting it done. He listened carefully as I waxed fulsomely over the perfect job for Etta Mae and how pleased she would be to have her future assured whether or not she ever walked down the aisle again.

"See, Sam," I said, summing up my plans, "I have a little money that needs to be put to work, and what better use for it than to put it into a going business. And Etta Mae is the perfect person to run such a business. She knows it from one end to the other, and she and I work well together. Just look at how she's managed the trailer park so that it's no longer a problem for me.

"Now, I know you're going to point out that The Handy Home Helpers isn't the best investment in the world, nor is the Hillandale Trailer Park, neither being on the New York Stock Exchange. But it's not a bad idea for me to invest in a local business, especially one that will help Etta Mae make a living."

Sam said nothing at first, just thought about it for a longer time than I'd hoped he would, then offered his opinion.

"Honey," he said, "you have a good heart and a good head for business, but think this through carefully. It seems to me that you're very close to planning Etta Mae's life for her. Now, I know that's not your intention, but to suddenly present her with this puts her in the position of feeling she has to accept it whether she wants it or not. She'll feel an obligation to you, and that wouldn't bode well for a good working relationship."

Well, that cooled my jets for a few minutes because I felt sure that Etta Mae would love to run, manage, and administer The Handy Home Helpers. I could just see her sitting in Lurline's office making out schedules, doing payrolls, and training new employees on exactly how to deal with the bedridden. No longer would she have to drive all over creation from one homebound patient to another, doing whatever was demanded of her from giving bed baths to bedpans, as well as lifting, turning, and walking uncooperative patients. And, of course, she would know how easy I was to get along with. We had, after all, a history of working together at the trailer park—my owning something and her taking care of it had worked fine for many years. I couldn't understand why Sam hadn't taken that into consideration.

When I said as much to him, he responded by making another suggestion.

"Think of this," he said. "Why don't you talk it over with Etta Mae and suggest that she buy the business?"

"Why, Sam, she doesn't have two nickels to rub together. How in the world could she buy a healthy business when she can barely pay her bills? And don't say she can get a bank loan. That single-wide is the only thing she owns, and, as collateral, it wouldn't make much of an impression on a loan officer."

"But would it impress you?"

"What?" I asked, staring at him.

"*You* could loan her the money. It would make no difference to you whether you buy the business outright from the present owner or loan the same amount to Etta Mae so she can buy it. But it would make a world of difference to her—she would be the owner, not the hired hand."

"Why, Sam," I said as the whole thing dawned in my mind, "that's a wonderful idea. I don't know why I didn't think of it, because you're right. Either way, it would cost me the same, but the difference for Etta Mae would be night and day." I flipped a page on my legal pad. "Now tell me exactly how to go about doing it."

"Talk to Etta Mae first. Make sure that she would want the business. You have to consider that she might not want the responsibilities that go with ownership. But, Julia," Sam went on, "you mustn't let her feel that you're just handing something to her. Make sure she understands that she'll be repaying you with interest, although you can offer easy terms. That's the only way she'll be able to accept help without being under a debilitating obligation to you. And it's the only way you can accomplish what you want—helping her and putting your money to work instead of letting it sit in a bank."

"Then," I said, starting to rise, "I'd better talk to Mr. Blair and find out how much Lurline wants for the business. I need to know what we're talking about."

"I'd wait on that if I were you," Sam said, smiling at my eagerness. "Etta Mae should approach him, not you, so he'll know he's working for her. And that means you should talk to her first, make sure she's on board and it's something she wants to do. To make it a legitimate business transaction that she's comfortable with, you should stay entirely in the background and let her do it all."

"You're right," I said, settling down. "I know you're right. And there's something else, Sam. Etta Mae will know if Lurline's asking price is out of line because Etta Mae will know how well the business is doing. She's in a much better position than I to know what it's worth."

"Exactly," Sam said. "And she'll know how to improve the business, where its weak points are, and possibly how it can be expanded. If you're going into the caregiving business, you couldn't find a more knowledgeable person to invest in."

I sat back and basked in the glow of seeing how things could work out in a way that would accomplish exactly what I wanted. Now all I had to do was to present it to Etta Mae in a way that would capture her imagination of what it would be like to own something that would ensure her future. And, I might as well confess, make a little money for me along the way.

"Uh, Julia," Sam said, interrupting my pleasant thoughts, "you should take into consideration that Etta Mae might not want a debt burden like that, to say nothing of not wanting to be responsible for the livelihood of her employees, as well as of the patients who would ultimately be under her care. It will all be on her shoulders, and some people are cut out for that kind of pressure and some are not. You shouldn't try to talk her into something that she's not prepared to accept. Being the boss," Sam concluded with a smile, "is not always what it's cracked up to be."

"Oh, I understand that," I said, "and I'd never try to talk her into something that I didn't think she could do." But of course, I was already picturing Etta Mae cringing at the thought of doing something she'd never done before. But how often had I seen her hesitate and hold back on some of our escapades, then in spite of her fears, jump in and save the day and quite often my bacon, as well? All she would need would be my assurance that she was not only capable, but the ideal person to own and run The Handy Home Helpers. I fully expected to have to push, shove, and constantly reassure her that she had what it took to succeed in an executive position.

"Well," Sam said, "just be aware that she might not be eager to take on so much. In fact, I'd be surprised if she is. She strikes me as someone who counts the cost before jumping in."

"That is true," I agreed, "except when it comes to men. That poor girl has jumped into marriage without counting the cost too many times already. Now, if I can just get her to want to be a business owner as much as she's wanted to be a wife, we'll be all right. Because I'll tell you, Sam, having a business under her control will be much more rewarding than any marriage she's ever had."

Chapter 13

❧

Sam was asleep almost as soon as his head hit the pillow that night, but I lay awake with first one thing then another streaming through my mind. I couldn't wait to present this wonderful idea to Etta Mae, convinced that she would be thrilled once she'd given it some thought. She'd probably be fearful at first, thinking that she wasn't capable of such an undertaking. I'd have to be at my best to effectively point out the rewards to her—and to me. Sam had been right in that I should not let Etta Mae think that I was doing it entirely for her benefit, which I was, because, let's face it, I was no more interested in a caregiving business than I was in watching golf on television.

Turning over one more time, I began trying out different ways to open the conversation I planned to have with Etta Mae. Her reaction would all depend on the way I presented this rare opportunity for her advancement.

I never decided on the ideal approach because the next thing I knew it was time to get up. I would have to play it by ear when the time came to present my plan. One thing, though, that I intended to stress—as a business owner, she would never again have to worry about being fired. That possibility seemed to be a constant threat to Etta Mae's peace of mind, and the Lurline woman apparently knew it and used it, which to my mind was no way to run a business or to treat an employee, especially one as loyal and hardworking as Etta Mae.

There would be, of course, other, different worries as an owner, but her employment would no longer depend on the whim of someone else.

While I was dressing that morning I gradually came to the conclusion that Etta Mae would have to be talked into making such a huge leap. I doubted that it had ever occurred to her that she could obtain a large loan, own a thriving business, run it effectively, and eventually pay off the loan, as well as make a decent living for herself. She simply did not think, or dream, in those terms. But I had seen in her a fierce determination to better herself and a willingness to dare—with a little push now and then—to reach for more.

She would need that push because she was fearful of even trying to reach for anything she considered beyond her. She lacked confidence in her own abilities while everybody around her stood back in awe.

It would be up to me to see that she seized the day and reached for the prize. If she didn't recognize her own abilities, I certainly did.

Of course it had crossed my mind that I was flipping back a leaf or two of what I had so recently decided to turn over. But that was my problem, not hers, and I intended to use every means of persuasion to get Etta Mae to at least look into buying The Handy Home Helpers. It would be for her own good.

So I called and invited her to lunch at my house the following day.

"Oh, I'd love to!" she said, as bright and perky as she always sounded. "And it's the perfect day—the only one of the week that I have a full hour to eat between patients."

I took that as a good omen.

"Can I bring anything?" she asked.

Bless her heart, she had just revealed how seldom she received a luncheon invitation.

"Oh, no, Lillian will prepare something for us. I just want to visit with you a while, maybe hear more about your employer's plans, and yours, of course."

She sighed. "That won't take long because I don't have any. And I guess I won't until Lurline lets us know what she's going to do. I declare, Miss Julia, it's hard not knowing from one day to the next whether I have a job or not."

That, to me, was an even better omen. I intended to put her mind to rest about that very matter.

"Lillian," I said as I hung up the phone and turned to her. "I guess you heard me invite a guest for lunch tomorrow. What do you think we should have? It'll have to be quick and easy because she doesn't have much time."

"I 'member Miss Etta Mae likin' hot dogs, so . . ."

"Well, I don't, but she is accustomed to fast food. What about hamburgers?"

"I can do that and have 'em all ready as soon as she gets here. You want to eat here in the kitchen or in the dining room?"

I thought about it for a minute, then said, "Let's do it here in the kitchen. She's almost like family, and I think she'll be more comfortable without making a big fuss over it." I thought about it for a while longer, then said, "And I might need you to help me out."

She frowned. "Help you out how? What you tryin' to get her to do?"

"Something that will put her mind at ease and maybe eventually put her on easy street. Don't worry, Lillian, I have her best interests at heart. I just might want you to chime in occasionally to help her see what a golden opportunity she has before her."

Lillian frowned so hard that she was practically glowering at me. "I don't know, Miss Julia. Sounds to me like you tryin' to talk her into doin' something she might not want to do."

"That's only because neither of you know what it is. And I think when you do, you at least will know that it's perfect for her. She, however, might need a little urging, a little push, to step out of her comfort zone. So to speak."

"Uh-huh, you gonna try to talk her into doin' something that you want done, but she might not. I might not want to be a part of that."

"Just wait until you hear what it is. I declare, Lillian, you can sure throw cold water on the best-laid plans, because I'm telling you that what I'm going to suggest to her is a once-in-a-lifetime opportunity. And the only thing that would keep her from jumping at the chance is the fear that it's beyond her, that she doesn't deserve such an opportunity. I want you to help me convince her that she has what it takes to do whatever she wants to do."

"That," Lillian said, scrunching up her mouth, "sound to me like it's gonna cost some money."

"Oh," I said, waving my hand, "everything costs money. Which of course I've thought about and have plans for, as well. It's just a matter now of getting her agreement to proceed."

"I don't know, Miss Julia," Lillian said again. "You better not be countin' on me. I'm not much good at talkin' people into doin' something they don't want to do."

"Well, that's just it," I said, somewhat sharply, "I don't want to talk her into doing something she doesn't want to do. I want to talk her into *wanting* to do it."

Chapter 14

❦

"Wha-at?" Etta Mae's jaw dropped and so did her hamburger—one stayed open and the other landed on her plate. "Miss Julia," she said, looking tired as she leaned back in her chair, "I don't have a pot to use when I need it. How in the world could I buy Lurline's business?"

"It's easy," I said. "People do it all the time. You borrow the money, and the business pays it back. Plus, of course, making a profit for you to live on. Now, look, Etta Mae, I am going to invest some money somewhere, either with you or with someone else. That's a given, so don't think I'm doing this just for your benefit. I'm looking for a sound local business run by someone I know and trust. The Handy Home Helpers and you seem to fit the bill. Because, number one," I continued, "if Lurline Corn is buying a half-a-million-dollar condo in Florida, then The Handy Home Helpers is a profitable enterprise. And number two, I know you, and I know what you're capable of, and if I hadn't trusted you in some of the tight spots we've been in, I probably wouldn't be sitting here now."

"That's the truth," Lillian chimed in as she leaned on the counter, listening to us. "No tellin' where she'd be if you hadn't been around to get her outta trouble. Pro'bly in the hospital or the jail, one or the other."

"Well," I said with a wry twist of my mouth, "I wouldn't go quite that far. But that's beside the point. The point now, Etta

Mae, is simply for you to be willing to take on a business and run it so that it continues to make a profit. And that brings up the next question—could you step into Lurline's place so there'd be no interruptions to the patients or problems with the employees?"

"I think maybe I could," Etta Mae said softly, as if she were thinking out loud. "Lurline put me in charge for a couple of months when she had her gallbladder out. But she wouldn't let me see the books. I had to take everything to the hospital so she could sign payroll checks. But I managed the schedules and brought in two new contracts while she was out."

"Well, see," I said. "You already know how to run the day-to-day routine. As for the books, Lurline will have to make them available so an accountant can look them over for you. You want to be sure that the business is making a profit and that you're not taking over some long-term debt that the business has incurred."

"It's the long-term debt *I'd* be incurring that worries me," Etta Mae said.

"I don't blame you," Lillian said. "That's what I'd be worried about."

"Lillian, for goodness' sakes," I said, "don't be a pessimist. Now, listen, Etta Mae, what you need to do is go to see Mr. Blair—he's a realtor who specializes in commercial real estate. Lay all your cards on the table for him, except for one thing—*where* you're getting a loan. There's no need to bring me into it at all. Just assure him that you have access to a loan if the price is right. You'll also want him to go over the books with you and tell you what he thinks. At that point, you and I both may decide that The Handy Home Helpers is not as thriving as we think it is. But Mr. Blair will find out what Lurline is asking for the business, and he'll help you decide if you want to make an offer, although I'll want to have some input on that, as well.

"Oh, and one more thing," I said, my usual skepticism coming to the fore, "make sure that he understands that Lurline is not to know who is inquiring. It wouldn't surprise me if she wouldn't want to sell to you. I don't mean you, specifically, but to anyone who has worked for her."

"Oh, it would be me, specifically," Etta Mae said, somewhat sadly. "She'd hate for me to take her place. She'd probably raise her price if she knew it was me trying to buy it."

"Well," I said, "that's why you use a realtor, and along the way, a lawyer, too. Now, Etta Mae, I don't want to talk you into something you don't want, but if you'll just see Mr. Blair, study the books, and get his advice, we'll know if it's worth pursuing. At any point during that process, you can decide against it and drop out. In fact, I'd want you to if it doesn't look as good as it sounds. I am not interested in putting money into something that's dying on the vine. So," I went on, "you don't have to make a decision now. All you have to do now is begin to look into it. Just keep my name out of it. You and I will come to an understanding when we know what we're getting into. How does that sound?"

"Sounds pretty good to me," Lillian said. "'Cause she don't have to say one way or the other right now. She can just wait an' see."

"Right," I said, "that's exactly right. We'd both be foolish to decide right now. But we *should* look into it. When can you go see Mr. Blair? You ought to go as soon as possible, because didn't you tell me that somebody else may be interested in it?"

Etta Mae nodded. "The Dollar Store, which had Lurline practically dancing in her office. But then we heard they're looking to build on a larger lot, so I don't know."

"Well, that's another thing to ask Mr. Blair to find out for you. And you'll want to know if the business and the property are being sold together or separately. I can't imagine the Dollar Store would be interested in anything but the property. But it's the business that we're interested in, although I would not turn my back on two lots on a main street, even in Delmont."

"Would you . . . ," Etta Mae began, stopped, bit her lip, then went on. "Would you go ahead and buy the business even if I backed out?"

Knowing that she was asking how much I was depending on her, I looked her in the eye and gave her a straight answer. "I would buy the property without you if it's being sold separately, because real estate is always a good buy in my book. But I would not buy the business without you, because I know nothing about running it and don't know anybody as capable as you to do it. Look, Etta Mae," I went on as I leaned toward her, "I'm really not interested in a caregiving business with or without you. I'm interested in investing in *you* because you would be a good investment. That's as plain and as simple as I can make it, because I don't give money away to just any Tom, Dick, or Harry."

"She sure don't," Lillian said.

Etta Mae took a deep breath. "So you think Lurline's business would make enough to repay the loan and make a living for me, too?"

"If it wouldn't, we won't do it."

"Let me think about it," she murmured.

"Of course, but don't think too long. If the Dollar Store makes a good offer for the property, Lurline will jump at it. Even," I went on, "if it means closing the business and putting her employees on the street."

She nodded, got up from the table, and put on her coat. Thanking Lillian and me for lunch, she said she had to get back to work. I walked her to the door, urged her to talk with Mr. Blair, then went back to the kitchen.

"Well, Lillian, what do you think?"

"I think she didn't eat her lunch," she said, pointing at half a hamburger left on Etta Mae's plate.

I couldn't sit still or turn my hands to anything else all afternoon. I kept thinking of what I should have said to Etta Mae, something more enticing than I had said. All I'd had to do was to draw her in far enough to speak with Mr. Blair, then an informed decision could be made. I wasn't sure that I had done that and kept planning what else I could say that would sway her to at least look into the possibilities.

The telephone interrupted my mental plans.

"Julia," Mildred Allen almost demanded, "do you know what that Tonya has done now?"

"Well, no, I guess I don't."

"You won't believe it anyway," she said, then began to cry.

"What is it, Mildred?" I said, gripping the phone for I had never known Mildred to cry about anything. "Tell me."

"Do you," she asked with a loud, wet sniff, "do you remember my telling you that I'd never have a grandchild?"

"Yes, of course I remember."

"Well, it seems that Tonya has produced one for me."

Chapter 15

❦

Stunned, all I could say was, "*How?*"

Then, stung that I had responded inappropriately to such happy news, I quickly said, "Why, that's wonderful, Mildred. I am so happy to hear that."

But Mildred was barely listening. After a few deep, sobbing breaths, she began her tale of woe. "She's sending the child to me, and what on earth am I going to do with it?"

"Wait," I said, "wait a minute. There's already a child? I thought you meant she was expecting one."

"Adoption, Julia," Mildred said with a wearing sigh. "She's adopted a child which she's too busy to look after. So she's sending it to me. As if I don't have my hands full with Horace." Mildred blew her nose.

"That's . . . ," I said with a gasp, searching for a word, "unbelievable." And selfish and presumptuous and a display of absolute gall, if you ask me. I said none of that, of course, but I had never known anyone to be so thoughtless as to do something this impulsively outrageous and expect someone else to pick up after her.

"So," I said, trying to get the conversation on track, "we keep saying *it*. Is it a girl or a boy, and how old is it?"

"It's a girl. Penelope, if you can believe, although I should be grateful for a normal name and not something like Blue Sky or Ashram or some other outlandish name. I keep thinking that maybe it's a sign, a good omen or something, because Penelope was my grandmother's name. But she's about seven years old, which, if you don't know, Julia, means that her personality and ethical sense are already formed and probably set in stone. And Tonya has had her only a few months—without one word to me *again*—so that child will be completely untrained, and for all I know, untrainable. What in the world am I going to do with her?"

"Oh, my, Mildred, what a shock it must be for you. But, listen," I went on, trying to find a bright side for her, "you will be so good for that child, and she will be for you, too. Remember how upset you were at the thought of never having a grandchild. Well, now you have one."

"It won't be the same," Mildred said mournfully. "Daddy would turn over in his grave at the thought of someone of unknown heritage sharing in his estate. I'll have to work on my will again."

Not wanting to get onto that subject, I posed another question. "Did Tonya say why she couldn't take care of the child? It seems strange that she'd be too busy so soon after getting her. I mean," I quickly added for fear of offending, "most new mothers want to be at home for the first few months anyway."

"Oh, Julia," Mildred moaned as if in pain, "it's just beyond belief. Do you know what she'll be doing? Of course you don't, so I'll tell you. She's making—and I mean, *starring* in one of those reality shows on television. It's going to be The Real Housewives of Somewhere. I don't know where and I don't care as long as it's not in Abbotsville. I mean they have Real Housewives in half the cities in the country but they'd better not come here."

"I don't think you need to worry about that," I said, fairly certain that Abbotsville would not be considered.

"Oh, I know, but I'm just saying. But I ask you, have you ever known a housewife like any of them? Not a one of them has ever mopped a floor or cleaned a toilet. Not that I have, of course, but

I don't walk around made up for a camera all day long, either. It's to be a weekly show, so Tonya's time is fully booked and guess who she turns to when she needs something. To *me*, that's who.

"Anyway," Mildred went on as if she needed to tell it all, "she'll be living in Los Angeles or somewhere—maybe Cabo—for the next year or so while they film two seasons. And while I take care of the child she's picked up from somewhere." She paused, then added darkly, "And from somewhere out of the country, too, because Tonya is sending no papers, no documentation, nothing. She said they're in the mail and you know what that usually means."

"Well," I said, hardly knowing what to say. "The Lord works in mysterious ways, Mildred, and I guess this is one of them."

"And I guess," she said, somewhat sharply, "that this will teach me not to wish for something I don't have. I might get it in another one of His mysterious ways."

Wanting to avoid a theological discussion of the workings of divine grace, I asked, "When will Penelope be coming? Will Tonya bring her?"

"Oh, no," Mildred said with more than a tinge of sarcasm, "Tonya is much too busy picking out wardrobes, talking to producers, and inviting camera crews into every nook and cranny of her life. Of course, I told her in no uncertain terms that she did not have my permission to discuss *me* in any way whatsoever. So if that show intends to include her relationship with Horace or me, or our reaction to her transformation, well, they'll just have to think again. I told her I wouldn't stand for it, and I told her I'd have every lawyer I know suing the producer, the director, and all the stars, including her, for defamation of character."

"My goodness," I said, appreciating the fact that Mildred was on a first-name basis with more lawyers than I even knew by sight, "that should make them all think twice."

"Well, it should, but then Tonya told me that Meryl Streep is being offered the mother's part, so I'll have to wait and see."

Rolling my eyes just a little, I changed the subject again. "Are you doing anything special to get ready for Penelope? It might be good to have a few toys and books for her, maybe fix up one of your guest rooms to appeal to a little girl."

"Yes, I suppose I should," she said, as if resigned to her fate. "I have all of Tonya's outgrown books and toys packed up and stored in the attic, waiting, you know, for a grandchild. Who would've thought one would come this way?"

"There are worse ways," I briskly reminded her. "So, if this is the way it's going to be, Mildred, you might as well make the best of it. Who knows? Having that child may end up being the best thing that could've happened."

"Don't be such a Pollyanna, Julia. You know I already have my hands full with Horace. I don't need somebody else to look after and tend to, because he's getting worse by the day. I declare, it's as if he's forgotten everything and everybody he ever knew. He told me the other day that I was the best mother anybody could have. Can you believe that? So now it looks as if I'll be mothering not only a strange child, but an even stranger husband."

"Uh, Mildred," I said, very carefully, "have you had Horace evaluated? I mean by a neurologist or by somebody who specializes in similar disorders? It may be that something can be done to help him. Although I must say that he seems healthy and happy, or so Sam tells me."

"Of course I've had him looked at and examined from one end to the other. I just hate to advertise how much he's declined. He's been diagnosed with symptoms of Alzheimer's."

"Oh, I'm sorry to hear that, but at least it's just a few symptoms, not the actual disease."

"That's true," she said. Then after a deep breath, she added, "Except the only way to diagnose the actual disease is through an autopsy which I am not ready to authorize."

"Oh, my goodness, I should say not. But, Mildred, it may help

Horace to have a child around to give him something to think about and enjoy."

"Yes, I'm trying to think on the bright side. But I'll tell you, I don't know how much longer Ida Lee and I can manage him. He will just walk off at the drop of a hat. Ida Lee found him wandering halfway to town just yesterday, and what if he takes that child with him one of these days? If I don't get help with him soon, I may have to put him away somewhere."

"Weren't you going to talk to Miss Wiggins? If she can't help you, she may know somebody who can."

"Yes, she called this morning and said that something had come up that will take all her free time for a few weeks, so she can't do it. But she's asking around to try to find somebody for us."

Giving Mildred a few more encouraging words to end the call, I hung up feeling guilty for doing her out of the help she badly needed, but mentally rejoicing that apparently Etta Mae was filling her free time with looking into buying The Handy Home Helpers.

Chapter 16

❧

We should've put Etta Mae on the hunt for help with Horace much earlier because it was not two days later that she sent Mr. Grady Peeples to ring Mildred's doorbell.

"You should've seen him, Julia," Mildred told me after the interview. "I almost chastised Ida Lee for letting him in, which should teach me not to judge by appearances. But at second glance, I realized that he had dressed for the occasion. His jeans had a crease in them which meant he'd gone to the trouble of ironing them. His flannel shirt—checked, no less—was buttoned to his throat and sported a thin knit tie. His lace-up boots had been polished and shined to a fare-thee-well, and his L.L.Bean jacket looked spanking new. He also had the courtesy to remove his Panthers ball cap when he came inside. If you don't get the picture with all of that, I'll just say that he was country down to his knobby red hands. Thank goodness, though, he didn't have a beard, just a slightly bushy mustache.

"And, thank goodness," Mildred went on, "I didn't act on my first impulse, which was to tell him the position was already filled. Because the more I looked at him, the more I became aware of the care he'd taken in preparing for the interview. That meant something to me, as did his manner in general. He told me that he'd worked at a sawmill until it closed down a few years ago when he had to take whatever he could get. Then he said his wife

'up and died,' on him, and ever since he's done a little bit of everything from carpentry work to being a janitor and driving a school
bus. I immediately took note of that because if there's one thing
Horace needs it's a good driver, so I hired him on the spot."

"A young man?" I asked.

"Young enough. Fiftyish, I'd say. He has some gray in his hair
and in his mustache. I liked his attitude, Julia. Sometimes you
just have to go on your intuition. So I did."

Thinking to myself that she should've checked his references,
I refrained from second-guessing her. She needed help with
Horace and may have been grasping at straws, but who could
blame her? She'd be just as quick to fire him if he displeased her.
Meanwhile she had someone who would entertain, distract, and
tag along with Horace wherever he decided to go without worrying that he'd never get home again.

"And, Julia," Mildred said, taking up her tale, "he's actually
worked for an elderly man—a neighbor, he said—who needed
help with getting in the shower and changing clothes. And, I'll
tell you, though I hate to admit it, but that's exactly what Horace
needs. As fastidious as he's always been, he just will not take a
shower, and Ida Lee says she hasn't washed any of his underwear
in over a week. Can you imagine! So that was the first thing I set
Mr. Peeples on doing. I sent him right upstairs and told him to
clean Horace up. I wanted him shaved, his hair washed, teeth
brushed, and clean clothes on him, and I wanted that done every
day. Mr. Peeples said, 'Ma'am, you got it.' And sure enough, he
brought Horace down an hour later, sparkling clean and smelling
like Bay Rum, and best of all, in good humor. I think I've found a
jewel, thanks to Miss Wiggins."

"I'm so glad for you," I said, then thinking of Horace's attach-
ment to his little red Porsche in the garage, I asked, "Are you going to let Mr. Peeples drive Horace's car?"

"Honey," she said, relief obvious in her voice, "if he's good enough to drive a school bus with twenty or thirty screaming kids in the back, he can drive any car he wants to, including mine.

"Now," she went on more soberly, "if I could find someone of equal ability for childcare, I could rest easy. Ida Lee found Doreen for me—you'll probably see her flitting from room to room like a little scared rabbit. But better that than someone who chatters all day long. Ida Lee needed help because the room that connects to mine will be Penelope's, and right now I'm using it as a closet. So we're moving everything out and making it a bedroom again."

"Oh, that's thoughtful, Mildred," I said. "I was thinking that a child might be lonely off in one of your guest rooms. I'm glad you're doing that."

"Well, I'm trying to make the best of it, but, I declare, I feel as if I've become nothing but a hiring agency. Now I have to start looking for a nanny or an au pair or somebody to look after *Penelope*." The name was pronounced with a tinge of distaste, after which she paused, then cautiously asked, "Do you think Granny Wiggins might be interested?"

"Mildred," I said, shocked that she'd even consider such a thing, "don't you dare go after her. Why, she's practically a member of the Pickens family, and how in the world would Hazel Marie manage the twins without her?" Granny Wiggins, Etta Mae's grandmother, in her oversized tennis shoes and rolled-down stockings, had been with Hazel Marie since the twins were born. "And if you were to try to tempt her away, I wouldn't be surprised if J. D. Pickens came after you with a shotgun or, who knows, a kitchen knife. You know how he is."

Mildred giggled. "Oh, I do know. But I'm just talking. I wouldn't do that to Hazel Marie, although Granny Wiggins would be perfect for me." She heaved a deep sigh. "I'll just have to wait and see. Maybe somebody else will show up at the door like Mr. Peeples did."

For the next few days we grew accustomed to seeing Horace and Mr. Peeples strolling together like two old friends up and down the Allen yard and around the block, weather permitting, of course. To see them, though, you would never think that one was looking after the other, and I commented to Sam that Mildred seemed to have lucked out again.

Not only that, though, Mr. Peeples—I mean, Grady, as he insisted that he be addressed—established a schedule that seemed to ease Horace's late afternoon agitation. It had become noticeable that Horace grew more anxious about wanting to go somewhere as the day drew closer to sundown. Grady arranged to show up at the Allen house in the early afternoon, took Horace for a walk "to wear him out," saw that he ate a good dinner, then sat and talked with him until bedtime. And, Mildred told me, he usually had planned some entertainment to keep Horace's mind occupied. They watched television, talked about their childhoods, tried to put puzzles together, and even, she said, played with toy cars. And once, she told me, Grady had brought his fiddle and played music for him.

"That didn't go over so well," Mildred said. "Horace tried to dance a jig—something he's never done before—but tripped over his feet and fell. Why in the world he was moved to try such a thing, I don't know. He's a lovely ballroom dancer, but after falling, that was the end of that."

Nonetheless, the schedule set up by Grady seemed to help Horace settle down, until the morning I walked into the kitchen and found Horace eating breakfast with Sam.

I looked from Lillian, who shrugged her shoulders and flipped a few more pancakes, to Sam, who smiled and welcomed me to the table.

"We have a guest, honey," he said, moving the syrup pitcher across the table from Horace. "Come join us."

I did, taking note of the pajama top that Horace wore, his uncombed hair, and his obvious enjoyment of Lillian's cooking. I spoke to him, but the only comment he made was when he leaned over to Sam and loudly whispered, "Who's that woman sitting over there?"

Sam walked Horace home, while I called Mildred to let her know that her wandering husband was on his way back. Not being up herself, she'd not known that he was gone. For myself, I'd been relieved to find when Horace stood up from the table that he was wearing a pair of pants and not the matching bottoms to his pajama top.

That little escapade created another problem for Mildred because it now seemed that Horace needed someone with him twenty-four hours of the day. She never considered getting up early and filling in until Grady arrived in the afternoon.

Instead, she moved Grady into the guest room next to Horace's room, had an intercom system set up between them, and probably paid a mint for both.

"Mildred," I said cautiously, after seeing Grady's pickup truck arrive with some of his belongings, "do you think it's wise to have a strange man in the house all the time? I mean, Ida Lee's apartment is out over the garage, and you and Penelope will be alone and, well, you really don't know Mr. Peeples all that well, and . . ." I trailed off, letting the rest of my concern hang in the air.

"That's not a problem," she said with a wave of her hand. "Grady and Horace will be at one end of the hall, and Penelope and I will be at the other end. All the doors lock, and I have the keys, and, furthermore, I told Grady that the only weapon allowed in the house was the shotgun under my bed. I'm not at all worried."

"Mildred . . . ," I began.

"I know," she said, nodding. "With a child in the house, I've put it in a safer place. But Grady doesn't need to know that."

So, after getting Grady moved in and a room prepared for Penelope, Mildred said she'd done all she could do. Although much relieved to have Horace so capably cared for, she nonetheless mourned over what she called the loss of her husband's companionship.

"It's as if thirty-five years of marriage never existed," she said. "We have nothing to talk about. He still refers to me as his mother and thinks he's living in Virginia where he grew up. Actually, I think that's where he was trying to go all those times when he walked off. He keeps talking about getting ready to go home, and it just does me in to have all our years together erased as if they'd never been."

After hearing that, I thanked the Lord that both Sam and I still seemed to know each other, although it scared me to death when I forgot a hair appointment with Velma not two days later.

So, as Mildred's household seemed to settle down with Horace in good hands and Ida Lee, with Doreen's help, managing everything else, the days were soon accomplished that a child was added to the mix.

Chapter 17

❧

After a phone call from Tonya about a week later, Ida Lee and Mildred went to the airport to pick up Penelope, with Ida Lee driving since Mildred was too nervous. Tonya, it seemed, was much too busy to accompany the child to her new home, so Penelope was flying in alone.

I waited at home, almost as nervous as Mildred, to hear what the child was like and to try to stop imagining a few harrowing events that would unhinge Mildred and scar the child for life. Let's face it, the Allen household was not an ideal place to raise a child, especially one who had just been adopted from who knew what awful circumstances, and then been upended from that new home to be sent off to live with another set of strangers.

And let's face this, too, from the thoughtless way Tonya had adopted Penelope without a word to her mother, it was fairly clear that Mildred hadn't done such a good job with raising the child that she'd had under more normal circumstances.

I feared for Penelope, not for her physical well-being—she would have the best of everything—but for her little soul. She had been seemingly tossed aside by both natural parents and adoptive parent. Needing some reassurance, I said as much to Lillian.

"Chil'ren can overcome, Miss Julia," she told me. "They's a lot of 'em that have worse than that happen, an' they come out all right. All they need is one somebody that cares, an' that can be anybody." And she gave me a good, long stare.

I didn't quite know what to make of that, but I filed it away for future reference.

"So," I said, "what do you think of asking Penelope over to play with Latisha some afternoon? Would Latisha like that?"

"She sure would," Lillian said, turning back to peel more potatoes. "You know how she like to be the teacher, so she'll take that little girl under her wing." Lillian chopped up the last of the potatoes, then said, "I jus' hope Penelope don't mind bein' bossed half to death."

"Miss Julia?" Etta Mae Wiggins said when I answered the phone that afternoon. "I did what you said and talked to Mr. Blair. He was real nice, except he kept asking if I was sure I wanted to buy a business." She paused as if thinking of what he'd said. "I think he was making sure that I could afford it, and of course I can't. But I didn't say that, just thought about what you would've said. So I told him that it depended on how good the business is and how much the seller wants for it, just like you told me to say."

"That was good, Etta Mae. I'm sure you did fine. So," I went on, "what've you found out? How much is it?"

When she told me what Lurline Corn wanted for the business alone, then more than doubled it for the business with the property, it almost took my breath away. "What," I gasped, "did Mr. Blair say?"

"He said she must think she's sitting on a gold mine. I guess that means she's asking too much. I mean, I thought it was too much, but anything would be for me."

"Etta Mae," I said, quite firmly, "you have to stop thinking that way. You have access to a reasonable amount for that business—it's as good as in your pocketbook—so you have to begin acting like it."

"Well, I'll try, but, Miss Julia, I've never bought anything that I couldn't put on layaway, and this seems so far out of my reach that it's hard to believe."

"Believe it, because we're going to look into it and make an offer if the business is worth it. Did Mr. Blair get any records that'll show how the business is doing?"

"Yes'm, he gave me some copies, but I'm not sure I know how to read them."

"Don't worry about that. I wouldn't know, either. But bring them by when you get through and we'll have Sam look at them. We need an idea of how many patients Lurline has under contract, what she charges for each one, how many employees she has and what she pays them. Then we'll know if the business is profitable."

"I know about the employees," Etta Mae said. "She has five full-timers, including me, and a bunch of ladies she can call on if somebody needs a sitter or a driver—you know, for a doctor's appointment or some such. They're temps, though I think one or two would like to go full time."

"That's good. Now, if you know or can estimate their wages, we can begin to find out what the business costs to run."

"Oh, I know all that, too," Etta Mae said. "The full-time girls moan all the time about what they make, and I pretty much know what the temps make per hour, although that varies."

"Well, here's another thing. Does Lurline supply anything? I mean, like cars, or paying for gas or your mileage? Tell me how she has things set up."

"Well, we use our own cars and turn in our mileage, and she checks it down to the inch. She supplies a medical bag for each of us that makes us look real professional. We carry the basics for checking blood pressure and temperatures and so on in them. All the full-timers have them." Etta Mae paused, then said, "Lurline buys a lot of things in bulk, so every morning we stock up on what our patients will need that day—things like protein drinks, bandages, all kinds of pads for the incontinent like Depends and so forth. We keep a record so she can charge extra for them. She trains the girls when they come on full time—how to give a bed bath, change sheets, help somebody out of bed or into it, as the case may be. And we learn how to check medications, like to see if somebody's taking too much or not enough or if they need a refill. But Lurline has stopped doing any of the training. She gave all that to me a few years ago. It's why I make a little more than the other girls."

"Well, see," I said, "you're as good as running The Handy Home Helpers already. I would think that the entire business depends on how well the employees are trained. Actually, that's what the business is selling and what the patients are paying for. The training has to be top-notch, Etta Mae, and if Lurline has entrusted it to you, then you're already in charge of the most important part of the business."

"I hadn't thought of it that way," she murmured, although I hoped that she was beginning to think of it that way. And maybe, I thought, beginning to realize her worth to the business, as well as her capability to step into Lurline's shoes.

"Okay, then here's another thing. Can you tell from the records or do you know if the patients pay on time? In other words, if Lurline has a contract with a patient, can she count on the money coming in as it should?"

"I don't know about that," Etta Mae said. "All I know is that she has a CPA come in every now and then, and they close the office door so nobody can hear them. Oh, and I know that most of our patients are on Medicare or Medicaid."

"That's good," I said, nodding to myself. "That means the business is accredited, approved, or certified—whatever it takes to get government money. And that reminds me. You're going to need a good CPA. Who does your personal tax returns?"

"H & R Block."

"Hm-m, well, you'll need somebody more business oriented. So here's what you should do. Make a copy of all the records you have and take them to C. J. Sims. His office is right off Main Street. I'll call and ask him to advise us about the state of the business, and I'll tell him you're coming in. Now, Etta Mae, you can speak openly to him, because I'll be telling him that I'm involved. He'll know eventually, anyway, because he does our taxes."

"Okay," she said, somewhat subdued. "I don't know him, but I've always heard he's the best in town. I'll run by tomorrow and drop everything off to him. But, gosh, Miss Julia," she said, blowing out her breath, "I didn't know how complicated it was going to get."

"We're just doing our due diligence to find out if it's worth doing at all. Don't worry about it, Etta Mae. Once you're set up as the owner, all you have to do is keep it running and stay straight with the IRS. But you can trust C.J. to keep you out of Atlanta."

"What's in Atlanta?"

"The federal pen."

"Oh, my goodness. Are we going to get in trouble?"

"I'm teasing, Etta Mae," I said, feeling bad for scaring her. "But, no, we're not going to get in trouble. That's why we're doing all the complicated stuff up front. And that's why we have Mr. Blair, C. J. Sims, and Sam to help us through it."

And I went on to encourage her and to assure her again that we were doing a good thing in spite of how it felt at the present. I knew she was feeling overwhelmed and that it wouldn't take much for her to back out completely. Yet I was convinced that The Handy Home Helpers was made for Etta Mae Wiggins, and I was determined to see that she got it.

If, that is, it proved to be a profitable business.

Etta Mae dropped off a manila envelope full of papers later that afternoon for Sam to look over. She was between patients, so she couldn't stay. I think she might have had enough of my encouragement, to tell the truth. Which was just as well, for by that time, I was taken up with worrying about Mildred and her new houseguest.

I knew they were back from the airport, so I kept thinking that Mildred would call to tell me the latest, as she had done almost every day since learning of Tonya's high-handed conduct.

And I was worried about that child, thinking how lonely she must be in a strange house with strange people. Homesick, even, although from the sound of it, Penelope had never really had a home to be sick about. But, still, Mildred didn't call, and I didn't want to intrude.

"I expect she's busy," Sam said after I'd moaned to him about it. "They'll be getting to know each other, and there'll be a lot to do. Unpacking, for instance, and showing the little girl around the house, and maybe just sitting and talking."

"Oh, I know," I said, "but Mildred has involved me in everything that's happened for so long that now I'm feeling left out. Which is silly, I know, but having had an unknown child once thrust on me, I could be of help to her."

I was referring to Lloyd, of course, the son of Hazel Marie Puckett, now Pickens, and my long-dead first husband, Wesley Lloyd Springer, conceived while his father was married to someone else, namely me. So I was familiar with having an unknown and unwanted child suddenly underfoot, and I was familiar with how a child could change one's life if one was even slightly open to the possibility.

"*Sam!*" I said, suddenly struck by even more similarities between Mildred's situation and mine. "It was Christmastime then, too."

"What?" he asked, lowering *The Abbotsville Times*. "What was at Christmastime?"

"When I stopped seeing Wesley Lloyd's face every time I looked at Little Lloyd. Remember? You went with me to Walmart to buy presents for him."

Sam smiled. "I remember. You almost bought out the store."

"Well, Mildred needs to be told how that came about, and we—you and I—need to start getting ready for another Christmas. Let's put the tree up early this year, and let's have some folks over for Christmas dinner, and let's remember that Lloyd is practically grown with a driver's license, and let's be thankful that we've had him all these years and how empty they would've been without him. Mildred needs to know that." I sat back and drew a deep breath. "Who do you want to invite for Christmas dinner?"

He laughed and said, "Get your pen and paper, and we'll make a list."

Chapter 18
❦

No need, however, to make out a guest list until the most important person was consulted. With that in mind, I took myself to the kitchen where Lillian was getting ready to leave.

"Lillian," I said, "do you and Latisha have plans for Christmas?"

With only one arm in her coat, she stopped and stared at me. "No more'n usual, I guess. We'll put up a little tree an' make some pound cakes for the neighbors. An' make sure I got all Latisha's Santy Claus off of layaway. Why?"

"Well, Sam and I are thinking of inviting some friends over for Christmas dinner—say, around two or three o'clock that afternoon. And, of course, we want you and Latisha with us." I stopped, for of course it wasn't as if Lillian would be a guest, but rather the provider of the feast. "I'm sorry, Lillian. We do want you both and not just to cook, but, well, nobody can cook like you. If it was left up to me, I'd have to serve frozen pizzas and probably burn them. Please don't think it's something you have to do. If it's too much to ask, I'll figure something out."

She laughed. "I'll tell you what's the truth, Miss Julia, it gets real lonesome on holidays with jus' me an' Latisha. Seem like them days oughta be happy days, but they jus' long and lonesome. So I'd as soon be cooking for a crowd of happy folks than settin' at home with nothin' to do but wait for bedtime."

"Oh, Lillian, thank you, but let me tell you what I have in mind.

I'd like you to hire some help, maybe for several days beforehand to get things ready and to serve and clean up on Christmas Day. Maybe Janelle? Or whoever and however many you think we'll need, because I do want you and Latisha to be guests, just with you supervising the food. I wouldn't trust anybody else to do it as well. And since Christmas is on a Wednesday this year, you can plan to take the rest of the week off and you can count on the usual, as well." The usual was extra pay which was a given, but it didn't hurt to mention it. Whenever I had a tea or a dinner party—anything that added to Lillian's workload—I added a bonus to her salary.

Lillian slipped out of her half-on coat, hung it on a chair, and asked, "You sure you want Latisha?"

"Yes, of course. I'll be asking the Pickens children and Little Gracie Bates, and Penelope Allen, too. We'll have a houseful of children, which means we have to have gifts, as well. Oh, I know! Maybe the adults can draw names beforehand and bring just one gift for whoever's name they get. That'll be fun, especially with a price limit on them. I wouldn't want anybody to get carried away. Sam and I will provide the children's gifts. How does that sound?"

"Sounds good to me, an' Latisha, she'll love it. But you better start countin' up who all you gonna have, so we can figure out where they all gonna set."

"Oh, you're right. Let's see, there're five in the Pickens family. No, let's ask Granny Wiggins, too, because I'm going to ask Etta Mae. And James, too? What do you think about asking him?"

"Well, you know what I think about him. That man's not worth th'owin' out, but I was already thinkin' of gettin' him to help with the cookin'."

"That's perfect. So that makes seven for the Pickens family. And Etta Mae makes eight, and Binkie, Coleman, and Gracie make eleven. Oh, wait, Binkie and Coleman are taking Gracie to Disney World for Christmas, so we're back to eight. You and

Latisha make ten, and the Allen family will make three more. But what about Grady Peeples and Ida Lee? Should we ask them, too?"

"If Mr. Horace come, we might better have Mr. Grady 'less he have family to eat with. Ida Lee, I don't know, she like to have some time to herself, so she might wanta come and she might not. But you left somebody out."

"Who?"

"You and Mr. Sam."

"Oh," I said, laughing, "I guess we should put us on the list, too. My goodness, Lillian, that'll make close to twenty people. Can we manage all that?"

"We've done it before, but dinner'll have to be set out on the buffet so people can help theirselves. We can put card tables up all over the house, but if somebody want to eat on their knees, they can do that, too. What we gonna feed 'em?"

"An old-fashioned Southern Christmas dinner with all the fixin's. You be thinking of what we'll need, and I will, too. Christmas is only a few weeks away, so the sooner we get started, the easier it'll be."

So, with Christmas plans buzzing in my mind, I had to make an effort not to jump too far ahead. For all I knew, all those I wanted to invite were already making their own plans. To circumvent that, I set to work writing invitations to send out the following day. It's a well-known fact that wedding invitations should be mailed six weeks before the event, so I figured that a great and wonderful Christmas dinner deserved no less. Maybe no one would notice that I was off by a couple of weeks.

Yet in spite of my head suddenly being filled with Christmas plans, thoughts of what was going on at the Allen house kept jumping to the forefront of my mind, intermingled now and then with anxiety about Etta Mae. I knew that she needed constant reassurance, being one of those people who thought less of themselves than others thought of them. I made a mental note to call her when I finished with the invitations.

And, I decided, since Mildred hadn't called me, I'd call her, too. Maybe she was waiting for me to show some interest. Maybe the child was so worrisome that Mildred had taken to her bed. Maybe a lot of things, none of which I'd know until I called and asked.

So, when my hand had become stiff from writing, I put down my pen and picked up the phone. Ida Lee answered, so I quickly asked to speak with Mildred. I had long before understood that I could not count on learning anything from Ida Lee—no matter what she thought, she'd never share it.

"Oh, Julia," Mildred said as soon as she picked up the phone. "I don't know how this is going to work out. I am beside myself, trying to figure her out."

"Why? What's she doing?"

"Nothing, and that's the problem. She doesn't say anything or do anything. Just sits where she's told and waits to be told what else to do. Why don't you come over and meet her?"

"I'd love to, but it's getting late so I won't stay but a minute."

Wrapped in a heavy coat against the wind, I hurried through the hedge that lined our side yards, across Mildred's wide lawn, and rang the doorbell. Ida Lee welcomed me and led me to the sunroom where Mildred was ensconced in her usual chair.

Glancing around, I saw a small girl, her back to me as she sat on the floor in a corner, holding what looked to be a Barbie doll. A play-sized footlocker held the doll's wardrobe. My first impression was that Penelope was much younger than Mildred had been told.

"Have a seat, Julia," Mildred said. "I'm so glad to see you, but you must forgive me for not calling you over before this. We, Penelope and I, have been busy getting ourselves situated." Then, leaning forward in her chair and surprising me by raising her voice considerably, she said, "Penelope, this is Miss Julia from next door. Can you say hello to her?"

The child looked around somewhat quizzically at Mildred, giving me my first good look at her. Her complexion was very close to that of Ida Lee's—a smooth, tan shade. Her eyes were large and black, and her abundant hair was equally dark and as straight as a stick.

Penelope glanced at me, then lowered her eyes. She mumbled something that I took to be a greeting and turned back to the doll in her hand.

Mildred rolled her eyes just the least little bit. "She's very quiet," she said, "which I much prefer to the noisy kind. But quite solemn, as well, and sadly lacking in basic manners. I'm not sure she's smiled even once since she's been here."

I frowned and shook my head at Mildred's thoughtless and perhaps hurtful comment. "I'm not sure we should be talking—"

"It's all right," Mildred assured me. "Watch this." Mildred turned to Penelope and, without raising her voice, said, "Penelope."

There was no response from the child by either word or movement.

"She's deaf," Mildred said. "At least partially, because she seems to hear if she's looking at me. Maybe she reads lips, I don't know, but I'm taking her to be checked next week. Isn't it just like Tonya not to say one word about the child's handicap."

"Uh, Mildred, I don't think they use that word these days."

"Well, I do because that's what it is. But," she said with a put-upon sigh, "she is quiet and easily entertained, and I should be happy she's so amenable. All I have to do is get her attention when I speak to her and she does whatever I say. But there's no telling what else is wrong with her because one abnormality usually indicates something else is wrong, too. I declare, Julia, she's just one more thing that Tonya has saddled me with."

I felt increasingly uncomfortable discussing the child with her in the same room even if she was as deaf as a post. Somehow it seemed impolite to say the least and hurtful to say the most. I wanted to leave and mull over this new complication.

"Well," I said, gathering myself to go, "tomorrow is Saturday, and Latisha usually comes with Lillian for a few hours in the morning. Would Penelope like to come over, say about ten, so the girls can play? We'd love to have her if you think she'd enjoy it."

"I'm sure she would," Mildred said, "so thank you for inviting her. Ida Lee and I plan to go through Penelope's clothes—a lot of things are sadly lacking. I need to start a list of what she'll need, especially with the weather so inclement. I'll have Ida Lee walk her over about ten, but, Julia, if she becomes a problem or you get tired of having her, don't hesitate to send her home."

I assured her that I would and hurried out before she could say anything more. I didn't like hearing the child referred to as a problem, even if she couldn't hear a word that was said.

Chapter 19

❧

Mildred was not generally known for speaking in a thoughtless way. In fact, she bent over backward to be kind, generous, and complimentary in referring to other people, especially within their hearing or to others who might repeat what she'd said.

So I was shivering with more than the cold by the time I entered my warm kitchen. Irretrievable damage could be done by Mildred's so openly making known her displeasure not only with Tonya, but with the child herself. It had been unmistakable to me that Mildred was not thrilled to have Penelope on her hands.

"Lillian," I said, coming out of my coat as I entered, "please tell me that Latisha can come over tomorrow and play with Penelope. That little girl needs some normalcy."

Lillian's eyebrows went up as she turned to look at me. "Well, I don't know as I'd call Latisha all that normal if you're talkin' about actin' right. She's a handful, as you oughta know, but I'll bring her 'cause she'll have a fit if I don't."

"Good. But, Lillian, there is a problem. Mildred says the child is deaf, and it really seems that she is—at least a little. Mildred called her by name in a normal tone of voice and Penelope made no indication that she'd heard. Of course her back was turned so she wasn't able to read lips, which Mildred thinks she can do. Tonya, however, said nothing about it. She didn't prepare her mother for anything like that."

"That Tonya something else," Lillian pronounced, shaking her head. "Ev'rybody waitin' to see her on television an' see if she's gonna flip a table or slap somebody's face or what."

"Oh, Lillian," I said, laughing in spite of myself, "do you watch those shows, too? They're so trashy, but fun, too. And I suppose if we'd been offered a starring role in one of them, nothing else would seem quite as important. However, it's a crying shame to discard a child in favor of a few minutes of fame. Or rather," I went on after a deep sigh, "of notoriety, considering that the subject matter is not in the least edifying."

After glancing out a window the next morning and seeing a few tree limbs heavy with ice, I worried that Lillian and Latisha wouldn't be able to come in and I'd be stuck with entertaining a half-deaf child. So it was with relief that I heard Latisha's voice as she and Lillian came into the kitchen downstairs.

"Where is she, Great-Granny?" Latisha said, or rather yelled, for her piercing voice carried easily from kitchen to master bedroom upstairs.

I heard Lillian shush her, then begin to close interior doors. Sam had risen early to have breakfast at the Bluebird café with a few of Abbotsville's movers and shakers. I hurried through my toilette to be prepared to welcome Penelope, devoutly hoping that the morning would be a success with the little girls enjoying each other.

After quickly finishing my breakfast and taking my plate to the sink, I watched as Latisha made her preparations. She'd brought her pink backpack and was proceeding to empty it of books, papers, crayons, Magic Markers, pencils, and who knew what else—all onto the small corner table that was hers alone.

"I'm gettin' ready for that girl," Latisha announced with authority as she leafed through a coloring book. "An' I'm gonna let her color whatever picture she wants to, except maybe this hummingbird. I been saving it."

Smiling, I made my own preparations, bringing my invitations and address book to the kitchen table so that both Lillian and I would be around to supervise the meeting of Latisha and Penelope.

Almost on the dot of ten, Ida Lee knocked on the door and presented Penelope, who looked lost swaddled in a jacket too large for her.

"Mrs. Allen said to call us if Penelope needs to come home," Ida Lee said.

"She'll be fine," I assured her. "Come in, Penelope. We're so glad to have you."

After introducing the child to Latisha, I turned her toward Lillian. "And this is my best friend in the world," I said. "This is Lillian."

Lillian stooped over, spread her arms, then wrapped them around Penelope. "What a pretty little thing you are! Now you know the way, little honey, you jus' come on over here any time you want to. We always glad to have you. Now, you just set down with Latisha, she got all kinds of things to play with."

With the girls settled at the play table, I spread my work on the kitchen table while Lillian busied herself with making a thick vegetable beef soup for supper. Gradually my attention focused more and more on what I was doing as the little girls seemed to be happily playing together. Only occasionally did Latisha break my concentration with a bossy comment to tell Penelope what colors to use.

They seemed so busy that there was little talking between them—just a few mumbles back and forth—until Latisha screeched, "*What!* Great-Granny, did you hear that! This girl's almost got my name!"

"What?" I asked, smiling at Latisha's imagination. "How does Penelope's name sound like yours?"

"'Cause, Miss Lady, her name's not Penelope, which I'm glad of 'cause it's not much of a name to start with. Her name's Lisha, almost 'xactly like mine! We could be twins."

Intrigued, Lillian and I gathered around the table as Latisha said, "Lisha, write your name down. Let 'em see what it is."

Penelope, or as it seemed, Lisha, gripped a number 2 pencil and, bearing down hard, printed on a page from the coloring book the name ALICIA, which when pronounced did, indeed, sound close to Latisha.

"Well, my goodness," I said as a few worrisome things began to clear up. "Lillian, this child's not hard of hearing at all. She just doesn't respond to the wrong name, as neither you nor I would either. I expect that Tonya changed her name in the same high-handed way she's done everything else. Not," I hurriedly added, "that I'm being critical, but . . . Well, sweetheart, which name do you prefer?"

For the first time, I saw the beginnings of a smile on the child's face. "Alicia," she whispered.

"Then, around here you will be Alicia, and we'll tell your grandmother that you have a beautiful name all your own."

But, I thought to myself, of all the thoughtless things to do, it would be to change a child's name in midstream, so to speak. It was as if the child's basic identity was unacceptable and had to be altered. What in the world had Tonya been thinking? Probably, I thought somewhat unkindly, she assumed a family name would endear the child to Mildred, but so far that hadn't seemed to have worked so well.

After a lunch of peanut butter and banana sandwiches, eaten with a lot of giggles, the little girls went upstairs to the room that Lillian used when she stayed the night and where Latisha kept a few toys. When I went up to the bathroom, I heard them talking— Alicia almost as much as Latisha.

At one point, Latisha said, "Now you be the mother, and I'll be the baby." Then in an even higher-pitched voice, "Wah, wah, I want my bottle." Giggles broke out from both girls. It was the first time I'd heard Penelope—I mean, Alicia—laugh, so I smiled to myself and went about my business.

Grateful for a successful playdate, I went back downstairs, getting more and more indignant with each step.

"Lillian," I said when I entered the kitchen, "I can't stand this. I'm going to march myself over to Mildred's and tell her that absolutely nothing is wrong with that child. Not only can she hear as well as anyone, she's perfectly normal in every way. And not only that, I'm going to tell her that Penelope is now Alicia and always has been. And if Tonya doesn't like it, she can speak to me. And I'm going to tell Mildred that she has to curb her tongue and quit making snide remarks about either Tonya or Alicia. If she can't bring herself to warm up to that little girl, better that she send her back to Tonya. I am not going to stand by and watch as Mildred thinks only of herself and how she's being put upon."

I snatched a coat from the closet and headed for the door. "I may lose a friendship, but that's better than damaging a child for life."

Chapter 20

❧

I should've known better. Mildred did not take kindly to criticism of her social skills, going so far as to lecture me for misunderstanding her. Still, I said what I'd come to say, most of which seemed to go right over her head. That, though, was better than enraging her. Maybe some of it would eventually sink in, although at the time Mildred pounced on the name change and ignored everything else I said.

"Alicia?" she asked, frowning. "Then why in the world would Tonya tell me it was Penelope?"

"Think about it," I said, in no mood to commiserate about the giddiness of a failed potter-turned-reality-TV starlet.

"Oh," Mildred said as if suddenly enlightened. "Giving her my grandmother's name was Tonya's way of including her in the Beasley family. How thoughtful of her!"

"Undoubtedly," I said dryly, as my eyes rolled back in my head.

"Well, now," Mildred went on, "I wonder if it should be Penelope Alicia Beasley or Alicia Penelope Beasley. Think how important a girl's initials are since they'll go on so much of her trousseau. Hers will be either PAB or APB, neither of which is very auspicious. With PAB, I'd always think of pabulum, and I think APB stands for something in law enforcement."

"All points bulletin," I said, having once or twice in past years been the subject of such a designation. "But speaking of names, what does she call you?"

"Me? Why, nothing so far, but at least she speaks English— when she speaks at all."

"It's the grandmother's prerogative, you know," I said, "to decide what the grandchildren should call her."

"I haven't thought about it," Mildred said. "What do you think?"

"Well, I've heard Granny, Grams, Gammie, and Grand-mommy . . ." I stopped at the face she made at the suggestions. "What about Nana? That's a sweet name."

She shook her head. "I wouldn't know to whom she was speaking. *Grand-Mère* is a possibility, but, no, I'll stick with Grandmother since it's been foisted on me anyway. There's a certain distinction about it."

Yes, I thought, and a certain distance about it, too, but I let it pass.

"So," Mildred went on, "she's not deaf at all? That's good news because I can cancel her appointment with the audiologist. I wasn't looking forward to that, anyway. Well, Julia," she said, shifting in her chair, "I've finally gotten some papers from Tonya by FedEx, and I have to tell you that nothing looks very legitimate. I wouldn't be surprised if we have to send her back, but I've already called my lawyers in Atlanta to put them on the case. It seems that Penelope, oops, I guess I mean Alicia, has been in an orphanage somewhere in South America. How Tonya found her, I don't know, and I don't know what her legal status is in this country. Tonya says that her attorneys have it well in hand.

"Anyway," she went on with a wry twist of her mouth, "the child is of South American heritage of some sort, which is of some relief to me. There're certainly some very high-ranking families of South American origin, and Alicia has the fine facial features that are their hallmark." Mildred sat back with a sigh of contentment. "And the name, Alicia, indicates a certain social standing, don't you think? I should've known that Tonya wouldn't have just picked up someone off the street. I'm much relieved to know that she chose not just a physically normal child but perhaps a child of some standing. How good of you to have recognized that."

"I'm happy to've been of help," I said as I mentally threw up my hands.

"Lillian," I said as I entered my kitchen and began to undo my coat, "it is absolutely amazing how we can talk ourselves into believing what we want to believe. Mildred Allen is one of the most clear-eyed women I know, yet right there before my eyes she convinced herself that Alicia is of noble birth. But," I went on, hanging my coat on the back of a chair, "I guess if it works for her, it shouldn't matter to me. And it doesn't, because whatever makes that child more desirable, acceptable, or whatever to her has to be a good thing. I just kept my mouth shut."

"It's pro'bly a good thing you did," Lillian said, "'cause sometimes you jus' have to let people find out what's what for theirselves. Tellin' 'em don't do no good. Jus' give it some time, Miss Julia, that little girl'll make her own way."

"She's a sweet little thing, isn't she? Not a bit of trouble, and Latisha seemed to really take to her, don't you think?"

"She did, an' she's ready to do it again. One thing, though, we was both wonderin' about. Where's Alicia goin' to school?"

"That's a good question," I said, sitting at the table. "I assume she'll go to the local elementary school, but Mildred hasn't said. She'll have to be tested to determine what grade she's in. Mildred should get on to that right away." I leaned my head on my hand, then said, "I'd better mention it to her because she's been so taken up with all that's wrong with the child that she can't think of what she should be doing to help her."

"Well," Lillian said, "now I think of it, I better mention that Miss Etta Mae wants you to call her."

"Oh, good," I said, rising. "Maybe there's some good news for a change."

There wasn't, for when I returned Etta Mae's phone call, she immediately said, "You won't believe this, but Lurline's been dancing all around her office. She told us that somebody else is interested in The Handy Home Helpers—I mean, besides the Dollar Store people. And Lurline thinks that'll make the Dollar Store eager to snatch it up before this new somebody can get it. What're we going to do, Miss Julia?"

"Well, wait a minute, Etta Mae," I said. "Does Lurline know who this new somebody is?"

"No'm, just that somebody else wanted to look at the business records."

"That would've been us, remember?"

"I thought of that, but it doesn't matter if it is or not, all it's doing is making her think she can hike up the price. Or at least that she won't have to lower the price. She's tickled to death thinking there'll be a bidding war. What're we going to do?"

"Not a thing," I said. "Now, listen, Etta Mae, I don't think the Dollar Store is all that interested. If her place had met all their needs, they would've already made an offer—not what she's asking by a long shot, but they would be in negotiations. And they're not, are they?"

"I don't guess so."

"So Lurline can dance all she wants, because so far it seems that no one has made an offer and that includes us. Just hold on, Etta Mae. If the Dollar Store people want to meet her outlandish price, then more power to them. They'll close The Handy Home

Helpers because all they'll want is the property, and you and I will step in and open a new home care business of our own. How does that sound?"

"Um, real good, I guess," Etta Mae said. "Real scary, though."

"Don't worry about it. Let's wait a few more days till we hear what Mr. Blair, C. J. Sims, and Sam think the business is worth."

"Well, that's a problem. I called Mr. Sims's office for an appointment and his secretary said he wasn't taking any new clients. I could go back to H&R Block, I guess."

"No, just wait. He's taking new clients though he doesn't know it yet. He'll call you in a few days, and as far as Lurline is concerned, let her think what she wants to . . ."

"She thinks she should've asked for more."

"She'll get over that when the Dollar Store buys something else and our offer comes in."

"Well, okay, but I get all jittery thinking what'll happen when she finds out it's me who wants her business."

"Oh, I doubt that, Etta Mae. She'll be thrilled to have it off her hands so she can move to Florida. It won't matter to her who gets it."

"Maybe, but you don't know her like I do."

With that, I launched into another encouraging lecture, reminding Etta Mae that she was fully capable of stepping into Lurline's shoes as soon as we could get rid of her and that she shouldn't feel we were doing anything underhanded by not disclosing our interest.

"That's the way these things are done," I said. "Everybody plays their cards close to the vest. It all depends on how quickly Lurline wants to move to Florida. If she's not in a hurry, she can string it out for a year or so until somebody meets her price. Or if nobody does, she can just close it down or stay in business herself."

"Oh, do you think she'll do that?" Etta Mae sounded as if she was near tears at the thought.

"No, I don't, but here's something you can do. Keep reminding her of how beautiful and warm Florida is, especially on one of our really cold days. Tell her how you envy her being able to live there. If she feels in competition with you—which you seem to think she does—she'll be more eager to do something you can't do, which is to move to the Sunshine State."

"I hadn't thought of it like that," Etta Mae murmured.

"That," I told her, "is because you're a nice, trusting person, Etta Mae, and unfamiliar with the way business is done."

After several days of gusty winds, heavy rains, and a few icy mornings, the weather turned mild again and we stopped worrying about the heating bills sending us to the poor house. Actually, I'd gotten over worrying about heating bills soon after interring Wesley Lloyd Springer, my late first husband. The first thing he'd done every day when he came home from work was to turn down the thermostat. The man had been absolutely loaded, the extent of which I hadn't known until he'd passed, yet he could not bear to spend an extra penny on heating the house.

The first winter he was in his grave, I kept the thermostat set at a comfortable temperature and turned it up when I wanted to. I much preferred to pay Duke Power than freeze to death.

So, after a taste of winter, a few balmy days with the temperatures in the fifties and sixties, with the occasional inching up into the seventies, reminded us of why we preferred to live in the South. I sat in the library in a wing chair beside the east window, enjoying the sun beaming through as I made a few more Christmas lists.

Lillian stuck her head around the hall door and said, "Miss Julia, come look at something out here in the kitchen."

"What is it?" I asked, putting aside my legal pad and rising.

"You gotta see it," she said, smiling, as I followed her to the window behind the kitchen table. "Look out there," she said, pointing toward Mildred's well-kept side yard.

"Well, I never," I murmured, as I peered through the glass at Horace Allen and Alicia, holding hands as they strolled along together.

"That's the second time they come around the house," Lillian said. "'Cept this time they set down on one of Miss Mildred's yard benches for a while. An', Miss Julia, they was jus' talkin' away at each other, an' Mr. Horace, he stopped one time an' look like he was tellin' 'Licia about a flower or something. An' it looked like he know what he was talkin' about, too."

"That is just so sweet," I said, "but I wonder where Grady is." Mr. Peeples was supposed to be watching Horace every minute to prevent him from wandering off. "You think he's keeping an eye on them?"

"Maybe he's in the backyard, waitin' for 'em to come back around."

"I hope so," I said, wondering if I should call Mildred and tell her that Horace was on a looser rein than usual. It's not easy to be a desirable neighbor. One never knows whether to report everything observed, thereby being referred to as nosy, or to keep one's distance and be accused of being unneighborly. "Let's keep an eye on them, Lillian. If they head for the sidewalk, I'll call Mildred."

"Yes'm, 'cause we know Mr. Horace don't know what day it is, and 'Licia don't know where in the world she is, so somebody gotta watch out for 'em."

"That is the truth," I said, "and furthermore, I sometimes wonder if Mildred herself knows up from down. Do you know what she was thinking just the other day?"

"No'm."

"She was looking into boarding schools for Alicia. I couldn't believe she'd send that child off to another new home, and I told her it was cruel to even consider such a thing."

"I'm glad you did, Miss Julia," Lillian said. "That little thing jus' a baby an' she been moved around so much, she pro'bly think nobody wants her."

"That's exactly what I told Mildred, and she told me not to get so exercised over it because she couldn't find a school that would take a child so young. At least in Virginia, which is where she'd been looking. So she's stuck with the local school and a tutor to catch Alicia up to whatever grade she's in. And I'm glad. Public school was good enough for Lloyd, excellent for him, in fact. I told you about his PSAT score, didn't I?" I stopped and allowed myself a moment of pride. "Public school will be good enough for Alicia, too, and good *for* her, as well."

I went back to my wing chair in the sun, but couldn't get my mind focused on Christmas lists. Instead, I began thinking about the state of our schools. Granted, I was not exactly well-informed, having had no children of my own enrolled in them, but I'd picked up a good bit from hearing conversations among women who did.

And it seemed to me that lately public schools in general, elementary through the high schools, were committed to turning out technicians, rather than well-rounded *educated* graduates. Yes, of course I knew that we were in the so-called Electronic Age, but was it really necessary to replace Ancient History and Latin with Web Design, Coding, software, hardware, and memes—whatever any of that was?

I had read that in an earlier age, only those who knew Latin were considered even basically educated. Yet it had taken a temper tantrum by J. D. Pickens to persuade the school board to offer two semesters of Latin and Ancient History so that Lloyd and a few other students could have the basics of a classical education before going off to college.

So maybe I'd been wrong in pushing a public school for Alicia. Maybe only private schools were still committed to an education beyond how to use a keyboard. But, no, I couldn't believe that Alicia would benefit from being uprooted and sent away again. It could be that she'd be emotionally prepared for a boarding school in a few years, but at the present time, I strongly felt that what she needed was a stable home.

And if Mildred didn't understand that, I feared for that little girl. In fact, from the wider viewpoint of education in general, I feared for us all.

It's been said that those who don't know history are bound to repeat it, and if you don't believe that, just read even a little about the decline of the Roman Empire and compare it to what you read in the morning newspaper or hear on the news. High taxes, constant wars, large bureaucracies, falling birth rates, multiple divorces, social license, decreasing agricultural acreage, increasing city populations on the dole, incompetent governance, porous borders, rebellions, and increasing demands for government handouts. Does any of that sound familiar?

Ah, well, bemoaning the state of affairs is the armchair version of getting up and doing something to help matters. But what could I do? Far be it from me to march in a protest or run for office. The only thing I might be able to do was to put in my two cents about the care and education of one small girl, and even that could be seen as none of my business. But, well, the same could've been said concerning Lloyd, my dead husband's illegitimate son, but thank goodness I hadn't said it.

Sometimes, regardless of how determined one is to mind one's own business, there are good and imperative reasons to speak one's mind and to go as far as to meddle in the affairs of others in order to make things come out right. In such situations it really doesn't matter how many new leaves you try to turn over.

Chapter 22

❧

"Can you come over?" Mildred asked when I answered the phone. "I am at my wit's end."

So I went and was now sitting across a tea table from her, waiting to hear how she was bearing up.

"It's Grady," she said, heaving a great sigh. "Grady Peeples, who has so relieved me by looking after Horace. He's come down with the flu or something. I had to send him home for fear that all that wheezing, sneezing, and nose blowing would infect Horace, who, as you know, Julia, simply cannot afford to get sick. He's so vulnerable to everything that comes along even when he's healthy, so in his present state I dare not expose him to anything that would make things worse than they are."

"Of course not," I said, gingerly holding a cup and saucer. "You take such good care of him, Mildred. But I am sorry to hear that you've had to send Grady away. He seemed the answer to prayer."

"Oh, he certainly was—*intense* prayer, in fact. But now," Mildred said with another sigh, "I'm right back where I was, trying to keep Horace occupied so he won't wander off. But I have had help from a most unexpected source. You won't believe this, Julia, but Penelope or Alicia or whoever she is has stepped up to the plate, so to speak."

I smiled. "Yes, I've seen the two of them walking around the yard. And, Mildred, they seemed to be engaged in an active conversation. She was holding his hand, and they were talking back and forth. Of course, I couldn't hear what they were saying, but Alicia was talking much more than I've ever seen her do before. Just chattering away, in fact."

"Yes, you're right about that. It has certainly been a pleasant surprise that they've taken to each other so well. She even reads to him, which is particularly helpful around dinner time when Horace usually gets so restless. Of course even as thankful for it as I am, it also saddens me. I mean, just picture me looking in on them in the upstairs sitting room and seeing that tiny little girl reading about Jack and the Beanstalk to my husband of so many years. And seeing him completely engrossed in the story.

"Of course," she went on, "Horace was never much of a reader in the first place, so perhaps he'd never heard that story. That would explain his interest."

"Yes, I suppose it would," I said, agreeing even though my heart sank at the thought. "But I'm sure it encourages you to know how well Alicia reads."

"Well, it would have if she'd been reading something appropriate to his age and education. But," she said dismissively, "a nursery rhyme book? I don't think so."

"Oh, Mildred, the child is only, what? Seven years old? Eight? As small as she is, she could be even younger. I think you should be grateful that she's helping him pass the time. Better Jack and the Beanstalk on his mind than a little red Boxster car."

"You're right," Mildred said. "I know you're right, and there's something very dear about her concern for him. She's not asked one question about his condition. She just seems to know that he has to be watched and cared for. It couldn't have come at a better time since Grady's out of the picture. Temporarily, I devoutly hope, because I'm the one who has to see that Horace showers and dresses. After that, she seems to take over. I'm so glad I ordered the Ken doll along with the Barbie, because Horace is entranced with all the outfits to put on and take off. Of course, he's always been interested in fashion—Armani, especially—so it's quite sweet to watch them select the styles for their various outings."

"I'm sure it is," I murmured as a wave of sadness swept over me at the decline of such a once-dashing man-about-town. Then to steer the conversation away from that depressing subject, I said, "Latisha is coming over after school at least one day next week. I'll let you know when, because we'd love to have Alicia, too, if you can spare her."

"Thank you, I'm sure she'll want to although Horace will miss her. That is, if he even notices that she's gone. But," Mildred went on, "I also wanted to tell you that I've decided to honor my grandmother's memory and Tonya's choice by calling the child Penelope. I've thought long and hard about it, Julia, and since Tonya is making her a Beasley legally, then we should firmly embed her into the family and the sooner the better."

I was nonplussed, whatever that meant. "But, Mildred, won't that confuse the child? I don't think . . ."

Mildred waved her hand. "I'm doing the best I can for her, and right now it has to be Penelope so I can at least pretend she's a Beasley. Although when I look into those black eyes which no Beasley has ever had . . ." She sighed as if long-suffering were her portion in life. "I might as well tell you, Julia, that I have little choice in the matter. Tonya called last night and I was so excited to tell her that we'd learned that Alicia is the child's name. But she'd known it all along and told me in no uncertain terms that it has to be Penelope—some legal matter apparently pertaining to Tonya's trust fund, which she herself changed. So Alicia is out. We are all to call her Penelope. I know it's a mouthful, but, please, no Penny. Tonya was adamant about that. In a sense, she gave me my marching orders—so different, you know, from my Tony—but, it is a family name so I'm inclined to agree with her. You don't mind explaining it to Lillian and Latisha, do you?"

To Lillian and Latisha? And who, I wondered, would explain to Alicia? I opened my mouth to say something but nothing came out, so shaken was I at the absolute gall not only of Tonya but of Mildred for playing so fast and loose with a child's sense of herself.

"Well, anyway," Mildred went on as if having taken care of one problem she was moving on to the next, "speaking of school, I've discussed the situation with the powers-that-be, and since it's so close to the Christmas break, they've advised me to wait until the next semester to enroll her. That way she'll have more time to become acclimated before starting school."

"That sounds like good advice," I said, wishing she'd had some of the same when it came to names. The cup tinkled in my saucer, and I realized my hand was shaking. Pulling myself together, I murmured, "What grade will she be in?"

"Well, I've found some papers that say she's eight years old, so she should be in the third grade. But since she'll start with only half a year to go, they say it'll be better to hold her back in the second grade." Mildred sighed. "Which, in a way, is a shame. Tonya was such a good student, you know."

I blinked at the non sequitur, since it did not follow that Tonya's abilities would've had any effect on Penelope Alicia, her having been adopted and all. So, using all my accumulated social skills to manage an untenable situation, I commiserated again with the loss of Grady, confirmed the playdate, and took my leave, wondering all the while if Mildred, herself, hadn't become slightly unhinged.

Blowing through the kitchen door, shedding my coat as I came, I sang out, "Lillian, Mildred Allen is losing her mind. Do you know what she's doing now?"

Lillian looked up from the sack of beans in her lap. "No'm. All I know's it's too early to be buyin' a mess of green beans."

"Well, she's . . ." I looked around. "Alicia's not here, is she?"

"No'm, she still walkin' with Mr. Horace, last I looked."

"Oh, well, good." I pulled out a chair from the table, sat down, and caught my breath. "She doesn't need to hear this, except sooner or later, she will. And it will be a miracle if she doesn't turn out to be the most confused child in three states. Now, Lillian," I said, leaning toward her, "you heard just as I did that Alicia told us—well, told Latisha first—that her name is *Alicia*. Didn't you?"

"Yes'm, I cert'ly did."

"Well, and you know that Tonya in the most high-handed way possible took it on herself to change that perfectly good name to Penelope, which is what she told her mother, I mean, Penelope's grandmother . . . I mean, told Mildred what her name was to be. So, Mildred didn't know that it was actually Alicia until we told her. Right?"

"That's right." Lillian snapped a green bean. "You tole her."

"And she went back and forth about it right in front of my eyes, saying first that Tonya was to be commended for naming the child Penelope so she'd feel a part of the family. But then she—Mildred, I mean—turned on a dime and decided that Alicia was a name that reflected a certain high South American heritage, something I never knew, and was, therefore, the preferred one. But now, *now*, Lillian, she's decided that it has to be Penelope after all because it honors a Beasley ancestor and it might hurt Tonya's feelings if it's not used. Well!" I flung out my arms in frustration at something so simple having been made so complicated. "Who cares about Tonya's feelings? Who's thinking of *Alicia's* feelings? Or *Penelope's*? Or whatever her name is?"

I sank back into the chair, surprised by my own vehemence. "Anyway," I said, calming myself, "at least now Mildred has tacked both names onto the child, though she can't decide which should come first to make the most attractive set of initials for mono-gramming."

"So," Lillian said, "what we s'posed to call her?"

I thought for a minute, then, reassuring myself, said, "Alicia. Alicia, because that's what she herself told us. Who should know better, I ask you. I mean," I went on, "you don't just change a child's name willy-nilly on a whim. Why, Lillian, your name is your identity. It's who you are, and what your parents chose for you. And that little girl doesn't have her parents anymore and she's been dragged all over creation, and now, strange people keep changing her name. She won't even know who she's supposed to be. I could just cry." And to my surprise, I just about was. "It's hurtful, Lillian, and I am just done in at Mildred's lack of sensi-tivity for Alicia's feelings. Or if she happens to be Penelope—hers, either."

"Well, Miss Julia," Lillian said, "Miss Mildred, she got a lot on her right now, an' she tryin' to please ev'rybody while tryin' to decide who need pleasin' the most."

"You're right, Lillian, as you usually are and I think, deep down, that it's Tonya who burdens her the most. And with good reason, I should think, considering the thoughtless way Tonya is treating her.

"And then there's Horace. I should be more sympathetic, I guess, but I do worry about the child and what kind of damage all this up and down, back and forth, in and out about her name is doing to her." I rested my head on my hand and sighed again. "So what do we do? Keep on calling her Alicia here in our house, but refer to her as Penelope in Mildred's? I declare, I don't know if I can keep them straight at the right place at the right time. How in the world will that little girl?"

"Well," Lillian said as she dumped a handful of snapped beans in a pan, "I tell you the best thing to do."

"What?"

"Come up with another name that'll work at both places and won't make nobody mad for not sayin' the right one at the right place."

"*Another* one? My word, Lillian, she has a gracious plenty already." But then, because of a knowing smile lurking around Lillian's mouth, I leaned forward and asked, "Like what?"

"Think about it, Miss Julia. We all already do it all the time with Lloyd, an' nobody think a thing about it. I think maybe Honey be a good one 'cause that's what I call her now. It come kinda nat'ral, an' it say a lot to her without botherin' anybody else."

"Well, they Lord!" I said, blowing out my breath. "An *affectionate* name. Of course! That's brilliant, Lillian. We won't add to her confusion by using Alicia or upset Mildred by going against her wishes, and, you know what? I don't really care what it does to Tonya." I slapped my hand lightly on the table. "*Honey*, it is."

Chapter 23

❧

Friday morning, bright and early, I took myself to the office of C. J. Sims, CPA, to discuss the purchase of The Handy Home Helpers. C.J. was a short, thin man with thick glasses, a slight paunch, and a large head filled with numbers and figures. Mathematics had pared him down to bone and baldness, leaving him with no interests other than the practice of accounting. He had no wife, no hobbies, and no social life, being too shy or too disinterested to pursue anything outside his office. He was precise and picky to a fault, but that's what you want in the one in whom you put your trust when it comes to state and federal taxes. Besides, Sam thought highly of him, even though he said that C.J. was the most boring person he knew unless you were up for an IRS audit. Then, he said, C.J. was the man you wanted.

That morning C. J. Sims was, as usual, all business, seating me at a round table in his conference room, and placing himself, an envelope full of records, and a yellow legal pad beside me.

"So you're thinking of going into business," he said, shoving his glasses up on his nose. "I wouldn't advise it."

"Oh, my," I said, my spirits dropping. "Is it that bad?"

"What? You mean Ms. Corn's in-home care business? No, it's the only one in the county and it's profitable. All it needs is a good manager and a plan for expansion before a competitor steps in. That's not you."

"Well, I know that, C.J.," I said, thinking to myself that knowing someone too well and too long had its drawbacks. "It's not my intention to manage it myself. I'm looking at it as an investment because I have the perfect person to run it. Actually, I'm not even thinking of buying the business myself, but rather to loan the money to someone who knows the business backward and forward."

"Hm-m," he said, laying down his pencil. "That means you'll be investing in the person, not the business. Might be better to buy the business and hire the person. That way you'd have something to sell if it didn't work out or you got tired of it. Can't sell a manager, you know."

"I do know, and you may be sure that I've thought it out quite thoroughly. What I'd like to know from you is how much the business is worth. To my way of thinking, Ms. Corn is asking an unreasonable price, which means she either has stars in her eyes or she doesn't really want to sell. What do you think?"

"I think that you're right—it's overpriced, probably because the Dollar Store showed a little interest."

"Oh? You know about that?"

"I keep up," C.J. said, slightly smugly. "And I know they're looking elsewhere. She'll know it soon, too, so a reasonable offer might be disappointing, but on the other hand, it could also be quite welcome."

He leaned over the table, drew the legal pad near, and wrote a dollar sign on the page. "Here's what I would offer if I were interested in a purchase." And he jotted down a figure beside the dollar sign. "She'll turn it down—it's much too low. But if she makes a counteroffer, you'll know she's serious about selling. You can go from there."

Pleased to have gotten what I'd come for, I began to gather myself to leave. "Thank you, C.J., we'll try your price. Actually, we'll let Joe Blair try it for us, because I'm staying in the background."

"Not a bad idea," he said, standing as I did. "The less the seller knows about where the money's coming from, the better."

"One other thing," I said, as he reached for the doorknob. "I know that officially you're not taking any new clients, but I'd like you to consider taking on The Handy Home Helpers, or rather its new manager, if and when this sale goes through. Well, even before that. She needs a tutorial in how to read the books as well as how to keep them. It can be considered part of my investments, which you're already handling anyway."

He whipped out a large white handkerchief, wiped briefly at his nose, and stuffed it back into his pocket. Giving himself time to think, I thought, and to consider if refusing a new client would entail the loss of a prized one—namely me.

"I'd take it as a personal favor," I said, not at all reluctant to do a little arm-twisting.

He pushed his glasses up on his nose again, flashed a tight smile, and said, "I'd be pleased to do so. Send your manager to me whenever you're ready."

"Her name is Etta Mae Wiggins and she knows the business backward and forward. She may, however, know absolutely nothing about *managing* a business."

His eyebrows went up just slightly, his only indication of surprise or dismay, I wasn't sure which. Then he opened the door for me and said, "I'll take it as a personal challenge. Thank you for the referral."

I left, unsure of the edge of sarcasm in his last remark, but it didn't matter. Etta Mae would be in capable hands.

Sam and I talked it over during the weekend, and he, too, thought that the business was sound, although overpriced.

"There's a good, steady income," he'd said, pointing to a line on a page. "And her patients seem to stay with her, which could be because she locks them in with contracts. But there're several who've renewed over and over, so they must be pleased."

"Either that," I said, "or they can't afford or don't want to go into a nursing facility."

"That's true," Sam said, nodding in agreement. "She's had several patients for years, and that could be because she's had little or no competition. Which could change, of course, so Etta Mae would do well to stay ahead of the curve and think of offering new or different services as she's able to. A business can't just stand still."

"She's mentioned that there're some part-time workers who'd like to go full time. She could expand that way, and take on more patients. If," I said, suddenly aware that an eager new owner could quickly run a business into the ground, "she doesn't get carried away."

"Oh, I doubt she'll do that," Sam said. "Etta Mae seems quite levelheaded and deliberate to me."

"Yes, she is that, even hesitant in fact. Except," I went on, "in marital matters. But that's neither here nor there. The big question, Sam, is this: Is the business worth what Lurline Corn is asking?"

"No," he said. "She's overvalued it, and she'll never get her asking price. And, if she's any kind of businesswoman, I expect she knows it. She's just sticking a toe in the water to see what the Dollar Store will do."

"That's exactly what C.J. said," I said, "but nobody's heard anything about them for a while. For all we know, they're looking in Fletcher or Mills River, or some other county entirely. C.J. implied that he knew something, but he didn't say what." I stopped and drummed my fingers on the arm of the sofa. "Sam, why don't you try to find out what they're up to? Surely somebody at the Bluebird has heard some rumors."

Sam smiled. "That's the place to find out, all right. In the meantime, you should make sure that Etta Mae is committed to taking over. You don't want to end up with a business on your hands and nobody to run it."

"Goodness knows *I* don't want to run it. But what do you think of C.J.'s suggestion of making a low offer in the hope that Lurline will come down on her price?"

"Well, she'll either be insulted or she'll negotiate. Actually I'm impressed that C.J. thought it was worth anything. He's not in the risk-taking business at all."

I perked up. "What do *you* think it's worth?"

When he wrote down a figure, I sat back and smiled. It was a reasonable offer and more in line with my own thinking than C.J.'s crushingly low number. It was a figure that, stretched over the years, would not overwhelm Etta Mae with debt, and it was a figure that I could live with while she paid it off.

Come to find out, though, I'd overestimated Etta Mae's ability to live with debt. When I showed her Sam's suggestion, she was not just overwhelmed at the thought of it, she was sick to her stomach.

"I don't think I can do it, Miss Julia," she said, whispering as she gasped through the words. "I've never seen that much money in my life, much less spent it."

We had met for lunch at my choice, the Tete-a-Tete Tearoom, which was proving to have been a poor choice. It had not occurred to me that her usual workday outfit—a colored tunic, matching baggy pants, and rubber-soled nurse's shoes—would draw the eyes of the ladies who lunch. The tables were fairly close together, as well, so we ended up whispering across the table, which attracted even more attention.

Etta Mae lost her appetite early on—as soon as I wrote two figures on a paper napkin, in fact.

"Look," I said, leaning close with my hand covering the napkin. "This is what Mr. Sims suggested, which I know would be rejected out of hand. C.J. is extremely conservative in his investment advice. Now, this is what Sam said we should offer so we won't insult Lurline. He thinks it's a fair price and one that she ought to jump at. What do you think?"

"Neither one," she said, swallowing hard. "Miss Julia, I can't borrow that kind of money. I'd never pay it off. I just can't do it."

I sat back and looked at her. Far be it from me to talk anybody into doing something simply because I thought it was a good idea. Of course I didn't want to do that, nor did I want to make a life-changing decision for anyone else unless it was absolutely necessary. Hadn't I just recently turned over a new leaf and gotten out of the knowing-what's-best business?

Still, Etta Mae was just the type of person who needed a little encouragement, a little push, a little hand-holding, and I was good at all three. I changed the subject.

"C. J. Sims wants to see you," I said.

"He does? I thought he wasn't taking new clients."

"He's making an exception for you," I said, then plunged on. "After looking over Lurline's books, he thought it was the perfect opportunity for someone like you. I'd told him, of course, of your background and how well you know that particular business. In fact, he was so impressed by the possibilities that he implied that if I didn't want to follow through, he might be interested in backing you himself."

"*Really?*"

"Yes," I said, hoping for forgiveness as I pushed on toward getting a good deed done. "Well, he *implied* an interest. He didn't come out and say so, but C.J. never totally commits himself to anything but correct tax returns. Anyway, he wants you to come in to see him, and he'll go over everything with you. If you still feel it's too much for you after that, we'll let it drop. How does that sound?"

A flush of color had come back into Etta Mae's face by then, so I sat back and waited to see if she'd give me a little more time to bring her around.

"Okay," she said, glancing away as if looking for an exit. "I can do that, I guess, if you're sure it's okay."

"I'm sure. Call today and make an appointment. And call me or come by after you've seen him, and we'll decide if we want to proceed to making an offer, or if we want to forget all about it."

Chapter 24

❧

I didn't know I'd just opened a can of worms, but apparently I had. Not hearing from Etta Mae for several days after that last conversation, I feared that I'd scared her off. For all I knew she'd packed up and moved to Florida herself. I called her a couple of evenings after work hours when she should've been home, but wasn't. I was beginning to think that I'd pushed her too hard and too far.

Finally she called me right after we returned from morning services that Sunday, asking if she could come by to talk.

"Of course," I said. "I've been wondering how you're doing. Come right on. Sam has gone with Lloyd and Mr. Pickens to Charlotte to see the Panthers play, so we'll have the house to ourselves."

"Oh, good," she said, but with a noticeable lack of her usual perkiness. "I was going to suggest we take a ride, but that'll be better. I'm too nervous to be driving, anyway."

I laughed and said, "It's going to work out just fine, Etta Mae. You don't have a reason in the world to be nervous."

"I think I do. I'll tell you when I get there."

And with that, she hung up, leaving me to pace the floor while waiting for her, going over and over the possible problems that might have suddenly sprung up to foil our plans.

Maybe Lurline was taking The Handy Home Helpers off the market—that would certainly cut us off at the knees. Maybe C.J.

had ignored my directions and, instead of soothing her concerns, had inflated them.

Good grief! I stopped in the middle of the hall. What if she'd jumped into another marriage when I wasn't looking? But, no, surely she wouldn't have done that just as she was about to become an independent woman.

I went to the kitchen and put on a pot of coffee. By the time I walked back to the hall, she was coming up the front steps.

"Come in," I said, opening the door. "Goodness, it's cold. Let me take your coat."

We walked back to the kitchen with me chatting away and her saying little in return. In fact, she looked down in the mouth, as Lillian would've described her glum expression. I feared the worst and kept talking to put off hearing whatever bad news she had.

"So tell me," I said, after pouring coffee and pulling out a chair at the table. "How're you getting along with learning the ins and outs of business? Sam's been telling me that you'll need to know things like payroll withholding taxes, FICA, property taxes, quarterly payments, vacation schedules, OSHA, and a dozen other things. It sounds overwhelming to me, but you're bright and probably know a lot of that already. Just as soon as you feel ready, I say let's go ahead and make an offer. What do you say?"

"I say," she said, staring into her cup, "I've already had one."

"One what?"

"An offer."

"What're you talking about, Etta Mae? We're buying, not selling."

She slumped back in her chair and sighed aloud. "Mr. Sims wants to take me to dinner, and I know what that means."

I blinked. C. J. Sims? That old bachelor who'd slouched slightly splay-footed from file cabinet to computer and back again day after day for thirty years? What was he doing asking out a woman young enough to be his daughter, or almost young enough if he'd ever had the gumption to get a wife?

"Well, I never," I said, breathing out a long breath. Then, with a quick look at her: "Are you sure?"

She nodded. "I'm sure. And I kinda need to know what you want me to do."

"*Me?* Why, Etta Mae, you can do whatever you want to do. I have nothing to do with it."

"Well," she said, "he's your friend, and I don't want to create a problem. And I know he's been working overtime to help me. I've been going to his office after work every evening and he's showed me how to do QuickBooks and a lot of other things, and I know it's because of you and the kindness of his heart, so I—"

"Etta Mae," I said, putting my hand on her arm, "he's doing it because he's getting paid to do it. It's a business deal, and you owe that old goat absolutely nothing.

"Listen," I went on, "how much more do you need to learn?"

"He says another month might do it, except we're already going over the same stuff. He wants us to bring our suppers every night and eat together to save time and eat at the cafeteria on the weekends. He says he'll pay for that."

I couldn't believe it, and said so. "Listen to me, you call his office in the morning and tell his receptionist that I'll be by to pick up your papers. The idea of stringing it out over weeks just to make time with you! That is unacceptable, and I'll tell you one thing, Etta Mae—Mr. C. J. Sims has just given his last lesson in how to run a business."

"I am outraged," I stormed to Sam when he got home late that evening. "Have you ever heard of such a thing—that randy old goat thinking Etta Mae would be interested in him? He's lost his mind, and I think we ought to take our business elsewhere."

"It's certainly out of character," Sam said, slightly amused at the thought of a love-smitten accountant. "But Etta Mae is a very attractive young woman—"

"Don't you blame it on her, Sam! He's just a crazy old man, and she'd be no more interested in him than in . . . in, well, I don't know who. But believe me, it wouldn't be him! Why, she was sick at the thought, and, bless her heart, she was worried that I'd want her to accept his advances. Well, I put a stop to that, all right. She is not going back into that office, so if any more lessons need to be taught, he can teach *me*. We'll just see if he offers me a cafeteria dinner—the stingy old bachelor. He's as tight as a tick on top of everything else."

Sam laughed. "He's not getting a chance at you. I'll help you with the books if you need it, and I'll take you to a nicer place for dinner."

"Oh, you," I said and threw a sofa pillow in his lap.

I had, however, understood from Etta Mae before she'd left that she was just beginning to see how she could afford to borrow money and be able to pay it back while making a decent living for herself. C.J. had been true to his word, having shown her what would be coming in and what would be going out and what would be left over.

Not much, as it turned out, but enough to encourage growth and expansion to improve the bottom line.

"I can do that," she'd said with a touch of wonder. "People're all the time asking me if I can help them with somebody who's sick or disabled or just plain old. Lurline has pretty much stopped taking new patients because she doesn't want to hire any-body else."

"That's understandable," I said, nodding. "She wants out and has no interest in making more work for herself. But it's perfect for you if you get on it before somebody else slips in and begins to compete with you."

She had left my house that afternoon with a new lease on her future. She'd walked out with a smile on her face and a bounce in her step, having been reassured that she had no obligation whatsoever to C. J. Sims and that I was more than ready to entrust money to her. She wanted to sleep on it for a few days before we committed ourselves, but I felt that we were now very close to entering negotiations for the purchase of The Handy Home Helpers.

"We'll find another accountant," I'd told her. "Someone who'll keep you on track and his mind on his business." Maybe a woman, I thought, to forestall any further monkey business.

After closing the door behind her, I thought that things might be well in hand and moving right along except for one worrisome possibility. What if there was somebody else lurking around who was thinking along the same lines? Surely we weren't the only ones to have recognized the potential of a home health care business.

I did not want to get into a bidding war, but of course a bidding war would send Lurline Corn into the stratosphere with excitement. The thing to do, I told myself, was to make our first offer too attractive for her to refuse, thereby cutting out any other interested party.

Sam wouldn't approve, but he was always willing to drop something if it didn't work the way that suited him, whereas I tended to get stuck on one perfect idea, then do whatever it took to see it through.

I had to curb my enthusiasm, though, for Etta Mae's sake. I couldn't encumber her with a debt that she could neither live with nor repay.

It then occurred to me that I would do well to pray about the situation, the first petition being that no one else was even vaguely interested in making an offer for The Handy Home Helpers. Barring a positive answer to that, my next petition was that our first offer be accepted forthwith with no further back-and-forth negotiations.

Although I wished her no ill will, it also occurred to me that Lurline's doctor might be led to tell her that she needed salt air and sunshine for her health, thereby making a move to Florida urgent. So I added that to my list of petitions as a possibility for the Lord to consider.

I admit that I have a tendency to make suggestions of how I think things should turn out, just in case He wants to know my preferences. But after I'd put forth several possibilities, I did what I always do and whispered, "Not my will, Lord, but Yours," figuring that in the long run He knew best even if He turned down every petition I made. I knew that, disappointed or not, Etta Mae and I would fare well in His hands, although I didn't see how anything could be better than the detailed plan that I'd laid before Him.

Monday morning, there was a hue and cry in the neighborhood. People were out and about along the sidewalks and two police cars were patrolling the rain-streaked streets. Lillian was glued to a window when I came down for breakfast and Sam had already left to join the search parties.

"It's Mr. Horace," Lillian said, looking around as I came in. "He's gone somewhere an' nobody know where."

The phone rang as I passed it. Grabbing it up, I heard Mildred gasp, "Julia! May I send Penelope to you? Ida Lee and Doreen are out looking and the police need to talk to me. Oh, where is Grady when I need him!"

"Send her on," I said. "I'll meet her at the hedge."

I shrugged on a coat, wrapped a scarf around my head, and dashed out the back door. Finding the gap in the boxwood hedge,

I slipped through and saw the tiny child just leaving Mildred's front porch. I waved to her, then waited to lead her back into our warm kitchen.

"You have two people here who need breakfast, Lillian," I said as we entered. "Here, sweetie, let me take your coat. Sit down right here and we'll warm up."

Easily led, though looking unsure of why she was there, or perhaps even of who she was, the little girl kept looking around the kitchen, finally whispering, "Latisha?"

"Why, Honey," Lillian said, "that chile's in school. But they's lots of things for you to play with till she gets back. Now, how you like your eggs?"

Not wanting to put the child through an interrogation, I nonetheless burned with questions. How long had Horace been gone? When had they noticed his absence? Where were they looking? And on and on, yet she looked as bewildered as I was feeling. In fact, she was still in her nightgown, so somebody had gotten her up and out before she'd known what was going on.

"Law, chile," Lillian said, "we got to find you some clothes. I 'spect Latisha got something here for you to wear. It'll swaller you, but better that than runnin' 'round in your nightgown. Le's go get 'em on, then come back down here and make us some cookies."

Alicia or Penelope or Honey, one of the three, looked pleased at that prospect and immediately took Lillian's hand and off they went.

That left me free to wonder what I should do—join the hunt, and if so, where? Sit and wait until Horace turned up? Bother Mildred with a phone call when her phone was probably ringing off the hook? Or were they keeping the phone free in case Horace called, as if he would remember the number?

I called her, and the phone was not already in use. She answered on the first ring.

"Mildred? It's Julia, what can I do to help?"

"Oh, Julia," she said, "you're already doing it. Keeping Penelope occupied is one less problem on my hands, so thank you for that."

"She's no problem. Just let her stay as long as you need her to, but tell me—what happened? When did Horace leave?"

"We don't know!" she cried, her voice breaking under the stress. "He just wasn't in his bed this morning, and it was hardly messed up. He could've left at any time during the night. Nobody heard a thing, and you know how cold and wet it was all night long. I am just sick with worry. He could have pneumonia by now."

"Surely they'll find him soon. You have to stay strong, Mildred, and not make yourself sick. Why don't you plan to have lunch here?"

"Thank you, but no. I've called Ida Lee to come back in and fix lunch for everybody. Julia, you wouldn't believe the number of people who're out beating the bushes, looking for Horace. The least I can do is provide a meal for them. I'm getting out extra plates now. There'll be a crowd, you know."

As I've said before, you can always count on Mildred to rise to any social occasion, and this one was no exception.

"That's good of you," I said, although if Sam were to go missing I wouldn't be planning lunch for anybody. "Where all have you looked, Mildred? I mean, are you sure he got out of the house? Wouldn't your security system have sounded?"

"I don't know, Julia. I just don't know anything except he wasn't in his room and I called 9-1-1 and Ida Lee right away and people just started flooding in. They've figured how fast someone his age could walk and made coordinates to estimate how far he might have gotten. But what if somebody's picked him up out on the interstate? He could be miles away or he could be lying somewhere in a ditch. I am about to pull my hair out."

And she certainly sounded it, and understandably so. Panic edged each word she uttered. "Listen," I said with some urgency, "you'll feel better if you're doing something besides sitting and waiting. I'm coming over and you and I are going to search the house and the grounds. I know, I know, it's already been done, but it'll give you something to do besides worrying yourself to death."

Calling upstairs to Lillian that I was leaving Honey with her, I left for the Allens' large house next door.

Chapter 25

❧

Mildred was securely settled in a fauteuil moved from the main reception room to the middle of the foyer. Small tables covered with papers, maps, empty cups, and phones surrounded the chair, making the area Search Central for Horace. One police officer with no stripes on his sleeve stood against the wall behind her, and I figured him for a figurehead to keep her occupied while the search was directed from elsewhere. People in town knew Mildred and what she expected.

"Where have you looked?" I asked, pulling a straight chair up close.

"Everywhere. He's not here."

"Well, think about it again," I urged. "Ida Lee was storing things in the attic, wasn't she, when you redid the room for Alicia, I mean, Penelope? Could he have climbed up there and gone to sleep? What about the garden house? And the pool house? The basement? If yours is like mine, it's filled with places he could hide. Or the garage? You know how fixated he is on that."

"I do know," she said, "and it was the first place we thought of. But it's locked tighter than Dick's hatband and has been since he hid in there once before. They've looked everywhere, Julia. A highway alert will be going out within the hour, which should've already been done in my opinion, but better late than never, I guess." Tears glittered in her eyes, and I was moved to pity. It's a terrible thing to lose a husband.

"Well, listen," I said, "it's doing you no good just to sit here and wait. You know this house better than anyone, and you know Horace better, too. You know places to look that no one else would think of, and you'll be better off doing something than just waiting around."

"They think he's out walking somewhere," she said, reaching for a tissue. "That's what they said, that dementia patients usually head for a highway, thinking they're going home or something."

"I don't see how he could've gotten out. Weren't the doors locked?"

"The front door wasn't. I can't believe we all slept with a door unlocked. Ida Lee is just devastated, but it was Doreen who forgot. Grady came by yesterday afternoon to see how we were doing although he still had a hacking cough, and Doreen saw him out. We think she forgot to lock up behind him, although she denies it. As of course she would.

"And by the way, Grady came in this morning when he heard Horace was missing, so he's looking around the house again, too. He's still half sick, but I blame all this on him. If he hadn't gotten a cold, he'd have been here and so would Horace." Mildred took a deep, shuddering breath, then went on. "So see, Julia, we're double-checking and back-checking and everything else we can think of."

"Well," I said, stymied for any other suggestion or for a way to help. "Well . . ."

"*Look who I found!*" Grady Peeples voice, hoarse and rasping, rang out in triumph. Appearing in the foyer, his hand firmly on Horace's arm, Grady led the lost sheep over to Mildred.

"*Horace!*" Mildred sprang to her feet, or rather she tried to but she was fitted so snugly into the chair that it came partially up with her. She shook it off and threw her arms around Horace.

"Where have you been? Are you all right? Oh, my goodness, you are a mess!"

And he certainly was. Bleary-eyed, hair sticking out at all angles, and a dazed look on his face, Horace looked a good deal worse for the wear. Bedraggled and grease-stained, in fact, and far from the dapper dresser for which he was known.

"Where was he?" Mildred demanded.

Grady, clearly pleased with himself, said, "In the garage. Actually, asleep in the back seat of the Town Car."

"How could they have missed him?" Mildred cried. "The garage was searched."

"Maybe not," Grady said, a trifle smugly. "He'd locked the door behind him, so they bypassed it, figgerin' he couldn't get in. But I broke a window and there he was." Grady pulled out a key ring and dangled it in front of Mildred. "Had it in his pocket. Ida Lee said it's s'posed to be in the kitchen pantry, but I guess he knew that."

"Oh, Horace," Mildred wailed, "how could you put me through this?" Then, leaning in close to him, she peered into his eyes as if she could see his brain working. Or not. "Do you know where you are?" she demanded.

He gave her a loopy grin and nodded. "Home."

"Well, do you know who I am?"

"My wife, Jane. Jane Smith."

Mildred let out a heartrending screech and collapsed into the chair again. "Jane Smith! Jane *Smith*?" Then, gathering herself, she straightened up and took control again. "Grady, take him upstairs and clean him up, if you will. Put him to bed if he'll go. But don't let him out. His wandering days are over."

"Yes, ma'am," Grady said, turning Horace toward the stairs. "I don't think I'm catching now. I'm about well."

"It doesn't matter," she said as if it really didn't. Then, to the bemused police officer, she ordered, "Call off the search. The lost has been found."

As they scurried off, she rang a bell for Ida Lee. "This mess has to be cleaned up," she said as if speaking to herself. After another deep, shuddering breath, she waved the hovering Ida Lee away and nodded coolly at me. "Thank you for coming, Julia. We'll be fine now. Send Penelope back whenever you want."

I was being dismissed, but I was more than ready to leave. Still I ached for her and wanted to offer some comfort. "They say," I said, "that the disease erases recent memories, but brings back old ones. He probably recalls a Jane Smith from school."

"Probably so," Mildred said, as she gazed up into the far corner of the foyer. "Attention, however, must be paid."

Now what in the world did she mean by that? I didn't know, but it sounded ominous. I hurried across the lawn toward my house, anxious to be out of the cold weather and away from the closed-off look on my friend's face. One never knew what Mildred would do, mainly because she had the means to do whatever she wanted and she did not mind using those means.

I will tell you this, though, the rich are different from you and me, as somebody else has already noted. But it's not the amount that makes the difference, it's the willingness to use the power it gives.

"They've found him," I announced to Lillian as I walked into the kitchen. "In the garage. He'd locked himself in the garage, and nobody but Grady thought to look inside." I blew out my breath and looked around. "Where's our little Honey?"

"She's in there asleep on the sofa. They had her up 'fore she got her nap out."

"Then let's let her sleep. Better here than over there, anyway. I tell you, Lillian, I am quite shaken with all that's going on."

After recounting the events of the morning to her, I said, "It wouldn't surprise me if Mildred decides to ship him off to a locked facility. And maybe that's what he needs. I don't know. It just seems that he's gone downhill awfully fast, and I'm not convinced that he's that bad off. I mean, if she had no way to care for him, I could see it. It would be terrible if it were just the two of them, and she had to watch him every minute. Some people have to do that, you know, but Mildred doesn't."

"Yes'm, I do know. You remember ole Miss Reenie Patterson that got so bad nobody could stand her? Mr. Tom took care of her for years 'cause he didn't have nobody else."

"That wasn't the reason," I said, adding a dash of cream to my coffee. "He did it because he didn't want to spend the money to hire some help. I was in Velma's having my hair done one day when he brought her in. Lillian, I'll tell you, Reenie didn't know where in the world she was. She screamed like a banshee when the girl wet her hair, and I saw with my own eyes when Tom walked over to the chair and pinched a plug out of her arm. She started crying like a baby. It was awful, but Tom had everybody convinced how loving he was to be taking care of her."

"Law, I didn't know that."

"She got so bad, though, that he had to stop taking her to get her hair done. She flailed around so in the chair that one day she practically knocked Pattie down, so Velma had to tell Tom that he couldn't bring her in anymore." I nibbled on a cookie and glanced at the hall door to be sure that Alicia hadn't joined us. "She hated having to do that, but her other customers were getting skittish."

Lillian shook her head in sympathy with Velma or Reenie or maybe with the other customers. "Did you hear 'bout that man down in Florida, I think it was. The one that shot his wife 'cause she got where he couldn't handle her? Had to put her out of her misery, I think he said. Although it sounded more like it was his misery he was gettin' out of."

"Well," I said, thinking that perhaps we'd talked too openly in case a child was listening, "thank goodness, Horace is nowhere near that. Nor is Mildred. She'll do the right thing when she faces the fact that he's not altogether responsible for who he remembers and who he doesn't."

"Yes'm, she a good-hearted lady, all right."

"She is that," I said, although I couldn't help but wonder who in the world Jane Smith was.

Chapter 26

❦

After Lillian walked Alicia home after lunch, I spent the afternoon wondering about that lonely little girl and her two half-crazed grandparents, each alone in their own worlds. And, as is often the case, having one thing to wonder about led to another. Not only was the question of Jane Smith's identity playing around in my mind, so were the most recent actions of Horace Allen. I think we had all begun to assume that Horace no longer had sense enough to come in out of the rain. His activities of the previous night, however, were making me revisit that assumption.

First of all, I knew that there was a small cabinet high up in Mildred's kitchen pantry where master keys to all the locked places in the house were kept. And I knew that the garage had rarely been locked when both Horace and Mildred, to say nothing of Ida Lee, had the run of the garage, going in and out to the cars for various errands. They only bothered to lock up when they were out of town for any length of time, so the garage key stayed on the hook.

Located on the other side of the Allen house from ours, the garage wasn't within our eyesight—not that we would've noticed a night visitor anyway. A covered walkway, for Ida Lee's convenience, led from the kitchen door, also on the other side, to an entrance to her second-floor apartment above the garage space. Would she not have heard something when Horace went in among the cars during the night? Maybe not. She could've been taking a shower, not at all expecting a sick man to be up and rummaging from Mildred's Cadillac to his Boxster, and from Ida Lee's SUV for grocery runs to the new Town Car that had been bought to distract him from the pleasure of wind in his hair.

It was a clean, spacious garage, not at all cluttered with odds and ends as most garages are. I could've slept in it, myself. The thing about it, though, was what was Horace doing in there again? Yes, I remembered that he'd spent a night in his little Porsche not long before and had come out so stiff and cramped that they'd thought he'd never straighten up. Since he'd chosen the back seat of the Town Car for his most recent overnight stay, I'd say he was still able to learn from experience. That said something right there for the functioning of his brain.

And another thing it said was that he'd known—and remembered—where the garage key was kept, and he'd known to lock the garage door behind him so that it would appear to be unoccupied. To me, that indicated the retention of more than a little cognitive ability.

But not enough. For, after his previous attempt to go for a night drive, Mildred had kept the keys to the cars up in her room.

At least, I think she had. What it came down to, it seemed to me, was that there was something sly and crafty about what Horace had done. There was no particular rhyme or reason for any of it—what good had it done him to sneak into the garage when he didn't have access to keys to the cars? He'd gotten in, but not out.

Maybe he hadn't been able to think that far ahead. Experience, however, had taught him that, for a restful night, the back seat of a Town Car was more comfortable than a bucket seat in a Porsche.

I was putting all that together while recalling the glint in his eye when he had looked straight at Mildred and called her his wife, Jane Smith. There had been something cunning in the tone of his voice, as if he knew he was cutting her to the bone and didn't care. Yet he had gone docilely enough with Grady to be cleaned up and put to bed, perhaps because the night had already been erased from his memory or because another foray was already being planned. The human mind is capable of dredging up wondrous, as well as dangerous, things.

"Sam," I said, as I snuggled up to his back in bed that night, "please, please don't lose your mind. I couldn't stand it if you weren't you anymore."

I felt him smile as he said, "I'm not planning to lose anything anytime soon."

"I feel so sorry for Mildred," I went on. "And for Horace, too, although he doesn't seem to know that anything is wrong. How do people like that think, Sam? What do they think about if they don't remember yesterday or look forward to tomorrow?"

Sam sighed. "I don't know, sweetheart. It's as if they live in the constant present—the always present, perhaps with unconnected flashes from the past popping up now and then." He turned onto his back and blew out his breath. "You know, that's exactly what we're occasionally urged to do—stop moaning about the past, which can't be corrected, and don't worry about the future, which can't be controlled. Seize the day, they tell us. It's all you have. Seize the day, and make the most of it.

"Good advice?" he asked. "I don't know."

"Well, I do," I said, looking up into the dark room. "How could anybody live without learning from the past or sleep at night without planning for tomorrow? No, thanks. Horace can seize the day if that's all he has to grab, but I'll gladly let it go and hope tomorrow will be better."

"It will be." He patted the arm I had around him, and I smiled in the dark. "Now, tell me how your Christmas plans are coming along."

"You're changing the subject."

"I certainly am. There's only so much you can do to help somebody else, and Mildred is perfectly capable of taking care of her own. She just has to have a big production before she does it. Where do you think Tonya got her dramatic flair?"

"You have a point," I said, "but I worry about what it's doing to that little girl. She must be totally confused in that crazy household with having her name changed a dozen times and playing Ken and Barbie dolls with somebody who's supposed to be her grandfather. I wonder if Tonya knows what's happening with Horace."

"Mildred hasn't told her?"

"I don't think so. Doesn't want to spoil her big starring role, I guess. Anything Tonya wants, Tonya gets, it seems, and Mildred is left holding the bag."

"That's Mildred's own fault."

"I know, but look, Sam, she's all but lost Tonya and now she's losing her husband." At a sudden thought, I sat straight up in bed. "That's it. They're both gone for all intents and purposes, and look what she's gotten in their place. A selfish, headstrong daughter and an empty-headed shell of the man she once married. She's all alone."

"Lie back down, honey," Sam said, pulling me back. "Maybe that's where the little girl comes in."

I sighed and settled back. "Maybe so, but it's strange, now that I think about it. I am convinced that the Lord sent Lloyd into my life just when I thought I would never overcome the hurt and shame of what Wesley Lloyd had done. But that little boy changed my life. Now, Mildred's also suffering hurt and shame—because even though she puts a good face on it, she's suffering over Tonya displaying herself on television in those low-cut dresses they wear, to say nothing of Horace becoming the talk of the town with his escapades. Mildred is like me—we're old school and she feels she has a certain position to uphold which doesn't include ridicule. People do look up to her, except she also knows that they love to see the mighty fall. But, Sam, if she could just see what's right before her eyes, she might see that the Lord has sent her a child who could change her life, too."

"He's good about that."

"What?"

"Sending a child to change lives."

Chapter 27

❧

I stayed home the following day and tended to my own knitting—placing some Christmas orders, accepting a few holiday invitations, and checking the silver for tarnish. Mildred knew where I was. If she wanted company or help or someone to babysit, she would call. I had other things on my plate and it was time to take care of them.

Number one, well, maybe the only pressing one, was Etta Mae and The Handy Home Helpers. We needed to do something fairly soon, declare ourselves an interested party or something. If we kept delaying a move, Lurline Corn could sell out from under us or even decide to take the business off the market.

I'd not heard a word from Etta Mae since she'd said she wanted to sleep on it before making a decision. Was she still sleeping? Had I pushed her so far so fast that she was using a delaying tactic to slow things down? Maybe she really didn't want the responsibility of owning a business and owing money on it. Maybe she wasn't cut out for entrepreneurship. Some people aren't, you know.

Yet I had seen something in that young woman that deserved an opportunity, a helping hand, a chance to better herself—the very thing she'd once told me she wanted more than anything else. All she lacked was self-confidence and a financial backer. I was ready to provide both, but if she wasn't ready to accept them, the best thing for me to do was to back off.

So, with a sigh, I decided that I would push no further. You can't help someone who won't help themselves, and as much as I hated to give up on Etta Mae, perhaps it was time I did.

Besides, what had happened to my intention to stay out of other people's business? That new leaf I'd turned over had apparently fallen back in place as I'd flown off in all directions, trying to rearrange Etta Mae's life and Mildred Allen's, too.

It was a shame, though, because I could see so clearly how both of them would gain so much if they had my foresight. Etta Mae would have independence and a secure future. She'd no longer be open to every blandishment by any man who made promises he couldn't keep. And Mildred, my dear friend Mildred, who had lost so much yet couldn't see what was right before her eyes.

"Miss Julia!" Etta Mae's voice on the phone late that afternoon jarred me with its edge of panic. "I have to talk to you. Can I come over? I won't stay long, but something's happened and I don't know what to do."

"Come right on," I said, then went in to tell Sam and Lillian that something had come up to put Etta Mae in a state and for them to go ahead with supper. "We'll talk in the living room. But stay close, Sam, there's no telling what has her so upset, but something sure has."

When Etta Mae arrived, she looked frayed around the edges with lipstick bitten off and mascara smudged around her eyes. She kept dabbing at them with a damp tissue. I led her to the sofa in the living room, then closed the doors and sat down beside her.

"Now, what happened?" I said.

She drew in a rasping breath and said, "Lurline is about to sell The Handy Home Helpers to somebody else. She told me today. She called me to her office and said she wanted me to understand that she was doing what was best for me, even though it might mean the sale won't go through. I didn't know what she was talking about, because as far as she knows I don't have anything to do with selling her business."

"What did she say?"

Etta Mae's hand shook as she mopped at her eyes. "Well, she said there's somebody ready to buy it as an investment. He doesn't want to run it, so all that's holding him back is finding somebody who can run it for him. He asked Lurline if there was anybody already working for her who could step in with the right set of managerial skills—that's what she said he said—the right set of managerial skills. And she said she'd immediately thought of me because I've been there the longest and I have my CNA degree and I know the patients and so on and so forth." Etta Mae stopped and sniffed as tears poured out again.

I nodded, realizing that another buyer was thinking almost along the same lines as I was—invest in a sound business and put it in good hands. "She knows what you're worth."

"No," she said, shaking her head. "I'm not worth anything to her. She reminded me of how long we've been friends and how she's helped me over the years and how she knows me backward and forward and how she knows what I can do and what I can't. So, she wanted me to know that even though I look good on paper, that's what she said, *on paper*, she knew that it would be too much for me. So she couldn't recommend me to him, and she wanted me to know that for my sake she was probably passing up a golden opportunity to sell out and move to Florida, and it was all because she didn't want me to be in a position to fail and ruin the business she'd started so long ago and end up having to wait tables or something. She said she hoped I appreciated her watching out for me."

"She actually *said* that?" I leaned back against the sofa, just done in by Lurline's idea of what a friend does to help a friend get ahead. If that was what she really thought of Etta Mae, why tell her about it? She'd devastated Etta Mae's self-worth while expecting to be appreciated for her thoughtfulness in not recommending her.

Etta Mae nodded, then covered her eyes with a shaking hand. "I thought . . . I thought I meant something to her. I mean, she gave me a job years ago and helped me go to the technical college for my degree and gave me the worst cases, the hardest patients to deal with, and the longest hours, and so on and so forth. So I thought I was a real help to the business because she depended on me so much. And all that time she was just . . . just *carrying* me."

"Oh, for goodness' sakes, Etta Mae, get a grip." I stood up and stomped around a little, so distraught that she'd accepted Lurline's opinion without question. "Can't you see what she's doing? I don't know how close you think the two of you are, but I can tell you one thing—she is not your friend."

"Well," Etta Mae said, frowning as she thought about it, "she was always there for me whenever I got divorced, and she showed me how to open a bank account and buy insurance and told me where to get my car fixed when it needed it. She always knew what to do if I got sick or needed anything. And she gets her feelings hurt if I don't tell her every little thing so I thought she cared about me, although it did get to be too much sometimes—her meddling, I mean." Etta Mae stopped, looked around as if just seeing where she was, then she said, "She's been running my life, hasn't she?"

"Yes, and you've let her do it."

"Well, kinda, I guess. I thought she just liked having somebody look up to her and ask her advice. So I always listened, then did what I wanted to, anyway. But I didn't know that she thinks I don't have sense enough to run the business. But I do, Miss Julia, I know that business as good as Lurline does. Maybe better, because she's not around half the time."

"That's exactly what I've been trying to tell you," I said, sitting down again. "Maybe Lurline has done you a favor, backhanded though it was. Maybe her trying to tear you down is enough to wake you up to some facts."

"But why would she do that? I mean, she wants to sell and she says she has a buyer, so it looks like she'd jump at the chance to get the business off her hands. She knows I'd work just as hard for him as I have for her, except I guess I haven't done as good a job as I thought I had. I don't understand it."

"Well, I do," I said, just as sure of it as I was sitting there. "The woman is eaten up with jealousy."

"Jealousy?" Etta Mae's eyebrows went up almost as far as Sam's when he was surprised. "Why would she be jealous of me? I'm her helpless little tagalong who can't keep a husband and has to be told what to do."

"Yes, and you're the one she puts in charge when she wants to be off. She doesn't think you're so helpless then, does she? Think about it, Etta Mae. You're young, you're as pretty as a picture, you draw men like flies, and you're highly capable. What is she? Sixty? Sixty-five? And she's nothing to look at with that hair dyed so black it's like Shinola shoe polish on her head. Men aren't swarming around her, are they?"

"No'm, but ever since Raymond passed, she's had Bug Timmons living with her off and on, and—"

"Who? Did you say Bug? Who is that?"

"Oh, he's Raymond's sister's boy. His mama said he was cute as a bug when he was little and the name stuck. Lurline waits on him hand and foot, but somebody has to 'cause he's so shiftless he won't hit a lick at a snake. He's been in and out of trouble all his life—never did finish high school—but Lurline thinks the sun rises and sets on him even though he's not worth shootin' and everybody knows it. He's been living off her for years because his mama got married again and moved to Tennessee. And, now that

I think of it, that may be why Lurline wants to get out of Delmont. Maybe she's had enough of him, too."

"Well, see," I said, pointing out the obvious. "You have a fun, carefree life living on your own and doing as you please, while she has a useless nephew dragging her down. She's jealous of you, and she hides it under a pretended concern for your welfare. She'd like nothing better than to see you fail at something she's made a success of, which makes me wonder why in the world she wouldn't recommend you just to see it happen."

Then I knew why Lurline hadn't given Etta Mae a recommendation. "Because, of course, she knows you *wouldn't* fail."

With an almost bewildered look, Etta Mae said, "I guess I never thought Lurline was all that underhanded. Nosy and bossy, yes, but not downright mean and hateful." Etta Mae's eyes filled again.

"Well, now you know," I said, deliberately refusing to sympathize with her feelings of loss. We had no time to wallow in recriminations and what-should-have-beens. Time, in fact, was being wasted as we talked.

"Etta Mae," I went on with a spurt of urgency, "did Lurline tell you who it is that's thinking of buying the business?"

"Yes'm, she did. And he's certainly able to buy it. Wouldn't even have to get a bank loan, either. He's loaded, and he ought to be because he won't lift a finger unless he sees money up front. And I know that, because he kept me out of jail one time for something I didn't do."

"Who in the world are you talking about?"

"Mr. Ernest Sitton, Esquire, Delmont's number one attorney-at-law."

Chapter 28

❧

Ernest Sitton? *Ernest Sitton!* Why hadn't I listened more carefully when Sam was talking about him? It pays to know with whom you are dealing when the stakes are as high as they certainly were now. Ernest Sitton could slip in and buy out Lurline Corn before we turned around good. And Etta Mae was absolutely correct in saying that he could afford to buy The Handy Home Helpers. He could probably buy up everything that was for sale in the dinky little town of Delmont, to say nothing of anything he wanted in all of Abbot County. He had the wherewithal to do it, and he was a formidable adversary not only in the courtroom, but would also be one in a bidding war over a coveted property.

But why in the world would he want to own a home health service? There was only one answer—he'd seen the potential just as I had.

"Etta Mae," I said, "we are at the Rubicon."

"The what?"

"It's time to put up or shut up. You have two choices, but you have to decide which way you're going right now, right this minute. Your first option is to hurry over to Mr. Sitton's office and tell him that you're the one he's looking for. You can tell him what you've been doing for Lurline all these years, tell him to ask the patients what they think of you, and tell him that if he's looking for someone with the right set of managerial skills, he's looking at her. You'd have to *sell* yourself, Etta Mae. That is, if you want to answer to somebody else for the rest of your working life.

"On the other hand," I went on, taking a deep breath, "you can decide to put the same time and effort into your own business, thereby reaping the benefits for yourself rather than for an owner who does nothing but rake in the profits. Although if I know lawyers—and I do—Mr. Ernest Sitton would be looking over your shoulder all the time. But if you're ready to strike out on your own—with a little help from me—then call Mr. Blair right now and tell him to prepare an Offer to Purchase The Handy Home Helpers."

Etta Mae raised her head as a blank look passed over her face. Her eyes skittered from side to side, and a frown drew her eyebrows together as she considered each option in turn.

I didn't say a word, just sat there and let her think it through. I'd already said all there was to say, anyway, and it was now up to her.

Finally coming out of her thinking mode, she asked, "What's an Offer to Purchase?"

"It's an official, well, offer to purchase," I said. "It'll show the amount you're offering for the business which Lurline can accept, decline, or counter. If she accepts it, then you're committed to buying the business for the amount you've offered. Mr. Blair would then guide you through to the closing, which is when you write a check to Lurline and walk out as the new owner. If, however, she doesn't like your offer, but wants to keep you interested, she'll come back with a counterproposal for more than what you've offered but a little less than what she's listed it for. You can keep going back and forth like that until you reach a figure both of you can live with. Of course," I continued, "at any point either of you can decide you've gone as far as you can go and that'll be the end of it. Neither of you would be obligated to the other, and she'd be looking for another buyer."

"Yes, but she'd know it was me doing it, wouldn't she? And if we couldn't agree on a price, she'd fire me for sure."

"Not if we play it right, she wouldn't. Mr. Blair will be representing you, so lay your cards on the table for him. Tell him he has to make sure that your name doesn't come up at all. Now, there is a line on the Offer to Purchase for the buyer's name, but he can put down whatever he wants to and add something like 'or Assigns' which means your name will be added when it's too late for Lurline to back out. Also," I said, frowning as I recalled a few other Offers to Purchase in the past, "there's a line for the signature of the buyer, so you'll have to sign it. I want you to start practicing a scribbled signature, one that's absolutely illegible."

"Won't Lurline think that's suspicious or something?"

"No, if anything, she'll think it's a doctor wanting to buy her business. Just remember that all the offers will come and go through Mr. Blair. Lurline won't know who the buyer is until the closing day when both of you show up. But that'll be too late for her to back out. She'll have to go through with the sale."

"Oh, Lord," Etta Mae moaned as she scrunched up her shoulders. "I wish she'd never have to know."

"Forget about her," I said with a wave of my hand. "She wants to sell and you want to buy. That's all there is to it. And remember this, she's moving to Florida. She won't be hovering around afterward with advice and criticism, and you can run the business the way you want to.

"So what's it going to be, Etta Mae? But," I quickly added, "understand that it's not me who's pushing you on this, it's Ernest Sitton. He knows everybody in the county, so he'll find somebody who'll jump at the chance to run the business for him."

I sat and waited for her to make up her mind, watching as her eyes skittered back and forth again. Then, just as I was beginning to wonder if I had completely misread her, she sat up straight, took a deep breath, and jumped in with both feet.

"I think I can do it," she said. "I mean, I know I can, and I *want* to do it because it's the best opportunity I'll ever have. And, furthermore, I can do just as good a job as Lurline, maybe even better. Miss Julia," she went on, turning to me, "if you're still willing to loan me the money, I promise I will work my tail off to pay you back, and I'll be grateful to you for the rest of my life."

I smiled. "This is a business deal for me, Etta Mae, based on sound economic reasons. Your only obligation to me is to make the payments on the loan, so gratitude doesn't come into it at all."

Which, I admit, wasn't exactly true because who doesn't want a little appreciation when lending money or a helping hand?

"Get out your phone, Etta Mae," I said, standing, "and call Mr. Blair. Tell him to prepare an Offer to Purchase which you'll come by and sign. Tell him to make sure that Lurline gets it tonight or first thing in the morning."

"He's probably already gone home."

"Doesn't matter. He's a realtor. They work all the time any time. Give him the amount we talked about as your official offer, and while you do that, I'll get Sam to help us with a loan agreement."

Although Sam no longer practiced law, having sold his practice to Binkie Enlow Bates some years before, he went over everything with Etta Mae to be sure that she understood what she was doing. Once a lawyer, always a lawyer.

He drew up a private loan agreement, leaving blank the amount until Lurline came to her senses and accepted a reasonable offer, as well as leaving blank the signature lines.

"When you and Ms. Corn agree on a price," Sam told Etta Mae, pointing to a page, "you'll enter the amount you're borrowing here. And this paragraph," he said, turning a page, "will spell out the terms of repayment—how much a month and for how long, which you and Julia will have agreed on. Then the two of you will go to a notary public and have your signatures notarized. Now, understand that this agreement is just between you and Julia—Joe Blair and Ms. Corn have nothing to do with it and need to know nothing about it. So you should get this signed and sealed between the time that Ms. Corn accepts your offer and the time set for the closing, which is usually a few weeks later. That'll give Julia time to transfer funds to your bank account so you can write a check at closing. You understand?"

"Uh-huh," Etta Mae said, staring at the papers in his hand. "Yes, sir, I think so."

"Well, just hold on to this copy and Julia will have a copy, too. You'll have plenty of time to ask any questions that come up because it's all in Ms. Corn's hands now." Sam turned to look at me. "Joe's sending the Offer to Purchase tonight?"

I nodded. "Yes, at least to Lurline's realtor, but I expect he'll contact her right away."

"Well, don't expect a response tonight," Sam said. "She'll not want to appear too eager, and she'll want Sitton to know she has an offer, hoping it'll spur him to make one, too. But whatever he does, I expect she'll make a counteroffer—you're too far apart for her not to. Unless," he went on with a smile, "she feels insulted enough to just ignore your offer."

At that, Etta Mae's face got a shade paler, but I would be surprised if Lurline got offended enough to discard our offer. She'd want to keep us on the hook, so I fully expected a counteroffer. I was prepared for that, hoping only not to get so carried away with getting what I wanted that I put a burden on Etta Mae that she couldn't bear. I had to be able to let the business go if Lurline stood firm on her listing price or if she got Lawyer Sitton to run up the price.

"Etta Mae," I said, "there's a cold front coming in with snow and sleet possible. Remind Lurline what the temperature is in Orlando."

———

When Etta Mae left an hour or so later, she still had a fine tremor in her hands, but it was the only symptom I saw of any lingering apprehension. She was both excited and more than a little fearful of the gigantic step she was taking. But she was taking that step, and I knew that, once committed, she would never back down. If all went well, she would own The Handy Home Helpers and I would have a good investment in her.

At least I hoped so. It all depended on how badly Lurline Corn wanted rid of the business and Bug Timmons so she could bask in the sunny Florida weather for the rest of her days.

Chapter 29

❧

Sam mumbled in his sleep that night, waking me enough to turn over and open my eyes. Then I sat straight up in bed, wondering if it was daylight. Everything in the room was as clear as day, yet the clock read one-thirty-five in the middle of the night.

I threw off the covers and ran to the side window. Every light in the Allen house was on, as were all the yard lights. The entire neighborhood was lit up so that it seemed Mildred was having a party to which we hadn't been invited.

"Sam," I called. "Sam, wake up. Something's going on at the Allens'. Oh, my goodness, there's an EMT truck pulling in, and a fire truck, too."

Horace, I thought, as Sam joined me at the window. Maybe he'd had another heart attack or maybe he'd wandered off again. But no, there'd be no need of emergency medical services if he'd simply walked away. This looked as if there'd been a medical crisis of some sort.

"Looks bad," Sam said, agreeing with my assessment, "although they all respond when a call comes in. We'd better get over there."

We hurriedly dressed and made the slog up the Allens' side yard to the columned porch where a gurney was being wheeled into the EMT truck. Somebody—or some *body*—was on it, but by the time we got to the porch the gurney was inside the truck and the door was closed. The truck pulled away down the curve of the driveway and turned onto Polk Street, its siren clearing the way although at that time of night there wasn't another vehicle anywhere in sight.

I caught a glimpse of Ida Lee inside the foyer, so Sam and I edged our way between first, second, and third responders, as well as a few neighbors, who were congregated at the front door.

Reaching Ida Lee, I asked, "What happened? Where's Mildred? She must be worried sick. We'll drive her to the hospital and stay with her as long as she needs us."

Ida Lee stared at me for a long minute, then she said, "She's already gone. They just took her away."

"Already gone?" My heart dropped a mile, as I thought of my friend dropped in her tracks. I leaned against Sam, overcome with grief at the suddenness and finality of death in the night. "Oh, Ida Lee, what happened? I am just devastated. Are you all right? Thank goodness, you were with her before . . . ," I swallowed hard over the lump in my throat, "before she went."

Clinging to Sam's arm, I made a supreme effort to pull myself together so I could render assistance to my friend for the last time. "What can we do to help?"

"Maybe," Ida Lee said, her voice quivering, "maybe, if you don't mind, it would be better for Miss Penelope to be with you and Miss Lillian. She's quite upset, as we all are."

"Of course we'll take her and keep her until Tonya can get here. She doesn't need to be around to hear about services and funeral preparations."

"Funeral preparations?" Ida Lee asked, frowning. "Whose funeral?"

"Why . . . why Mildred's, of course. Didn't you say she'd died?"

Ida Lee almost laughed, if the surprised expression on her face was any indication. "No, not yet anyway, although she had some kind of attack that nearly scared *me* to death."

"Oh, thank goodness," I said, weak with relief. "Sam, did you hear that? Mildred's fine, I mean, not fine, but alive at least. Yes, let's get Penelope, and, Ida Lee, please do let us know how Mildred gets along. We'll visit her in the hospital as soon as we can." I turned away, hardly knowing what I was doing, so relieved to know that Mildred was still among the living.

"What about Horace?" Sam asked. "Is he aware of what's going on?"

"It's hard to say," Ida Lee said. "Mr. Peeples is with him. Mr. Horace heard the commotion at one point and came out of his room. He became quite agitated at the sight of so many strangers in the house, but Mr. Peeples calmed him down and put him back to bed."

"Good," I said. "We'll go up and pack a few things for Penelope and take her home with us. But, Ida Lee, please keep us up to date with Mildred's condition. I am so worried about her."

"Yes, ma'am, I am, too."

As Sam and I walked up the curving stairs, I wondered how Tonya would take the news of Mildred's illness. Would she break away from her chance at stardom and rush to her mother's side, to say nothing of coming to care for her daughter? If her previous self-absorbed actions were any indication, I feared she might not.

We found Penelope huddled in her bed, the covers up around her head with only her little round face peeking out. She was awake, as how could she not be with all the shuffling and stomping of a dozen pairs of shoes and boots going in and out, and up and down the stairs?

"Honey," I said, sitting on the bed beside her, "it's been scary, hasn't it? Especially when you don't know what's going on. But they've taken your grandmother to the hospital where she'll be well taken care of. I'm not sure exactly what happened, but the hospital is the best place for her right now. We'll know more a little later on and I promise to tell you everything, because there's nothing worse than being in the dark. Now," I went on, smoothing the damp pillow under her head, "would you like to go home with me and Mr. Sam? You can sleep in Latisha's bed, and I expect we can find one or two of her dolls to keep you company."

She nodded, then sat up and lifted her arms to be picked up. Sam took her while I gathered a few clothes, knowing I would come back later and pack a decent wardrobe for her.

"I don't see a coat, Sam," I said. "It's probably in a closet downstairs, but here, wrap this around her." I stripped the bed of its top blanket and Sam bundled her up and off we went.

After a bathroom stop at our house, we put Penelope in Latisha's twin bed—the one next to Lillian's when they spent the night—tucking her in with a baby doll and a small Steiff bear. She had not said a word throughout our entrance into her room, being carried through Mildred's house and out onto the lawn, or up the stairs in our house to Latisha's bed.

So I talked constantly to her, using a soft, comforting tone as she curled up in the bed. Slightly worried that she was asking no questions or expressing any concern, just agreeing to whatever anyone wanted from her, I sat in a rocking chair beside the bed. And talked and talked to keep her company and to reassure her that somebody was there looking after her.

"Julia?" Sam said, poking his head around the door. "You're not going to sit up all night, are you?"

"No, I guess not. There'll be too much to do tomorrow. I mean, later today. But I hate to leave her. She might wake up and not know where she is."

"Then crawl into Lillian's bed," he said. "Here, I'll turn the covers down for you. Now, come on. You need to get some sleep. But," he said, his encircling arm guiding me toward the bed in the dim room, "don't get used to it. I want you back in our bed where you belong."

I smiled in the dark, feeling a surge of gratitude for this good man. Then I got into Lillian's bed, pulled up the covers, and was asleep before Sam was out the door good.

Daylight came too early as it always does after a night of interrupted sleep. But I heard Lillian downstairs, so I left Penelope sleeping and hurried to dress and go down to tell her of the night's events and to prepare her for our houseguest. If anybody could calm a child's fears of abandonment, Lillian could.

"Oh, that poor little thing," she said after I'd brought her up to date, filling in what Sam had left out before he'd headed for the Bluebird. "I'm glad you brought her home with you, Miss Julia, a baby like that don't need to be in all that turmoil. You jus' go on an' do whatever Miss Mildred need you to do, an' I'll look after our little Honey. An' Latisha'll be here after school so we'll be fine."

"Thank you, Lillian. I don't know if Tonya has been contacted about her mother yet, or if Ida Lee is waiting for Mildred to tell her to call. I guess it'll depend on Mildred's condition, don't you? Which is another thing to worry about—just what kind of attack was it and will she still be able to look after a child?" I did a little handwringing over my friend's condition and the possible limits it could impose on her activities. "I declare, I shudder to think of Penelope—I mean, Honey—being carted off to those dens of iniquity in California and put in a crowded daycare center so Tonya can concentrate on show business. But I'll tell you this, Lillian, when you have a child, that child should come first before anything else—especially when you didn't get it by mistake or miscalculation, but got it deliberately by adoption. I mean, if you don't have time to raise a child, why in the world would you go out of your way to have one?"

"Here, Miss Julia," Lillian said, pulling out a chair, "why don't you set down and have some coffee? You jus' rest a few minutes, while I go up and see if Honey's awake. She need to see a friendly face when she open her eyes."

"Yes, good, that's fine, Lillian," I said, gratefully sitting down. "And I need to run back over and get her some more clothes. We just grabbed a few things last night, but I'm thinking we may have her for several days. And it may be that Ida Lee has heard something by now."

She hadn't, for as soon as Lillian left the kitchen I got up and called Ida Lee. She'd heard nothing from the hospital or from Dr. Hargrove, Mildred's primary physician.

"But, Miss Julia," Ida Lee said, worriedly, "I may not hear anything. You know how they are about giving out information on patients. The patient has to give permission as to whom to give information, and as far as I know, Mrs. Allen has only given Mr. Allen's name. And, well, you know that he won't even know to ask." Then she hurriedly added, "I don't mean to pass judgment on his condition, but I don't quite know what to do."

"I don't either, Ida Lee," I said. "But if Mildred's condition is critical, Tonya should be notified or maybe Mildred's lawyers in Atlanta. They may have her Medical Power of Attorney in their files." I paused to consider that. "On the other hand, we don't want to go off half-cocked and upset everybody when she could well be on her way to recovery by now."

"It didn't seem that way last night," Ida Lee said, expressing for the first time I'd known her some hesitation about how to proceed. "I thought she was dying and all I knew to do was call 9-1-1."

"You did exactly the right thing. Mildred was fortunate to have had you with her, and in all likelihood, you saved her life." It never hurts to give praise where praise is due, and if anybody deserved it, Ida Lee did.

Chapter 30

❧

The morning was taken up with the walk back over to Mildred's house for Penelope's clothes, toothbrush, and other needful things, as well as with constant worry about Mildred herself. I kept trying to decide if it would be intrusive of me to call Dr. Bob Hargrove and try to wheedle some information from him. And amidst all of that, I tried my hand at entertaining a silent little girl by reading aloud some stories, admiring a picture she'd colored, and serving a tea party at a table too low for my knees.

So it came as a jolt of reality when a phone call from Etta Mae brought me back to the business deal in which we were so heavily involved.

"Miss Julia," Etta Mae said against a backdrop of road noise, "I'm in my car on the way to a patient's house, but I had to tell you that Lurline got our Offer to Purchase, and she's going up one side and down the other. She's thrilled to have somebody actually ready to buy, but she's outraged at what they want to buy it for."

"Did she talk to you about it?"

"Oh, no'm, she wouldn't do that unless it was something to brag about. Which I guess our offer wasn't. I just heard her talking on the phone to her realtor when I was restocking my car this morning—you know, with patient supplies like Depends and mattress pads and the like. You wouldn't believe how much of that stuff we use. Anyway," Etta Mae went on after blowing out a breath, "I guess she's not going to accept our offer."

"We really didn't expect her to," I said, reminding her of our strategy. "This is just the starting point. So now we wait to see how she'll respond."

"I think I know how she'll respond," Etta Mae said in a dejected tone. "I couldn't hear everything she said—she was in her office and I was going in and out of the stockroom—but I heard her mention Ernest Sitton several times." Etta Mae emitted a tiny moan. "He's going to buy it, isn't he?"

"Hold on. Let me think a minute." After a second or two of wondering if I dared, I decided that I did. "Etta Mae, how close are you to the other women who work there?"

"Pretty close. We all like each other and help each other out when anybody needs it."

"Well, I mean between you and Lurline, which one would they prefer? Which one would they support if they had to make a choice?"

"Gosh, Miss Julia, I don't know. I think they might like me better, because they all say they like it when Lurline takes off and leaves me in charge. They say conditions are better when she's not around, whatever that means. But of course it's Lurline who signs their checks and they like that. Why?"

"I'm wondering," I said, somewhat hesitantly because I'd not had time to think it through, "what Mr. Sitton would do if word got around that those ladies might quit if somebody they don't know takes over. And it's possible that they would," I quickly added, "because they might not like working for an outsider who wasn't promoted from within and who might change their schedules and pay scales and everything else. Lurline has already told him that her best employee isn't capable of stepping up, remember? What would he do if he had no employees at all? You could also mention to one or two of the ladies that you'd been considered, then rejected as not being good enough, and, because of that, you're thinking of quitting and moving to Charlotte for a better job. You mentioned that possibility to me one time, so it's not too far from the truth."

After a minute of silence, I went on. "I guess what I'm asking is this: Would they support you or Lurline? I mean, if they knew what she'd done to you—which affects them, too—would they threaten to quit in protest?"

"They might feel like it," Etta Mae said, "and they might mumble about it, but getting a check every week is more important than protesting."

"A few mumbles are all we'd need," I said. "That might be just enough to put Mr. Sitton off investing in a business with unhappy employees. It's something to think about, anyway."

I heard a lot more road noise as Etta Mae took her time considering my suggestion.

Then she said, "I don't know, Miss Julia. I'm not real good with doing sneaky things. I'd probably mess it up."

"That's because you're an open, honest person and unaccustomed to deceit of any kind. So just forget it. It wasn't that good an idea and probably wouldn't have worked anyway. But keep it in mind, just in case, because employees do get unsettled when there're changes at the top."

"Okay, I can do that, because I know more than they do, and I'm already pretty unsettled."

Mentally wringing my hands and physically pacing the living room floor, I tried to conjure up something else to keep Ernest Sitton from starting a bidding war. If that happened, I wouldn't put it past Lurline Corn to tell him every offer we made so he could top it by a few dollars.

With that dire possibility looming, I made myself sit down and calmly reconsider our strategy. What if, I thought, I were to go see Mr. Sitton and explain to him that I was trying to do a good turn for a deserving person—would he be sympathetic enough to drop out of the bidding?

No, because he was a businessman and buying The Handy Home Helpers was a good business move. Why else was I trying to buy it?

Mr. Sitton wouldn't care who I was trying to help, except if he knew it was someone already working for Lurline, he'd wonder why she hadn't been recommended to him. Should I tell him? With a word or two, I could confirm Etta Mae's credentials and lock in the managerial position for her. And, I reminded myself, lock her into being an employee for the rest of her life. Well, of course that's what most working people were, anyway, so what was so bad about that? Nothing, unless you had one opportunity to own a business, and you, or rather *I*, let it slip away.

I called Etta Mae, but got her voice mail. Knowing that she was working with some bedridden patient, I very firmly said, "Etta Mae, call Mr. Blair as soon as you can and see if Lurline has made a counteroffer. If she has, let me know right away. I'm ready to up our offer."

I had made up my mind not to go down without a fight. Ernest Sitton might be rolling in money, but that didn't mean he was eager to part with it. Most likely he was not, which was the reason he had so much of it in the first place.

And, I thought, he might be unpleasantly surprised to learn that an offer had been submitted. Up to this point, he'd had no idea that anybody else was interested in The Handy Home Helpers. Our offer, even as low as it was, coupled with his lack of a manager, might be just enough to put him off completely—a result devoutly to be wished.

Just as I was heading for the kitchen to check on Penelope, the phone rang. Thinking Etta Mae was returning my call, I was momentarily confused to hear Ida Lee's voice.

"Mrs. Murdoch," she said, "someone from the hospital just called. She wouldn't tell me anything about Mrs. Allen's condition, just that she wants me to send some gowns and personal things up to her room. I'm hoping that means she's much better—not wanting to wear a hospital gown, that is."

"I hope so, too. In fact, I'd say that's very good news. So if you'll pack what she needs, I'll take them to the hospital. Unless, of course, you'd rather go yourself."

"No, ma'am, I don't think so. I think you might be able to learn more than I would. About her condition, I mean. So if you don't mind going, I'll come get Penelope."

"No, please don't do that. She seems quite content here, especially with Lillian. And Latisha will be out of school in a little while." And to change the subject since even I would dread going back to rattle around alone in that huge house, I said, "Have you thought of calling Tonya? Do you think one of us should?"

"No, ma'am, not unless something dreadful happens. Mrs. Allen wouldn't want me to overstep like that."

"I understand," I said, but didn't. "I'll ask when I take her things to her. If you'll have everything ready, I'll be by to pick them up in about thirty minutes."

Hating to leave with Etta Mae's phone call pending, yet eager to learn how Mildred was faring, I hung up and turned to go to the kitchen. Lillian met me in the hall.

"Miss Julia," she said, frowning, "I'm worriet about that baby girl. She's not said one word all day long. That's not the way a little girl s'posed to act, 'specially since Latisha, she talks from sunup 'til sundown."

"I noticed that, too, Lillian, but I thought it was because I was talking so much to her. Trying to keep her distracted, you know. Where is she now?"

"Takin' a nap in the lib'ry. I didn't want her to be upstairs by herself, so I put her on the sofa. But Latisha'll be here in about an hour, so she'll be up then."

"That's good," I said, relieved that Latisha would take over the entertainment chores. I was far from knowledgeable in the range of interests of a seven- or eight-year-old. "Ida Lee is packing some things that Mildred wants, so I'm taking them to the hospital for her. I'm hoping to find out just what happened last night and what the prognosis is."

"And if you get a chance," Lillian said, "find out if Mrs. Allen's gonna get better, 'cause that little girl don't know what to think, an' it seem to me she could use some good news for a change."

Chapter 31

❧

A brisk wind with gusts up to twenty miles an hour, according to the latest weather report, lashed at me as I walked up to Mildred's house. What had I been thinking, I thought, not to have driven the car around? But assuming that would've been foolish just to pick up a few silk gowns in a tote bag, I had braved the weather. Ida Lee must've been watching out for she opened the door as I walked onto the porch.

"I have everything ready," she said, pointing to a Louis Vuitton suitcase of considerable size, a matching carry-on, plus a cosmetic case, also matching. "But, Miss Julia, you can't carry all this. Why don't I ask Mr. Peeples to go with you?"

I thought for a minute or two, knowing full well that I was not about to trudge around the hospital lugging enough luggage for a two-week cruise.

"That might be the simplest," I said. "Sam's downtown at some meeting and Lloyd's still in school. But what about Mr. Horace? Will he be all right while Grady is gone? Although," I quickly added, "I don't plan to be gone long. Mildred may not be allowed to have visitors yet."

Ida Lee frowned, then her face lit up. "Mr. Horace could go, too. Mr. Peeples was planning to take him for a drive this afternoon anyway, so a trip to the hospital would serve the same purpose."

I mentally rolled my eyes, but it seemed that I was stuck with delivering Mildred's luggage as well as providing an outing for Mildred's husband. That's the problem with offering to help. You're often taken up on it.

But I plodded back to my house, got in the car, drove up Mildred's driveway, parked by the porch, and waited while Ida Lee and Grady Peeples loaded suitcases in the trunk, then loaded Horace in the back seat.

I spoke to Horace, asking how he was and being my usual mannerly self.

To my befuddlement, he replied, "How very nice to meet you, madam. I hope you don't mind driving, but my car is parked for the time being and I'm having to depend on the kindness of strangers."

Since he had known me for twenty years, I hardly knew how to respond, so I mumbled, "Not a problem. I'm happy to do it," and was thankful when Grady crawled into the back seat with him.

When we got to the hospital, there was another round of discussion about who would deliver the luggage to the second floor—Grady and Horace while I waited in the car, or Grady alone while I kept watch on Horace, or all three of us.

"You go, Grady," I said, making the decision. "Horace and I will wait here."

"Don't you think she'll want to see him?" Grady asked. "I could take the suitcases and you could hold onto him."

Since holding onto Horace was not a pleasing prospect, I demurred. "I'm thinking she's in no condition for visitors," I said, also thinking that this was turning into a three-ring circus or a Who's on First situation. "At least for the three of us trouping in at one time. If she wants to see him, come back down and get him."

Grady finally left, loaded down with Mildred's luggage, leaving me with Horace, who sat behind me in the back seat. Have you ever had a conversation with someone in another world? It isn't easy, especially when that someone keeps reaching for the door handle. I could just see me chasing Horace all around the hospital parking lot, so I locked the doors and tried to distract him by saying the first thing that came to mind.

"Horace, who is Jane Smith?"

"Who?"

"Never mind. I don't know her, either." Then I quickly went on to the usual topic of conversation when you can't think of anything else. "It's a beautiful day, isn't it? A little cold and windy, but at least the sun is shining."

There was a moment of silence, then Horace asked, "How're your children? Are they all working?" And I knew that he, too, in his polite, but spacey, way was searching for a topic.

"Um, yes, they're all fine," I said, loath to explain what he should have known, i.e., I had no children. "Grady Peeples is a good friend to have, isn't he?"

"Who?"

Well, that didn't work, so I tried something else. "It's getting close to dinnertime. What would you like to eat tonight?"

"The food's good where I'm staying," he said. "I like it there. That's why I come back every year."

To my profound relief, Grady opened the door and got in beside Horace. "You were right, Mrs. Murdoch," he said. "No visitors, so I left everything with the nurses. They said they were fixing to move her to a private room anyway."

"Oh, my word, she's been on a ward?" I could just picture Mildred sharing a room with two or three other patients and the uproar that would engender.

"No'm," Grady said. "ICU."

"She's been in *intensive care*? Oh, goodness, that's worse than a ward, but I guess we should've expected it."

"Well, they're moving her to a private room so that's better than either one."

"Did you ask how she's doing?"

"Yes'm, but the nurse said she couldn't give out that information, though you'd think she could've said something one way or the other."

"Well, that's the way they are," I said, quickly turning the ignition in my eagerness to get home to learn what Lurline had thought of our offer. "It's a legal thing, I think."

"Pro'bly," he said, then went on. "Why don't we ride downtown and give Horace a chance to look around? He'd like that. Or we could drive up to Jump Off and walk him around so he can view the scenery. I like to give him lots of things to do, different things to think about, you know. And it's nice for him to have company and be out and around for a while."

"That's all well and good," I said, turning onto the most direct route home, "and you're to be commended for the care you take of him. But I have obligations at home, and that's where we're going."

I couldn't blame Grady for wanting a diversion from the constant company of one with whom conversation was impossible, but I had a real estate venture on the front burner and I'd had enough of Horace's company.

But Horace spoke up at that moment. "My car's parked around here somewhere. Just let me out when you come to it."

"No," Grady said in a humoring way, "it's in the garage at home, remember? You put it there the last time you drove it, and it's still right where it belongs."

"It is?" Horace asked. Then he sighed. "Well, I guess I did if you say so, but I sure don't remember it. My memory isn't so good these days."

"Mine, either, Horace," I said, wanting to make him feel better. "I think it's just part of growing old, don't you?" But I thought to myself that I'd hate to get so old that I couldn't remember where I'd left my car.

Nothing else was said as I drove directly to the Allen house. As I parked at the front, Grady opened his door and came around to lend a hand to Horace, who was noticeably unsteady on his feet.

As Horace started out of the car, he turned back to me and said, "I'm not that old."

Chapter 32

Hoping, indeed expecting, to hear the chatter and giggles of small girls playing, I walked into a silent house. I stood for a second inside the door and picked up the murmur of a television cartoon in another room.

"How's Mrs. Allen doin'?" Lillian asked as she turned from the counter where she was rolling out biscuits.

"She couldn't have visitors and the nurses wouldn't tell us anything, so I don't know. I assume, though, that she's doing well enough to want something decent to wear. And they've moved her from ICU to a private room, so that's encouraging. But I declare, Lillian," I said, coming out of my coat, "conversing, or rather *trying* to converse with Horace Allen is like pulling teeth. He is in another universe." Then, noticing the neatness of Latisha's table in the corner, I asked, "Where are the girls? They've not been coloring?"

"They in the lib'ry watchin' TV. An' no'm, Honey didn't do nothin' but watch Latisha when she wanted to color, so that didn't last long. But, Miss Julia," Lillian said as she held up flour-coated hands, "I'm still worriet about that chile. She jus' shake or nod her head without sayin' anything. 'Course Latisha, she take up the slack, but it's not right for her not to be talkin'."

"Oh, my," I said, sinking into a chair at the table. "You're right, it's not right and it's not normal, either. I just wonder exactly what happened last night to put her into such a state. I'm guessing that she was forgotten in all the hubbub of whatever happened to Mildred. And Ida Lee told me that Horace was disturbed by it, so he was up and wandering around. Then all the first responders descended on them. It must've been like an invasion of some kind, and there was nobody who thought to go in and comfort a small girl."

"Yes'm, I 'spect Ida Lee and Mr. Peeples had their hands full."

"Oh, you're right about that. I know for a fact that Mildred does not suffer in silence. And Horace apparently needs somebody holding onto him all the time. I'm not criticizing—just explaining how Honey could've been overlooked. Of course," I went on with an edge to my words, "if her *mother* had been here . . ." I trailed off, for there was no use stating the obvious.

"No use cryin' over spilt milk," Lillian said, finishing my thought. "'Sides, they's other things to take care of. Miss Etta Mae needs you to call her soon as you can. She already called two times."

Struggling to my tired feet, I said, "Yes, I expect she's getting anxious. I'll call her right now."

"Miss Julia!" Etta Mae said as soon as she recognized my voice, even as I recognized the distress in hers. "I've been trying to reach you. Lurline's made a counteroffer, and she wants an answer in twenty-four hours. Mr. Blair is waiting for me to do something, and I don't know what to do."

"It's all right, Etta Mae. I'm sorry I was out of touch, but a neighbor needed help. But don't worry, we don't want to appear too eager to respond. So tell me, what's her counteroffer?"

"You won't believe it," Etta Mae said, sounding on the verge of tears. "I didn't think she would do it this way. I thought she'd either stay with her first number or she'd make a decent counteroffer. I don't think she's playing fair."

I smiled at Etta Mae's innocence. "Nothing says she has to play fair. Just tell me what she's done."

Etta Mae took a deep breath, then said, "She's lowered her price by a thousand dollars. By *one* measly thousand dollars and that's all."

I almost laughed, although it was disappointing. "Well, she's a sharp lady, Etta Mae. But you see what she's doing, don't you? She's indicating that she's open to negotiation, and she wants to keep us on the hook. It may also indicate that she's had no other offers, especially from Mr. Sitton."

"Well, but what do we *do*?"

"We let her dangle overnight. Nothing says that we have to immediately respond. In fact, we let her think that we're seriously considering her offer." I let that sink in for a minute, then asked, "Have you talked with Mr. Blair? What does he say?"

"He says I should make another offer, higher than the first, but it's up to me how far I want to go. And, Miss Julia," she said as her voice broke on a sob, "I don't know how far I want to go. I'm already worried sick about paying back our first offer."

"Etta Mae," I said, "you've got to be strong now. I promise you that I will not let you get in over your head. I've counted the cost, and I know what the business will bear in the way of repayments." Actually, it had been Sam who had counted the cost, but it sounded better to have come from me. "So," I went on, "if Lurline won't negotiate a decent price, we'll drop out. I know how far to go, and I know when to stop."

"Okay," she said with a tremble in her voice. "It's just that I'm not used to all these big numbers."

I wasn't all that used to them myself, but I trusted Sam who was.

"I know," I said, "but let's sleep on it tonight, so we don't appear too eager. Besides, we have twenty-four hours to respond, anyway. We'll go up with our counter, but I'll let you know tomorrow just how much. In the meantime, let's hope that our, or rather, *your* silence will give Lurline a restless night."

It was a busy evening, enlivened by Latisha's monologue at the table, a phone call from Mildred, and a discussion of where Penelope would spend the night. Lillian suggested that she go home with Latisha and her, but she had been left in my care so I felt she should stay with us. Penelope herself did not indicate her preference, remaining as quiet as she had all day.

The phone call from Mildred both reassured and disturbed me. She called about seven that evening to tell me that she'd had several tests during the day, none of which had determined the cause of her attack.

"It was my heart," she'd said. "It had to be a heart attack, I don't care if all the tests in the world say different. I know what I felt, and you would not believe how terrifying it was. I couldn't catch my breath, and I broke out in a cold sweat, and there was this awful pain in my chest, and I thought I was going to die. I've never had anything like it, and if it hadn't been for Ida Lee, I would've died right there in my bed. And now," she said with a catch in her voice, "all I can think about is when I'll have another attack."

"But, Mildred, you may never have another one," I said, wanting to encourage her. "Especially since they're telling you it wasn't a heart attack. It should be a great relief to know that it wasn't."

"Oh, it would be, if I didn't know better. The cardiologist said my heart is as strong as a horse, which isn't all that comforting when you think about it. But there're other things it could've been that they're still looking into, although I don't know what they could be. One doctor even said it could've been indigestion—can you believe that? I told him in no uncertain terms that I knew the difference between a heart attack and heartburn."

Then, in an aggrieved tone, she went on. "I have been poked and prodded all day long, Julia, and I've had one test after another. They're going to do even more tomorrow. I don't know if I can survive much more, but Ida Lee tells me that you have Penelope, so I want to thank you for that. Let me know if she gets to be too much for you, and I'll make other arrangements."

Although wondering what other arrangements could be made with both the child's mother and grandmother taken up with their own concerns, I let that hang in the air.

But fearing, as Ida Lee had, that I could be overstepping, I dared to ask, "Would you like me or Ida Lee to call Tonya and let her know you're in the hospital?"

"Absolutely not!" Mildred said in a tone so abrupt and harsh that I almost dropped the phone. "No one is to call her, not Ida Lee, and certainly not you."

"I understand," I said, although my mouth was so stiff that I could barely get the words out. "I'll let you get some rest. Call if you need anything."

Just as I was about to hang up, Mildred whispered, "Wait, Julia, wait. I am so sorry. Please forgive me. It's just that . . . that I'm afraid if anybody called Tonya, she, well, she wouldn't come, and that would be more than I could bear. I'd rather she just not know."

"Oh, Mildred," I said, my heart aching for her, "there's no need to apologize. I do understand."

Of course I didn't fully understand anything other than that she was under terrible stress, and I didn't at all understand how she could ache for her child without realizing that her grandchild could be aching for her.

That evening I told Penelope that her grandmother was much better and had sent her love and a good-night kiss. I'm not in the habit of out-and-out lying, but it seemed to be called for in this case.

I put her back in Latisha's bed, suggesting that she think of what she would ask Santa to bring her for Christmas, hoping that such thoughts would put her to sleep with sweet dreams. Just as I was about to leave the room, I turned back and sat on the side of the bed.

"Let's say your prayers, Honey," I said, then had my usual period of tongue-tied silence at the thought of praying aloud.

To my surprise and for the first time all day, Penelope spoke. She began to whisper, "Now I lay me down to sleep," and I joined in, elated that somebody at some time in her erratic life had been concerned enough to teach the child to pray.

Chapter 33

❧

After discussing Lurline Corn's ridiculous counteroffer with Sam, who had a good laugh over it, I settled on our counter-counteroffer. It was a nice jump from our equally ridiculous first offer, but not our best and final although it was getting close.

Etta Mae, of course, was shaken by the increase when I called her the next morning. I reassured her that we were still well within what I, or rather, Sam, thought the business was worth.

"And, still no word from Mr. Sitton?" I asked. "Are we sure that Lurline isn't playing us off one another?"

"Pretty sure," Etta Mae said. "If she had two offers, she wouldn't keep it to herself. We'd hear about it all day long."

"Then pass our new offer along to Mr. Blair, and be sure to impress on him the need for secrecy as to who you are. Lurline is not to know who's buying her business until the closing."

"Yes'm, I tell him that every time we talk. If Lurline found out it was me, she'd kick me out on my you-know-what so fast it'd make my head swim. But she's not said a word about Mr. Sitton in several days. Maybe he's looking at something else."

"That would be nice," I said, but thinking that if so, I'd like to know what it was. Ernest Sitton had an eye for a good business deal.

Later that morning, after a stop at The Flower Basket for a nice bouquet, I made the trek back to the hospital to see Mildred. I considered taking Penelope with me, but recalled that with flu season on us, she would not be allowed to visit.

Instead, I told her that when Latisha got home that afternoon, I would take the two of them wherever they wanted to go.

"We could go to the library and check out some books," I suggested, but was met with a blank look. "Or if there's a decent movie playing, we could go see it, or maybe we could go downtown to the ice cream parlor. You be thinking about what you'd like to do, although Latisha will probably have some ideas, too."

Lillian laughed. "I 'spect she will."

So, hopefully leaving Penelope with something to look forward to, I went to see her grandmother.

I found Mildred resting against her raised bed. Wearing one of the gowns and a bed jacket that Ida Lee had sent, she looked tired and somewhat forlorn.

"How're you feeling?" I asked, because what else do you ask a hospitalized patient?

"Terrible," she said, reaching for a tissue. "Julia, I'm thinking of going somewhere else. I'm just not sure that I'm getting the quality of care that I should."

"I'm sorry to hear that. I thought that for a small town we have excellent physicians. I know they're quick to refer patients when they need to."

"Well," Mildred said with a loud sniff, "I'm about ready to refer myself. That cardiologist that Dr. Hargrove brought in is the most next-to-nothing I've ever seen. He patronizes me, Julia, and tells me I'm fine when I know I'm not." She adjusted her bed jacket and sighed pitifully. "I'm thinking of going to Duke or maybe to the Mayo Clinic where cutting-edge medicine is practiced. The doctors around here are too set in their ways. They don't listen to their patients."

"I'm sorry you're not pleased with the care you're getting," I said, hardly knowing how to reassure her. "I thought they were doing every test under the sun."

"They were. They have, but they're wrong in their conclusions. Julia," she went on, struggling to sit up higher, "you won't believe this, but they've decided that my heart attack was nothing but a panic attack. Now, even I know better than that. But they want me to have some psychological tests and talk to a psychologist. Or maybe even to a psychiatrist. Now, listen," she went on, grasping my arm, "don't tell anybody about that because I do not want it discussed all over town. But you know that I am the last person who needs psychological counseling."

"Well, but, Mildred, you've had a lot on you lately, what with the Tonya situation, and Horace's heart attack, and now his memory problems. Then to be surprised by the appearance of a grandchild, it's no wonder that you've been under extreme stress. It might be a real relief to talk with a counselor. It might prevent another panic attack."

"*Heart* attack," she said firmly, "and talking to a counselor is not going to prevent another one of those." Then she leaned back against the bed and looked away. "I really should talk to my lawyers again—to be sure I'll be leaving everything in good order, you know."

Before I could respond to such a despondent comment, a nurse came into the room with a stethoscope around her neck. It was an opportunity to take my leave, so I did, knowing that once Mildred had her mind set, there was little chance of changing it.

As I approached the elevator to leave, I realized that Mildred had not asked about Penelope—a clear indication to me of where her interests lay, or didn't lie, as the case might be.

The elevator door slid open and I stepped aside to allow an orderly to push a patient in a wheelchair out into the hall. Avoiding a direct gaze in case the patient preferred anonymity in an incapacitated state, I started to enter the elevator.

"Well, Mrs. Murdoch," the patient said, holding up his hand to stop the orderly, "if you came to see me, I'll be receiving in my room. If you didn't, I bid you good day."

Almost tripping at being spoken to, I stepped back in confusion. "Why, Mr. Sitton! Ernest, I mean. My goodness, I didn't know you were in the hospital. How are you?"

"Oh, I'm fine," he said. Then, with an edge of sarcasm, said, "That's why I'm here. Push me out of the way, Roy. People want in the elevator."

Moving out of the door of the elevator, the orderly pushed Mr. Sitton to the side, and I, nervously mindful of the competition we were in and wondering if he knew it, followed.

"I expect you'll soon be home," I said, as cheerily as I could manage. "You're looking quite well."

Actually, he wasn't, but a flannel bathrobe is a poor substitute for a three-piece suit. Ernest Sitton was a small man in stature, but a rotund one in girth. His powerful personality, though, made up for any physical lack as, according to Sam, he dominated a courtroom by intimidation and pure legal knowledge. To tell the truth, the man scared me, especially since I knew something he didn't. At least I hoped he didn't know that I intended to buy something out from under him.

"Just in for some tests," he said. "A minor matter, and nothing to be broadcast around town." Then, reverting to his usual courtly manner, he went on. "I sincerely hope you don't have someone incarcerated here. How is Sam?"

"Sam is fine, thank you. And, no, I'm here visiting a neighbor—a friend who may soon be discharged. But I must let you get on to your room. Is there anything I can do for you? Bring you anything?"

"Thank you, madam, but no," Mr. Sitton said quite formally. "Please don't burden yourself with concern for me. I expect this little unexpected meeting qualifies as fulfilling your Christian duty of visiting the sick, so nothing more will be required." Then, with a finger pointing forward, he motioned to Roy to push him on.

Startled by the clear sarcasm I heard in his words, I turned on my heel and left. But what had brought that on? Sick people, I knew, often expressed their discomfort in ways that they wouldn't ordinarily do. Maybe Ernest Sitton was suffering from some extreme discomfort, like from hemorrhoids, for instance, which would make anybody slightly prickly in their choice of responses.

On the other hand, if he had even an inkling that Etta Mae and I were after The Handy Home Helpers, he would view me as an unwelcome competitor and give me the cold shoulder, as I felt he had just done.

Still unsettled by the chance meeting with Ernest Sitton, I started home while going over in my mind every word spoken between us. So intent on trying to determine the meaning behind his, I almost ran a stop sign. Did he know something or didn't he?

Finally deciding that there was nothing to be done about it either way, I pulled into the driveway at home and tried to put it out of my mind. I also decided not to tell Etta Mae the details of the conversation, but I would tell her that I had seen Mr. Sitton and, especially, *where* I'd seen him. It was no wonder that bidding on The Handy Home Helpers wasn't at the top of his list of things to do.

Then it suddenly occurred to me that with him temporarily out of commission, this might be the time to present our best and final offer. That would really put Lurline Corn between a rock and a hard place. She would have to decide between accepting our offer or turning it down to await one that might never come. It all depended on just how ill Ernest Sitton was.

So, I thought to myself, I would suggest to Etta Mae that she make sure Lurline knew of Mr. Sitton's precarious physical condition. When one is hospitalized, one is unlikely to be all that interested in making a major purchase. Lurline would know that, and that would make our lone bid for her business much more attractive.

I was met by two excited little girls when I entered the kitchen, Latisha leading the way. The two of them sounded like a herd of wild horses as they ran from the library into the kitchen, Latisha shouting, "We're ready! We're ready!"

Penelope, saying nothing, ran in behind her, then stopped short and looked expectantly at me. I noticed a flush of excitement on her face.

"Have you decided what we should do?" I asked.

"*Yeah!*" Latisha yelled. "I mean, yes, ma'am, we know. And we're ready to go."

"All right, where're we going?" I asked, hoping that she would not put me on the spot by saying they wanted to go for a hike in Pisgah Forest or some other bizarre outing that would test both my limbs and my stamina.

"The *PlayPlace!*" Latisha yelled, as she jumped up and down. "That's where we want to go! Can we? Can we?"

Penelope gave a little jump and chimed in, "Can we? Can we?"

I looked to Lillian for help. "What and where is the PlayPlace?"

"At McDonald's," she said. "You know, it's that fenced-in place some of 'em have with the slides and ladders and big balls to fall into. 'Cept ours don't have a PlayPlace. You have to go to the McDonald's over at the airport."

"Well, that's easy enough," I said, relieved that no walking would be required of me. I could sit at a table beside a window and sip coffee while watching the girls wear themselves out in a gigantic playpen. "It's perfect, in fact. Get your coats on, girls, and let's go. Lillian, there's no need for a heavy supper. I expect all that physical activity will call for a snack or two before we get home."

"I want some fries!" Latisha announced, then turned to Penelope. "You want some fries?"

"Yes, I want some, too!" Penelope said, and for the first time raised her voice in excitement.

So we bundled ourselves into the car, the girls, mostly Latisha, chattering constantly. I drove us out to the interstate, then the ten or so miles to the airport exit and turned into the lot of the newer, larger McDonald's that featured a large fenced-in appendage. And all the while I was offering up silent thanks for the girls having chosen such an easily fulfilled promise. I was, in fact, looking forward to having some quiet time inside as I watched through a window thick enough, I hoped, to drown out the squeals and screams. And looking forward, as well, to having a cup or two of McDonald's excellent coffee, thinking that I might also order a hot apple pie to go with it.

By the time we started for home, a good hour and a half later, both girls were worn to a frazzle from all the climbing, sliding, and jumping they'd done. Stuffed with fries and milkshakes, they crawled into the back seat and buckled themselves in. Latisha was uncommonly quiet during the short drive, too tired to talk, and I didn't expect to hear much from Penelope. But that little girl leaned her head back and, with a beatific smile on her face, said, "That was the best time I ever had."

Neither of them was interested in supper that evening, with Latisha openly yawning and Penelope almost nodding off. Not even Sam could get a rise from them, although they took turns telling him of all the acrobatic gyrations they had engaged in during the afternoon.

"Miss Julia," Lillian said as we finished supper, "before I take Latisha home, you remember that muscadine jelly we made back in August? I'm thinkin' you better decide who you gonna give it to, else you and Mr. Sam gonna eat it all up 'fore Christmas gets here."

"Oh, my goodness, yes," I said, recalling the several days that the sweet aroma of muscadine grapes boiling on the stove filled the house. And recalling also the hours of crushing, cooking, and ladling the hot liquid into small jars and then sealing and placing them in the pantry to await Christmas. "With all that's been happening, I had about forgotten them. Penelope, Honey, that's something you and I can do tomorrow. We'll get out some Christmas labels and decide who will get a jar of the best jelly in the world.

"And," I continued, looking at Penelope, "I think it's time to get out some Christmas decorations and begin to dress up the house for Santa Claus. I am so glad to have you here to help with that.

"Oh, and another thing," I continued, "we'll need some greenery for the mantels, so we'll go look for a roadside stand and get it fresh from the mountains."

"Well," Sam said, expansively, "with that on the agenda, I'm canceling my Bluebird visit tomorrow. I need some Christmas spirit, so I want to help decorate, too."

"Well, I do, too," Latisha said, then glanced at Lillian from under lowered eyelids. "But I guess I'm gonna have to go to school 'less somebody thinks I need a day off."

Sam and I laughed, but Lillian said, "Don't nobody think you need anything 'cept a good night's sleep."

"Don't worry, Latisha," I said, "there'll be plenty left to do, and we'll finish up on Saturday when you can be here to help."

I declare, it was beginning to look as if I ran a day care center, what with having Penelope on my hands and Latisha, as well. But Latisha with her exuberance was good for Penelope, who still seemed closed in on herself and much too somber for a child of her age. I wondered if she missed her mother. But if so, which mother? Did she even remember the woman who bore her? As for Tonya, it was hard for me to think of her in motherly terms. As far as I knew, the adoption was of fairly recent occurrence, so perhaps the child had not formed much of a bond with her new mother. If that was the case, she might not miss her at all, which meant, it seemed to me, that Penelope had no conception of where or to whom she belonged.

Dangling in midair, I thought, must be the way the child felt, aware that at any minute she could be shipped off to another strange place and another group of strange people. Why couldn't Mildred and Tonya see that a child needed stability and a sense of belonging?

Right at that moment, I decided that, in spite of my determination to stay out of the business of other people, I would tell Mildred in no uncertain terms how she was endangering Penelope's well-being. And, if my outspokenness infuriated Mildred, then I would just accept the loss of a friendship. There are some things worse than living next door to someone who strikes you off her invitation list.

With that decision made, I put it aside until Mildred was home and out of danger of another attack of whatever had caused the first one. And, speaking of that, I hoped to goodness that Mildred would not take herself off to Duke or to the Mayo Clinic because what would she do with Penelope? Mildred would not go anywhere without Ida Lee at hand, which would mean leaving the child with Horace and Grady Peeples. Surely she wouldn't do that, which left either sending her back to Tonya or leaving her with me.

I prepared myself to insist that Penelope stay with us if Mildred considered sending her to Tonya. Not that I wanted to offer childcare for what could be weeks, but I could not bear the thought of Penelope being bounced back and forth across the continent, knowing that she was unwanted at either end.

And I kept thinking of Lloyd, often seeing in her his wan little face when he first came to me. What he had added to my life could not be measured and Mildred was a foolish, self-absorbed woman if she would not seize the opportunity to enrich her own life.

But one thing at a time, I thought, and at that time the one thing needing my attention was The Handy Home Helpers.

Chapter 35

❧

I finally connected with Etta Mae later that evening after watching the little girls pick at their suppers, then getting Penelope
ready for bed. It was with effort that I turned my mind to our
business deal, for it had been a long, busy day what with visiting
Mildred in the hospital, having that run-in with Ernest Sitton,
and drinking enough McDonald's coffee to float a battleship.

"Oh, I was hoping you'd call," Etta Mae said as soon as she
heard my voice. "I wanted to call you, but didn't want to bother
you. Miss Julia, I am so nervous I'm about to jump out of my skin.
Mr. Blair hasn't heard one word from Lurline, and he sent her our
new offer first thing this morning. Or maybe it was last night, I
don't know. But I don't see how we can go any higher, so if she
turns us down this time, I guess that'll be it for us."

"Wait, Etta Mae," I said, responding to the panic as well as the
disappointment in her voice. "It's not as bad as you think. Remember that it was a full twenty-four hours before she responded the
last time. And she has a lot more to think about now than she did
then because Ernest Sitton is in the hospital."

"He *is*? What's wrong with him?"

"He said it was a minor matter, but he was in a wheelchair
coming back to his room after having some kind of test. So I'm
thinking that if he's unable to walk . . ."

"No, Miss Julia," Etta Mae interrupted, "that doesn't mean

anything. Hospitals never let patients walk to and from tests. They're afraid somebody'll fall and sue them."

"Oh. Well, I don't know what his problem is, but do you think Lurline has heard about it? That would make a difference if she thinks our offer is the only one she'll get."

"Gosh, I don't know," Etta Mae said. "But she was awfully quiet today, though I only saw her early this morning and then again around quitting time. But she sure wasn't walking on air like she's been doing." Etta Mae paused, then in a brighter tone she said, "I bet she does know, and it's got her thinking that our offer is all she's going to get. Miss Julia, she may really be thinking of accepting ours. Oh, my goodness, what if she does?"

"Then," I said, "we will have a thriving business on our hands. Now, Etta Mae, don't get too excited. She may still be waiting to see what the Dollar Store will do."

After a few more minutes of conversation, we hung up with promises to stay in touch at the least little indication of what Lurline Corn might do.

Sam snapped the newspaper open and looked over at me. "I heard you mention the Dollar Store," he said, "but you can forget about them. I heard today that they've bought eight acres out on Springer Road."

"They *have*? *Where* on Springer Road? Sam, why didn't you tell me?"

"Because I wasn't sure it was true. It was Jack Maybin who mentioned it, and you know how he is. He gets something right about once a year." Smiling, Sam turned back to the newspaper. "I'm going to the Bluebird for breakfast in the morning. I'll find out for sure then, unless you want me to help decorate for Christmas."

"Well, yes I do. But I want to know about the Dollar Store more than I want boxes down from the attic. Christmas is still a ways off."

With Lillian's help the following morning, I was able to find the leftover-from-last-year Christmas wrapping paper, ribbons, and tags. Mixed in with all of that, we found one sheet of small labels with adhesive backs, and that was exactly what we needed.

Placing the jars of jelly, the sheet of labels, and a couple of red ink pens on the kitchen table, I helped Penelope climb up to sit on a thick tome so she, too, could reach the table. I had earlier made a list of those to whom I wanted to give a jar of jelly, but as I counted them out I realized there were not enough jars to go around. Somebody had to be struck off the list.

"Oh, Lillian," I said, "why did you let us eat so much jelly?"

"I tole you," she said with a noticeable lack of concern. "Sides, Mr. Sam like that jelly."

"Yes," I said, laughing, "and around here what Mr. Sam likes, Mr. Sam gets. Well, Penelope, somebody will just have to do without. We have a list of twelve names and only ten jars of jelly." Pulling over the sheet of labels, I went on. "Why don't I write the names and you paste the labels on the jars?"

And that's what we did, although I drew out the project for as long as I could simply because I couldn't think of anything else with which to entertain Penelope. She seemed to enjoy pasting the labels, frowning with serious intent to make sure that each one was level and securely adhered to the jars.

With the kitchen radio turned low to an early selection of Christmas carols, Lillian preparing dinner with a soft clatter of pans, and the child busily entertained, you would think that my mind would be pleasantly occupied. It wasn't, for I kept thinking of the cutting sharpness in Mildred's voice when she told me in no uncertain terms that Tonya was not to be summoned. Even worse, she had made it plain that *I* was not the one to place a call. To tell the truth, no one had spoken to me like that since Wesley

Lloyd Springer had been laid to rest. He was known to belittle anyone who did not measure up, and he had cut me down to size more often than I cared to recall. To have heard the same critical disparagement in my friend's voice had cut me to the bone.

Yes, she had quickly apologized, and her reason for not wanting Tonya notified had moved me with deep sympathy for her pain. I had easily forgiven her for speaking to me in such harsh tones, but, being human, I had not forgotten. I would from now on watch my step and measure my words in her presence. It was a crying shame, but I would not risk another outburst from her again.

There's such a thing as too much of a good thing, as too close a friendship, and as getting too involved with someone else's problems. Oh, I would of course continue our friendship and do what I could when she wanted help, but I would always be holding back just a little for fear that she would lash out at me again.

To tell the truth, I had had my fill of verbal lashings from Wesley Lloyd, who could never be completely pleased with me. I didn't have to take the same abuse from anybody else. So, yes, I could forgive Mildred for blurting out her true feelings, but forget her belittling tone of voice? No.

"Miss Julia?" Lillian asked, interrupting my thoughts. "If y'all 'bout through with the jelly jars, you want me to start pullin' out Christmas decorations?"

"No," I said, putting down my pen, "I don't want you going up and down the attic stairs. Sam said he would do that this morning. But where is he? Down at the Bluebird, as usual."

"Well, he tole me 'fore he left that there was something he had to check on down there."

"Huh," I said with a laugh. "He just doesn't want to miss any news. But don't worry, Honey," I said to Penelope, "he'll be back soon and we'll test the Christmas tree lights and check on the ornaments. We'll be ready to put up the tree, but we can't do that without Latisha, can we?"

Penelope smiled and shook her head.

Lillian leaned on the counter and said, "Y'all got to get a tree 'fore you can put it up, with or without Latisha."

"Well, I think," I said, "that would be a good thing for Honey and Sam to do this afternoon, don't you? Then it'll be ready for decorating when Latisha can be here." Then, carefully wrapping each jelly jar in newspaper to prevent breakage, I stacked them in a large basket, ready for delivery. "Thank you for your help, sweetheart," I said to the child. "You did such a good job, and our friends will be delighted to get a jar delivered by a little elf like you."

Penelope smiled again, and I began to try to think of other little jobs for her to do. It wasn't easy, for everything I could think of would take five minutes or less, and with her help, twice as long, but still not long enough to fill the morning.

"Miss Julia," Lillian said, leaning over to look out the side window. "Something's goin' on over at Mrs. Allen's house."

Chapter 36

❧

I hurried to the side window to look out over the boxwood hedge that separated our lawns and through the bare branches of a row of Bradford pear trees, getting just a glimpse of the columns on Mildred's porch and a glint of black metal.

"Oh, my goodness," I said, "that looks like a limousine to me. Maybe it's . . ." I stopped myself from saying *Tonya* in front of Penelope for fear of exciting then disappointing her in case it wasn't.

But Lillian knew who I meant for she said, "Wouldn't nobody be driving all the way from California, would they?"

Shaking my head, I whispered, "No, but they would from the airport."

"Oh, look!" Lillian said, clutching my arm. "It's got a back door, an' they openin' it. It's a ambulance, Miss Julia."

And of course it was, for I could now make out the long, sleek, highly-polished lines of the vehicle normally leading a string of cars on the way to a cemetery.

I looked around for Penelope, not wanting to speculate too much in her hearing, but she was still sitting at the table seemingly engrossed with the red ink pens.

"They pullin' somebody out, Miss Julia," Lillian said, her face pressed against the window. "I b'lieve it might be Miss Mildred. It sure look like her on that stretcher."

"Let me see." I took Lillian's place at the window and found that she'd had a clearer view through the branches. I watched as men maneuvered a heavily laden stretcher out of the ambulance and onto the ground. "I think you're right. That has to be Mildred, coming home in style. Penelope," I went on as I turned to her, "I do believe your grandmother has come home. Isn't that exciting?"

She looked up at me with those big, black eyes, then, without a word, slid off the chair and left the kitchen for the library.

"Oh, me, Lillian," I said, "what do we do now?"

"Only one thing to do," Lillian said, turning to go after the child. "We make us some cookies."

While Lillian distracted Penelope with cookie dough in the kitchen, the hours passed as I sat stewing in the library. Why hadn't Mildred let me know she was coming home? What was I to do with her grandchild—take her home immediately or keep her until Mildred deigned to summon her home? And where was Sam? How long did breakfast last at the Bluebird? Then I switched back to Penelope, wondering what to do with the child.

She was no problem for any of us, certainly not to me. In fact, she'd fit into our daily routine easily and she'd been a pleasure to have around. We would miss her when she returned to Mildred, but when would that be? It wasn't that I wanted rid of her. It was the principle of the thing—the feeling of being used and of being taken for granted.

If Mildred had called to announce her homecoming, if she'd said she still felt unwell and asked me to keep Penelope another day or two, I would've quickly agreed and thought nothing more of it. But for Mildred to assume that I was always available for her convenience did not sit well with me. No one likes to be taken advantage of, yet on the other hand I found that I would be reluctant to let Penelope go. I knew the child would grieve in that big, lonely house where everything and everybody revolved around its owner. I hated the thought of sending Penelope back, even while I fumed at Mildred's assumption that I, too, revolved around her needs.

When Sam finally came in, I waited to unload my concerns on him until after lunch and after we'd sampled the cookies and after Penelope was in Latisha's bed, taking a nap.

Sam had assured me over our cookies that the Dollar Store had definitely bought an eight-acre parcel of land on Springer Road. That was good news to me, not only because that meant they were out of the running for The Handy Home Helpers, but because it couldn't hurt the value of the Hillandale Trailer Park to have the area become commercialized.

We discussed the future possibilities for a while until I could no longer hold in my present concerns.

"I know I'm sounding unsympathetic, Sam," I said, faintly fearful that he would think the less of me for feeling used. "But the least Mildred could do—in fact, what any thoughtful person would do—would be to *ask* me to keep Penelope. And I would gladly do it, you know I would."

He nodded. "I know you would. But here's something you could do—why don't you take the situation in hand yourself? I mean, why don't you call her and tell her that we want to keep Penelope until she—Mildred, I mean—is feeling better? That way you won't feel used. It would be your decision, not something that you'd been roped into doing."

I thought about his suggestion, then I smiled. "And we'd get to keep Penelope a little longer, but on our terms. I think that's the answer." I reached over for his hand. "How did you get so wise?"

He clasped my hand and grinned. "Oh, I don't know. Just born that way, I guess."

A little later Sam brought down the boxes of Christmas decorations from the attic, and Lillian, Penelope, and I carried them on down to the living room. That tired me out so much that I announced we should wait for Latisha before beginning to open them.

"Besides," I said, "we need a tree before we strew everything all over the floor. Sam, you have a good eye for Christmas trees. Why don't you and Honey go pick one out for us?"

"Today?" he said, raising his eyebrows.

"Yes, it's as good a time as any. And why don't you see if Lloyd can go with you? You'll need help getting it off the car anyway, and the tree will probably need trimming, too."

"I still think it's a little early," he said, and if I didn't know that he wasn't the grumbling kind, I would've thought that was what he was doing. "We could end up with a few bare branches by the time it gets here."

"We'll water it," I said, determined to entrance Penelope with Christmas preparations even if the holiday had been a month away. "Just get a full, well-shaped one at least nine or ten feet tall."

"As early as it is, we may not find any trees anywhere, much less the perfect one. Well, Penelope," he said, taking her hand, "we may be on a fool's errand, but we'll have a good time anyway." So off the two of them went with Sam wondering whether to go first to Lowe's or to a garden center.

It wasn't all that early. Many people put up their trees weeks beforehand, but to my mind that wasn't the point. The point was to give that somber little girl something exciting to think about.

They had barely pulled out of the driveway when Lillian called me to the kitchen. I found her peering through the side window again.

"Come quick," she said, waving me over, "an' see what you think about this."

"What is it?" I started toward the window, then stopped with a sudden awareness of how inquisitive we had become, especially about the comings and goings next door. "Lillian, we have got to stop keeping tabs on the Allens. Do you realize how often we've been spying on them? Prying into what they're doing? It's really most unbecoming, and we'll get a reputation for being nosy neighbors before we know it."

"Yes'm, I know it, but you got to see this. Hurry, 'fore she goes inside."

She? Could it be *Tonya?* With an inward lurch and all concerns of nosiness suddenly gone, I hurried to Lillian's side to peer through the window toward Mildred's house. Just in time, I caught sight of the flip of a white skirt—and it being the dead of winter, too—before the door closed behind her.

Chapter 37

❧

"Was that *Tonya*?" I whispered, forgetting that Penelope wasn't around to hear me. "I mean," I said in a normal speaking voice, "was it Tonya?"

"Not 'less she's taken to wearing white stockin's," Lillian said.

"Well, they were quite the in-thing a while back, but I can't imagine Californians wearing anything out of fashion."

"No'm, or a little white hat on her head, either."

"What?" I turned to stare at Lillian. "White dress, stockings, and hat—that wasn't Tonya. Lillian, it was a *nurse*, and probably one with a bachelor's degree on top of her nursing degree." I sighed and left the window. "Leave it to Mildred to have the best of everything whether she needs it or not."

"I bet she's a nursemaid for Honey," Lillian said.

"And if I were a betting woman, I'd take you up on that. No, mark my words, that woman has been hired to take care of Mildred. And Grady Peeples is hired to take care of Horace, while Ida Lee takes care of the house. So where does that little girl fit in? Nowhere, and she's the one who really needs taking care of."

Well, it wasn't any of my business what Mildred did or whom she hired or why she hired them. Except in a way, it was, because I was one of those who were providing services. I declare, I didn't want to feel used, but when I analyzed my feelings, I realized that I was more aggrieved on Penelope's behalf than on my own. And that made me feel better.

While waiting for Sam and Penelope to get back with the tree, I went three times to the phone, and each time failed to pick it up and call Mildred. She should've called me, and if her excuse was that she was too ill, why then had she left the hospital?

The fact of the matter was that I was working myself up into a state of agitation again until I recalled Sam's advice. That gave me the impetus I needed, and I dialed Mildred's number, expecting Ida Lee to answer it.

Instead, it was Mildred herself. "Julia!" she said as if I'd been missing for a week. "I was hoping you'd call. How are you? When you didn't come see me this morning in the hospital, I was afraid you were sick. How is everybody?"

"Everybody, including your granddaughter, is fine," I said, more than slightly offended that she had put me on the defensive. "And I didn't come to the hospital this morning because I was busy doing what you'd asked me to do. But that's neither here nor there. How are you?"

"Oh, don't ask," she said with a deep sigh. "I'm not well at all, but I checked myself out of the hospital because they were doing nothing for me. But thank goodness I redid that room for Penelope so close to mine. It's perfect for having a registered nurse live in until I have the strength to make the trip to Duke next week."

Quickly taking the opening to do as Sam had advised, I said, "Then you must let us keep Penelope. There's really no need to move her to your house, then back here when you leave for Duke. It's easier for her just to stay."

There was a moment of silence while she considered my proposal. "Are you sure?" she asked somewhat hesitantly or perhaps hopefully. "I don't know how long they'll keep me at Duke. I don't want to take advantage, but it would really be a help to know that she's in good hands."

"Then consider it settled," I said firmly, knowing that I could no longer feel used since I'd done this to myself. Somewhat surprisingly, though, I felt quite good about it.

"Thank you, Julia," Mildred said. "You are a good friend, but I ask you, where is LuAnne? And Helen? To say nothing of Emma Sue? Not one soul has been to see me. Except you, of course, but you'd think friends would visit friends when they're in the hospital, wouldn't you?"

"Well, actually, I've not seen anybody for ages," I said, trying to excuse their absences. "But LuAnne works full time, and Helen has her hands full with Thurlow. And who knows what Emma Sue is up to—saving the world, probably. But maybe you weren't in the hospital long enough for the word to get around." I paused to think for a second, then asked, "Did you see Ernest Sitton while you were there? He was a patient on the same floor."

"Really? You know, I thought I saw him go past my door, but I wasn't sure who it was. What's wrong with him?"

"I don't know," I said. "He wasn't forthcoming when I saw him in the hall. In fact, he was a little tetchy on the subject."

"Oh, Julia, forgive me," Mildred said with a little groan. "Here's Inez with my sleep medication. I'll have to hang up, but do come over soon and meet my Florence Nightingale. She is the answer to a sick woman's prayer."

It was much too late in the day for a social call, especially with darkness falling so early, so I told her that I would see her the following day and bring Penelope with me. Besides, Sam had just driven in with a huge tree roped to the top of his car and both front and back seats filled with helpers.

I had to laugh because Sam was always thinking, and he'd

thought ahead enough to have gone by and picked up not only Lloyd but Mr. Pickens, as well, to help with the tree.

"Law," Lillian said as she saw the four of them get out of the tree-laden car, "we better start movin' furniture 'fore they bring that thing in."

Lloyd and Penelope came in to help us rearrange furniture in the living room so the tree could be put in the front window alcove. As always it was a pleasure to see Lloyd, except these days he seemed to have become more muscular and maybe an inch or two taller. He was growing up and, thank goodness, looking less and less like his father, Wesley Lloyd Springer. In fact, he had about him an air of easy competence and self-assurance, the lack of which Wesley Lloyd had covered with bluster. I could only credit Mr. Pickens with setting an example, although there were many of his former habits that I devoutly hoped Lloyd would never emulate.

Maybe, I thought as Lloyd took charge of clearing the way for the tree, proximity counted for more than genes in some cases.

Sam and Mr. Pickens unroped the tree from the top of the car and quickly trimmed the trunk to fit into the tree stand. In minutes, it was in front of the windows with the top barely grazing the ceiling. The two of them turned the tree a little this way, then a little of that, until Lillian and I decided which was the best side. Penelope watched wide-eyed as Lloyd crawled on his hands and knees to pour water in the stand and to get the tree skirt arranged around it.

"I hope you know," Mr. Pickens said, "that this means I'll have to put ours up any day now. Sam, you're setting a bad example."

Sam laughed. "Just call me when you're ready."

Lillian offered around the cookies she and Penelope had baked, giving Penelope credit for being a number-one cookie maker.

"She can bake cookies for me any time at all," Lloyd said, taking a second one. "These are good." Penelope edged toward Lillian, but didn't hide the smile that lit up her face.

With that, I decided to string the lights on the tree then and there and not wait until we could trim the whole tree. As Sam took Mr. Pickens and Lloyd home, Lillian and I, with Penelope's help, got out the several strings of lights and plugged them in to weed out the dead bulbs. After screwing in replacements, we strung out the lines to unsnarl them. I don't care how carefully we put them away when Christmas is over, they somehow get tangled up during the summer.

Penelope was entranced with the lights, especially as we wound the lines around the tree, then adjusted them to make sure that the bulbs were evenly placed. She gasped and clapped her hands when Lillian turned off the lamps in the living room so that the tree glowed in the dark.

It was always a magical moment for me, as well. I put my arm around the child's shoulders. "We'll hang the ornaments on it tomorrow morning," I said, "and I'm so glad that you're here to help."

I did something that Saturday morning that caused Lillian to roll her eyes and shake her head in anticipation of an impending disaster. But I didn't care. I was no longer obsessed with having everything just right—the doing had become more important than the outcome.

"Sam," I said as we finished the pancakes that Lillian had prepared, "thank you for skipping the Bluebird this morning and deigning to have breakfast with us." I glanced from Penelope to Latisha, then went on. "I should visit Mildred this morning, so I want to leave the tree decorating in your hands. You have two excellent helpers who will do the hanging while you sit back and point out the empty spots. Then, when they've hung ornaments as high as they can reach, you can take over and they'll point out the empty spots for you.

"And, oh my goodness," I said, "I almost forgot. You must put the tinsel around the tree first, Sam, and make sure the swags are evenly placed. And, Lillian, you're the overseer of them all. I expect to see a fully and beautifully decorated tree when I get back."

The little girls looked ready to begin, exchanging grins of anticipation, while Sam tried to look woebegone at being given a decorating job.

"Hey, everybody!" Lloyd sang out as he opened the kitchen door and came in. "Nobody's cooking at my house so I decided to come over."

My heart lifted as it always did when Lloyd came over and I smiled at him. "Did you walk in this cold weather?" I asked, knowing that he wasn't yet old enough to drive alone.

"No'm, rode my bike," he said, grinning. "When you're hungry enough, the cold doesn't matter."

"Lloyd!" Latisha yelled. "You wanta help us? We're the tree decorators. You can help if you want to."

Lillian said, "Set on down at the table, honey. I'll have you a stack of pancakes in two minutes."

"I can always count on you, Miss Lillian." Lloyd divested himself of his heavy coat and knit cap and sat down beside Penelope. Although she had not added words of welcome, she glowed when he chose to sit beside her. He just naturally seemed to recognize her need to feel special, especially to a big boy.

When they'd finished eating, they got up and went en masse and noisily to the living room. I noticed that Lloyd took Penelope's hand as she skipped to keep up with him. Smiling, I took my coat from the pantry to make my call on Mildred.

"Miss Julia," Lillian said, nodding toward the sound of retreating footsteps, "I hope you know what you're doin'. No tellin' what that tree gonna look like."

"I'm not a bit worried," I said, pulling on my coat. "In fact, I don't care if it's not even close to perfect. It'll be beautiful to them—well, maybe not to Sam because he has a good eye—but he knows, as you and I do, what's important."

Chapter 38

❧

Telling myself that I would not make this an everyday habit, I trudged across the lawn to Mildred's front porch and rang the doorbell. In fact, after having a few second thoughts about leaving the tree trimming in untried hands, I had almost decided not to make a visit this morning at all.

"But just this once," I'd said to Lillian. "She'll expect me since she's just home from the hospital—on her own orders, I might add."

"Well, take these to her," Lillian said, handing me a small package of cookies. "That's all that's left from what Honey made yesterday."

"Hm-m, yes. Good thinking, Lillian, maybe they'll remind her that she has a granddaughter."

Ida Lee welcomed me in and walked with me up the stairs to the bedroom where Mildred was ensconced in bed, a breakfast tray on a nearby table.

"Julia!" Mildred cried when Ida Lee announced me. "I'm so glad you've come. You can't imagine how boring it is to lie abed all day with no visitors. Inez," she said, turning to the tall, skinny, uniformed woman by the bedside, "take a break while I visit with my friend. This is Mrs. Murdoch. Julia, this is Inez Freeman, who's taking such good care of me."

The nurse and I exchanged nods on her way out of the room, while I wondered at the sour expression on her face. It wasn't the tender, loving, and caring look that I had expected after hearing Mildred's enthusiastic endorsement of her. In fact, her face was gaunt, careworn, and looked tired to the bone, although she strode out of the room with alacrity.

"Grady Peeples recommended her," Mildred said as if that explained everything, and perhaps it did.

It was a brief and would've been a pleasant visit if I had enjoyed the litany of aches and pains and worries that Mildred had about her health. I gave her the package of Penelope's cookies, which were put aside with Mildred commenting that her diet did not include empty calories.

"How is Horace doing?" I asked in an attempt to move away from discussing the odds of her having another attack. "I expect he's glad to have you home."

"He doesn't know I've been away, much less in the hospital. But I'll tell you, Julia, he is worrying me to death. Do you know what he's doing now? He's getting up in the middle of the night, dressing himself, then trying to get out of the house. Grady found him last night going around trying every door. The poor man hardly got a wink of sleep."

"Oh, that's too bad," I said, thinking that Horace needed the sleep. "But maybe he'll nap during the day."

"How can he? He has to watch Horace like a hawk or he'll be out and gone before we know it." Mildred frowned, smoothed out the sheet, and went on. "I talked with one of the nurses at the hospital who's had experience with senile patients. She called what he's doing *exit-seeking* and said it was common to a phase of Alzheimer's disease. She said these patients have an urgent need to go out to get something done. It can be anything that's weighing on their minds—the need to get to work on time or to pick up children from school or to meet an appointment, things like that." Mildred sighed heavily. "The only thing is, Horace has never had an urgent need to do *anything*, so where it's coming from now, I'm sure I don't know."

Exit-seeking? I'd never heard the phrase before, but it reminded me to seek my own exit and get home to see how our Christmas tree looked.

Not very evenly trimmed, if you want to know the truth. It was heavily laden with ornaments up to about four feet, but sparsely decorated above that. Sam had built a fire in the fireplace, and he sat beside it smiling at the job he'd overseen. "I hung those two up near the top," he said.

I laughed and congratulated him on the good job he'd done. "Where's Lloyd? In fact, where's everybody?"

"Lloyd took the little girls to play with the twins. He'll have them back in a little while, and Lillian is upstairs doing whatever she does."

I sat down in the wing chair across from him, then commended him on the fire. "There's nothing like a wood fire, is there? The gas one in the library is certainly more convenient and less work, but I love a real one. Is that apple wood you're burning?"

He nodded. "Yes, I got us a cord of it when they cleared an old orchard out beyond Edneyville. So they can build some apartment houses, I think, which is a shame even if it's called progress."

"Anything is called progress if there're people against it. It's supposed to make us feel bad."

He smiled. "So how's Mildred doing?"

"She's fine, but not to hear her tell it. But it's Horace who concerns me." And I went on to tell of his latest attempt to leave the house. "Apparently the need to get outside and go somewhere is quite common. They just don't know how to find what they're looking for when they get out."

I looked up as Lillian appeared in the doorway. "Miss Julia, Miss Etta Mae wants you to call her. She called right after you left."

"Maybe," I said, my heart lifting as I rose from the chair, "she's had a response from Lurline Corn. I'll call her from the library, but stay close, Sam, if you will."

"Etta Mae? It's Julia Murdoch," I said when she answered. "Have you heard anything?"

"Hey, Miss Julia. Yes, but it's the strangest thing. Mr. Blair said it's real unusual, but he recommends that we go along."

"Go along with what?"

"Well, you know we submitted another offer, going up a good bit more than her coming down only a thousand dollars, so now she wants more time."

"Why?" I asked. "Twenty-four hours is what she gave us when she responded to our offer. What more does she want?"

"She wants the whole weekend—today and tomorrow until Monday morning. She claims that a personal matter has come up that prevents her from giving our offer the consideration it deserves—that's what she wrote to Mr. Blair."

"Well, for goodness' sakes," I said. "She may be hoping for more time to hear from Mr. Sitton, but we might as well give it to her. You know her better than I do, Etta Mae, what do you think is going on?"

"I don't know," Etta Mae said in a troubled tone. "She didn't come in to work yesterday, but that's not real unusual. Just called me to make sure everybody knew what to do." Etta Mae paused, then went on. "I've a good mind to call her and see if everything's okay, but I'm kinda scared to. I'm not supposed to know she's had an offer, so how would I know she needs more time to consider it?"

"That's right. You'll give yourself away unless you have a real good reason to call her on a Saturday."

"Well-l," Etta Mae said, drawing it out with a tinge of excitement underneath. "I might have one. Guess who's back in town?"

"Who?"

"Bobby Lee Moser, and Lurline would expect me to tell her about it."

Oh, my word, I thought with a sinking feeling. If I wasn't careful, I could find myself in Lawyer Sitton's situation—ready to buy a home care business but having no one to manage it.

"Etta Mae," I said, realizing that I had no right to interfere in her personal life, but feeling an urgent need to issue a warning. "Etta Mae, are you in danger of taking your eyes off the prize? Because if you are, I need to know."

"Oh, no," she quickly said. "No, I'm not. Don't worry about that. I know what Bobby Lee is like, and I know I have to think of my future. It's just, well, he's real exciting."

I heard the little gasp in her voice, so her words did not reassure me. "He's been away a good while, hasn't he? Is he just visiting now?"

"No, he's back for good because the sheriff wants him to run for sheriff next year when he retires. See, Miss Julia, Bobby Lee's been working for the State Bureau of Investigation down in Raleigh, so he has a real good résumé and the sheriff wants to leave his office in good hands."

"Well, that speaks well for both of them," I said, but it did not relieve my anxiety that Etta Mae would lose her head again and turn up married to another footloose man. That wouldn't prevent her from taking the helm of The Handy Home Helpers, but it could certainly divide her attention. "But," I went on, "back to our original question. Call Lurline and tell her about this Bobby Lee person if you would ordinarily do so. Just don't slip up and let on that you know she's considering an offer."

"Oh, I wouldn't do that. But I don't know, Miss Julia, I might better not call her. She knows me so well that she might suspect something. And she's never liked Bobby Lee, anyway. She might wonder why I'd call to tell her he's back."

"Then let's let her alone to consider our offer in peace. We'll know the answer Monday morning, and it sounds as if you have enough to keep you occupied over the weekend anyway."

"Yeah," she said, blowing out her breath, "I sure do. Bobby Lee's taking me to the Outback Steakhouse tonight."

Chapter 39

"If it's not one thing," I said, sighing heavily as I returned to my chair across from Sam, "it's two more. I've always been able to count on Etta Mae's basic good sense and her tenacity when something has to be done. But apparently that assessment was made during the times that Bobby Lee Moser was out of town."

"What's he got to do with it?"

"Everything, maybe. Do you know him?"

"Know *of* him," Sam said. "A good man from what I hear. Well-trained, in fact he may be the best-trained officer the county's ever had. If he's back on the force here, I'm glad to hear it."

"Well, you'll have a chance to show your approval next year. Etta Mae says he's going to run for sheriff."

Sam's eyebrows went up. "Ah, so the old man plans to retire? That's good news. But how does Etta Mae know about it?"

"Because Bobby Lee Moser is the one she's lost her head over time and time again and probably this time as well."

"Oh, yes," Sam said, "I seem to remember that they were an item a few years ago. They were dating a good long while, weren't they?"

"Well, yes, if dating is what you call it."

Sam laughed. "Well," he said, "I'm in polite company. But Moser shouldn't affect your business plans."

"Maybe not, but it worries me. Etta Mae seems quite vulnerable to a handsome man's attention. I need her to stay focused, because now Lurline Corn has asked for extra time to consider our offer. She'll let us know her decision Monday morning."

"Hm-m," Sam said, "that sounds as if she's thinking of accepting."

"That's what I'm hoping, but tell me this. What will I do with a home care service if the new owner can't get her head out of the clouds long enough to take charge of it?"

"I don't think you have to worry about that. Etta Mae will come through for you."

"I hope so," I said, but I wasn't totally convinced. "I just wish Bobby Lee Moser had stayed where he was, at least until Etta Mae had settled in. There's no telling what the two of them will be up to now."

"Oh," Sam said with a wry smile, "I expect we could guess."

Well, yes, I could guess, and it filled my head with worries all weekend. In fact, it took up so much of my time that I didn't visit Mildred, and I didn't call her. It was all I could do to put those concerns aside for just the hour and ten minutes of the Sunday-morning services.

Actually, though, I could've better used the time to worry than to listen to the new pastor tell us that faith without works is dead. I couldn't disagree with that since it was Scriptural, but I could disagree with his definition of works. According to him they were made up of giving until it hurt to the church, to foreign missions, to the homeless, to the jobless, and to every professional nonprofit agency with its doors open and its hands out. And you don't even have to think about it. Most of them will tell you exactly how much they've figured you can afford to give—just check a box and write your check. Or to make it even easier, put it on your credit card.

Not one word came from the pulpit about the real work of every Christian, which is to save souls by way of the Good News.

Ah, well, in my small way, I was doing what I could, which was to have Penelope seated beside me in the pew and occupied with a New Testament coloring book.

But as Monday morning drew near, I found myself getting more and more excited by the thought of Lurline Corn actually committing herself to selling for our most recently quoted price. What a coup that would be! Etta Mae would be Chief Executive Officer of her own business and set for life regardless of who moved back to town and who didn't. I talked myself into believing that Bobby Lee Moser would be downgraded to at least second place on her list of concerns if Lurline would just sign that Offer to Purchase The Handy Home Helpers.

It was five of twelve, after I'd waited impatiently all Monday morning, before Etta Mae called to tell me what Lurline Corn had done.

"Mr. Blair didn't hear from her until eleven thirty!" Etta Mae reported, the outrage obvious in her voice. "I had about decided she was just going to ignore us, and on top of that, she didn't accept our offer! What're we going to *do*?"

"Hold on, Etta Mae," I said, although my hopeful expectations were fast deflating. "Did she just reject our offer or did she send a counter?"

"Oh, she sent another one," Etta Mae said as if it were of no account. She told me what it was, and I did a fast computation in my head. "At least," Etta Mae went on, "she's come down more than the thousand she came down the first time."

"Yes, and it's sizable enough to have possibilities. Give me a few minutes, Etta Mae, to do some figuring. I'll call you back within the hour." Actually, I wanted to check my figuring with Sam before making another offer.

"Well, wait, Miss Julia, there's something else. I think I know why Lurline needed the weekend to think. She didn't come in to work this morning, so I'm holding down the fort, which always upsets the other girls. They have to add my patients to their lists, so they were about half mad about the added work and it being a Monday morning, too. Anyway, they were all talking about Bug— you know, Lurline's worthless nephew. Well, he went on such a bender over the weekend that Lurline had to call 9-1-1 because he took her car and drove it through a cornfield and ended up nosedown in a drainage ditch because, he said, he was changing radio stations and missed the turn-off. And the cops came, too, and they arrested him even though Lurline wouldn't swear out a warrant on him even though he'd ruined her car. But they say he went after a deputy with a tire iron, so they didn't need a warrant. They put him in jail, and everybody in Delmont's talking about it."

I'm sorry to report that my heart gave a leap of renewed hope at that news. "Oh, my goodness, Etta Mae, you know what that might mean, don't you?"

"She'll have to go his bail?"

"No. I mean, yes, probably, but I'm thinking of something else. She may really want to sell now, or even *need* to sell. You see?"

There was a moment's pause, then Etta Mae got it. "Oh, man, yes! If there's one thing Lurline hates more than anything, it's being gossiped about. She's real close about her private life, but her reputation's going down the drain when word gets around that her nephew is even goofier than we thought and, believe me, it'll get around. I mean everybody already knows it anyway, but it'll just kill her that it's out in public now. She'll be done in with people whispering that she's not as high-toned as she makes out she is. I kinda feel sorry for her, because she really tries to keep up appearances."

Well, don't we all? But I let that alone, and said instead, "I'm sorry for her troubles, too, but it might play right into our hands. We'll just do what we would've done anyway, which is to make another counteroffer. I'll call you back within the hour."

Clicking off the phone, I turned toward the library and called, "Sam?"

"We ought to strike while the iron is hot," I said, leaning over to look at the figures on Sam's legal pad. "I don't want to take advantage of Lurline's personal problems, but I guess that's what we're doing. But then again, we were already in negotiations before that boy ended up in jail, so it would be strange if we suddenly backed off, wouldn't it?"

"Probably," Sam said, nodding. "If Ms. Corn is as concerned about appearances as Etta Mae says, she might assume her unknown bidder had heard the gossip and didn't want to do business with her." Then he added, "Having kinfolk in jail wouldn't deter most bidders, though. I think you should go ahead with whatever you would've done anyway."

"Well, I had halfway planned to make one last offer this morning, and if she turned it down, I was going to tell Etta Mae that we were through. I just don't want to appear to be taking advantage."

"You won't." He pointed at the figure we had been discussing. "This is a good, reasonable offer, and she'd be smart to accept it whether her nephew is in or out of jail."

"Good, I'm glad you agree. But I'd better be ready to deal with Etta Mae's disappointment if Lurline holds out for more." I leaned over and tapped the last figure on the page. "This offer, I'll have to tell her, will be our best and final."

Chapter 40

Steeling myself to stand firm in spite of an urge to meet Lurline's price regardless of the consequences, I stiffened my intent to protect Etta Mae from a loan she could not repay. So, to prepare her for disappointment if Lurline turned us down, I made sure that she understood we were making our final offer.

"It doesn't make sense to go any higher," I told her on our next phone call. "You'd be strapped to make the loan payments, and I told you that I wouldn't let you go beyond what the business will support. Of course," I went on, adding a little encouragement, "if you expanded the business, it would, but we can't count on that at this point. I want you to enjoy being the owner, not constantly worrying about making ends meet. And another thing, if this doesn't pan out, we'll look around for something else. In other words, Etta Mae, it will work out one way or the other."

A lot of platitudes, I knew, but facing facts is when comforting platitudes are needed.

"I appreciate that, Miss Julia," Etta Mae said, "I really do. But when I look at what Lurline wanted for the business in the first place and compare it to our final offer, there's still an awful big difference."

"Yes, but she had it overpriced to begin with, and she has to realize that we're the only interested party she has. It may be that she'll have to sell to us or to nobody. With the Dollar Store out of the picture, it's down to take-it-or-leave-it time for her. Well, wait," I said as a certain image loomed in my mind. "Have you heard anything more about Ernest Sitton? Has he ever made an offer?"

"As far as I know, he hasn't. In fact, I haven't heard anything at all about him. You think he's still in the hospital?"

"That's a good question," I said. "I'll call the hospital and see if he's been discharged. Not that it matters to us where he is, unless he suddenly jumps into the bidding. Just be prepared, Etta Mae, neither you nor I can afford to go any higher than the bid we're about to make."

"Do we tell Lurline that? You know, so she'll know we won't make a better one?"

"Well, *we* won't tell her anything, but Mr. Blair will submit it as our best and final. She'll know from that."

"Oh-h, Lord," Etta Mae moaned. "My stomach is all torn up with not knowing one way or the other. I get so excited thinking of actually owning the business, but then I have to come back to earth since I know how crazy that is. And," she said, swallowing hard, "worrying myself sick about Lurline finding out about me and firing me. One good thing, though, is Bobby Lee being back in town. He kinda takes my mind off all the worrying for a little while at least."

I expect he does, I thought.

"One other thing, Etta Mae," I said, ignoring Bobby Lee's ability to soothe her concerns, "let's give Lurline a little time to worry, too. Hold off on getting back to Mr. Blair with our best and final until a full twenty-four hours are up tomorrow. She'll be busy getting Bug what's-his-name out of jail today anyway, so it won't hurt for her to have a little nagging worry about what we'll do. I mean," I hurriedly went on, "she doesn't know it's us, but let's let her worry about what her only bidder will do."

Etta Mae was silent for a minute, then she said, "That seems kinda mean."

"Well, it kinda is, but on the other hand, she'll be so busy with lawyers, judges, and bail bondsmen today that she might reject our offer out of hand. Then regret it later on. I'm just saying that she doesn't need to make a decision while so much else is going on." I stopped, then added, "We're really doing her a favor."

"Well, okay, I guess. Should I let Mr. Blair know? I mean, tell him it's our best and final?"

"Yes, go ahead and tell him that you're *considering* your last offer and will let him know tomorrow what it is. But in the meantime, do not under any circumstances tell anybody what our final offer will be, and I mean not even Mr. Blair." I stopped, started to add Bobby Lee Moser, then thought better of it. "The reason is that I could change my mind between now and tomorrow. Just let me know right away if you hear anything from or about Lurline or Mr. Sitton."

"Miss Julia," Lillian said as I went into the kitchen, "Mr. Horace is out walking around if you want to look out the window at him."

I didn't think twice about appearing nosy, just went to the window and peered out. "He looks quite normal, doesn't he? A little wobbly, but surely he's not out by himself. Is Mr. Peeples watching him?"

"Yes'm, I seen him a little while ago, but what I'm wonderin' is why don't we see if Honey wants to walk around with her granddaddy?"

"What a good idea, Lillian. She needs some connection to her so-called family even if her grandmother doesn't give her a thought."

Penelope, assenting in her quiet way to any suggestion, left the showing of cartoons on television and let me bundle her up in a parka, scarf, hat, and mittens.

"It's a pretty day," I said, "but cold, so I don't want you to stay out too long. I'll walk you over there and keep an eye on you from here. But come on back in any time you want to."

After putting on my own coat, I took her hand and we walked to and through the hedge and waited until Horace rounded the corner of the house.

"I'll let Mr. Peeples know you're out here, too. And, Honey, hold your grandfather's hand while you walk. I want the two of you to stay together."

She nodded and gave a little skip, while I wondered if sneakers kept her feet warm enough. Fur-lined boots, I thought, making a mental note to tell Mildred what the child needed. And if, I continued to think, Mildred forgets, I'll get them for her myself.

As Horace came shuffling into full view, Penelope dropped my hand and ran to him. I stopped and watched as she took his hand and he, startled at first, smiled down at her. Mr. Peeples edged around the corner, saw the child, then me where I waited at the edge of the yard. After exchanging a few nods and waves with Horace's keeper, I turned to go back inside. As for being dressed for the weather, I wasn't, so I hurriedly regained the warm kitchen.

"That wind is brisk," I said to Lillian as I shivered from the cold. "And clouds are rolling in from the west. We're likely in for something pretty soon, so Penelope shouldn't stay out too long. Right now, though, I'm going to sit right here," I said as I took a chair beside the window, "and make sure they come back around when they're supposed to."

The odd couple made two more circuits while Lillian and I discussed how preparations were going for our Christmas dinner party. Then just as I'd told her we might need another place setting for a certain recently returned deputy sheriff, I saw Mr. Peeples motion to Penelope that Horace had to go inside. I watched the child run across Mildred's lawn to the hedge, so I went to the back door to welcome her back. She came inside with a rush of icy air, her face red from the cold.

"Did you have a good time?" I asked, helping to remove her coat.

She nodded. "We looked for his car."

Oh, for goodness' sakes, I thought, he's still obsessed with that car. "Well," I said, "the doctor says he shouldn't be driving, but I think he forgets how sick he's been. As people get older, you know, their memories aren't quite as good as they once were."

She nodded again. Then, frowning, she said, "His hair's not white, so he's not old."

I laughed. "Yes, that's what he told me. But it was very good of you to keep him company for a while. I'm sure he enjoyed it. Now," I said, going to the pantry to hang up her coat, "I think Lillian has some hot cocoa to warm you up."

As Lillian joined us at the kitchen table with three steaming mugs, I looked over my list of things to do before Christmas. Most of the gifts I'd ordered had come in, so they needed to be wrapped and labeled. After checking that off my list, I looked over the names of those who had accepted our invitations.

"It looks as if most everybody we've invited is coming for dinner," I said. "But don't worry about breakfast that morning, Lillian. Hazel Marie is having us over so we can see what Santa brought the children."

"That's good," Lillian said, nodding her approval. "That way you and Mr. Sam will be out of the way while we get everything ready. Honey," she said, turning to her, "what you want Santy Claus to bring you?"

"A baby doll and some color crayons," Penelope said in her soft voice.

One of Lillian's eyebrows cocked up as she looked at me. "Well, I bet a baby doll and some color crayons is already on his list, don't you, Miss Julia?"

"I wouldn't be a bit surprised," I said, making a mental note of her requests, which I would add to a few other items. "And, you know," I went on as a new thought sprang up, "we might need to go on a shopping trip ourselves. Be thinking, Honey, what you'd like to give your grandmother and grandfather for Christmas. We'll go shopping, then have fun wrapping presents and putting them under the tree."

Her dark eyes lit up. "I know what I want to give him. He told me what he wants."

"Oh? And what does he want?"

"A big ring to keep his car keys on. He said he used to have one, but he can't find it, and he said his pocket's empty without it."

"Well," I said, leaning back. "Well, that should be easy to find." But even as I agreed to help her find a key ring, I was thinking hard about what kind of key could go on it, not only to fill his pocket, but to keep it from being used.

Lillian must've been thinking the same thing for her eyes rolled back in her head. She didn't say anything, just got up and went back to emptying the grocery bags on the counter.

Pulling out a small bottle of yellow liquid, she said, "Look here, Honey, I bought you some Johnson's no-tears baby shampoo. Now we can wash your hair without it hurtin' your eyes, an' I think we ought to do that right now so it'll get dry before nap time."

Penelope didn't seem too thrilled at the prospect, but as usual she made no objection.

"Use the hair dryer in my bathroom," I said, lifting a strand of Penelope's long, straight hair. "Her hair is so thick it'll take forever to dry. You know," I went on as I turned her face toward me, "wouldn't it look good with bangs?"

"No'm," Lillian said, shaking her head, "don't go cuttin' no bangs. Mamas don't like somebody else cuttin' hair."

"Well, you're right, of course, and I wouldn't do it without permission. But I'm just saying. Honey," I said to her, "you have beautiful hair and it looks good any way you want to wear it."

She smiled and said, "I like bangs."

As the two of them went upstairs to the shower, I headed for the living room to cogitate on our next move in a real estate transaction.

Chapter 41

❧

"*Miss Julia!*" Etta Mae screeched almost before I could say hello when the phone rang later that afternoon. "You won't believe what's happened! I'm so mad or scared or something I don't know what to do. Hold on, I've got to get off the road."

I waited, holding tightly to the phone, as she parked the car.

"Now," she said, her breath rasping as she spoke into the phone again. "I'm parked, and I really shouldn't be driving at all the way I feel right now."

"Take a deep breath, Etta Mae, and tell me what happened."

"Okay. Well, I finished my schedule early today and went back to the office to check out. Lurline makes us keep track of our hours to make sure we put in forty for the week. And, well, anyway, I thought she'd be busy getting Bug out of jail, but she was in the office—*singing*! Can you believe that?"

"Singing?"

"Yes, just blaring out 'This Little Light of Mine' like she didn't have a care in the world. She even called me in to tell me her good news, and believe me it wasn't about her jailbird nephew. Well," she went on with a rasping breath, "I guess some of it was. She got Bug out of jail, and now she's thinking of suing the deputies for false arrest. But that wasn't why she was on top of the world. Miss Julia, she got an Offer to Purchase from Mr. Sitton!"

"Oh, no," I said, with a sinking feeling. "Well, I guess that means he's back on his feet and ready to do business. Did she give you any idea of how much he offered?"

"No, but I wanted to ask her so bad it was like needing to go to the bathroom and not going. She went on to tell me that she now has two people who want the business, and she intends to come out of it smelling like a rose. What're we going to *do*, Miss Julia?"

Well, there wasn't anything we could do except let it play out however it was going to. My first order of business, though, was to reassure Etta Mae and calm her down to the point of accepting whatever happened.

"There's not much we can do, Etta Mae," I said, sounding much calmer than I was feeling. "Here's the thing: we haven't yet submitted our final offer, which I'm still convinced is the best we can safely do. If we go any higher, you'll be in trouble before you even start and we don't want that. It's very likely that Mr. Sitton has submitted a lowball offer, especially if he doesn't know about us. Of course, she'll tell him that somebody else is interested, and she'll let him know exactly what we're offering so he can top it."

"Can she do that? I mean, is it legal?"

"I'm afraid so. For her to do it, I mean. The realtors involved can't do it, but she can."

As Etta Mae considered that, I took a deep breath and said, "I say that we proceed just as we'd planned and go ahead with our best and final. What I'm hoping is that Mr. Sitton's offer is a lot lower than ours—it's his first, so likely it is. That will put her on the spot, because we'll have a short time limit on ours in which she'll have to accept or decline. And if she declines, hoping that Mr. Sitton will go higher, she'll have lost us for good because her realtor will tell her that final means final. And with us out of the picture, Ernest Sitton can sit on his offer because it'll be the only one she has. All we can hope for at this point is that she'll figure that a bird in the hand is better than two in the bush."

There was a long silence on the line as Etta Mae processed either our plan or the meaning of an old saying. But she finally accepted the fact that all we could do was wait and see what Lurline would do.

After hanging up, I sat down to do some processing of my own. There is such a thing as outsmarting your own self, and I certainly did not want to do that. The last thing I wanted was to get into a bidding war with Mr. Sitton in which Lurline Corn edged the two of us up by a few dollars on each offer. No, the best thing to do was to make our best and final, then make sure she knew we'd stick to it regardless of what Ernest Sitton did.

So with pen and paper in hand, I refigured the number of years and the amount of monthly loan payments that Etta Mae would take on, *if* our final offer was accepted. It still looked do-able to me, so I figured how it would look if I raised our best and final up by a few more thousand dollars.

No, I told myself firmly. Better to stick with the amount that both Sam and I had agreed on. It was a fair offer, all things considered, and one that Etta Mae could repay in the time allowed even without expanding the business.

I knew that I had to keep my eyes on the purpose with which I'd started, and that was to ensure a safe future for Etta Mae. If I allowed myself to get into competitive bidding, I would quickly defeat that purpose.

Leaning my head back against the chair, I thought that if Lurline would just accept our offer and stop trying to make a killing, things would work out just as I'd planned. You would think, however, that by now I would've learned that most people don't listen to me regardless of how often I'm proven right.

But, something suddenly occurred to me as I sat straight up with a surge of hope. If she turned us down there was still another way. I could set Etta Mae up in a competitive business. Over the past few years, Abbot County had gradually become a haven for retirees from the long-winter states, and the local population had become top heavy with golden-agers. Home care services were set to become a premium type of business, and there was no one better prepared for such a start-up business than Etta Mae Wiggins.

I came to my feet with renewed purpose, thinking, So there, Lurline Corn, do your worst!

With a great relief of anxiety, I saw that whatever Lurline did, Etta Mae could still have her own business, and who was to say that one way of accomplishing that goal was better than the other?

The day had begun to darken after lunch as clouds thickened overhead, so we went around switching on lamps to relieve the dreariness. After wrapping a few more gifts to go under the tree, I called The Flower Basket and ordered a Christmas centerpiece for the dining room table. Fresh greenery, I thought, and made a note to stop at a roadside stand and buy some garlands for the mantels.

Then, feeling on top of my list of things to do, I sat on the sofa in the library with Penelope on a stool in front of me while I brushed her clean, damp hair. It really was beautiful, so dark and thick, and it gave me a comforting feeling to be the one to brush it dry.

Parting it into three strands, I tried my hand at one long plait, pleased that I still remembered how to do it.

"Do you like it like this?" I asked.

Penelope yawned as she felt it with her hand, then nodded.

"Then I'll find a rubber band and a ribbon to tie it off with, but right now we'll take it down so you can nap better."

We got up as Lillian came in with the nap blanket and a pillow. Penelope slipped off her sneakers and crawled onto the sofa. Lillian brought in the small kitchen radio and tuned it to an FM station softly playing Christmas carols, while I lowered the gas fire and turned off the lamps. Then she and I slipped out of the room—Lillian going to the kitchen and I to the living room.

Taking with me a yellow legal pad and a pen to make a few notes, I wished for an open fire in the fireplace. But having one would've meant going outside to the woodpile, so I decided to turn the Christmas tree lights on instead.

Smiling at the haphazardly decorated tree, I moved one ornament to a bare space. I figured that if I rearranged just one ornament every now and then, the children wouldn't notice and by Christmas Day, the tree would be quite evenly decorated.

Stretching out with my feet on an ottoman, I caught the first wisp of cinnamon and cloves from the spiced tea brewing in the kitchen. It smelled like, well, like Christmas. Barely hearing the music from the library and the occasional soft clatter of pans in the kitchen, I put my head back and drifted off.

The relief of having a backup plan for Etta Mae's future didn't last very long. After discussing the pros and cons of starting a new business with Sam that evening, I was wound up so tight I could hardly sit still. He had pointed out the many pitfalls we would face if we started from scratch, most of which I had not only not considered but hadn't even known of. It seemed to me that whatever happened, I was going to end up disappointing Etta Mae.

Maybe I should've never brought up the possibility to her, but if Ernest Sitton had stayed in the hospital only a few more days we would have had time to wrap things up. But he'd been discharged with obviously no lingering consequences from his hospital stay since he'd immediately jumped into the bidding. Even though I was fairly well convinced that he'd made a low offer, any offer at all would show Lurline that she had more than one fish on her line. And she would play us for all she was worth.

As bedtime approached, the house began to get colder and, as we undressed for bed, Sam remarked that we should consider replacing our old windows with new double-paned ones.

I had no response to that. My head was too full of other worries, but I said, "You'll be warm enough tonight. I'm wearing a pair of socks."

"Well, thank goodness for that," he said, and I had to laugh since I was known for letting my cold feet creep closer and closer to his warm ones.

I didn't think I could turn off all the possibilities and questions and problems running around in my mind, but I fell asleep fairly quickly. But then, sometime in the middle of the night I came wide awake, staring up into the dark of the room. Etta Mae, Lurline Corn, Bobby Lee Moser, Mildred, Penelope, and Ernest Sitton were streaming one after the other along the back roads of my mind and it was all I could do to lie still and not disturb Sam.

What if *this* happened? I thought. Or maybe *that*? Or what if my entire idea of letting Etta Mae borrow more money than she'd ever dreamed of had been foolish to begin with? What if she indebted herself, then the business fell apart from some unforeseen catastrophe? On the other hand, what if we dropped out in favor of Mr. Sitton and the business took off on an unsuspected trajectory so that a national home care service bought him out to the tune of several million dollars? Which could've been Etta Mae's if I hadn't been too squeamish to let her get so far in debt.

Finally, I slipped out of bed, unable to lie still any longer. I put on my thick quilted bathrobe and the lined hightop bedroom shoes, and tiptoed out into the hall. Looking in on Penelope, I made sure that she was warm and sleeping, then went downstairs in the dark. Streetlights lit up the familiar rooms, so I went straight to the kitchen without disturbing those who were able to sleep.

Closing the door behind me when I got to the kitchen, I felt for the light switch, then drew back my hand. Light from the street didn't reach the kitchen, but Mildred's accent landscape lighting did. Small path lights and foundation lights and lights around flower beds gave the kitchen a pleasant glow—not too glaring and not too dark. So, instead of turning on lights and plugging in the coffeepot, I made my way to the table and sat by the window, hoping that I'd soon be tired enough to go back to bed.

The clock on the stove showed two twenty in the a.m., still much too early to start a day, so I briefly considered going back upstairs for my book of devotions. It's an unfortunate fact that serious reading soon brings on a haze of sleepiness.

But I just continued to sit, resting and clearing my mind, and lazily glancing out the window across the hedge and through the leafless Bradford pear trees that lined the boundary of my yard and Mildred's.

Suddenly drawn by something on the side of Mildred's house, I frowned and strained to see what it was. Then I stood up and pressed my face to the cold glass. What was that? Squinching up my eyes and wishing for a telescope, I peered long and hard at what looked like a huge white spider suspended on the vine-covered trellis on the side of Mildred's house, an open window above it. Frowning, I thought, That's not right, and recalled the time Horace had climbed the trellis outside that very same window, trying to sneak in, and also recalled the skeet-shooting shotgun that Mildred had fired, thinking that someone was breaking and entering.

Was somebody breaking in now?

Oh, my word, I gasped, electrified by the realization that no one was breaking *in*. It was Horace, breaking *out*! And breaking out in a state of undress that would get him arrested in a New York minute.

Flapping my hands and jittering around the kitchen, not knowing what to do first, I started toward the stairs to wake Sam.

Then stopped. Horace would be down and gone before Sam could get up and get over there. Call Mildred? How long would it take to rouse her from a medicated sleep? Too long. Ida Lee? She was on the other side of the house. 9-1-1? They were fast, but Horace, with his head start, was faster.

I grabbed my cell phone from the charger and flew out the back door, scrambled through the hedge, and bounded up the incline of Mildred's lawn to the foot of the trellis. The closer I got, the higher up he seemed. High ceilings make for elegant rooms but a long way down from a second-floor window.

Chapter 42

❧

Looking up at the soles of Horace's bare feet, some ten feet above me where he clung like Spider-Man to the vine-covered trellis, I yelled, "Horace, what are you doing? Come down from . . . . I mean go back up! Go up to the window! You're going to freeze to death."

"Help," he moaned, and stayed where he was.

"I can't reach you. You have to crawl back up. Do it, Horace, it's just a couple of feet. Just climb straight up to the window."

"I can't," Horace mumbled. "I'm stuck." Then louder, he said, "I can't hold on!"

"Don't fall!" I yelled. "Hold on!" Thinking that if I climbed a couple of feet toward him he'd feel safer, I reached up to grasp the trellis and drew back a badly scratched hand. I'd forgotten that Mildred had replaced the wisteria vine that had once flourished on the trellis with a beautifully espaliered but treacherous pyracantha with glossy leaves and orange berries and long, sharp thorns.

So when Horace said he was stuck, he meant it. With trembling hands, I searched for Mildred's number on the bright face on my phone, finally found it, misdialed it the first time, but finally heard her phone ring. And ring and ring.

"Hold on, Horace," I called. "I'm getting some help. Just hold on. Don't turn loose."

"Help," he said.

"I'm trying, I'm trying," I mumbled, urging Mildred to wake up and answer.

Finally, she did, saying, "What?" in a sleep-befuddled voice.

"Mildred! It's Julia. Wake up! Are you awake? Horace is out here hanging on your pyracantha vine, and—"

"What?"

So I repeated it all over again. "Hurry, Mildred, I don't know how long he can hold on, and I can't reach him."

"Julia? Where are you?"

"*In your yard!* Your side yard under Horace's window. Let me in and I'll help you get him in."

A second of silence ensued, then Mildred took hold, and when Mildred takes hold, things begin to happen. "Hang up," she commanded. "Go around to the front. I'll call Ida Lee to let you in while I get Horace inside."

She would have a hard time doing that, but I followed orders and waited a few minutes by the front door until I heard Ida Lee running through the house from the back. Following orders also, she unlocked the door and let me in.

She was in the same stages of undress as I was, but neither of us cared as we hied up the stairs in a flurry of bathrobes and headed for Horace's room.

Inside the room with its four-poster bed and flocked wallpaper, the first thing I saw was Mildred's wide, silk-covered back end filling the open window as she leaned over to reach Horace. The room was freezing, making me wonder how long the window had been open, which also meant wondering how long Horace had been impaled on the trellis.

Ida Lee ran to Mildred's side and wedged herself into the open window beside her. There was no room for me, thank goodness, for I had about reached my limit and needed to catch my breath. I leaned against a wall, listening as they encouraged Horace to reach up and clasp their hands.

"Pull, Ida Lee!" Mildred cried. "Get his other hand and pull!"

Horace yelled, crying and cursing, but Mildred urged him and Ida Lee on. Finally in a voice of command, she said, "Just hush, Horace. Just hush and lift your foot to the next slot in the trellis."

"It hurts!" he cried.

"Oh, suck it up, and do what I say." Mildred had no pity when she wanted something done.

With a mighty heave and a piercing scream from Horace, Mildred and Ida Lee pulled him over the edge of the window and onto the floor of the room.

Ida Lee snatched up a coverlet from the bed and wrapped it around Horace's scratched and bleeding body. She helped him to a chair, then went to the adjoining bath for what was needed to patch him up.

"Outside in his underclothes!" Mildred said with a snort as she slammed the window closed. "And him with a drawer full of silk pajamas." Then, with a glance around the room, she addressed whoever was listening. "There is just one thing I want to know—*where* is Grady Peeples?"

"That's exactly what I was wondering," I said, looking behind me down the dark, silent hall that stretched the width of the house and ended at the door to Mildred's room.

"I am simply furious!" Mildred said, stomping her foot. "I mean, *where is he*? We've all been running in the hall and calling Horace and leaning out a window, and him crying and yelling, and Grady is sleeping through it? Now, I ask you, Julia, does that make sense to you, especially since he's being paid to prevent just this sort of thing from happening?"

"Well, no, it doesn't," I said with another fearful glance behind me. "But, Mildred, something else might be going on." I edged away from the hall door as a shiver ran down my back.

We stared at each other with growing horror. Was Grady lying half-dead in his bed? Had there been a home invasion and Grady was tied up somewhere while criminals roamed the house? Had somebody else opened the window and pushed Horace out?

Mildred grabbed my arm. "We can't just stand here and wait for whatever it is. Come on."

We hurried to Grady's room right next to Horace's from which he should've heard the commotion we'd made. Mildred flung open the door and flipped on the light switch without one thought of his privacy, and *he wasn't there*! The bed had been slept in but Grady wasn't in it.

Mildred gasped and my heart sank. What in the world could've happened to him? And there we were—three helpless women and a wounded man at the mercy of who knew what.

"Inez!" Mildred cried, a note of panic in her voice. "We have to see about her."

The two of us ran down the hall and into the alcove that led to Penelope's room, now occupied by the live-in nurse. Mildred didn't hesitate, nor did I. She pushed open the door, flipped on the light switch, and stopped short. Blocked by Mildred's wide body, I both heard and felt the sound she made as if she'd been hit. She groaned as her breath came and went so fast and deeply that I wondered if she was nearing another panic attack.

"What?" I said, trying to see past her. "Is she all right? What is it?"

Mildred stepped back, pushing me as she came, and slammed the door. "They're there! Both of them!" she said, her eyes wild with fury. "In bed! Together!"

"Oh, no!" I said, shocked at what I hadn't seen but could vividly picture.

Mildred stood stock-still, her hand closed on the doorknob. "Oh, yes! You should've seen them, Julia, I scared them to death." Mildred managed a small laugh, but it had an edge of hysteria to it. "Grady must've levitated two feet. I don't mean to be crude, but that was an instance of *coitus interruptus* if I ever saw it."

"Oh, my word," I said, patting my chest as the image sharpened in my mind, to say nothing of my surprise at Mildred's knowledge of Latin. "You mean, they were actually . . ."

"I do mean it—full-blown and no doubt about it. Not a stitch on either one of them, and all the while poor Horace was hanging on the side of the house in twenty-degree weather, stuck full of thorns." Mildred took a deep, shuddering breath. "*Unacceptable!* This is *absolutely* unacceptable!"

She twisted the knob, opened the door, and stuck her head inside, eyes closed. "Pack your things, both of you, and get out! Tonight! Right now! I'll mail your pay through dinnertime last night, but no further. I'm not paying a cent for what you've been doing since then!"

And she slammed the door closed. "Come on, Julia," she said as she swept past me. "I don't want to lay eyes on either of them again. All I'd see is what I just saw, and my heart can't stand the strain."

"I can't believe the audacity," I said, following her into the hall. "You can't have that going on, but, Mildred, how will you manage without them?"

"I'll manage," she said with a heaving sigh. "I always do." Then, glancing down the hall toward Horace's room, she said, "Here comes Ida Lee, bless her heart."

Ida Lee walked to us and uncharacteristically put her arm around Mildred's shoulder. Mildred leaned against her, asking about Horace.

"He's asleep," Ida Lee said softly, "and I think he's all right. I pushed a chest against that window and locked the door. He won't get out again. Now, let me put you to bed. You need to rest."

Mildred raised her head and said, "No, not yet. I think I need to wind down a little."

"Then come downstairs," Ida Lee said soothingly. "And you, too, Mrs. Murdoch. I'll fix some hot cocoa. Doesn't that sound good?"

"We'll go to the kitchen," Mildred said, asserting her authority to occupy a room she rarely even visited. "Grady and Inez are moving out tonight, and I don't want to see either of them ever again. They're to go out the front door without stopping, Ida Lee, and good riddance."

Ida Lee raised her eyebrows as she looked at me, but she raised no questions. I nodded, so she turned Mildred toward the stairs. We settled at a table in the large kitchen, as far from the assigned exit of the shameless pair as it was possible to get.

Chapter 43

❧

"Well, I'll tell you this," Mildred said, her hands cupped around a hot mug. "I'll never again hire someone on the recommendation of a current employee. You know that's how Inez came to work for me—Grady recommended her and now I know why. So here they've been, both under the same roof, and who knows how many times in the same bed. And right under my nose! It just beats all I've ever heard."

"It really does surprise me, though," I said, recalling the one brief time I'd been in the company of Mildred's rawboned private nurse. "Inez seemed so cold and angular. She didn't look the type who'd do something like that."

"Oh, you'd be surprised," Mildred, the woman of the world, said. "That type is the most ravenous of all. It's the little, plump, smiling ones who tease but rarely act out, and it's the ones you least expect who can't get enough."

"I didn't know that," I murmured, learning something every day. "But what're you going to do without them?"

"Well, the first thing I'll do is buy new mattresses and get rid of the used ones." She shuddered at the thought of how they'd been used. "And I still have Ida Lee and Doreen. And Penelope. We'll make do until I find a suitable place for Horace, because I've come to the conclusion that he has to go. I just cannot risk having someone move into the house again."

"No, I wouldn't, either," I said, but thinking *Penelope*? "What about your plans to go to Duke?"

"Oh," she said, with a wave of her hand, "I can do without that. If I can survive a night like this one, I can survive anything. It's time to get out of bed and take control, which I intend to do. And the first thing I have to do is face the fact that Horace needs constant supervision and there're not many places that provide that—*suitable* places, I mean."

"Memory Care units, I think they're called," I said, having recently read an informative article. "I'm sorry, Mildred, but it does seem that he needs to be in a locked facility with well-trained personnel—to keep him from hurting himself if nothing else."

"Yes, and I hate doing it, but he is just determined to get out and go somewhere. So when I think of how he could've broken his neck falling from that trellis, a locked facility is sounding better and better. Anyway, I have to start investigating what's available but, in the meantime, I'm going to see that he has a safe, pleasurable last few days in his own home. That's where Penelope comes in. He likes her and never gets agitated or afflicted with wanderlust when she's around. I'll send Ida Lee for her later this morning, but thank you so much for keeping her. I hope she hasn't disrupted things too much."

"Not at all," I said as a feeling of loss almost overcame me. "But, Mildred, I hope you don't mean to put too much responsibility on her—she's only a child, you know."

"I do know, but it'll only be for a few days while I find a place for Horace. Of course, it's almost Christmas so that might delay things a bit, what with personnel being on holiday breaks. But Penelope is such a calming influence on him, and I have to use who and what I have available."

My heart sank even further at the thought of Penelope being available for use. It wasn't as if Mildred didn't have the means to avail herself of suitable help. It was all I could do not to ask, What about Tonya? What about hiring a responsible adult? What about *you*?

Mindful of my intention to stay out the affairs of others, I restrained myself from saying what I was thinking, but it was hard. All I could do was remind myself that Mildred had been, and might still be, ill, and that she was not normally so self-involved. Besides, if I had a husband in the shape of her husband, there's no telling what ill-advised means I would use to help him.

"Well," I said, "we'll miss Penelope, but of course her home is with you. But, listen, I've promised to take her Christmas shopping so she can get gifts for you and Horace. She's looking forward to it, so let us keep her today, and I'll bring her home after dinner."

"Wel-l," Mildred said, "I was counting on her reading to Horace this afternoon, which is when he gets so insistent on going out. But then again, I don't want to disappoint her, so I'll just give Horace two of those anti-agitation pills the doctor prescribed."

"And," I pointed out, "it's likely that he'll be so exhausted from tonight's excursion that he won't even think of going anywhere."

"That's true!" Mildred said, as if she'd just realized it. "He should be completely wiped out for the rest of the day, so that's one thing we can be thankful for. And who knows, I may be back in bed myself. All right, Julia, she can stay one more day so you can take her shopping. I mean," she said with a laugh, "after what I've been through, I'm certainly not up for shopping, Christmas or otherwise. So better you than me, if, that is, you really want to do it."

"I really do," I said even though the night was far gone and I had lost hours of sleep. "In fact, I'm looking forward to it."

"Well," she said, "she'll need some shopping money, so let her pick out whatever she wants. Ida Lee," she said, turning to her, "would you run up and get my purse? And maybe look in on Horace while you're there?"

When Ida Lee returned with the purse and the key to Horace's room, she said, "He's sleeping. I don't think he's moved since I put him to bed. And," she continued, "Mr. Peeples and Miss Freeman just left. I locked up behind them."

"Good," Mildred said as if that was exactly what she'd expected to hear. "Thank you, Ida Lee, but why don't you run along and get some sleep yourself?"

Mildred rummaged in her purse, then, thrusting a roll of bills at me, she went on. "If that's not enough, just let me know and I'll reimburse you."

"Goodness, Mildred, we aren't going to New York, or even to Atlanta. We won't need this much."

"You never know, and better to have too much than not enough. So," she said, pushing back from the table, "we both need some sleep, at least for what's left of the night. Julia, I can't tell you how much I appreciate your help. There's no telling what would've happened if you hadn't seen Horace hanging out there. How did you happen to see him, anyway?"

"Oh," I said, passing it off as a happenstance, as indeed it had been. "It was one of my 'couldn't sleep' nights. I went down to the kitchen so I wouldn't disturb Sam and just happened to glance out the one window which gives a clear view of the side of your house—something I'd rarely noticed before." I cleared my throat and went on. "And there he was. But you need to go back to bed, too, Mildred. You've not been well, you know."

"I know," she agreed, "but I think I'll doze in a chair in Horace's room. I won't have him much longer, so I'll spend this night with him."

That seemed quite touching until I recalled, according to her own admission, that it had been a rare night she'd ever spent with him. But I passed no judgment. What worked in one marriage might not in another and either way it was no business of mine.

Mildred began to rise, saying, "I'll start calling around for a place for Horace this morning. I'll start with his doctor first, I guess, but if you have any suggestions, let me know." Then, turning to me, she said, "Thank you, Julia, for everything, especially for looking after Penelope. With all that's on my plate right now, it's good to have one thing not to have to worry about."

And perhaps, I thought to myself, even as my heart went out to her, that's the one thing you should worry about.

Chapter 44

❧

Sam and I were late going down for breakfast the next morning, my having taken time to tell him of the night's escapade through which he had soundly slept.

"You should've gotten me up," Sam said, amazed that so much had gone on, including, he said, his wife out gallivanting half the night while he was out like a light.

"My first thought was to wake you," I told him, "but I was afraid Horace would be down and gone before you could get over there." I finished with my hair, then said, "I didn't know about the holding power of pyracantha thorns."

Sam gave a short laugh, then shook his head with pity. "If I ever get in Horace's condition, just shoot me."

I put my arms around him and said, "Never, never in this world. I'll take you in any condition I can get you."

When we joined Penelope at the table, neither of us brought up the subject of her grandfather's escape attempt or his imminent departure for a locked room. That should be left to Mildred, although I intended to stand by, as Lillian would as well, for any comforting that needed to be done.

To start the day as normally as possible, Sam asked, "Are you two ladies going to Asheville to shop?"

"Not if we can help it," I said, stifling a yawn. "Traffic is awful on the interstate. I think we'll start downtown. I've heard good things about that new gift shop on Main Street."

"If I was you," Lillian said as she wiped the kitchen counter, "I'd go to the Dollar Store."

"Why, Lillian," I said, "they haven't even built a store yet. They just bought land in Delmont."

"No'm, there's another one out on the highway next to Walmart. It may be the Family Dollar or the Dollar Tree—something like that—but it's got everything anybody could want. An' Zaxby's is real close if you want chicken for lunch."

Penelope looked up. "I want chicken for lunch."

I laughed. "Then that's where we'll go. Have you made out a list so we'll know what to look for?"

She nodded and off she went, running up the stairs, but coming back not only with the list but with her hair brush, as well. "Will you make me a plait again?" she asked, holding out the brush.

"Of course," I said. "Come sit down. Lillian?"

"Yes'm, I know." And going to the kitchen catch-all drawer, she drew out a rubber band and a wrinkled, narrow red ribbon. "It needs ironin'," she said. "No tellin' how long it's been settin' in here."

"It's fine," I said, quickly plaiting Penelope's thick hair and fastening the rubber band around the end. When I tied a bow over it with the red ribbon, I said, "Now you look like Christmas."

Sam added his compliments and Penelope smiled as she felt the thick plait. I still thought that bangs would've set her hairdo off perfectly, but I didn't bring it up.

Penelope had been the first one up that morning, clearly excited about going shopping, and now after a larger than usual breakfast and sporting a special hairdo, she was ready to start.

"Here's my list," she said, handing me a slip of paper on which she had printed several names.

I could barely read it, for spelling words such as *grandmother* and *grandfather* were beyond her and almost beyond my ability to decipher. But Ida Lee's name was correctly spelled and Doreen's nearly so. To my surprise she had also included *Latesha*, *Miss J*, *Lilan*, *Sam*, and *Loid*. We just might need all the money that Mildred had handed over and then some.

Admiring her attempts at English, I realized that her first language was either Spanish or Portuguese in which my name may have been pronounced *Miss Yoolia*. Pleased to have been included, however she spelled or pronounced it, I smiled and made no comment. It wasn't until I sent her upstairs for a last bathroom visit before what she hadn't listed hit me.

"Sam," I said, lowering my voice, "and you, too, Lillian, she doesn't have Tonya on her list. What should I do about that?"

"I wouldn't do nothin'," Lillian said. "She knows who she wants to give a present to and who she don't."

"I think I'd leave it alone, too," Sam said. "Maybe remind Mildred and let her take care of it."

That suited me for I was not eager to cast a pall over our outing by reminding the child that she had a mother who needed reminding that she had a child.

I still had a task to do before leaving, so while Sam prepared to attend a finance committee meeting at the church across the street, I went to the library to telephone Etta Mae. Fearing that I'd left it too late and her phone would ring while she was giving a bed bath to a bedridden patient, I was relieved to hear her answer.

"Etta Mae," I said as decisively as I could manage even though I was tingling with nerves, "let's go ahead and give Mr. Blair our best and final offer just as we discussed. Tell him to send it at eleven thirty this morning and tell him that Ms. Corn has twenty-four hours in which to respond. After that, we're through."

There was dead silence on the phone for several seconds.

"Etta Mae? Are you there?"

"Um, yeah, I mean, yes'm, I am. I'm just trying to take it in. This is really it, isn't it?"

"Yes, my dear, it is." I closed my eyes, fervently hoping that I had not held out something to her that would now prove unattainable. "We have to stop sometime, and now is the time. But don't despair if she turns us down. I may have something else up my sleeve."

I had never before been on a shopping trip the likes of which Penelope took me on that morning. Maybe all children dawdle, I don't know, but it seemed that she looked at everything on every counter throughout a shop before making up her mind.

The only exception was our first stop at the new gift shop on Main Street, because there on a rack beside the cash register was a display of key rings. She quickly chose one with a car etched on the fob for Horace, then hesitantly selected one with a tennis racket on it for Lloyd and another with an open book for Sam. She held them out for my approval which I quickly gave, impressed that she had so unerringly picked up on their interests. And impressed also with the speed with which she'd found what she wanted.

Thinking then that shopping with her was going to be a breeze, we left after she made a tour of the shop with nothing else catching her eye. On to the Dollar Store we went, and that's where it seemed that she examined every trinket on every counter on every aisle in the store. After straggling along behind her up and down the aisles, I was about to give out when she suddenly chose a fancy paint set for Latisha.

Then she went straight across the store to a counter where she had lingered on her first lap. She selected two pairs of thick, fuzzy knee socks, one pair pink and the other aqua.

"These are for Ida Lee," Penelope said, holding up the aqua

pair, "because Doreen likes pink." Smoothing the fuzzy texture with her hand, she said, "Pink is my favorite color, too."

"I'm glad to know that," I said to be saying something, but inwardly congratulating myself on the choice I'd made in a certain gift already under the tree. "Anything else you want to get?"

"No, ma'am," she answered, "but can we go back to the other store?"

So back to Main Street we went as well as around the block several times before finding a decent parking place. As I prepared to get out and go in with her, she asked if she could go by herself. As I could see the shop door from the car, I smiled knowingly, gave her some money, and told her to take her time.

And she did, during which I caught a few more moments of sleep. Waking suddenly, I realized how quickly the car had cooled down. Cold had seeped in and my feet were freezing, making me wonder just how long Penelope had been gone. I was just before going in after her when she came out with two large shopping bags. Penelope had finished her shopping, so we put everything in the trunk as she announced that she was ready to have chicken for lunch.

So back out onto the highway we went, to Zaxby's, where we joined other almost-last-minute shoppers for lunch.

"Did you find everything you were looking for?" I asked to make conversation as well as to assure myself we would soon be on our way home where, unaccustomed to being up half the night, I could lie down.

"Uh-huh," she said with a small, self-satisfied smile. "I got Miss Lillian the best present of all—some bedroom slippers with a cat face on both of them. She likes kitty cats."

"I didn't know that," I said, wondering what else I didn't know about the people closest to me. "Can you tell me what you got your grandmother? I won't tell her."

"Wel-l, I'm trying to decide which one to give her—the lavender one or the lemony one." Penelope leaned toward me, her face lit up with anticipation of presenting her gift. "It's a whole set," she whispered, "with soap and everything."

"Either one would be lovely," I said, assuming that she'd just told me what my gift would be, as well. "You are very good at finding just the right gifts."

She beamed. "There was really something else I wanted to give her, but they didn't have gerbils at either store."

"Well," I said, swallowing hard at the thought that I might've just missed getting a gerbil myself, "she'll love a soap set regardless of which one she gets."

"I think so, too," she said, then frowning, she went on, "but I wish I'd picked something else for Latisha."

"She loves to color, so I expect she'll really like the paint set." When Penelope didn't reply, I asked, "Do you want to look for something else?"

Her face brightened. "Can we go back to that other store? Her pink book bag has a hole in it, and I saw a purple one there. Purple is her favorite color."

"Then we'll go back and get it," I said, trying to keep my eyes open. "Will you give her the paint set, too?"

"I'll give that to Lloyd's little sisters. It has enough brushes and paint for both of them."

Hazel Marie will love that, I thought, and gathered myself for another tour of the Dollar Store. And by the way, it carried a number of items that cost more than a dollar, including purple book bags.

Chapter 45

❧

In the car on our way home, Penelope was noticeably basking with satisfaction over her selections. There was a rosy glow on her face and she kept twisting around to check on the bags, which she'd moved from the trunk to the back seat.

It was getting late in the day and colder by the minute, and I was not all that anxious for the day to be over for I knew how it would end. But Penelope didn't, and I realized that Mildred, having left it so late, assumed that I would be the one to prepare the child for a call to duty.

"Honey," I said, resigned to telling her what Mildred had not. "Honey, your grandmother wants you home tonight. I don't know what we'll do without you because we're going to miss you so much. But you'll be right next door and you can come back any time you want."

I glanced over at her and saw that she was staring straight ahead, her little face without expression. "When we get home," I went on, "why don't you take your presents up to Lloyd's old room? I have a table set up there and plenty of Christmas paper, bows, and ribbons. You can leave everything there, and nobody will bother them. Then you'll have a reason to come back to wrap them."

She turned away and looked out the window.

"Your grandmother needs you," I said, seeking to offer a measure of comfort. "Your grandfather isn't well, you know. It seems he'll have to go to a special place where he can be taken care of. And that's been hard on your grandmother, but you can be a great help to her. I think she's been missing you very much."

Getting no response, I glanced again at her. Her head was still turned away, her eyes on the window or perhaps on the door handle.

"Oh!" I said. "I just thought of what we can do. I'll tell your grandmother that I need you to help me wrap my presents, and we'll fix a special time for you to come over every day. Would that be all right with you?"

She nodded as I parked in our driveway, so at least I'd elicited a tiny response. She got out and opened the back door to retrieve her shopping bags.

"Can I help you take them in?" I asked.

She hesitated, looked at the two large bags and one small one, and said, "Don't look."

"Oh, I wouldn't. Not for the world." And in we went, laden with both Christmas surprises and leaden hearts.

Penelope made two trips up the stairs, carrying her presents to Lloyd's room. Before she came down the last time, I told Sam and Lillian what had transpired in the car.

"Oh, that poor baby," Lillian said. "She don't want to go back to that big, ole, lonesome house. I don't know why we can't jus' keep her."

"I wish we could," I said, hanging up our coats in the pantry. "But she's not ours to keep, more's the pity."

Sam said, "She'll know we're here, and that'll help. But I'll miss having her around."

"Well," Lillian said with a sigh, "at least I got fried chicken for supper."

"Why, Lillian," I said, "we had chicken for lunch. On your recommendation, as I recall."

"That little girl likes chicken," she said as if that was reason enough. And for me, it was.

Supper was a quiet affair even with Sam's efforts to draw Penelope into the conversation. I didn't have much to say, either, and Lillian kept touching the child every time she brought something to the table.

After supper Lillian took Penelope upstairs to pack her things as Sam and I lingered at the table.

"It's really getting cold outside," Sam said. "The weatherman said down in the teens tonight. Why don't you stay in while I walk Penelope home?"

I put my hand on his. "Thank you, Sam, I don't think I could bear walking away and leaving her. I wouldn't mind so much if she wanted to go back and if I knew Mildred would give her more than the time of day. I am so angry with that woman. I could just shake her."

"Well," Sam said, smiling, "she'd be a handful if you tried it." Then, as if he'd just thought of it, he said, "Why don't we send that little bear with her? She's been sleeping with it every night."

"Oh, yes, let's do," I said, brightening with another thought as well. "And I've just remembered something else."

While Sam ran upstairs to add the Steiff bear to Penelope's packing, I went to the living room to retrieve a present from under the tree.

When we were all back in the kitchen and Lillian was buttoning Penelope's coat for her, I held out the gift.

"Honey, years ago when Lloyd was your age, we always let him unwrap one present before Christmas, so I think you should unwrap one before Christmas, too."

She looked up at me with those big, dark eyes and a small smile appeared. We watched as she unwrapped the large box, and when she opened it, a look of wonder replaced the smile.

"Can I wear them now?" she asked, holding up one fur-lined boot that was as pink as any little girl could want.

"Absolutely," I said, "we want to see how you look."

It took only a minute for her to slip off her sneakers and pull on the boots. She looked down at them on her feet, wiggled her toes in them, then, looking up at us, she said, "I can't wait to show my grandmother."

If anything could ease the pain of seeing her go, that was it.

In bed that night, I was all but asleep when Sam said, "Mildred hasn't put up a tree. At least I didn't see any signs of one when Ida Lee came to the door."

My eyes popped open. "Mildred wasn't there to welcome Penelope home?"

"No, and I didn't ask for her. Just went in the foyer to put down the suitcase, and left. But there were no decorations at all, not even that remarkable crèche set she has. And you know she usually goes all out for Christmas, so she may be sicker than we realize."

"Maybe she is. I hope not, but she's able to get up and do what she wants to do. You should've heard her dress down Grady and Inez last night. They were out of there before, well . . ." I stopped to laugh at what I'd said, then went on, "almost before they could get dressed at all."

Of course I'd told Sam all the sordid details of the previous night, including the variety of curse words from Horace on his way back inside and Mildred's description of what I'd not seen but could vividly picture going on in what was supposed to be Penelope's bed.

"After all that," Sam said, as I felt him smile, "maybe we should give Mildred a little slack. That's enough to traumatize anybody."

"I just hope she got that mattress changed. And," I went on, "I hope Penelope is sound asleep on it now with her little bear and not lying awake feeling lost and abandoned."

Sam patted my back, awkwardly because I was lying on his

arm, but any kind of pat was appreciated. After a few minutes just as my eyes were about to close for good, he said, "Have you heard anything from Etta Mae? You made your final offer today, didn't you?"

"No, nothing from her yet, and, yes, we made the final one, and I'm trying not to worry about it. I doubt we'll hear anything, though, until around noon tomorrow. I just hope Lurline Corn recognizes a decent offer when she sees it, and I really hope that Ernest Sitton will take his little red wagon somewhere else. He could spoil everything."

Doors opening and closing and the rumble of voices from the kitchen aroused us early the next morning. Christmas was fast approaching, and Lillian was gathering her forces for our great, wonderful Christmas dinner. I heard James's deep laugh as well as a lighter one which I took to be Janelle's, Lillian's energetic teenage neighbor.

"Busy day today," Sam said as he swung out of bed. "You remember that I'm helping the Men of the Church deliver Christmas Angel gifts, don't you? We should be through by early afternoon if you need me for anything."

"Okay, but from the sounds downstairs, we have plenty of help." I yawned and began to dress, thinking of all I still had to do before Christmas. Penelope crossed my mind as I wondered what the day held for her. But resolutely, though reluctantly, I had to put her aside to concentrate on immediate concerns.

In fact, my heart started to race at the thought that Lurline Corn might actually agree to our best and final offer and sell The Handy Home Helpers to Etta Mae on this very day.

By the time I got downstairs, James and Janelle had already brought up five card tables and stacks of folding chairs from the basement and were rearranging furniture in the library.

"We didn't know how many we'll need," James said, pointing to the folding tables leaning against the wall. "Miss Lillian said the number keeps changing."

"Well, that's the truth," I said, "so just set up all five and if there're empty places, it won't matter. And if more than twenty show up, there's always the kitchen table."

"We gonna serve from the dining room table?" he asked. "I got a new chef's hat if you want me to carve the turkey."

"That's wonderful, because I do want you to carve. You put us all in the holiday spirit, James."

I walked into the living room to plug in the tree lights, thinking that I needed all the holiday spirit I could get. Presents piled up beneath the tree reminded me to make sure that Penelope was relieved from her duties long enough to come over and wrap her gifts.

Going into the kitchen, I found fresh coffee and cinnamon rolls waiting on the table, and Lillian emptying a row of grocery bags at the counter.

"You've already been to the grocery store?" I asked. "I didn't know they were open this early."

"Yes'm, an' I'll pro'bly be goin' back a half a dozen times more. But I can stop and fix you some eggs."

"No, cinnamon rolls are perfect. But why don't you stop and have some with me?"

"I already had some," she said, wadding up plastic bags to save. "I tell you, Miss Julia, they's a lot to do to get ready to feed a bunch of people. I make out lists, then always find out I need something else, so back to the store I go. But if I ever get things situated where I know I got everything in one place for ev'ry dish I'm gonna cook, that's half the job done. See, everything I need for the broccoli casserole is settin' right here, except the broccoli and the eggs and cheese that's in the 'frigerator. An' everything for the Jell-O salad is over in this corner, so when I'm ready to put it together, I don't have to go lookin' for anything. It's a whole lot easier to stir up a dish if you got everything you need in one place."

"Goodness, Lillian," I said, "I don't know how you do it all. The army ought to put you to work on strategic planning."

She laughed, then looked toward the door as we heard a soft knock. I opened it to see Penelope standing there in her pink boots.

She didn't come in, just stood by the door and said, "My grandmother said it was a good time to wrap my presents if it's all right with you."

"Any time you can come is all right with us," I said. "Come in, Honey, we're glad to see you."

Lillian dried her hands and went to the refrigerator. "You need a cinnamon roll 'fore you start, an' a glass of milk to go with it."

After getting her settled at the table, I asked, "Did your grandmother like your new boots?"

"Yes, ma'am," she said without looking up. "She said she guessed they're what all the girls are wearing these days."

Not exactly a ringing endorsement, I thought, and probably said with just enough flippancy to take the joy out of anything.

I really could've shaken Mildred and shaken her hard, handful or not.

Chapter 46

❦

Getting Penelope settled in Lloyd's room upstairs, I pointed out all the wrapping necessities and told her to use whatever she wanted. I saved Christmas wrapping supplies from year to year, supplementing them with new purchases as needed, so Penelope had a wide choice. Finding several small colorful bags, I suggested that she wrap the key rings in tissue paper then put each one in a bag.

"Then all you have to do," I went on, "is put labels on them with the name of who gets which one, and of course your name so they'll know who came up with such perfect gifts. And here's the Scotch tape. You'll need it when you wrap the larger presents." Then, with an urgent thought, I said, "You want me to cut the paper for you? These scissors are quite large and very sharp."

"I can use scissors," she said, "and Ida Lee let me borrow some little ones." She held up a pair of small, blunt-ended scissors, a little larger than kindergarten size and perfectly suited for her small hands.

"All right then. When you finish, bring your presents down and put them under the tree," I said, avoiding the fact that there was no tree to receive them at her house. "We'll all be opening gifts on Christmas Day, and I can't wait for everybody to see yours."

Seeing her settle in to her tasks, I left her alone and went downstairs, ending up moving from room to room as Janelle followed with the vacuum cleaner. If I hadn't been expecting a call from Etta Mae, I would've just left the house and fiddled around downtown. But as the morning wore on and the deadline for Lurline's response approached, I found myself more and more on edge. What would that woman do? If she accepted our offer, it would be a wonderful Christmas for Etta Mae. I could just picture her beaming with the joy of ownership, tempered of course with her usual fear of anything new. But I could also picture her taking hold of her new responsibilities and proving to herself and everybody else how competent she was. Bobby Lee Moser just might find himself in second or third place in the mind of a blossoming entrepreneur.

The likelihood of everything working out as I'd planned, however, was looking more and more doubtful. What with Lawyer Sitton getting in on the bidding and Lurline singing as she worked in spite of her nephew's incarceration, I had a bad feeling as to our prospects. Still, there was nothing to do but wait for Lurline's response and, I thought with a deep sigh, start planning something else for Etta Mae. If, that is, she didn't lose her head and get married again.

After a while Penelope came downstairs, her arms laden with wrapped and bagged gifts. Surveying the pile of presents already under the tree, she asked, "Is there room for mine?"

"Of course," I said, jumping up to help. "Here, let me re-arrange a few things." Ignoring the creaking of rarely used joints, I got down on my knees and began to make room for her gifts around the tree. I declare, though, the gifts that were wrapped had more Scotch tape on them than wrapping paper. A couple of sizable square ones which I assumed were mine and Mildred's were glistening with see-through tape.

When the last gift was placed, I sat back on my heels and looked up at the tree. "It's beautiful, isn't it? And your presents add just the right finishing touch."

She held out one small Christmas bag and said, "Is it all right if I don't put this one under the tree?"

"Of course, Honey, they're your gifts. You can do whatever you want with them."

With her eyes still on the tree, Penelope said, "My grandmother said he's too sick to come for Christmas dinner, so I want to give him his present today or maybe tomorrow."

Understanding that the *he* and the *him* referred to Horace, I didn't question her, saying as I rose with difficulty from the floor, "That's an excellent plan. You're sure you have the right key ring in that bag?"

She nodded. "Uh-huh, I'm sure."

"All right then, but it's lunchtime so why don't you stay a little longer and have lunch with us?"

"No'm, I have to go. He likes to eat with me."

So what Horace liked appeared to be what Horace got, regardless of what anyone else might prefer. That was understandable, considering his current condition, but I was saddened by the thought of a child being used to accommodate someone else.

There was nothing I could do but help Penelope with her coat, make sure that she had Horace's gift as well as Ida Lee's scissors, and watch her safely across both lawns until she disappeared inside the house next door.

I'd just finished eating a sandwich in the living room, the kitchen having been commandeered by Lillian, James, and Janelle, who were designating for specific usages, it seemed, every pot, pan, and dish that we owned. I stretched my feet toward the fire that James had started for me, made note of a bare place on the tree and decided I'd fill it the next time I had to get up. The living room was a peaceful retreat on a raw day, although there was precious little peace in my mind.

I'd not heard one word from Etta Mae even though the time limit we'd given Lurline Corn had come and gone. Was Lurline just ignoring our best and final offer? Or was she holding off in the hope that Mr. Sitton would outbid us?

Surely, I thought, she'd have the courtesy to formally decline if she had no intention of accepting our offer. But maybe not, maybe total silence was her response. Whatever the case, my stomach was roiling with anxiety and my mind was filled with first one thing, then another.

When the doorbell rang, I nearly dropped my plate in my haste to answer it.

"I'll get it!" I called toward the kitchen, as I flung open the front door. "Etta Mae, thank goodness! I've been waiting to hear from you."

She stood there a minute with her teeth clenched tight and her hands balled into fists. Her face was red from crying, her nose from the cold, and she was steaming with anger.

"Miss Julia, I am so mad I could spit fire! You won't believe what she's come up with."

"Come in," I said, reaching for her, even as my spirits fell. "Come in and tell me."

She followed me into the living room, but when I stopped at the sofa, she kept going, stomping to the fireplace, then turning on her heel and stomping back. "I can't *believe* her! How she came up with this idea, I don't know. I could just slap her to kingdom come for even thinking I'd do that, and, and . . ." She stopped, swallowed hard, and the tears poured out.

"Come sit down, Etta Mae," I said, patting the sofa cushion. "Come tell me what happened. It's all right if she turned us down. It just means something better is on the way."

She plopped down beside me, her face crumpling with misery. In a strangled voice, she said, "It couldn't get any worse."

So Lurline had turned down our best offer. I wouldn't be telling the truth if I didn't admit that I was disappointed at the news, but Etta Mae was in such a state that I had to pretend that our loss was simply the price of doing business.

"Oh, now," I said soothingly, "just losing out on a business proposition can't be that bad. It happens to people all the time. What you do is pick yourself up and start looking for something else. And that's what we'll do. I told you I was already thinking of something else, remember? So we'll just start working on that."

"No," she said, shaking her head, "it's too late. I won't be here."

"*Won't be here?* What do you mean? If Lurline sells to Mr. Sitton, you know he'll keep you on. And at the same time we'll be getting our ducks in a row for something else, because I'm not ready to quit by a long shot. Now listen, you can't let this get you down. It may turn out to be the best thing that could've happened."

"Miss Julia," Etta Mae said with a groan of pain. "She's not selling it at all. She's taking it off the market."

"What?" I said, sitting back in surprise. "Why? What in the world brought that on? She's changed her mind about moving to Florida?"

"Uh-uh, no, she's still going." Etta Mae stuffed a handful of wet tissues into one coat pocket and drew out a handful of dry tissues from the other one. "She'll just fly back every month or so to make sure everything's all right."

"And leaving you in charge as she always does? But with a pay raise, I hope. A sizable one?"

She shook her head and groaned again. "No, not me, and no raise, either." Etta Mae sniffed, wiped her nose, and went on. "She called me to her office and told me it's come home to her that blood is thicker than water. Which I already knew, but I didn't know what it had to do with The Handy Home Helpers. Then she said that what Bug needs to straighten himself out is a little responsibility. He just needs to grow up, she said, and be a man. But, Miss Julia, he's so goofy, he stumbles over his own feet. So what is she doing? She's keeping the business and putting him in charge, and she expects me to back him up and," Etta Mae stopped and pressed the wad of tissues to her eyes, "and she said that I was the only reason she could leave Bug in charge because she knows I'll be there to keep him out of trouble and keep the business going."

I let a number of seconds pass in silence as I tried to absorb this revolting development. "In other words," I finally said, "she's leaving the business with you, but Bug will have the title, the office, and the authority, as well as the credit and the salary." She nodded, too broken up to speak, and I went on. "And Mr. Sitton is out of the running, too?"

"I guess. She didn't mention him. But it doesn't matter. I can't work *with* Bug, and I can't work *for* him. He's a mess, Miss Julia. He's lazy and as dumb as a post, and he'll run the business straight into the ground. Patients will leave and the other girls will quit and when nothing's left but debt he's gotten into, Lurline will blame it on me." Her shoulders shook as the unfairness of it all hit her again.

Then with a deep sob, she said, "I'm going to quit. It's the only thing I can do."

"I don't blame you," I said, still stunned by Lurline's assumption that Etta Mae would do for Bug Timmons what neither his mother nor Lurline herself had been able to do, and not only that but she'd take on the manager's job without the manager's pay. "But it most certainly is not the only thing you can do."

Chapter 47

❧

I didn't tell Etta Mae what I had in mind, not wanting to disappoint her again if it didn't work out. But I had something in mind, all right, and only wanted to run it by Sam before proceeding. After she'd pulled herself together—more or less—she had gotten up to leave, saying that she still had two more patients to see that afternoon. And that just showed the kind of person she was. If it had been me, I would've already handed in my resignation and left those patients for Lurline to see.

How in the world, I wondered after Etta Mae had left, could that woman leave a thriving business in the hands of an overgrown boy who drove through a cornfield and ended up in jail? I mean, if you were lying sick in bed and somebody named *Bug* came with your medicine, how safe would you feel?

I paced the floor for a while, my nerves stretched to the breaking point as I wondered how Lurline Corn had gained a reputation as a sharp businesswoman. Of all the foolish ideas she could've had, putting Bug in charge took the cake.

Still, I had two possibilities in mind that would turn a sow's ear into a silk purse, but I couldn't decide which of the two should be pursued. One of them, of course, was to forget about Lurline's business and set about opening a new one. The downside to that was Etta Mae being without work until we had it up and running. That could take months. We'd have to apply for a business license and a tax number, to say nothing of finding a suitable location, hiring employees, and so on.

Still, I mused, Etta Mae could earn a salary by doing all the planning, hiring, and running around that a new business required. She'd need help getting all that done, though, which meant hiring someone else since I didn't want to do it.

And, to tell the truth, I was really leaning toward the second possibility—something that had popped in my head while watching Etta Mae cry her eyes out. I so wanted to make it right for her, and since money was already earmarked for her benefit, I decided then and there that if Sam gave me the slightest encouragement I would forget about opening a new business.

When Sam came in about midafternoon, he turned on the Christmas tree lights and sat down in the wing chair by the fireplace. Then he began to regale me with the details of delivering gifts donated by church members to children who might otherwise not have received any. He'd enjoyed every minute of it, even though it had meant driving all over the county. I listened, enjoying his pleasure and waiting for an opportune time to bring up my plans for The Handy Home Helpers. Finally as he yawned, it came.

"Sam? What do you think about my buying Lurline Corn's business?"

"I thought that's what you were doing."

"Well, not exactly. I was going to make a loan to Etta Mae so she could buy it. But now, Lurline has suddenly decided to take it off the market and put her good-for-nothing nephew, Bug Timmons, in charge. And to top it off, she expects Etta Mae to prop him up and keep the business going."

Sam frowned. "That doesn't sound so good for Etta Mae."

"I should say not! So here's what I'm thinking: What if I jump in with an offer that meets or maybe exceeds Lurline's last counteroffer and buy it my own self?" I leaned toward him, wanting him to feel the excitement of my new plan. "See, what I could do is knock her socks off with a large enough offer that she'll forget about rehabilitating Bug. I want her so thrilled with it that she'll take the money and run."

Sam cocked an eyebrow at me. "Won't that defeat the purpose you started with? I mean, of loaning the money to Etta Mae so she can buy it?"

"No, because I'll turn around and sell it to her at the price we agreed the business could sustain. She'll make monthly payments to me, just as we'd planned in the first place."

"Wait," Sam said, "let me get this straight. I thought you've been worried about paying more than the business is worth. But now, you're planning to buy it for Lurline's price and sell it to Etta Mae for a lower one?"

"Yes, but without Etta Mae knowing about it. It's not any of her business, anyway. What do you think?"

"Well, Julia, it's your money and you can do what you want with it. But you do realize, don't you, that you'll be losing money on a deal like that?"

"Not really," I said. "Since it's going for a good cause, I'll just count the difference as part of my tithe for the next few years."

Sam started laughing. "Honey," he said, "you must have a unique relationship with the Almighty."

I nodded. "I do. He understands me."

Sam stood up, shaking his head but still smiling. He backed up to the fire for a few minutes, his mouth twitching with amusement. "Then do it," he said, "and more power to you. All I want is a ringside seat."

The day was getting long in the tooth and the holidays were looming which meant there wasn't much time to get anything done.

On the other hand, I thought as I hurried upstairs to use the phone in privacy, the time constraint could work in my favor.

"Mr. Blair?" I asked when the real estate broker answered his phone. "Julia Murdoch here. I know it's late and you may have holiday plans, but I understand there's a property in Delmont for sale. I want to buy it."

"Uh," he said, as if switching off a part of his brain that had been focused on going home. "What property is that?"

"The Handy Home Helpers, actually not only a property but a business."

"Well, Mrs. Murdoch, there might be a problem with that. I have nothing official, but . . ."

"All the more reason for haste," I said, not wanting to discuss Lurline's threat to take the business off the market, something that I shouldn't have been in a position to know. "Mr. Blair," I went on, "I want to submit an offer today—tonight if that's what it takes. I'd like you to prepare an Offer to Purchase right now, and I'll run down and sign it before your office closes."

"No problem," he said and I heard the shuffling of papers on his desk. "What kind of offer do you have in mind? Although I should tell you that several offers have already been submitted and rejected. There's been a lot of interest in that particular property lately."

I wanted to say, "Yes, I know," but I restrained from mentioning my previous participation. Instead, I gave him the knock-Lurline's-socks-off price along with a hefty percentage as earnest money, heard him draw in his breath, then laconically say, "Well, that should get her attention."

Then, clearing his throat, he said, "I'll call the owner's broker now and put him on notice that an offer is coming."

"Yes, do that, because I don't want to have to track him down through half a dozen Christmas parties. There are, however, a few requirements that should be included with the offer. First of all, this is my first and *only* offer, so no negotiations at all. Don't bother giving me a counteroffer. I won't accept it. Secondly, I want an immediate response and, if affirmative, I want the owner's signature on the offer tonight. The luxury of sleeping on it is off the table. My offer will be withdrawn before the sun comes up in the morning. I am in no mood for dillydallying."

"Yes, *ma'am*," he said. "I'm on it and a Merry Christmas to you, Mrs. Murdoch."

Wishing him the same, I hung up, drew in a deep breath, and thought, I'm not only at the Rubicon, I'm up to my neck in it. I fiddled with my hair a little, thinking that Velma needed to trim it at my next appointment, then I went downstairs, stopping at the hall closet for my coat.

Sam looked up as I, buttoning my coat, entered the living room. He grinned and said, "You did it then, did you?"

"Yes, I did, and I have to get to the bank for a certified check for the earnest money, then run to Mr. Blair's office to sign the Offer to Purchase, and do both before either of them closes. I've also followed your advice and put a short response time on the offer because I don't want Lurline Corn to have time to think."

"Want me to go with you? We could have supper downtown since I've noticed a considerable silence from the kitchen."

"I sent Lillian home early, that's why. She needs the rest. So, yes, let's do."

On the way downtown, Sam said, "If this doesn't work out, you might not want Ms. Corn knowing your business."

He went on to explain, so as we went into Joe Blair's office, I was flexing my right hand in preparation. After handing over the certified check for the escrow account, I leaned over the desk and signed the Offer to Purchase in a scrawl that would take a paleographer to decipher. Then we watched as it was faxed to the office of Lurline's broker.

"I hope," I said, "that you've impressed on her broker the need for a timely response."

"Don't worry about that," Mr. Blair said. "I know for a fact that he has his car warming up. He'll have your offer in Ms. Corn's hands within the hour." Mr. Blair stopped gathering his papers, looked up at me, and said, "Do you have a closing date in mind? If she accepts, that is."

"Yes, the sooner the better."

"Good," he said with a knowing smile. "End-of-the-year statistics are coming up."

I smiled back, knowing a thing or two myself, namely that a broker's fee from a large transaction can make a difference in a broker's bottom line for the year.

Chapter 48

❦

I slept well that night, the result, I thought, of having made a decision and acted upon it which, to me, meant it had been a satisfying day. Sam and I had had a nice meal at a restaurant on Main Street, topped by a phone call from Joe Blair as soon as we got home.

According to Lurline's broker, she had taken the bait and accepted my Offer to Purchase—at least, he said, she'd made a verbal commitment and had given every indication of her imminent approval. She had not, however, signed in her broker's presence nor had she given the offer back to him. Something, he'd told Mr. Blair, concerning a family member who she wanted to consult before fully committing herself. As such, Mr. Blair explained, there would be a slight delay in completing the transaction, and he hoped that I would understand since we were so close to confirming the sale.

"I explained," Mr. Blair went on, "that we wanted this completed tonight. I know you said sunup, but I gave them only until midnight to get the signed offer back to me."

"Call me as soon as you get it," I said, "no matter how late."

Although slightly edgy at the delay, I was nonetheless pleased that I'd gotten Lurline's attention. It had taken not quite three hours from start to finish for me to make an offer and for her to forget Bug and grab the money. For all I knew, she was already packing for Florida.

But first, she'd called Etta Mae to "crow about getting more than she expected," as Etta Mae put it when she, in turn, called me before I had my coat off. "So it's gone," Etta Mae had said as if in the depths of despair. "Somebody else bought it right out from under us. Lurline said she didn't know or care who bought it—the signature was so scribbled she couldn't read it, but money is money, she said, regardless of where it comes from. She was flying high, Miss Julia, thinking she'd made the deal of a lifetime. And," she went on, "and I had to pretend to be happy for her when I could get a word in edgewise. And I don't mean to sound like I wish she hadn't sold it because I sure didn't want to work for Bug. But I just hate losing it when we came so close to getting it. I guess," she said, then broke off to clear her throat, "I guess it was too much to hope for in the first place. Anyway, Miss Julia, I'll find out who bought it and let you know. Maybe it was Mr. Sitton, but thank you for everything even though it didn't work out."

"Etta Mae," I said, "I apologize to you for not telling you ahead of time, but I didn't realize that Lurline would call you so quickly. But get yourself in gear, girl, because Lurline is selling it to me."

Dead silence ensued. Then, "Wha-at?"

So I went through it for her, omitting only the price to which I'd committed myself, and ended by saying that I hoped she was still willing to buy it from me. "It's the same for you either way. But instead of you borrowing from me to buy from Lurline, I've cut out the middle man so to speak, so that you'll be buying directly from me. You'll be making the same payments under the same terms that we've already agreed on.

"I hope that's still agreeable with you," I went on, "because goodness knows, I don't want to run the business. All I want is a good investment, which is you, Etta Mae. On the other hand," I quickly added, "I don't want you to feel obligated."

But of course I did. If she changed her mind, I'd be up a creek without a paddle or else crawling on my hands and knees to

Ernest Sitton to entice him into taking The Handy Home Helpers off my hands.

"You *did*?" Etta Mae asked with a note of wonder in her voice. "I mean, *really*? You bought it?"

"Well, yes, I guess it's all but bought. I don't have the signed offer in hand, but I just heard from Joe Blair that Lurline told her realtor that she definitely accepted my offer. I was right before calling you, not knowing that she'd beat me to it. I tell you, Etta Mae, I think it was the timing. I think she was having severe second thoughts about leaving Bug in charge, so she might've accepted any decent offer that came along." And that thought immediately made me wonder if I could've gotten the business for a lower price. But you can't second-guess yourself all the time, so I put that aside, wished Etta Mae sweet dreams of ownership, and went to bed feeling content with what had been accomplished.

So, as I've said, I slept quite well that night, resting on my laurels for having made something turn out right. Even though I had committed myself to staying out of other people's business, I didn't think that lending a hand now and then really counted as interference or micromanagement, and certainly not meddling by any stretch of the imagination.

We woke early on the morning before Christmas Eve to the sound of Lillian, then James and Janelle, talking and laughing down in the kitchen. The laughter jangled with my sudden realization that I had not heard from Joe Blair. My heart sank as I knew he would've called if he'd received the signed offer. His silence seemed to mean that Lurline had had a change of heart, or else another, better offer.

Wanting to bawl in frustration on Sam's shoulder, I decided instead to soldier on in hopes that there was a simple and understandable explanation for Lurline's continued delay.

"Busy day ahead," Sam said as he threw back the covers. "Anything I can do for you today?"

"I don't think so. Well, maybe clean the living room fireplace and lay a fire in case company drops by. And finish wrapping your gifts so I can straighten Lloyd's room. We'll need it for everybody's coats on Christmas. The florist is coming by this morning with the centerpiece for the table, and . . . oh, my goodness, I almost forgot." I came out of the bed in a hurry, reminded of something I'd almost let sneak up on me. "I meant to ask Mildred about Penelope going to the Christmas Eve service with us tomorrow. In fact, I'd almost forgotten about Mildred altogether."

"And she's gotten along just fine, hasn't she?"

"You're right," I said, smiling as I slowed down, "as you usually are. However, I should show a little interest after Horace's near escape, even though she's apparently done nothing for Penelope's Christmas which, now that I think of it, makes me mad all over again."

"Well," Sam said, "we'll do the best we can to make it a good Christmas for her. Which service are we going to? Not the one at midnight, I hope."

"No, we'll go at six o'clock, which is the children's service. Penelope wouldn't be able to stay awake for the later one."

Sam yawned. "Me, either. By the way," he said, turning to me, "you should check with Joe and be sure your offer has been signed and returned. It's not binding until he gets it back."

Well, that took even more wind out of my sails. I sat down abruptly, just done in at the thought of having come so close yet losing out after all. What if Lurline had changed her mind? What if Mr. Sitton had sent another offer? What if she'd decided Bug needed the responsibility?

Oh, Lord, now I'd have to tell Etta Mae that it was not a done deal after all.

———

"Have you heard from her?" I asked when Mr. Blair answered his phone. Then I quickly said, "Oh, sorry. Good morning, this is Julia Murdoch. Has Lurline Corn sent the signed offer?"

"Well, no, and I just hung up from talking with her broker. It seems that Ms. Corn is asking for extra time."

"No! I am not playing that game, Mr. Blair. She is just trying to tempt another bidder to top it, and I thought I'd made it plain that I am not interested in negotiating. You can tell her that I'm withdrawing the offer and . . ."

"No, no, wait," Mr. Blair said, seeing his commission beginning to grow wings. "She's accepted. Her broker saw her sign it. But she didn't want to send it back until she'd explained a change of plans to her nephew. It seems," Mr. Blair continued in a wry tone of voice, "she wanted to show him in writing the amount you'd offered, so he'd understand why she was selling. Apparently she'd led him to believe that she would leave the business to him. But, believe me, Mrs. Murdoch, she is more than pleased with your offer."

"Well, how long does she expect me to wait? I want this thing settled and set in stone, and I don't want to have to wait until sometime after Christmas."

"Hold on, ma'am, I've got another call coming in. It may be her broker. I'll put you on hold."

So I stood there, steaming and stewing and dreading telling Etta Mae that Lurline still had us dangling.

"Mrs. Murdoch?" Mr. Blair was back on the line. "That was her broker. She just called him from her cell phone to tell him she's in Easley, South Carolina, and—"

"What? She's out of town?"

"Yes, it seems her nephew's in a hospital down there and she's on her way to see about him."

"Bug?" I asked.

"No, car wreck. Anyway, she wanted to assure us, well, actually you that the offer is signed and she'll get it to us as soon as she gets back. She's asking for your patience because of a family emergency."

"Well, I guess there's nothing else I can do, but I don't like it. Did she give any idea of when she'll be back?"

"No, but I expect she'll want to be back for Christmas if he's in any shape to be moved. Why don't we say we'll expect the signed offer tomorrow afternoon by three?"

"All right," I said, sighing. "But that's it."

I hung up, just drained by the disappointment, and now I had to tell Etta Mae, which would put her in the same condition.

Chapter 49

❦

During a light breakfast, a lot of bantering went on in the kitchen between Sam and James, while Lillian, laughing at their carrying-on, stood at the counter chopping celery and onions.

When I asked if she wanted a cup of coffee, she wiped her face with her arm and said, "I already had some, an' I got to get all this chopped for the dressin', an' then I got to be sure I got everything for the Jell-O salad. I keep thinkin' I forgot something. You know," she went on, looking up, "the worst thing about cookin' a big dinner is timin' ev'rything jus' right. The turkey has to start thawin' days ahead of time, an' the dressin' has to be ready to go in the oven early Christmas mornin', and the Jell-O salad ought to be in the 'frigerator no later than Christmas Eve mornin', an' sweet potatoes got to be baked and peeled that afternoon, an' at the last minute, I got to whip the whippin' cream to finish the dessert, an' I have to put Janelle to work peelin' oranges for the ambrosia. She can set and do that tomorrow. Ev'rything has to be ready to go in or on the stove on Christmas mornin'. Then I can set and rest while it's all cookin'."

"Well, as I've said before," I said, "you could lead an army, Lillian, and," I went on, leaning over to whisper so James wouldn't hear, "I'm glad you're in charge. But don't tire yourself out so much that you won't enjoy the day when it gets here."

Leaving her smiling, I went to the library and called Etta Mae while dreading every minute it would take to tell her.

"Etta Mae? Are you driving?"

"No'm, I'm just sitting in my car in a patient's yard, trying to get myself up for the next one on my list. I've heard, Miss Julia. Lurline called early this morning to tell me that Bug got upset when she told him she was selling the business instead of giving it to him. She said he broke her heart when he stormed out late last night, saying that nobody ever thought of him. And, Miss Julia, that's all that family has ever done—think of him, I mean." Etta Mae drew in a shuddering breath. "So go ahead and give me the bad news. She's backed out, hasn't she?"

"No, at least not yet," I said and told her of Mr. Blair's call. "He seems to think she's worried that I'll withdraw the offer, but we're giving her until three o'clock tomorrow. So just hold on, Etta Mae, we're still in the running."

"I'm almost afraid to hope anymore," she replied in a mumble, as if to herself.

"Well, tell me this, why was Bug going to South Carolina? What's down there?"

"Oh," she said, "they have family down there, so I guess he was going to hang out with them for a while. Anyway, he had a wreck again—his was the only car in sight and he drove off the road, sideswiped a speed limit sign, and ended up in a ditch."

"That's the second time he's done that, isn't it? Maybe he needs glasses or something. Was he hurt?"

"I don't guess so," Etta Mae said. "They took him to the hospital, then to jail, which is mainly why Lurline went down there, to get him out."

"Goodness," I said, "I didn't know they put you in jail if nobody else was involved."

"They don't. It was all the empty beer cans in his car that did it. Those South Carolina cops don't mess around."

"Oh, well then," I said, no longer interested in Bug's run-in with a ditch and out-of-state law officers. "We'll just have to wait one more day, Etta Mae. I expect by this time Lurline wants nothing more than to be rid of both The Handy Home Helpers and Bug. Florida has to be looking more and more attractive to her."

After boosting Etta Mae's spirits, although doing little for mine, I said goodbye and then called Mildred. Before I could ask after Penelope, she insisted that I come over for coffee that afternoon.

"I thought you'd forgotten me," she said. "I know it's Christmas and everybody's busy, and I've certainly been busy, as well. But I'd really like to know what you think of the options I've found for Horace."

"I've found two places," Mildred said, pointing to a small stack of brochures as we sat in the chintz-covered chairs in her sun-room. "They're the best of the crop, although that's not saying much. Just reading about them saddens me. They make their facilities sound so nice, even desirable. Yet once you're inside, you don't get out unless someone with a key lets you out. But I just called to confirm one of them because I decided that I'd feel better if he's in a church-run place, so it'll be the Episcopal retirement center near Southern Pines. Of course it's farther away than the one north of Asheville, but I don't expect to be visiting very often, anyway. I mean," she went on as tears glistened in her eyes, "he doesn't even know who I am. He thinks I'm his mother or his sister or maybe that Jane Smith, whoever she is or was."

"I am so sorry," I said, and I was, imagining how I'd feel if Sam ever lost all memory of our life together. "But I'm glad you've found a place for him."

"Yes," Mildred said, dabbing at her eyes. "Ida Lee is going through his things and beginning to pack. We're taking him the day after Christmas. I've found a professional driver, so we'll take the Town Car."

"Ida Lee is going with you?"

"Oh, yes, I couldn't manage without her. We should be back late the same day, but I want to impose on you again and ask if you'd have Penelope while we're gone."

"Of course," I said. "We'll be happy to have her, and on that note I wanted to ask if she can go with us to the Christmas Eve service at the church. We're going to the early one at six, and," I quickly went on, taking advantage of the opening she'd given me, "we'd love to have her this afternoon. Latisha is coming for a little while, and the girls play so well together."

"You may not want her at all," Mildred said, reaching for her coffee cup. "I wouldn't take her anywhere if it was up to me. On top of everything else I've had to contend with, she has almost been the straw that broke the camel's back. I've been on the telephone for days, speaking with first one care center after another, calling to find a driver, going through Horace's clothes and all the stuff he's saved, trying to get him to shave and shower, and . . . ," she stopped to take a breath, then went on, ". . . and arranging a schedule of sitters. Did you know that there're people who will sit with sick people, and I do mean *sit*? That's about all they do, just *sit*. And they cost a fortune, but at least they let you know if there's a problem, especially with someone who's a flight risk, as Horace is. I told them that if he ends up hanging on the side of the house again, somebody was going to get sued. So now they sit by the window instead of in the hall. Anyway," she said after stopping to catch her breath, "what does Penelope do on top of everything else? She cuts her hair!"

"Oh, no," I said, and recalled Ida Lee's scissors, which Penelope had used so adroitly when wrapping her gifts. "She cut her beautiful long hair?"

"No, not all of it, but, Julia, you may not want to take her out in public. When she came downstairs this morning, I could hardly believe my eyes. I called Velma to see if she could do anything—even it up or something, and do you know she's closed her shop for the holidays already? You'd think Christmas would be her busiest time. I really think she needs some competition in this town. Anyway, Penelope looks like a little ragamuffin, so she really should stay home."

"I can't believe it's that bad," I said. "Remember when one of Hazel Marie's twins went to bed with chewing gum in her mouth? The next morning it was stuck all through her hair. They ended up having to give her almost a boy's haircut, so, you know, children do that sort of thing and nobody thinks anything of it."

"Well," Mildred said with a slight wave of her hand, "if you don't mind the way she looks, go ahead and take her. But where she ever came up with the idea of *bangs* is beyond me."

Startled, I blinked, then, hurrying to relieve Penelope of some of Mildred's displeasure, I admitted that she'd gotten the idea from me. "I'm sorry, Mildred, but don't be upset with her. She would've never thought of bangs if I hadn't said they'd look nice on her."

"Well," Mildred said in her dry way, "just wait till you see her now."

Chapter 50

❧

"Lillian?" I called as I opened the kitchen door and stepped in with Penelope in her pink fur-lined boots edging in behind me. The house was quiet with James having gone back to Hazel Marie's, leaving to Lillian and Janelle the final preparations for our Christmas dinner.

"Look who's come to see us," I said, urging Penelope forward, knowing that Lillian would know what to say.

When Mildred had called Penelope down so I could "see what she'd done to herself," I had not only seen what she'd done, but what she was feeling, as well. The child was in great need of someone with hairstyling expertise and an abundance of comfort to offer.

To say that the newly acquired bangs were uneven does not quite cover the description. One side was long enough to lap over her eyebrow, while the other side was little more than a wisp of hair, leaving her forehead only partially covered. I had been vaguely reminded of Veronica Lake, a movie star of long ago who was famous for a wave of hair covering one eye.

Penelope had stood before her grandmother with the miserable look of a child who knows she's done something wrong and has been told of it in no uncertain terms. Mildred would never use inappropriate words to anyone, but I also knew that her tone of voice could flay the skin off a miscreant. Penelope had the forlorn look of a scolded puppy, so I knew she'd been the target of Mildred's extreme displeasure.

Not wanting to hear any belittling comments Mildred might make, I jumped in to announce that Latisha was coming especially to see Penelope and that Lillian wanted them to frost some cookies she'd made. That was enough to get the child released for the afternoon. "Oh, take her," Mildred had said. "Maybe she'll stay out of trouble with you."

Now, as we walked in and Lillian got her first sight of Penelope's mangled hair, she said, "Oh, my goodness!" Which could be taken in several different ways, but her shock from the sight was evident enough to me. Lillian, however, quickly recovered. "Here's our pretty little girl come to see us again. Come'ere, little Honey, an' let Lillian give you a great big hug. I been missin' you."

Then, turning from hugging Penelope, Lillian looked at me and said, "Miss Julia, put this chile on a stool while I get a towel an' some scissors. We gonna even things up a little."

Spreading newspapers on the floor, I centered a counter stool on them and helped Penelope to climb up. Lillian draped a towel around Penelope's shoulders, stood back with comb and scissors at the ready, and said, "I don't think we want 'em as short as the shortest side, so how you wanta do this?"

"I thought you knew how," I said, just as Janelle walked in, having finished setting silverware on the card tables in the library.

Taking in the scene, she asked, "What y'all doin'?"

"Fixin' this chile's bangs," Lillian said, "but I'm studyin' on it first."

Janelle, a competent, reliable teenager who was third in her high school class and willing to work at anything for college money, took one look and said, "First thing, comb her hair over her face. Just comb it forward from the top of her head, then cut straight across right above her eyebrows."

Lillian hesitated. "You wanta do it?"

"Sure," Janelle said, taking the comb, "I've cut bangs before."

And in just a few minutes, long strands of black hair were falling on the newspaper and an even line of bangs was on Penelope's forehead. One side was a little thinner than the other side, but from a distance you could hardly tell.

"There!" Janelle said, brushing hair from Penelope's face. "You look terrific."

Removing the towel from Penelope's shoulders, I turned her around to get a good look. "They're perfect! Oh, Honey, bangs are beautiful on you. Janelle did such a good job. Now, would you like me to make a braid to go with them?"

She nodded, her face clearing of misery, as the hope of pleasing those who counted reappeared. When I finished the thick, loose plait and tied a green bow at the end, Lillian took her to the hall bathroom and lifted her up so she could see in the mirror. The pleased expression that swept over her face lifted my spirits.

"Wait till your grandmother sees you now," I said. "You're going to knock her socks off."

When Latisha was dropped off by her babysitter after choir practice later that afternoon, she took one look at Penelope and said, "Why, girl, you look just like a pesky kid in a movie that drives her parents crazy but gets them out of trouble in the end." Which of course pleased Penelope no end.

They played quietly for an hour or so with Latisha chattering away about the Christmas Eve service. I heard her tell Penelope about the sweet girl playing Mary, and about the manger with a baby doll in it, and about the shepherds wearing fake beards, and about the three kings wearing bathrobes until Lillian was ready to go home. It was time for Penelope to be home, as well, so both girls prepared to leave.

As we put on our coats, Lillian said, "Now, you little girls need to be in bed right after church tomorrow night so Santy Claus can come, an' if you listen real close right before you go to sleep, you might hear little reindeer hooves tappin' on the roof."

Waving goodbye to Latisha and Lillian as they left for home, I walked Penelope across the yards to the house next door.

On our way over, Penelope said, "I wish I could see three kings come walking in."

"But, Honey, you will see them," I said. "You're going with us to see the whole service and sing the songs and hear the Christmas story again. Didn't your grandmother tell you?"

She shook her head. "Maybe she forgot."

"Well, you just be ready because we're going." But there was another black mark against Mildred and it was all I could do to keep my feelings to myself.

Before ringing the doorbell, I leaned down and said to Penelope, "Sometimes grandmothers don't know what all the girls are wearing these days. But you are right in style, and bangs look wonderful on you."

Undercutting Mildred's authority like that was not something I'd ordinarily do, but I wanted to ease the sting of any other slashing comment that might be made.

As I walked home alone, I couldn't rid myself of the downcast look I'd seen on Penelope's face as the door closed behind her. It was bad enough to think of Mildred making snide remarks about the way the child looked. Even worse was the fear that Santa Claus did not have the Allen house on his list of stops the following night.

Slightly comforting, though, was the fact that I had a few gifts for Penelope under our tree. That, however, wasn't the same as discovering what Santa had left under your own tree.

Sam and I went to a party that evening at the Hargroves' home, taking literally it having been called a drop-in, for that was about all we did. Too many other things were on my mind to be in a party mood.

"Next year," I said to Sam on our way home, "I'm planning absolutely nothing. I am going to focus only on the spiritual meaning of Christmas and go to every church service there is. I'm not inviting anybody in, and I'm not accepting any invitations out. It'll be a Christmas celebrating what it's supposed to celebrate."

"Okay," Sam said as he turned onto Polk Street, "but you should write that down. You could forget as the year goes on."

I laughed. "I know. But my intentions are good right now."

I woke on Christmas Eve morning more determined than ever to lock down the purchase of The Handy Home Helpers and to do something about a sad little girl. My musings on exactly what could be done about either were interrupted by a phone call from Etta Mae, who still needed reassurance that The Handy Home Helpers would soon be hers.

"Miss Julia," she said as if trying to catch her breath, "sorry to bother you, but would you just tell me one more time that Lurline really said she'd sell to you and that you will really own it and that you will really sell it to me?"

I laughed. "It's really true, Etta Mae, or will be when we close, and she's committed to closing the sale." At least, I thought, Lurline has *said* she's committed. But if she couldn't get Bug out of jail and she didn't get the signed offer back to Mr. Blair by three o'clock, I had a big decision to make. I didn't, however, share my concerns with Etta Mae.

"Okay," she said, taking a deep breath. "I just wanted to be sure. I keep trying to picture Lurline deciding to actually sell. I mean, after telling me she was putting Bug in charge. Something really changed her mind, because she dropped him so fast, his head must still be swimming."

"I think she just came to her senses, and lucky for us that she did. Now," I said, so she'd know I was changing subjects, "can we expect you and your friend, Deputy Moser, for dinner on Christmas?"

A certain, very pregnant pause ensued. "I didn't RSVP, did I? Oh, Miss Julia, I am so sorry. You'll never trust me with a business if I can't do the right thing."

"Don't worry about it," I said. "I knew you had a lot on your mind, so the two of you just come on. Your places are already set and waiting for you."

"Well, thank you, but I want you to know that I do know better, and I feel awful about it."

"Oh, I counted on you both because Granny Wiggins is coming, and I assumed she'd be coming with you. And I'm looking forward to getting to know your friend better."

She giggled. "I am, too."

After hanging up, I was more determined than ever to hold Lurline's feet to the fire. If Bug played on her heartstrings long enough, she could try to renege on her commitment to sell. And if she did, I decided then and there, I would sue her up one side and down the other. I was through playing around with that woman and, as my patience ran out with her, I thought of another woman I was also through playing around with.

Chapter 51

❦

There were still many last-minute things to do to prepare for our Christmas guests, but I was undaunted in my intention to tell Mildred exactly what I thought of the way she was treating her grandchild. Just because it was Christmas Eve didn't mean that I had to be merry and bright all day long.

"Mildred," I said when she answered her phone, "I know you have a lot on you right now, but——"

"Oh, Julia," she broke in, "I'm so glad you called. You won't believe what I'm doing. I'm sitting here in Horace's office where he keeps his datebook, his calendar, and all the golf and tennis trophies he won at various country clubs. And," she went on with a sigh, "also, photograph albums, old notes from friends, and all kinds of mementos from the past. I never knew how sentimental he was to have kept all this stuff, and I have to decide what to send with him and what to throw out. But it's heartbreaking to look at the things he so obviously treasured."

Hearing that was almost enough to deter me from adding more to the burden Mildred was already bearing. But not quite enough.

"Mildred," I said again, "I know this is a poor time to bring it up, but time has almost——"

"I found it, Julia," she said so softly that I barely heard her. All I knew was that her mind was still stuck on the track it had started on, and that she was not listening to me.

"Found what?" I asked, being too easily deterred from my intention.

"Her picture," Mildred said, her voice muffled. "He's kept it all these years. And the minute I saw it, I remembered."

"Well, listen, Mildred, there's only one day left to shop and you really should—"

"She was a tiny, little thing," Mildred mused. "Everybody said she had a waist like Scarlett O'Hara's, but I remember Horace saying that she looked like an underfed waif to him, which was just to put me off because he's kept her picture all these years."

"Who, Mildred? Who're you talking about?"

"Jane Smith," she said and began to sob. "I'm talking about Jane Smith, the girl . . . the girl he thought he'd married. Well," she went on, obviously regaining control, "he can just dream on. I'm tearing this up right now. He'll have to get along on his memories if he has any left."

"Mildred . . . ," I began, hardly knowing what to say.

"Don't try to talk me out of it. I'm not having it in my house and I'm not sending it with him. The idea of still mooning over a girl who has to be sixty years old if she's a day is just unbelievable. And, Julia, this just proves I was right. He was seeing her while we were engaged. He denied it, but I knew in my heart after that last debutante ball that he was smitten. But I thought he'd gotten over her when we married because he never gave me any cause to worry after that." She stopped to blow her nose. "Of course that was after Daddy had a talk with him.

"Still," she went on, "it's just devastating to find out that she's still on his mind, and . . ." Full-fledged sobbing was all I could hear.

"Oh, for goodness' sakes," I said, losing all sympathy and recapturing my reason for calling. "Get over it, Mildred, and count yourself lucky that you've had a faithful husband. Some people, as you know, haven't been so fortunate. And, besides, Horace is no longer responsible for anything he does or has done in the past.

Tear up that picture if you want to, but let the rest of it go. You have more important things to think about, and the main one is your granddaughter. You have just today to shop so she can have a halfway decent Christmas from you."

"You mean," Mildred said with more than a touch of bitterness, "the granddaughter foisted on me by a thoughtless daughter who I barely even know anymore? You mean the one who chopped off so much of her hair that I can hardly bear to look at her?" Then just as quickly, Mildred's voice took on a self-pitying tone. "I am trying my best, Julia, to put up with what I have to deal with, but it's just one thing after another. I don't know how I can stand much more. So the idea of going shopping today, and *where*, I ask you. Walmart? No, thank you. I have a couple of things for her, some socks and sweaters and a nice coat I ordered some while back. Penelope or whatever her name is will just have to understand that this is not the time for celebrating anything."

"Oh," I said, "I think she already understands that." And I hung up.

And, still steaming, called right back. "Sorry, Mildred, but I didn't finish. All I want to say is that Santa Claus needs to stop at your house tonight, and you need to make sure he does. You simply cannot let Penelope get up on Christmas morning and find that it's just another day of mourning over what should have been for you. In other words, start thinking of someone besides yourself, and if that makes you mad, then so be it. But get up from there and get that child some Christmas presents before the stores close. And now I'm hanging up again." And I did.

Still in the throes of righteous anger, I could barely recall what I'd actually said to my longtime friend from what I'd left out but wished I'd said. But at least *something* got said that I hoped would redound to Penelope's benefit.

Unless, I thought with an awful sinking feeling, I'd made Mildred so angry that not only would our friendship be ended, but Penelope would suffer the consequences as well.

And I immediately began to regret lashing out as I'd done. I should've stayed out of the business of other people just as I'd promised myself I would do. But then I thought of Etta Mae and how happy she was because I'd been involved just a little in her life. And that reminded me that we were still waiting on Lurline's official acceptance of my Offer to Purchase.

So, as the afternoon began to lengthen even the Christmas carols playing on Lillian's kitchen radio couldn't lift my spirits. All afternoon, I fretted over Mildred's state of mind and over the possibility of Lurline changing hers. Had I ruined a friendship and, in the process, made things worse for Penelope? Had I given Lurline too much rope and Bug had latched onto it? I declare, I was fast losing all the Christmas spirit that had been building during the week.

But then the phone rang, and it was Mildred. At least she was still speaking to me, unless she'd called to let me have it with both barrels.

Instead, she murmured, "I just called to remind you that I do have a couple of things for Penelope. I have Doreen wrapping them now. And I've been thinking that maybe you're right, and I should make it a better Christmas for her. There's no use making her miserable just because I am. I know it's getting late, but do you know what will be open?"

"Walmart," I said, "just as you said. That is, if they haven't sold out of everything. Go now, and get Ida Lee to go with you. I promise you, Mildred, you'll feel better when you make sure that Santa Claus comes to your house."

There was a long pause, then Mildred said, "You know what I could do? I mean, since I didn't put up a tree? I can have a treasure hunt, so Penelope has to follow clues all over the house to find her gifts. Yes, that's what I'll do. Sorry to cut you off, Julia, but I've got to get busy."

Not at all minding being cut off, I hung up with a smile on my face. And it stayed there until Joe Blair called at three o'clock.

"Ah, Mrs. Murdoch," he said, somewhat hesitantly, "I've just had a call from Ms. Corn, calling from her car. She's on her way back from South Carolina, and wants me to tell you that she has the signed offer with her. She'll drop it by my office in about an hour. She hopes you'll forgive her for being late, but it couldn't be helped. Her nephew . . . well, you know."

If it had been just me without Etta Mae's involvement, I would've dropped The Handy Home Helpers then and there. Some people can just push you to the edge, you know, and I was teetering on it. But I controlled myself and said, "Tell her that this is the absolute last extension, so she'd better not have a wreck on her way. And tell her I want a copy of that offer with her signature on it before five thirty. After that I'm going to church and Ms. Corn can look for another buyer."

"Uh, well, she really wants to know who the buyer is now. She says nobody can figure out your signature. Do you mind if I tell her?"

"I certainly do mind! She'll find out at the closing, which you can set up any time she wants—the sooner the better. But for now, she has to be satisfied with the price she's getting unless she comes up with another delay, in which case she'll never find out because I'll be through."

"Yes, ma'am, I'll bring you a copy as soon as I get the offer."

He was ringing my doorbell about an hour before the Christmas Eve service was to begin. I quickly scanned the copy, smiled at Lurline Corn's very neat and very legible signature, and wished Mr. Blair a Merry Christmas.

Showing it to Sam, I said, "I'd love to show this to Etta Mae, but I don't want her to know how much I paid for it."

Sam smiled. "That's between you and the Lord, right?"

I smiled back, and went upstairs to put the finishing touches to my attire for church when the phone rang again.

"Julia," Mildred said in a tone that got my attention in a hurry. "You won't believe what's happened now. I sent Ida Lee and Doreen to Walmart to buy some toys for Penelope. They went in my car because it has a trunk and Ida Lee's doesn't. You have to be careful about theft at this time of year, you know. And I was just too tired to face the crowds, and now Ida Lee just called to say that they've been in an accident. Somebody ran into them just as they pulled into the parking lot, and my new car's torn up and the police are there and the EMTs are on the way, and I am about to lose my mind!"

"Oh, no," I said. "Were they hurt?"

"Well, Ida Lee was able to call me, so I guess she's all right. Doreen, though, is being looked at, whatever that means. And on top of that, I've just been notified that Horace's evening sitter can't come, which means he'll be on his own until the next one comes at eleven. See, Julia, what I have to put up with? I hire sitters, then they don't come, which is a poor way to do business even if it is Christmas Eve."

When she paused to take a breath, I jumped in. "Can we do anything? You want us to go see about Ida Lee and Doreen?"

"No, I don't think they need that. Ida Lee is so capable, you know, and even though she's a little shaken up I think she has things well in hand. It's just a matter of waiting to get the accident report, and waiting on a tow truck—the car can't be driven—and waiting for a taxi to bring them home. I expect they'll both need to rest and unwind when they get here—whenever that'll be. I don't know what I'll do if either of them need hospitalization. But the reason I called is that I just cannot spare Penelope tonight.

She can go to church with you another time, but without a sitter, I need her to keep an eye on Horace. She can read to him until somebody shows up."

A dozen things to say flashed through my mind, but I was so dismayed and disappointed that I couldn't get anything out. I finally managed to express my condolences on the loss of her new car, the evening sitter, and the constant attendance to her needs by Ida Lee and Doreen.

After hanging up, I stood by the phone for a few minutes, trying to sort through the situation. Of course I was sorry about the accident and glad that Ida Lee and Doreen weren't hurt, but that didn't negate the fact that Penelope would miss not only the Christmas Eve service but the arrival of Santa Claus, as well.

Then I thought of something. "Sam?" I called, tracking him to the living room. "Do we have time to go to Walmart before church or would it be better to go afterward?"

When I told him what had happened, he folded the newspaper and stood up. "Let's go now. The midnight service is the best one, anyway."

❀

Chapter 52

As Sam turned in to the huge Walmart parking lot a few minutes past six o'clock that evening, we passed a tow truck pulling out with Mildred's injured Town Car hiked up on its hind wheels.

"My goodness," Sam said, slowing to get a good look, "they really got whacked. Must've been a Mack truck to bend the frame like that."

"I guess it was a good thing that Mildred wasn't with them. I'd never hear the end of it." Then, feeling bad for sounding so unsympathetic, I said, "I'm glad, though, that Ida Lee and Doreen are all right."

We found a parking place seemingly two miles from the front of the Walmart store, and went in to find the place still full of anxious, single-minded shoppers. You'd think that people wouldn't wait till the last night to do their shopping, wouldn't you?

"Where to?" Sam asked as he disengaged a cart from the few remaining ones.

"The toy department," I said. "Mildred already has some clothes for her."

"Okay," Sam said, making a left turn with the cart, "but somehow this all seems strangely familiar." And we smiled at each other, recalling a similar shopping trip when Lloyd was so achingly young.

But that meant that we were experienced last-minute toy shoppers, so I led us straight to the almost empty bicycle display.

"My word," I said, surveying the leftovers, "I hope we can find something suitable. It's a settled fact there won't be anybody to help us. Look for a girl's bicycle, Sam, a small one, maybe one or two sizes up from a tricycle. I don't care if she outgrows it in a year."

We found one and only one without the masculine bar, but it was complete with streamers on the handlebars and a bell that dinged quite pleasurably. Unhappily, though, it wasn't pink, but at that stage of the game, blue seemed perfect especially since it was the only small one left. I liked to think that it had been waiting for us.

I took over pushing the cart because Sam pointed out that it wasn't safe to leave the bicycle unattended as we shopped. Other eyes were already scanning the empty display area with disappointment and zooming in on our bicycle with envy, so he ended up pushing it up one aisle and down another as I filled the cart as best as I could from the depleted shelves.

"I already have a baby doll and a crayon set," I told Sam, "and a good thing that was because the only dolls left are too mature for Penelope."

"Um-m, too mature for me, too," he said, eyeing the shapely dolls still waiting to be bought.

I placed in the cart a few boxes of toys and games of one kind or another—things Penelope might enjoy on rainy days—a couple of I Can Read books, and a large paint set on the assumption that she would not have bought the same for someone else unless she liked it herself.

"One more thing, Sam," I said, "then we'll be through."

"Good, I'm getting tired of pushing this thing." And he wheeled the bicycle quickly out of the way of a harried-looking woman with a glint in her eye.

When we reached the jewelry counter, I was relieved to find a saleslady ready to help us. She was the only one I'd seen in the entire store, but her being there made sense because jewelry was too tempting to be left unlocked for the perusal of the shopping public.

I selected, with Sam's approval, a small—I hoped not too small—simple gold bangle, then, after looking with longing at a necklace with a tiny gold cross, bought it, too.

"You don't think we're getting too much?" Sam asked in his uncritical way of suggesting that I reconsider what I was doing.

"Yes, I do," I said, "but the necklace is for her birthday, because I don't want to have to come out here again."

"When's her birthday?"

"I don't know but whenever it is, I'll be ready."

After an interminable time waiting in line, we were finally able to check out and slog to the car with me pushing the cart piled with sacks of gifts, and Sam still pushing the bicycle. With the car full, the bicycle just barely fitting into the back seat, we collapsed in the front seats to catch our breath.

"I'm glad we only do this once a year," Sam said. "My back is killing me from leaning over that bicycle."

"Yes, and for just a penny I'd skip the midnight service and go to bed."

"No penny," Sam said, firmly. "You can nod off during the anthem."

"Yes, well, they're long enough sometimes." Then we smiled at each other, knowing that we'd be in our usual pew regardless of how tired we were.

As we neared Polk Street and home, Sam said, "How're we going to do this? Shall I go straight to Mildred's and unload there, or do you want to take everything in at our house?"

"I haven't thought that far ahead," I said, and proceeded to do so. "Let's unload at Mildred's. Surely Penelope is asleep by now, and we can pile everything up in the foyer for her to see when she comes downstairs in the morning. That is, of course, if Mildred hasn't come up with an idea of her own."

When we turned onto Polk Street, our best-laid plans had to be re-laid. Mildred's house was in total darkness, not even the soft glow of a night-light could be seen anywhere. And not only that, but her architecturally designed landscape lighting hadn't been turned on, either.

"I don't suppose we want to wake anybody, do we?" Sam asked, even as he turned into our driveway.

"No, we'll just unload here and call Penelope over in the morning. It's not the best idea in the world, but it's all we can do. Mildred," I went on a little defensively, "had a hard day, you know."

So we unloaded the gifts from the car, tromped through the house with each arm full to the living room, and placed them around the tree just as Santa might have done. Then we perked a pot of coffee and ate a quick sandwich, supper having been foregone in favor of the Walmart trip, and hurried across the street to the First Presbyterian Church of Abbotsville in time for the midnight service, which began before midnight. We just made it.

Stepping outside through the double doors onto the church portico, the organ recessional soaring out into the silence of the night, I looked up at the brilliant display of stars above us. After the warmth of the church, the midnight air seemed to penetrate the heaviest of coats, yet the small congregation lingered, passing along softly spoken Christmas wishes to each other.

Muting our responses to each other, the crowd gradually dispersed in various directions. It seemed to me that we were all once again awed by what had occurred so many centuries ago.

Sam took my hand as we walked along the side of the church toward our house straight ahead across Polk Street. It looked so welcoming in the chilly air with the few lights left on inside and the small gas lights flickering by the front door.

But as we passed the back of the church, a glare of lights from Mildred's house hit us full-force. Every light she owned must have been on.

"Uh-oh," Sam said as we stopped short of the street. "Something's happened again."

And surely it had, for a sheriff's car with bar lights flashing came zooming around the corner and pulled into our neighbor's driveway.

"Oh, my," I said, wondering how in the world Horace could have gotten out. But then with a sudden tightening in my chest at the squawk of an EMT vehicle headed our way, I choked out, "It could be Mildred. A real heart attack this time. Hurry, Sam."

He nodded, squeezed my hand, and glanced quickly about for oncoming traffic. As another siren began to wail in the distance, Sam hurried me across the street and onto our walk. As we gained the three steps to the porch, a large, shadowy shape flew at us from the dark corner of the porch. Sam threw his arm in front of me, as I yelped and almost fell off the steps as the creature enveloped me in its furry arms.

Almost smothered in Chanel-scented fur, I struggled to free myself as Mildred Allen cried, "*Julia!* Is she with you? Did you take her with you?"

"What? What?" Stunned, I could only turn to Sam and try to understand what was happening.

"Penelope!" Mildred cried as she flung out her arms. "She's gone, I can't find her anywhere! Tell me, *tell* me she went to church with you!"

Sam reached out to her, clasped her arms, and calmly said, "Slow down, Mildred. It's all right. She didn't go to church with us, but we'll find her. Now, come on inside and tell us what happened."

He unlocked the door and led Mildred, sobbing by this time, into the living room. I followed, still trying to slow my heart rate after having been accosted from out of the blue, or rather, from out of the dark corner of the porch.

Sam got Mildred seated in one of the wing chairs, gave her his clean handkerchief, then said, "Now tell us what's going on so we can help. But you have to hurry, deputies are pulling in at your place and you need to be there. What about Horace? Is he all right? Is it only Penelope who's missing?"

Mildred took a deep, shuddering breath, wiped her face with the handkerchief, and said, "Something woke me, I don't know what, but I got up to check on Horace, because the next sitter didn't show up, and, you know, he was alone. I'd made sure to lock his door before I went to bed, but well, you never know."

I sat down beside her and took her hand, noticing that she was still in one of her costly nightgowns with her full-length mink coat over it. "Take your time, Mildred," I crooned, although I wanted to shake the whole story out of her—where was that child?

"But," Mildred went on, "his door was wide open and he wasn't there, so I went to wake Penelope to help me look for him. In the house, you know. I didn't even think that he could've gotten outside. I mean, all the windows and doors were closed and locked. And, and, she wasn't there! I called and called her, got Ida Lee up to help me look, and . . . and, Julia, that's when we found a side door unlocked, and I hoped, prayed that she'd gone to church with you."

"Wait a minute," Sam said, "did you think they *both* went to church with us? I mean, if Horace is gone, too, did they leave together? Or separate, or what? It'll make a difference in how we look for them."

"I don't know, I don't know." And Mildred wept, then strangled out, "Maybe he took her or she took him, I just don't know."

"All right," Sam said with some urgency, "let's get you home. The deputies will want to talk to you."

"Ida Lee's there," Mildred said but she rose at Sam's urging. "She knows all I know, and I was so sure Penelope would be with you." And she broke into full-fledged crying again. "Because if she was, I knew she'd be all right."

As Sam led Mildred toward the door, I, shaken and fearful, whispered to him, "Check on the little Steiff bear. If it's gone, too, that might tell us something."

What it might tell, I didn't know, except that Penelope would not have left it of her own accord.

Chapter 53

Lord, it was a wretched thirty minutes of waiting and worrying while I, just in case, searched every room in our house, knowing all the while that Penelope could not have gotten in even if she'd wanted to. Looking out the side window in the kitchen every time I passed, I watched as the traffic increased in and out of the driveway next door. I had about decided to go on over there, hoping to be given something to do besides wring my hands over that child's whereabouts. And Horace's? Well, like Mildred, I barely gave a thought to his whereabouts.

But then Sam, looking drawn and concerned, returned. "Just getting some boots," he said, as I met him in the kitchen. "I'm on foot patrol down by Lily Pond Lake." As I gasped at what that might mean, he went on. "The deputies are well organized, just covering all the bases because it's fairly plain they're not walking. Or at least, Horace isn't. His car is gone, that little red Boxster, which should be easy to spot, and they've got Be-On-the-Lookouts all over the police radio bands. Highway patrol, too." Sam stopped and dropped into a chair, his shoulders sagging.

"*How*," I asked, "did Horace get that car? Not only was the garage locked up tight, but Mildred had the car keys upstairs in her room."

Sam shook his head. "I don't know about the car keys, except Mildred may have left them lying around. He broke a window to get into the garage as Grady Peeples did the last time Horace got out. I guess that proves his memory isn't completely gone. It's just," he said and stopped to rub his hand across his face, "they still don't know if Penelope is with him. They could've gone their separate ways. And I don't know which would be worse." He looked up at me. "Do you know where my boots are?"

"Oh, in here," I said and went into the pantry to retrieve them, hoping as I did that if Penelope was out on this cold night, she was wearing her fur-lined boots. "Sit down and I'll help you get them on." I stooped down to help, but my hands were shaking almost too much to lace up boots, but then so were his.

"Oh, Sam," I said and began to cry on his shoelaces.

"Don't, honey. Don't give up hope this early. Listen, they've put out a double alert, both Amber and Silver, so every driver in four states will be watching for them. Off-duty officers and people from all over are pouring in to help. We'll find 'em." He stood up and buttoned his coat, then found a cap in his pocket. "I'd better go, but I'll have my phone. Call if you hear anything."

I stood up, too, but not very quickly or as easily. "I guess I'll go sit with Mildred. She's really shaken by this, and I won't be able to sleep anyway."

Sam opened the door to leave, then said, "Go if you want to, but the EMTs gave her a sedative. Probably," he said with a touch of irony, "so they can do their jobs."

He gave me a quick kiss and left me thinking that Mildred had shown more concern over Penelope's absence than Horace's. In fact, she'd been close to hysteria, fearing for the child's safety and overwhelmed with a feeling of loss, proving once again that we often don't value what we have until we lose it.

Lights still blazed next door, but parked vehicles were down to one official car, as it appeared that everybody was out cruising the streets and beating the bushes. Mildred, I assumed, was sleeping through the agony of waiting for news.

But I wasn't. Alone in the quiet house, my fearful thoughts began to run amok. To keep busy, I heated up the leftover coffee then tried to drink it, as images of Penelope, alone and frightened, perhaps hurt, sprang up in my imagination.

Had she been kidnapped? Certainly, Mildred was a likely target—she made no secret of her wealth and she lived accordingly. If someone had gotten in while Mildred slept her routinely medicated sleep, could Horace have tried to follow them? As attached to the child as he seemed to be, it would've felt to him to be the sensible response to an abduction. If, that is, he could still understand the connection between cause and effect.

But was Horace able to drive? So many pathways in his brain had shut down that he might no longer be able to depend on the habits of a lifetime. Obviously, though, he thought he could because the car was gone, and Penelope couldn't have driven it. Actually, I had severe doubts that Horace still knew which side of the highway he should be on.

Which brought up another fearful scene: If they were together, where was Penelope sitting? Horace's car had no back seat, and I doubted that Penelope weighed enough to legally sit in the front seat. Was she strapped in? What if he hit another car? Ran off the road? Rolled over?

I jumped up from the table, almost upending the cup of undrinkable coffee. But I could no longer sit still while all the awful possibilities ran through my mind. I walked through the dining room, glanced at the table filled with silver serving dishes awaiting the food for our guests. Then I went on into the living room where I surveyed the pile of gifts under the dark tree. I knew that pots and pans ready for the oven waited in the kitchen, and perfectly appointed tables awaited hungry guests in the library.

It was already Christmas Day, the day for which we'd been preparing for weeks. I should have been happily anticipating the joyful hours to come, but now the day might be locked in my memory as one of the worst of my life. I shuddered, thinking that I'd almost rather be holding Mildred's hand than alone and fearing the worst.

But, I suddenly thought, what if everything was just the opposite of what we'd assumed? What if Penelope had seen or heard Horace leave and, worried about him, she'd followed him? She knew his state of mind to a certain extent and had already assumed a caring, even motherly, attitude toward him. But if that had been the case, why hadn't she awakened Mildred instead of following or going with him?

Well, if you'd been the target of Mildred's searing criticism, how eager would you be to rouse her from sleep? It made perfect sense to me that Penelope would try to manage on her own.

Still, other than the fact that they were both gone, there seemed to be no hard evidence that the two of them had left together. And that thought brought up a picture of Penelope, scared and lonely, wandering around town by herself, not knowing where to go, yet fully aware that she was unwanted at the place where she'd been deposited.

Maybe, I thought as a chill ran down my back, she'd come to our house where surely she'd known she would be welcome. My heart contracted at the thought that she'd knocked at our door while we were sitting in church thinking of another child for whom there had been no room.

I couldn't stand it any longer. I went back to the kitchen, picked up the phone, and tapped a number.

"Lillian . . ."

"What?" she asked, as I pictured her sitting up, immediately awake and alert. "What's the matter?"

When Lillian's car turned into the drive, I went to the back door to meet her. She came in with a worried look on her face and a heavy pocketbook under her arm. Latisha, still in flannel pajamas and wrapped in a trailing quilt, stumbled in behind her.

"Lillian," I said, on the verge of throwing my arms around her, "I'm so sorry for waking you, but thank you, thank you for coming. I'm so worried I don't know what to do."

"Don't worry 'bout wakin' me. I'd be mad if you didn't." She put her hands on Latisha's shoulders and turned her toward the library. "Go lay down on the sofa, honey, an' go back to sleep. An' don't bother none of them tables in there."

Latisha, still half-asleep, stumbled out of the kitchen as Lillian shook her head at the sight. "She goes ninety miles an hour all day long," Lillian said, coming out of her coat, "but when she lays down she's out like a light. Now," she went on, "you heard anything? What's goin' on over there?"

"Nothing, it looks like," I said, leaning against a chair. "At least, I've heard nothing from Sam and everything's quiet next door. As far as I know, they still don't know if they left together or separately. They have all kinds of bulletins out, and cars and trucks have been going and coming next door ever since we got home from church. I keep thinking, Lillian," I said and stopped to catch my breath, "that Penelope might've come here, either with Horace or without him, and we weren't here to let her in. It just breaks my heart."

"Come on an' set down," Lillian said, taking immediate charge, "while I put on some coffee. An' while I do that, I wanta hear everything, don't leave nothin' out, an' we'll figure out where they might be. 'Cause they're together, I b'lieve we can count on that. Neither one would let the other'un go off by theirselves."

"Yes," I said, gaining strength from Lillian's practical approach,

"I think you're right. Which means that Sam is tromping around a lake for no reason except that it has to be ruled out. But that's neither here nor there. The scary thing is the thought of them driving on the streets or on the interstate in the dark—I mean, is Horace aware enough to even turn on the headlights? And, if he is, why hasn't somebody reported seeing that unusual car? Sam said they'd put out alerts all over the place. But what worries me most is that Horace might be headed home, which he's tried to do before, and home to him is Virginia. Only he wouldn't know if Virginia is to the north or the south. For all we know," I went on, leaning my head on my hand, "they're somewhere in Tennessee, if they haven't already gone off the side of a mountain."

"Don't be thinkin' like that," Lillian said. "It's not a bit of help. I'm thinkin' they're not on the road at all, 'cause like you said, somebody would notice that car. What if they stopped somewhere to get something to eat or to take a nap? Nobody would see that car if it's parked somewhere in the dark."

"Great-Granny?" Latisha, still draped in the quilt, stood in the doorway.

Lillian started to rise. "You need to be asleep, little girl. Now go on back an' lay down."

Latisha propped one foot on her opposite leg and leaned against the doorway. "I think I might know where they are."

Chapter 54

❦

We flew around putting on coats, grabbing pocketbooks and cell phones, unplugging the coffeepot, and running out the back door. I stepped on Latisha's quilt and nearly unquilted her.

"Lillian, you drive," I called, running for the passenger side of her car. "It'd take too long to get mine out."

Latisha got into the back seat as Lillian slid behind the wheel and rammed the key in the ignition. "Put your seat belts on," she said. "Latisha, you hear me?"

"Yes'm, but I'm about to freeze."

"Wrap that quilt around you, an' be glad we don't have leather seats." Lillian looked over her shoulder and stepped on the gas. The car spurted out backward onto Polk Street where she whipped it around to head toward Main.

Holding on to the armrest, I leaned forward to urge the car on. "Step on it, Lillian. Nobody's going to be handing out speeding tickets this time of night. They're all busy searching, anyway."

She turned onto Sixth Street, saw a green light at the next intersection, and floored it. The car went airborne over a bump in the street, lifting us from our seats in spite of being strapped in.

"Whoa," Latisha said.

"I just thought of something," I said as my stomach settled back in place and Lillian, approaching the interstate, zoomed down the ramp and merged without slowing. Swallowing hard as a Roadway tractor trailer pulled alongside, I went on. "Does Mc-Donald's stay open this late?"

"This one does," Latisha said, "'cause of the airport, I guess. I saw a sign when you took us there."

Lillian hadn't said a word. She was hunched over the wheel and maintaining a steady sixty-five, except when she edged it up a little. We were making good time on the almost empty interstate as dark, bare fields flitted past on each side, until the vast glow of airport lights off to our left lit up the sky.

Then Lillian said, "Maybe we shoulda called somebody. The deputies coulda got here before us. Police cars might already be real close."

"I'm thinking that, too," I said, having had a few second thoughts along the way. "If we just miss them, we'll regret not calling. But I didn't want to scare them, especially Horace, who's been known to run. If he saw a bunch of cop cars headed his way, he's likely to speed off and wreck the car." I strained to see ahead. "It's the next exit, Lillian."

"I jus' hope they're there," she mumbled, flicking on the right-turn indicator.

"I bet they are," Latisha said. "Penelope said the PlayPlace is her favorite place in the world."

Lillian drove up the exit ramp and turned right onto a four-lane highway lined with stores, shops, gas stations, Mexican restaurants, and a McDonald's, all blazing with lights and fairly busy in spite of the early morning hour.

"There's the entrance," I said, pointing to a yellow arrow. "Go real slow, Lillian, so we can check the parked cars."

From the back seat, Latisha sang out, "But don't get in the drive-through lane, Great-Granny. We'd be goin' round and around a dozen times."

Lillian grunted in response and eased into a bare crawl while we scanned every car in the lot for a flash of red. As we neared the back of the restaurant, I saw the giant playpen enclosed by a partial wall and an exceedingly tall wire mesh fence. It was filled with huge tubes, tunnels, slides, and a pool of plastic balls. The place was still and quiet, almost as if it were closed for the night.

Lillian steered the car around the curve behind the PlayPlace, and there in the employees' dark parking area, wedged between a pickup and an SUV, was the little red Boxster.

"They're here!" I said, almost whispering in wonder. Then I cleared my throat and said, "At least the car is. Pull up in front of it, Lillian, so they can't leave."

"Them others can't, either," she said, even as she parked broadside to the front of the Boxster and turned off the ignition.

"We won't be that long." I opened my door, finding that Lillian had parked so close to the Boxster's grille that I had to slide out sideways. "Come on, let's go find them."

Getting out on her side, Lillian said, "Lock these doors, Latisha, and stay right here till we get back."

"But I wanta go, too!"

"In jammies and a quilt? No, ma'am, you lock the doors an' stay here."

"Well," Latisha conceded, slumping back in the seat, "tell that girl I'm waitin' on her."

Lillian and I hurried to the side door of McDonald's, fearing, or at least I was, that Horace and Penelope had gone somewhere else either by foot or by way of another ride. And that thought made me sick to my stomach. We'd never find them if they'd hitched a ride with someone else.

We approached the counter and clasped it, waiting for the tired-looking, hairnetted woman to take our orders.

"Have you seen a man and a little girl?" I asked, almost demanded.

She looked at me with heavy-lidded eyes, then thumbed behind her toward the PlayPlace. "In there, an' we can't get 'em out. I'm about to call the cops."

"Oh, don't do that," I said, as Lillian headed for the interior door to the play area. "We'll get them. They, I mean, *he* isn't well. Thank you for looking after them."

I caught up with Lillian as she stepped inside the seemingly empty area. We stopped and looked around—there were no children running or climbing, no shrill screams or yells, and not one adult—Horace or otherwise. The place was deadly quiet and only dimly lit.

Grabbing my arm, Lillian said, "Look over yonder, Miss Julia." She squinched up her eyes and pointed through a forest of bars and tubes and rungs to a little yellow stationary play car, about a third the size of a Boxster. The only moveable part on it was the steering wheel, and Horace, head nodding on his chest, had both hands on it at the correct ten and two position as he sat in the driver's seat with his knees up beside his ears.

"Oh, my word," I said, an immense load of concern lifting at having one down and only one to go, "but where is Penelope?"

"She wouldn't go off without him," Lillian said, "so she's here somewhere. Let's look in them tunnels."

And that's where we found her—curled up just inside the gaping mouth of a blue plastic tube, sound asleep, the little Steiff bear beside her, and her pink fur-lined boots tucked up close. Lillian gathered her up, holding both child and bear in her arms, and started for the door.

"Can you get Mr. Horace?" she asked.

"One way or the other," I said and hurried toward Horace, telling myself to stay calm and be kind because he wasn't responsible for endangering a child as well as himself, and scaring us all half to death. But I still had to restrain myself from lacing into him good.

I shook his shoulder. His head jerked up, and he turned to me with a smile and a vacant look. "Mildred?" he asked.

"Not by a long shot. Come on, Horace, it's time to go."

"Okay," he said, and shakily climbed out of the car.

He teetered on his feet, so I took his arm and followed Lillian with her armful through the restaurant to the exterior door, drawing mindless stares from a few sleepy diners hunched over Big Macs and Quarter Pounders with Cheese.

As we walked out into the frigid air, heading for the cars, Penelope nestled closer in Lillian's arms and mumbled, "Can I have some fries?"

While Lillian stowed Penelope in the back seat with Latisha, spreading the quilt to cover them both, I leaned over and asked, "Which car do you want to drive?"

"Lord goodness, Miss Julia," she said, closing the back door of her car. "I don't wanta drive Mr. Horace's car, 'specially with him in it."

I didn't especially want to either, but I was afraid that Horace would pitch a fit if we left his beloved car. Not to mention the possibility of theft if we left it.

"Give me the keys, Horace," I said, hoping that a commanding tone would get results.

"Where are they?" he asked, looking around as if they'd be hanging in the dark.

"Hold still a minute," I said and rammed my hand in his pants pocket, "and overlook the body search. I'm interested only in the keys so we can get your car home."

I pulled out a key attached to a certain key ring that had lately been wrapped in a Christmas bag.

"I want to go home," Horace said a little peevishly.

"Good," I said, "because that's where we're going." Lillian and I walked him to the passenger side of the Boxster, guided him backward into the seat, whacking his knee right smartly as we did, and strapped him in.

I locked and closed the door, thought for a minute, then said to Lillian, "We need to let somebody know so they can call off the search."

"Yes'm, they's a lot of daddies that need to get home for Santy Claus. Chil'ren'll be gettin' up in a little while 'cause it's already Christmas mornin'. Who you think we oughta call?"

"Sam," I said, taking my phone from my pocket. "I'll text him, then call Mildred, who'll take forever to answer."

So I sent Sam a text: BOTH FOUND SAFE. CALL OFF SEARCH. MEET YOU AT M'S. Then, dialing Mildred's number, I waited an interminable time for her to rouse from her sedated sleep and mumble, "What?"

"Mildred! Wake up!" I said, speaking loudly to penetrate the fog of whatever the EMTs had given her. "Are you awake? It's Julia. Listen, we've found them. They're all right and we're on the way home. Do you understand? Don't go back to sleep. We're bringing them home."

"Penelope?" Mildred asked with a catch in her voice. "Is she . . . ?"

"She's all right." Unless, I thought, she'd caught pneumonia in a blue plastic tube in the dead of winter.

"Thank you," Mildred whispered, "thank you, Lord."

I hung up since she was no longer speaking to me and started toward the driver's side of the Porsche.

"You know how to drive this thing?" Lillian asked, giving the sleek little car a worried glance.

"No, but how hard can it be?"

Harder than I'd thought as it turned out, for I was not proficient in managing manual transmissions. Having cautioned Lillian not to leave us behind in case of trouble, I think I drove the whole way home in the wrong gear—if a peculiar whining sound from the engine was any indication.

Chapter 55

I followed Lillian up Mildred's drive and stopped behind her car, which had stopped behind an Abbot County Sheriff's Department car. Relieved to be home in one piece, I clumsily crawled out of the low-slung, much-envied car, hoping that I'd never have to get in it again.

Lillian was already out and opening the back door of her car. Just as Penelope, fully awake by now, slid slowly out of the car, Mildred ran out onto the porch.

"Penelope!" she cried, her arms outspread as her silk negligee billowed behind her. "My baby, my little girl! Are you all right? Oh, my darling, I've been so worried about you!" And with tears running down her face, Mildred engulfed Penelope in her arms, lifted her up, and carried her inside.

"Julia!" she called through the open door where she bent down to kneel beside Penelope. "Thank you, thank you, and Lillian, how can I ever thank you enough! Where were they? How did you know where to look . . . oh, come in, come in, and tell me everything."

Ignoring the invitation, I checked my cell phone and found an almost unreadable text from Sam: PTL! ALL CALLED TO S'S OFFICE. HOME SOON, which being interpreted read: "Praise the Lord! I'll be home after a meeting with the sheriff."

I walked around to Horace's side of the car where he waited, still strapped in. He'd opened his door, but sat now with his hands in his lap, content to wait, I supposed, until somebody told him to get out.

"We're home, Horace," I said, unlatching his seat belt. "You want to go in?"

"No," he said, lumbering out of the car, "but I will. I forgot my suitcase."

Uh-oh, if that wasn't a warning sign, I didn't know what was. Mildred, however, was paying no attention to the status of her wandering husband. Maybe she was immune to his exit-seeking by this time, but not to Penelope's for she kept the child close to her side as she gave orders to the lone officer deputized to the house. He was already radioing the All Clear signal, calling in the searchers from all points in the county.

I walked Horace up the steps to the porch and aimed him toward the open door.

Mildred turned and saw him coming. "Ida Lee!" she called. "Take Mr. Allen upstairs and put him to bed. And lock his door so he can't pull this stunt again. Penelope, sweetheart," she went on, embracing her again, "I know you're tired, but let me get things straightened out here, and we'll go upstairs. You can sleep as long as you want and when you get up it'll be Christmas."

Mildred looked over and met my eyes with a sudden hollow recognition that Santa had long before passed over the Allen house. Tears streamed down her face, but I took no pleasure in her silent acknowledgment that I'd been right.

I walked into the foyer and leaned down to Penelope. "Honey," I said, "the most unusual thing has happened. Mr. Sam called to tell us that he'd just seen a miniature sleigh lift off from our house and zoom away across the sky. He thinks that Santa may have gotten the wrong information. Why don't you come over as soon as you wake up and see if he thought you were spending the night with us?"

Her wan little face brightened as she looked for permission from her grandmother. "That's it!" Mildred said. "And it's my fault because we didn't have a Christmas tree to guide him in. Well! *That* won't happen again. Now, run up and hop in my bed. When we wake up, we'll go see what Santa brought."

Still looking somewhat bewildered, Penelope did as she was told, but with a backward glance at Lillian, who called out, "We'll be waitin' for you."

Mildred reached for me with outstretched arms. Too tired to linger, I sidled aside, preparing to leave.

"Julia," she said, as humbly as Mildred had ever sounded, "how can I thank you? The lost has been found, and you did it."

"No, it was Lillian. I mean, Latisha. Latisha told us where to look."

"Whoever," Mildred said with a wave of her hand. "I'm eternally grateful to you all. Oh, Julia, I thought she was gone forever. You don't know all the horrors I imagined, and it brought me to my knees. Literally, I'm talking about, *to my knees*. If we hadn't already lost so much sleep, I'd be in church this morning."

"Hold that thought, Mildred, there'll be other mornings. Here," I said, handing over the key to the Porsche. "It needs a better hiding place, but come on over any time today. We may not be up, but I don't think Penelope will mind."

"Let's go home, Miss Julia," Lillian said. "We already done all we can do." She took my arm and walked with me to her car, where I got into the passenger seat again.

Glancing in the back, I saw Latisha, stretched out on the seat, still wrapped in her quilt, and sound asleep. Bored with the homecoming, I thought, and smiled.

Lillian started the car and eased behind the deputy's car as it went down the curved driveway. On Polk Street, she drove the few feet to the curb in front of my house.

"Don't look like Mr. Sam's back," she said. "Same ole lights still on."

"Yes, but why don't you pull in and just stay the night? You'll barely get home before it's time to get up."

"No'm," she said with a quick look in the back seat. "Latisha make out like she don't b'lieve in Santy Claus, but she'll be looking for him anyway."

"Oh, of course, I should've thought of that. Too tired to think, I guess. Anyway," I went on, reluctant to leave all the questions up in the air, "I wonder if Mildred will get any answers from Penelope. I'd sure like to know what she and Horace were thinking when they took off."

"Well," Lillian said, resetting the heat as the car rumbled in park, "Latisha and Honey, they got to talkin' on the way back, an' I heard Latisha say, 'Why'd you go off like that? Weren't you scared?' An' Honey, she say 'Uh-uh, my grandmother said not to let him go off by his self, so I went with him.' An' Latisha, she say, 'You coulda woke her up, couldn't you?' An' Honey say back, 'She was mad at me.' Then that Latisha, she say, 'Oh, shoo, girl, my great-granny gets mad at me all the time. What you have to do is . . .' an' they went to whisperin' an' gigglin', an' I didn't hear no more." Lillian shrugged her shoulders. "No tellin' what Latisha meant by that, but I sure wish I'd heard it."

I did, too, but at least we had a general idea of why Penelope had left home—she was obeying her grandmother and looking after Horace. As for why he left, who, including him, knew?

Lillian got a few hours of sleep before coming back to put the turkey in the oven. She brought an alarm clock with her in case she dozed off and missed putting the dressing in an hour or so later. I don't think I turned over at all once I hit the bed, and it was all I could do to get up again for breakfast at the Pickens' house.

I had no idea when Mildred would bestir herself enough to bring Penelope over for the gifts waiting under our tree. I hated to miss seeing Penelope's awe when she realized that Santa had not forgotten her, but Hazel Marie was expecting us, so we went. It would not have been Christmas for me to have missed being with her and Lloyd and the little twin girls. And J. D. Pickens, P.I., as well, since he was always where they were.

Suffice it to say that as the clock neared two o'clock we were home welcoming our guests for Christmas dinner. Some of us were giddy from lack of sleep, but the turkey, dressing, several casseroles, congealed salad, and even the dessert with its whipped cream on top were ready and waiting to be served. Mildred and Penelope had gotten there before Sam and I were back, but I had told Lillian that all the unwrapped gifts were what Santa had left for Penelope. The wrapped ones were to await the arrival of all our guests.

It was the bicycle that had taken Penelope's breath away. Mildred sat in one of the wing chairs and watched as the child climbed on and off a dozen times, unable to believe it was hers. Sam, bless his heart, rolled it outside to the sidewalk and kept it upright as she climbed on and dinged the bell to her heart's content.

Etta Mae, her boyfriend, and Granny Wiggins came together, laughing and expectant of a good time, and I got the inner jolt from the masculinity emanating from Deputy Bobby Lee Moser. Or it might have been a whiff of something by Calvin Klein.

"Etta Mae," I said, drawing her aside, "it's a done deal. I've seen the Offer to Purchase with Lurline's signature, written bold and clear on it, and furthermore, a certified check is in Mr. Blair's escrow account, so we'll be closing in a few days."

"I can't believe it," she said as tears glinted in her eyes. "I just can't believe it. Miss Julia . . ."

She bent her head to my shoulder, but I straightened her and said, "No tears, Etta Mae. This is a happy day for both of us."

She laughed as she mopped her eyes with tissues. "Yes, it is. But who would've thought that I'd get to have my own business and maybe Bobby Lee, too?"

"I'm happy to have helped with one," I said, smiling at her happiness, "but you're on your own with the other."

After dinner when those of us who had been up half the night were all but comatose, we opened gifts, laughed a lot, and counted ourselves most fortunate. I sent Lillian and Latisha home soon afterward, leaving Janelle and James to clear the tables, clean the kitchen, and take home extra envelopes.

As coats were retrieved from Lloyd's bedroom and hugs and good wishes were exchanged at the door, Mildred came up and drew me aside. "Julia," she said, "I've decided to take Penelope with me tomorrow. I can't bear to leave her, so we'll be leaving early to take Horace to the retirement center at Southern Pines. I hate to say that it'll be a relief to have him gone, but it's the truth. Sooner or later he was going to hurt himself or somebody else, so this is for the best. But when I think of what could've happened to Penelope last night, I just get cold chills. I didn't realize what an addition she is to my life. I've been grieving so much over Tony and Tonya and now Horace that I couldn't see her."

Even though I am not a hugging sort of person, I gave her a brief hug, then stepped back. "I'm so glad, Mildred. She's a very special little girl, and you're both blessed to have each other."

"Yes, well," she said, straightening herself, "I'm going to see to it that we continue to have each other. I'm calling my lawyers in Atlanta to start custody proceedings against Tonya. But thank you, Julia, for a lovely Christmas, and," she ended with an arched eyebrow, "for seeing that Santa stopped for Penelope."

Stunned by her custody plans against Tonya, I wished her a safe trip on the morrow and left unsaid the colliding thoughts in my head. It was just as well that I did, for I didn't know which one would've come out.

Recalling my determination to allow other people to stand or fall on their own and acknowledging that I'd failed to do so in a few recent instances, I wondered if I should redouble my intent to mind my own business. Still, when people I cared about rushed headlong into dangerous waters, I knew I could not and would not refuse a helping hand. Call it interference, call it meddling, I didn't care. I would be there for Mildred and for Etta Mae regardless of how many new leaves I turned over.

So tired by this time that all I could think of was crawling into bed, I leaned against Sam as he closed the door behind the last guest. Then, with a sigh, I walked into the living room, switched off the lights on the Christmas tree, and smiled at the memory of Penelope's face when she saw the bicycle.

"Sam," I said as he came in behind me, "I am so tired I may never get out of bed again. But what a Christmas it's been, so Merry Christmas to you if I've forgotten to say it before now."

"And Merry Christmas to you, too," Sam said, putting an arm around my waist as we turned and surveyed the room where a few ribbons and scraps of wrapping paper were still on the floor. "I'm feeling my night out at Lily Pond Lake, too. This will all be here in the morning, so I say that we ask Janelle and James to lock up when they finish and we go on to bed."

"Oh, Sam," I said, immediately sympathetic, "of course you're tired. You were out in the weather and walking all over the place for half the night. I'll check on Janelle and James—and by the way, James is thrilled with that electric drill you gave him. I'll be up in a few minutes, but you go on to sleep. I won't disturb you."

"Disturb all you want," he said, smiling his sweet smile. "I'm not that tired."

Miss Julia Happily Ever After

A Novel

Wedding fever hits Abbotsville and several of Miss Julia's friends have plans to tie the knot. Miss Julia wants to properly celebrate each ceremony, insofar as anyone will let her. In the middle of it all, a strange figure keeps showing up in town, streaking across lawns and vandalizing gardens. In the delightful final installment of the beloved series, Miss Julia once again finds herself trying to solve it all—matters of the heart and petty crime alike.